The Lost Pages Bookstore

STEVEN E. WEDEL

MoonHowler Press

MOONHOWLER PRESS

Acknowledgements

This is the book that almost wasn't. About halfway through writing it, I found myself suddenly and unexpectedly unemployed. This led to a terrible depression and eighteen months without writing. I thought my life as an author was over, and wished everything else was. Then the Universe (or God, or Fate, or absolute random chance) brought me a most unexpected friendship from deep in my past. In high school, I thought she was a "preppy snob" and she thought I was a "scary stoner." We were both wrong. Annie Sturdivant, I don't know how you knew to reach out to me when you did, but thank you for your friendship, your mentorship, and your patience. This book is for you.

Thanks, also, to Brianna Cuellar, who needed an internship and got stuck editing this book. May you have a brilliant career that makes you happy, fulfilled, and wealthy in every way.

Chapter One

The October wind flapped the collar of his coat against Donald Nelson's reddened cheek. A drop of persistent snot clung to his cold nose, threatening to fall, or worse, hang in a long string for all to see. Not that anybody *would* see, but still, it was embarrassing. The key to the shop was lost in the brown knit glove of his hand and he struggled to push it away from his palm enough to get it into the tarnished old knob of the battered wood-and-glass door while holding a paper bag of groceries in his other hand. A pickup drove past on Main Street and the driver honked once. Donnie nodded without turning to look.

The key slipped into the lock. He turned it and pushed the door open. Warmth, and the smell of old books and fresh coffee wrapped around him, pulling him inside, promising him the protection of solitude and the ache of loneliness.

Donnie closed the door and locked it behind him, making sure the CLOSED sign was still facing the street. The bookstore was dim, lit only by the orange salt lamps in the back corners and the iron gray light of the overcast morning pressing against the front windows. He made his way down the long aisle of romance fiction to the quartet of worn red Queen Anne armchairs crouched like tired gargoyles around a chipped and scarred faux oak coffee table. He put his brown paper bag down on the table, pulled off his gloves, and dropped them beside the bag. Next, he went to a shelf mounted on the wall and poured strong black coffee from the Mr. Coffee machine into his wide mug that still showed a few lines of the Shakespearean insults someone found funny when she bought him the cup in a different lifetime.

Sitting down, Donnie looked at the bag. Inside was a dozen eggs, a pound of bacon, and a loaf of bread that hadn't molded yet. He'd awakened wanting a bacon-and-egg sandwich. The half-loaf of bread he owned had turned green and fuzzy. There were no eggs and no bacon in his refrigerator. The cold walk to a little convenience store/bait shop had sapped his energy. The idea of hot eggs and bacon on toasted bread sounded good, but the thought of standing at the two-burner hotplate in the back room of the bookstore to cook the stuff just seemed like too much work.

He reached into the bag and took out the box of generic chocolate toaster pastries and tore open a silver package. He knew this was how it would turn out. He scolded himself for not at least springing for real name-brand Pop Tarts. The pastry was dry, chalky, and cold. Why had he even bought these? It was like admitting he wouldn't cook before he even paid for the groceries. He swallowed and sipped coffee and listened to the silence between the ticks of a brass clock mounted near the cash register at the front of the store.

His pastries finished, Donnie took the eggs and bacon to his mini-fridge and put the bread in one of the stacked plastic crates he called a pantry. He refilled his coffee and went to the front of the store to his worn black leather desk chair behind the counter. The imprint in the seat cushion was a lover's caress as he settled into the chair and gently swiveled back and forth while looking out the dirty windows at the mostly empty street.

There were a few pickups parked at the end of the block. They belonged to some of the older farmers who came into town to enjoy breakfast and fellowship at Annie's Café. They would be there in their faded overalls, plaid flannel or denim shirts, most with bald heads and thick guts, dirty work boots, but smiles and twinkling eyes, toothpicks dangling from the corners of their mouths as they told old stories or commented on politics or the early cold spell.

Donnie sighed and wished for a moment he could go join the conversation. It wasn't that the farmers would shun him. They simply didn't understand him and therefore didn't have much use for him. He was strange. An outsider to their profession, their way of life, and, despite living in the little town of Sagebrush, Oklahoma, for over seven years, Donnie Nelson was an outsider, a city boy who'd moved here for reasons no one understood, and he was "too damned close-mouthed" about his past for most people's liking.

He sipped his coffee and watched tiny snowflakes beat themselves against the thick glass of the window. The snow wouldn't stick. He knew that. This cold front, the first of the season, came on the heels of mild weather. The ground was still warm. The snow would melt on contact without leaving so much as a whisper of white. Later, though, in late November or early December, northwest Oklahoma was sure to get a real snowstorm sliding down from the peaks of the Rocky Mountains.

At ten o'clock, Donnie got up and unlocked the front door and turned the hanging sign around so it said OPEN. He turned on the overhead lights and went back to his desk chair and switched on his outdated laptop, waiting for it to boot up. When it did, he opened his word processing program, opened a file named WIP, and stared at the unfinished sentence on page 33 of the manuscript.

The pain he felt

What about that pain? How did it feel? How did it affect his barbarian warrior main character? Would it melt him to a puddle of muscle and tears, or harden him into a rage-fueled instrument of vengeance?

Donnie didn't know.

For seven years, he'd opened his laptop, opened the file that wasn't really a work in progress, and read that last sentence fragment.

The fan mail forwarded from his agent had stopped coming years ago. Email from the more enterprising fans no longer interrupted the deluge of spam in his inbox. The movie deal fell apart, thankfully after the generous option had been paid, and the muscular star that had been in talks to play the lead had disappeared from the public eye along with Bolkar himself.

"Things run in cycles, Donnie," Gene Adkins, his agent, had told him the last time they talked a few years ago. "George R.R. Martin is where you should be. HBO and Netflix and all that streaming shit would eat up your Bolkar stories. Everybody's looking for the next *Game of Thrones* or *The Witcher*. They need something to remind them about Bolkar. When are you gonna finish the next fuckin' book?"

They had both known it was a lie when Donnie promised he would finish it soon.

Bolkar, the death-merchant, was frozen in time, waiting, waiting, waiting for ... Donnie didn't know what his character was waiting for.

He left the laptop open and picked up the paperback mystery novel he'd begun reading late yesterday. He'd taken a liking to mystery novels since moving to Sagebrush. Agatha Christie was his favorite. *Shit actually gets solved in her stories*, he told himself.

At 12:13 p.m., the front door opened and Sherry Brown came in with the cold wind clinging to her like angry gremlins. She closed the door behind her and turned to face Donnie, a smile on her jowly face. She lowered the hood on her gray wool coat, revealing an equally gray short crop of old-lady hair. Her Dillard's perfume drifted through the store and tickled Donnie's nose.

"It's so cold out there!" she exclaimed.

"Sure is," Donnie agreed. "I guess it's lunchtime, huh?"

"It is," Mrs. Brown said. "I baked cookies last night. I brought you some." From one deep pocket of her coat she pulled a baggie of chocolate chip cookies. From the other, she removed the romance novel she'd taken yesterday. She extended the bag of cookies. "Shall I just reshelf this myself?" she asked.

"That'd be great," Donnie said, taking the bag. He opened it and held it to his nose and sniffed deeply. The aroma was semi-sweet chocolate and moist cookie dough and heaven. "They smell perfect," he said.

Mrs. Brown's face crinkled into a wide grin that made her eyes tiny brown-and-white pricks of light above her rouge. "I hope you like them. Edgar did."

"I bet he did," Donnie said, thinking how Mr. Brown's pickup had been at Annie's Café earlier and wondering why he didn't eat breakfast with his wife. "How was the book?"

Mrs. Brown looked at the paperback in her hand. "Eh. It was okay. A Viking fighting a werewolf for a woman I couldn't really make myself like very much."

Donnie took a cookie from the bag. He smiled at Mrs. Brown. "You win some, you lose some. With you, at least it isn't a huge investment of time."

It was true. Sherry Brown borrowed a book from the store every day. At first Donnie had charged her and given her the usual low price when she returned the previous day's book, but when she'd begun bringing him cookies, slices of cake or pie, or covered plates of chicken and dumplings, roast beef, and other complete meals, they'd made an arrangement that allowed the bank secretary to borrow a book a day every day. She never dog-eared a page. The one time she'd spilled tea on a book she'd apologized profusely and paid for the copy.

"I'm in the mood for something more contemporary today," she said as she made her way to the romance section of the store.

"There's coffee in the back, if you're interested," Donnie called, then popped a moist, chocolatey cookie into his mouth. If his mouth could have an orgasm, it would be screaming the name of the Lord right now, he thought as he chewed. Even his mother hadn't made cookies this good.

A few minutes and two cookies later, Mrs. Brown returned with two thin paperbacks from Harlequin. "Which one?" she asked, putting them both on the counter.

Donnie smiled and shook his head. "Take them both," he said. "One of those skinny books won't last you half a day. Especially today. I bet you haven't seen five customers."

"Only three," she answered, laughing. "I can really take both?"

"For this bag of cookies, I should give you a key to the store," Donnie answered.

Mrs. Brown laughed and deposited the two novels into her coat pocket. "I don't know how you stay in business, Donnie," she said. "Especially without a cat."

"Every bookstore should have a resident lazy cat," Donnie said in harmony with his customer. He nodded. "I know, Mrs. Brown. I just don't like cleaning up after them."

"Well, I know I won't change your mind today," she said. "I do hope this weather lets up. It's not even Halloween and it feels like Christmas." She made for the door, then stopped and turned back to face the proprietor. "Donnie, have you eaten lunch?"

"I had a sandwich just before you came in," he lied.

Mrs. Brown gave him a look that said she knew he wasn't telling her the truth. She shook her head and clucked her tongue. "When you moved here, you had a little bit of a tummy on you. Now you're as lean as a scarecrow. You're not eating right. I'm cooking chicken fried steak tonight. I'll bring you some tomorrow."

"You don't have to do that, Mrs. Brown."

"Nonsense. You stay warm and have a good day, Donnie." With that, she opened the door to the winter gremlins and slipped out. Donnie watched her hurry across the street, holding the bottom of her coat closed around her denim-clad legs as she went.

She's a good woman. Some kid's favorite grandma.

There were no more customers that day. At seven o'clock, Donnie closed the laptop, locked the store, turned off the lights, and flipped the sign around to CLOSED. In the back room of the store, he patted out some ground beef and dropped it into the little skillet on his hotplate. While it fried, he turned on the television to watch the six o'clock news rebroadcast out of Amarillo, Texas. Most of the talk was about the early cold snap, with a few forays into tales of a shooting at some low-income apartments and a city councilman being investigated for sexual misconduct with an employee.

Donnie flopped his hamburger onto a bun, squirted some mustard on it, added chips to his plate, and sat down in the single chair at a little café table he'd found at an antique shop. He ate and stared at the television until the food was gone, then he flipped idly through the channels he got with his digital antenna, but didn't find anything that caught his interest. He turned off the television. The only sound was the ticking of the clock at the front of the store and the howling wind prowling through the street and alley. The room was dark.

Donnie was about to get up and turn on a light and make his way to the shower stall he'd had put in where a second sink had been when he bought the shop, but the sudden, almost frightening ring of the cell phone in his pocket made him jerk in his chair. He fished the phone from his pocket, accidentally accepting the call before seeing who it was from. He put the device to his head.

"Hello?" he asked.

"Donnie? Donald Nelson?" a man's voice replied.

"Who is this?"

"Eric Francis. In Lawton. Remember?"

"I remember," Donnie said. "How'd you get my number?"

"It wasn't easy, but there are advantages to working for a newspaper," Eric answered.

"A newspaper?" Donnie asked, his stomach clenching. *Another story about the fantasy author who disappeared?* "What do you want?" he asked. He dropped into the chair he'd just left, waiting, dreading the rest of the conversation.

"I just wanted to tell you Mrs. Wilder died yesterday," the voice from his past said. "I thought you'd want to know."

Chapter Two

S troke.

    She was 86 years old.

Good life.

Funeral on Friday.

Donnie thanked the friend he barely knew for calling him and stared at his blank cell phone for a few minutes before dropping the hand to his lap. His eyes were on the wall across the room, but he saw backward in time, back to when he was a teenager, a sophomore in high school, just floating along with average grades and no real interest in school. A friend a year older had taken Mrs. Wilder's Creative Writing class and promised Donnie it was an easy A, so Donnie enrolled.

That first day, Mrs. Wilder came into the classroom in a dress she must have made herself, climbed onto the top of her desk without saying a word, and proceeded to ring a cowbell, shocking her students into silence. She hadn't seemed young, then, Donnie remembered. She wore big glasses like most bespectacled women of the time, with thick brown frames. Her hair was in some kind of old-lady poof thing, and she wore support hose with clunky brown shoes. For an older lady, though, she was nimble getting onto the top of her desk.

"What is the first thing a writer has to do?" Mrs. Wilder called out over the heads of her students.

Blank stares were all she got in return.

She held the black metal bell out in front of her and flailed her wrist around some more, setting off a low-pitched but very loud clanging.

"Do I have your full attention?" she demanded.

Donnie remembered that he'd nodded. A few others nodded. Somewhere behind him there'd been a girl's voice with a hesitant, "Yes." Some football player in the back of the room had whispered, "This old bat is crazy as hell."

"Then I've succeeded," Mrs. Wilder said. "The first thing a writer has to do is get the reader's attention."

It was a maxim that Donnie remembered and tried to put into practice with every story he wrote from that day forward.

I love how every book in the series starts off with Bolkar in some kind of trouble he has to get out of.

That line from a very early piece of fan mail had stuck in Donnie's mind for almost twenty years because it meant he was practicing what Mrs. Wilder had taught him.

Donnie lay on his twin-sized bed in the dark room in the back of The Lost Pages Bookstore and thought back to those early days of wanting to be a writer. Mrs. Wilder had always encouraged him, assuring him he had the gift and all he needed was practice. She encouraged him to enter writing contests, insisted he submit work to literary journals, and critiqued anything he asked her to read in a caring but brutally honest way.

When a tiny three-line poem he'd written on break at the retail job he hated was published in a regional college literary journal for no pay, Mrs. Wilder had brought bottles of sparkling grape juice and plastic champagne glasses to class so everyone could toast his success. Donnie smiled at the memory of how embarrassed but proud he'd felt that day. Mrs. Wilder had him sign her copy of the magazine in front of the other students, too.

It had been a rush to sign the pulpy page of that magazine, Donnie remembered.

And that was the first step on the road to ruin ...

Donnie looked again at the notes he'd scrawled in pencil on the pad he kept beside his bed for story ideas. There were no story ideas. Just a note about Mrs. Wilder's last celebration on this earth. The funeral was at 2 p.m. He had the name and address of the church.

"I'll send flowers," he said to the empty room. His voice was low, flat, and dead in the cool air. Outside, the wind whistled and blasted against the building, mocking him. Donnie hung his head.

"I should go," he mumbled.

He hadn't been back to his hometown in years. Not since the divorce.

"I can't go back," he whispered. "I can't."

He pulled up his blankets and turned off the lamp. The room was dark and he felt blinded. The space heater blew electric-smelling warm air toward the bed while the wind continued to prowl around the building, looking for some way to get inside and chill Donnie's bones. He lay on his back, facing a ceiling he couldn't see, and remembered Mrs. Wilder keeping him after class at least once a week to ask if he was writing, to encourage him to keep putting words on paper.

"Once every ten years or so, I get a student with real talent," she'd told him once. "You're it. Maybe the best I've ever had. But writing is like a muscle and you have to exercise it. You have to practice. You have to write thousands, maybe millions of words that aren't good enough for anybody to see before you get strong enough to publish. You can do it, Donnie. I know you can."

Donnie wasn't aware of the warm tears that ran down his temples. Eventually, he slept.

Chapter Three

T he morning sunlight was pale and weak, filtered through high, milky clouds and too diffused to offer any warmth. The wind continued to whip down Main Street, slashing at scraps of paper, scooping up dead leaves and throwing them around, and biting at any exposed skin.

Donnie locked the front door of his shop, pulled up the collar of his battered old coat with one gloved hand, holding a knit cap in place as he half-jogged across the street. He had awakened with the need for company, even if he was alone in a crowd. It was probably better that way, he reasoned. He didn't want to talk to anybody, but he also didn't want to feel so alone standing over his hotplate with bacon grease popping on his hands as he held a spatula.

Annie's Café was nearly full and oozed the smells of fresh black coffee, baking bread, and sausage when Donnie slipped through the door. A waitress in jeans and a striped flannel shirt smiled at him. She was in her late thirties, Donnie guessed, and was fairly new to the café. She had only been working there for a couple of months, by his estimation. He had never thought before about where she came from or what she'd been doing before coming to the café. Was she a local? Or had she come to Sagebrush to hide from her past like he had? Donnie had expected her name to be Flo, but it was Debbie. She wore heavy makeup to hide the scars of teenage acne, but she was pretty in a tired sort of way, offering just the right amount of banter at each table, never letting drink glasses get empty, and she had a nice smile.

"Be with ya in a minute, Mr. Nelson," she said as she hurried from the counter with the cash register, a damp cloth in hand.

"Just Donnie," Donnie said quietly after her. *Seven years*, he thought. *Seven years and still most people call me Mr. Nelson, like I'm a stranger. How long do I have to live here before they think of me as one of them? I'm from Oklahoma. It's not like I'm a New York yankee or California surfer dude trying to fit in.*

"Just one again?" Debbie asked. Donnie blinked and turned to face her. He hadn't realized he'd taken to studying a bulletin board of babysitting offers, lost pets, and church socials.

"Yeah. Same as always," Donnie said, trying to smile and feeling it splitting his face like cracking ice on a frozen pond.

"Follow me, Mr. Nelson," Debbie said, taking a single menu and leading him around tables of four, six, twelve people to a little out-of-the-way table with only two chairs. She put down the menu, pulled silverware rolled in a white napkin from her apron, and put that down. "One of these days you're gonna surprise me and come in here with a pretty woman hangin' on your arm." Debbie winked at him, then added, "I'll be right back with some water." She moved off before he could respond.

Donnie looked at the menu, a single yellow sheet, laminated, listing various breakfast combinations and then each item separately for those who wanted to build their own breakfast. He didn't really read the menu. He knew what he wanted.

Debbie put a glass of ice water on the table. Donnie wondered why they served ice water in winter, but didn't ask. "What'll it be?" she asked.

"I'll have the pancakes, with a side of biscuit and gravy and four strips of bacon," Donnie answered. Then he added, "And hash browns. With coffee."

"This cold weather makes a man hungry, don't it?" Debbie said automatically as she scratched his order out on a little pad. "I'll be right back with this," she said, giving his shoulder a quick pat, then hurrying away.

Donnie unzipped his coat and shrugged out of the sleeves. The café was warm and comfortable, decorated with pictures of local kids winning FFA awards dating back to the bellbottom era of the 1970s, and memorabilia from the high school, with a few pictures of Sagebrush's early years and some rustic farm implements. He listened idly to the conversations going on around him.

" ... had the old Ford for almost fifty years. Dad bought it new off a lot in Enid ... "

" … got her pregnant. Bill was fit to kill the boy. Ain't no wonder the kids ran away. Heard they went to Oklahoma City. He's working in a grocery warehouse … "

" … the old heifer didn't like me reaching in there, but that calf was breached. I broke one of its legs pulling it out and we had to put it down, but saved the mother. She's given me good calves every year but this one. I think I'll … "

" … my little Mandy is learning to drive. Yeah, she's old enough. Sixteen in two weeks. Tried to get her to drive the truck, but she kept popping the clutch, so Barb's teaching her in the Olds. She's doing fine … "

Donnie looked at his right hand and saw that he was slowly twisting the salt shaker in a circular pattern on the table. He stopped himself and pushed the plastic container back in place beside the pepper shaker. There was so much life happening all around him, he thought. Everyone had things going on, while he sat and moldered away in a used bookstore that lost more money each year.

Debbie brought his food on a long oval plate and set it down in front of him. The gravy and hash browns were steaming, and the smell of the food made Donnie's mouth water. He thanked the waitress before she was called away to another table, then took up his fork and dug into the biscuits and gravy. The food was as good as it smelled.

The plate was nearly empty when a large shadow fell over the table. Donnie looked up, a bite of bacon in his mouth, and found an older man with a big gut pushing out the front of a pair of faded overalls. Under the denim was a white T-shirt and over it was a red-and-black-checked flannel shirt with a Carhartt work coat over that. He had hands like hams and gray stubble on a round, weathered face. "You're the bookstore fella, ain't ya?" the man asked.

Donnie swallowed and nodded. "Yeah. Lost Pages. That's my store."

"I'm Sam Teskie. Susie's husband," he said, holding out his right hand. Donnie put his own hand into the hard, cavern-like grasp of Sam Teskie and offered a squeeze that must have felt like the last breath of a dying sparrow in the other man's grasp.

"Would you like to sit down?" Donnie asked. "I'm almost done here, but I'd be glad to buy you breakfast or coffee or something."

"That's nice of ya," Sam responded. "But I already ate. I was sitting over there with the guys when I saw you over here. I texted Susie to let her know I saw you. She wanted me to ask about the club meeting tonight since we were both here."

Donnie nodded. The club had no name, but met weekly in the old Queen Anne chairs in the back of his store. They'd been meeting there long before he bought the place, and he'd seen no reason to end the sessions when he took possession of the building. There were four older ladies who filled the graceful antique chairs, and sometimes younger daughters or nieces or even a granddaughter or two joined them. They talked about the books they were reading, gossiped, drank tea, and ate pastries for a couple of hours. The four matriarchs were loyal customers and nice ladies and Donnie had to admit he liked eavesdropping on their conversations.

"She's worried about the weather?" Donnie asked.

"That's it. The cold is bad on her knees," Sam admitted. "The cost of getting old, I guess."

"I understand," Donnie said. "To be honest, the group meets in my store, but I don't have much to do with it. Mrs. Brown, at the bank, would be the one to say if they're going to meet. She's kind of the leader, I guess. If they want to meet, I'll keep the store open. I enjoy having them."

Sam Teskie's moon face split into a grin. "I bet you hear more clucking than you'd get in a henhouse in a tornado when those women get together."

Donnie grinned back and took a bite of biscuit and gravy. The food was getting cold. "I've sure heard a few things from back in that corner," he confessed. He thought about asking Sam if he'd seen a doctor about his prostate yet, but decided not to. If the man didn't mind peeing every hour, that was his business.

"Well, I'll tell Susie to call Sherry and ask her," Sam said. "Sherry still reading a book a day?"

"She is," Donnie said. "I see her every day at lunch."

"She was like that in school, too," Sam said. "Teacher's pet every year."

"I'm not surprised," Donnie said.

"I'll tell her to call Sherry," Sam said again as he got to his feet. His belly bumped the table as he stood up but neither man mentioned it. He shook Donnie's hand again, straightened his sweat-stained red cap, nodded at the last of his friends still sitting at another table, and left the café.

Donnie returned his attention to his food, but the gravy had coagulated, and the hash browns were cold. He ate the bacon and swallowed some more water, then paid his check with Annie herself, a thick, round red-head who worked the register, and headed toward the door.

"Bye, Mr. Nelson," Debbie called from a nearby table. "Thanks for comin' in."

Donnie turned and waved. "It's Donnie," he said. "Just call me Donnie."

The waitress winked in response and Donnie turned up his collar and crossed the street to his own business.

Inside, he took off his coat and sat down at the chair behind the front counter, turned on his laptop and opened the file to the novel he suspected he would never finish, and stared out the dirty window, thinking about a funeral he both did and did not want to attend.

There weren't that many people he'd personally known whom he respected. Mrs. Wilder was certainly near the top of that list. A few other writers, one politician, an elderly civil rights protester, and Wanda Wilder, high school teacher. He wanted to pay his respects to her. He wanted to stand up at the funeral and say something about the influence she'd had in his life. Not to tell others about it, not to show off his own past glories, but to say to her spirit, in hopes it was hovering around, what she had meant to him.

Why did I never tell her that while she was alive?

During the successful years, life had been too hectic with the writing and touring and trying to balance a marriage with two kids. After all that crashed down around him, he'd simply retreated into the Lost Pages Bookstore of Sagebrush, Oklahoma, and kept his head down.

I could have written to her, he scolded himself. Mrs. Walker never would have told anyone where I am.

Shame.

If she hadn't heard what he'd done, he would have had to admit it to her eventually. Even if she hadn't asked outright, that invitation to confess would have been there and it would have been too strong to resist.

"I should go," he said aloud.

Melissa ...

And the kids.

And Dad.

Going home meant being in the same city as his ex-wife, his now teenage children, and his father in the nursing home. The chances Melissa would come to the funeral to make a scene were small. Not completely off the table, though. Brian and Lizbeth wouldn't talk to him at all unless Melissa made them. His father would probably never know he'd come to town, Donnie knew. There would just be his own guilt for not visiting.

He hadn't seen his father since his sisters had him committed to the nursing home, claiming his medical condition made it necessary. Donnie had gone along with it, though reluctantly. He hadn't wanted to rob their father of his independence. Despite the stupor he'd been in at the time, Donnie did remember that. But in the end, he agreed with his sisters.

Traffic outside the dingy window picked up slightly, meaning maybe a dozen cars moved on Main Street in ten minutes or so. It was lunchtime. Donnie blinked to focus his eyes and saw Sherry Brown crossing the street from the bank, yesterday's paperbacks held in one gloved hand and a plastic container in the other. Donnie remembered talk of chicken fried steak.

A cold blast of air rushed in around Mrs. Brown's flapping coat as she entered the store and closed the door behind her, using the hand holding the books. She made a disgusted noise that caused her red cheeks to puff out, then turned to face Donnie, her lips parting in a smile.

"I don't know what we did to deserve this cold weather so soon," she said. "I saw on the TV, though, that it should start warming up again tomorrow." She stepped up to the counter and put down the clear plastic container with the red lid. The plastic was steamed and opaque. She put the two thin paperbacks down and pulled the gloves off her age-spotted hands. "How are you today?" she asked.

"I'm good," Donnie answered. "How were the books?"

"Wonderful. Pure escapism. Fluffy as a summer cloud. I want something a little more serious today. Maybe a historical. Vikings or barons. Strong men, you know?" she said, winking at him.

"I understand," Donnie said. "Are the ladies calling you about tonight's meeting?"

"Yes. Yes, they are. I called it off. I was going to tell you. There's a chance of a little rain late this afternoon, and with this cold, it would freeze. Nobody should be on the roads, don't you think?" she asked.

"I agree," he said, thinking of the elderly women trying to maneuver their cars on the slick streets.

"I brought you the chicken fried steak I promised," Mrs. Brown said. "I heated it up in our breakroom. You have to be careful with chicken fried steak and microwaves because the breading will come off. There's mashed potatoes, gravy, and a roll. You go ahead and eat." She pulled the lid off the container and the smell of food immediately made Donnie's mouth water despite the big breakfast he'd had.

"Thank you, Mrs. Brown," he said.

"I love to see a thin man eat," she said, reaching into a coat pocket and pulling out a plastic fork and knife wrapped in a couple of napkins. She put them on the counter, picked up the books she was returning, and headed for the romance section of the store.

Donnie grinned and started cutting a bite of the tender steak. He was more than halfway done with the hot meal when Mrs. Brown returned with a thick novel set in ancient Briton. She put it on the counter and Donnie looked it over. It had the expected large-breasted woman with the shirtless man. He shook his head, wondering why publishers thought men of ancient times would have shaved their chests. He swallowed and asked, "That one sounds good?"

"I think so. The hero sounds like just the kind of rogue I'm in the mood for," she answered.

"Good," he said and lifted another bite of steak covered in cream gravy. "This is amazing," he added just before putting the food in his mouth.

"Thank you," she said. She gave him a concerned, motherly look. "You were staring out the window pretty hard when I was walking over. Like you were looking into another world. What's on your mind, Mr. Nelson?"

Donnie chewed and swallowed, his eyes on the elderly customer. He thought maybe, just maybe, he should add her to the list of people he truly respected. She was organized, reliable, involved in everything going on in this little town, and a genuinely caring person. She wasn't asking about him just to be nosy or spread gossip. He knew whatever he said would be kept in confidence, and she would give him the best advice she could.

"An old friend of mine passed away the other day," he said. "I'm debating whether or not to go to the funeral."

"Why wouldn't you go?" she asked.

Donnie thought about what to say. Finally, he shrugged and said, "Ghosts. Spirits from my past that I'm not ready to face."

"The person who died?"

"No," he answered quickly. "No, she was one of my high school teachers. Later, she continued to be a mentor to me. We'd fallen out of touch recently, especially after I moved. Most other people I know, I wouldn't go. But Mrs. Wilder ... It's tempting."

"Mr. Nelson," Sherry Brown began, "I've never questioned why you moved to Sagebrush and bought this struggling bookstore from Martha. That's not my business. I've never asked what you did before you came here. Again, not my business. It's obvious you're hiding from something. Why else would a young man move out here to the middle of nowhere? But that isn't my business.

"But I'll tell you this," she went on, "I know a few things about old people dying. I know that if this teacher meant a lot to you and you even think you should go to that funeral, you should go. This isn't something you get a second chance at. When they put her body in the ground, it's over."

"I could visit her grave," Donnie offered. "It would be less public. Nobody would be looking for me."

Sherry Brown clucked her tongue. "You are a man of mystery, Mr. Nelson. But that isn't my business. I say go to the funeral. You'll wish you had. Talking to a headstone isn't the same as looking at the person's face one last time, even if there's no life left in that face." She gave him a hard stare, her gray eyes almost glittering with light. "Now finish those last bites so I can take my container and get back to work before they fire me."

Donnie laughed out loud. "The bank would close down without you," he said. "This whole town would close without you."

"Nonsense," she said. "I'm just one little cog in this little machine we call Sagebrush. Same as you."

Donnie chewed as the smile faded. "I feel more like a piece of scrap wood someone dropped into the machine and it fell beside all the working parts. I'm not really doing any harm, but I shouldn't be there."

"I didn't know I was coming to a pity party," Mrs. Brown said. "You do more than you think you do." She closed up the plastic container as Donnie lifted out the last bite. "The bank's closing early so everyone can go home before that rain comes in. The whole town will shut down early today. You should, too."

Donnie nodded. "I think I might," he said. "I need to think about what you've said. Maybe I'll go camp at Mason's pond. I still have my fishing lease there."

"That's crazy," Mrs. Brown said. "It'll be below freezing tonight, with freezing rain."

"It sounds perfect," Donnie said, his mind made up about one thing, at least.

Chapter Four

S ilence.

Donnie stood for a moment in the little clearing among the pine trees and listened to the sound of absolutely nothing. There was no wind here. But it was the calm before a storm, which explained the lack of bird sounds. He was too far from any major roads for there to be the sounds of traffic. Above, no airplanes were visible; though they may have been there, above the heavy, thick canopy of dull gray clouds.

The rain would come soon. It would be cold rain.

Donnie made his first task gathering all the wood he could find on the ground. Beyond the little stand of pine trees were hardwoods, mostly cottonwood, that had dropped limbs here and there. He pulled them into his camp and used his little hatchet to chop them into small enough pieces to go into a campfire. He stacked the wood under the protective boughs of a pine tree and threw a blue tarp over it as an added measure to keep it dry when the rain came.

Next, Donnie pulled his five-man tent from his truck and spilled the contents from the bag on the ground. He scanned the place for small rocks and sticks that might stab into the floor of the tent, tossing a few stones out of the place where he would set up his shelter. He remembered buying the tent, long ago, when he was still a husband and father. He'd hoped his wife and kids would camp with him, and they had, once. But only once. The tent had been roomy enough, but nobody liked sleeping on the ground, not even with the foam mats he'd bought. No one liked breakfast cooked over an open fire. No one liked wearing bug spray, not having air conditioning, or running water for a shower. Nobody else had wanted to sit and stare into the fire or watch Nature in all its glory.

Nobody had shared his interest.

That's how it usually was.

Donnie threaded the collapsible poles through the loops and sleeves of the red-and-gray tent, drove stakes into the ground with the blunt side of his hatchet, and finally fitted poles into rings and had his structure standing up, the door facing south, away from the direction the wind would come from.

The tent up and firewood gathered, Donnie left the protection of the pines and walked thirty or so yards down to the shore of the large pond. He found a big rock with a mostly flat surface and sat down to look at the water reflecting the depressing gray of the sky. There was a slight ripple playing over the water and Donnie felt the cold wind caressing his face. He lifted his chin and closed his eyes and let the freezing fingers brush through his hair. He filled his lungs, held it, letting the breeze before the storm become part of his blood. Exhaling, he opened his eyes just as the first fat drop of cold rain slapped his cheek. Donnie smiled.

He thought how he'd like to sit here a while longer and feel the rain come for real, but he knew he'd have to sleep in his coat and gloves and jeans and he hadn't brought any others. He couldn't get these too wet. Taking one more deep, cold breath, he pushed himself from the rock and went back to his tent, sitting on the ground inside, the door flap pulled back, and he watched as the rain began as big, heavy drops and then became a pouring sheet of water.

The rain was still coming when the sun set somewhere beyond the downpour and the oppressive clouds that brought it. When it was dark, Donnie closed the flap of the tent, zipped it shut, and rolled onto his sleeping bag to stare at the ceiling of the tent. He listened to the sound of water plopping against the red nylon. The tent, though old, was still in good shape and didn't leak. As the night came down and the temperature dropped, the rain changed again, hardening as it froze on its descent to hit the tent and the trees and the pond and the earth.

Donnie thought of Mrs. Wilder. He thought of himself as a young man, working nights cleaning metal shavings from high production lathes in a machine shop. Aluminum, brass, a black iron alloy they called ductile. Pitchforks and shovels, burlap bags, heaving the heavy, wet sacks onto pallets and hauling them out on propane-powered forklifts from four in the afternoon until midnight. Making money to pay the bills and buy gifts for his young wife.

He hated his job. Of all his co-workers, there was only one other who read books. They talked together when Donnie cleaned the scrap metal from Bruce's machine, but it wasn't much. Donnie soon realized that Melissa wasn't a reader. She'd read a few books while they dated, she said, just to impress him, but she didn't like books and now that she was working full time and had her own house to keep up, she didn't want to read. And she didn't care to hear about what Donnie was reading.

She cared even less about what he was writing. Sure, she'd let him buy a nice electric typewriter for his twentieth birthday, but she didn't expect him to give up time sitting in the living room watching television with her to go to his workspace and type. "What's the point?" she asked over and over.

"I'm trying to get published," Donnie argued.

She shook her head. He stopped showing her the rejection letters. When they came, he studied them for hints about how he could make his writing better, then he filed them away. When he published his first story with a magazine based in southern California, he was only paid with a few copies of the issue with his story. Melissa was not impressed.

She missed a period. She peed on the plastic stick and the stick said she was pregnant. She wanted the spare room to become a nursery. Donnie remembered he was excited about the idea of a baby, too. He'd willingly given up his office. He moved his little desk, a piece he'd bought at Wal-Mart and assembled himself, to a corner of the living room, and put up a shelf for the reference books he used. They bought a used crib and decals of Winnie the Pooh for the walls of the new nursery.

Then the miscarriage happened.

Donnie sighed. The rain was pellets of ice outside the tent. The darkness was so deep that the ceiling of the tent was only a whisper of nylon barrier against the ice a few feet above his head. Ice rattled on the autumn leaves that still clung to the hardwoods beyond the pines. The wind was calm, though, and that was good.

They hadn't named the baby, Donnie remembered. Melissa had only been ten weeks pregnant, and there had not been anything recognizably human in the miscarriage. She hurt afterward, physically and emotionally, and though he tried to comfort her, there was nothing Donnie could do right for several weeks.

"Why are you pounding on that goddamn typewriter? Would you even have given a shit if Britney was sleeping?" she had shrieked at him one Saturday afternoon when she was trying to watch a TV chef. He hadn't dared move back into the baby's room, but had kept writing in the living room. Britney Nicole was one of the names they had talked about if the baby was a girl.

Donnie switched off the typewriter, he remembered. He took the old green canvas pup tent he'd had since childhood and went to a nearby state park and spent the rest of that day and night there. When he returned home, Melissa's mood had changed. She was glad to see him. She thought he might have left her forever. She apologized for how she'd been acting. Promised she would get over it. They would try again. She wouldn't lose the next baby. He did not ask why she'd used the name Britney to refer to the miscarried fetus.

Donnie never suggested that he move back into the spare room while they waited for her to get pregnant. He knew it would hurt her. He didn't type while she watched television, which is what she did most of the time she was at home. If inspiration hit and couldn't be put off, he took up a yellow legal pad and a blue ink pen and he wrote with those ancient tools until it was safe to use the typewriter, where he revised what he'd written.

Most of his writing was done weekdays between one in the morning and dawn, while Melissa slept. If it was a truly good night, he would write until he heard her alarm going off, then make her breakfast before she left for work and he finally went to bed.

He longed for others like himself, writers, to talk shop with. The local writers' group met on Tuesday evenings, though, and he had to work. He couldn't join them. But there was a poetry club that met in the local highway patrol conference room. Donnie got the information, and after missing a few meetings due to his shyness, he finally found the nerve to walk in one Saturday afternoon.

And there was Mrs. Wilder, holding a doughnut and talking to another elderly lady as they stood at a table of refreshments. Her head turned slightly as Donnie came in, he remembered, and she smiled at him. It was a knowing smile, small and confident and knowing, as if she'd been expecting he would come someday.

Though he'd won the poetry contest Mrs. Wilder hosted at the school, Donnie never really considered himself a poet. He wrote poetry for fun, mostly. It wasn't serious. He wrote pornographic poetry on the back of blank job tickets to amuse his co-workers at the machine shop. He tried writing poetry while he was in the poetry group, and the other members – all of them at least forty years older than Donnie – encouraged him. Some of the poetry was decent. Most was bad. But he was with people who loved writing, even if it wasn't the sword-and-sorcery or horror fiction he liked to write.

"Going to visit the nursing home again?" Melissa would ask before Donnie left for the club meetings. "I'll stay here and do laundry, then I'll do the dishes. Think you'll be home in time to mow the lawn?"

Conversations with Melissa were never about more than housework, what bills were due, how much money they had, or family gossip.

Mrs. Wilder, as always, encouraged him. She wasn't a fan of speculative fiction, but she looked at his short stories, most of it uninspired, copycat work, and offered suggestions and fixed his grammatical problems. She promised him that if he kept working, he would make it someday. He had the talent. He had the imagination. "Never give up the dream," she said, her old eyes moist and happy, her red-brown hair in the same poof she'd always kept it in when Donnie was in her class.

He kept writing, kept submitting, and eventually he sold a story for a real check. It was only a penny per word, totaling $2.91, but it was money for writing and he was encouraged. Melissa was dismissive.

Donnie began his second novel, having given up on his first one when Melissa said the plot he'd described to her once he was a hundred or so pages into it sounded too much like a movie they'd recently watched. The second one was more bizarre. Maybe *too* bizarre. He kept working on it, not talking to Melissa about it much. He talked to Mrs. Wilder, though. Every Saturday, she asked about his progress and Donnie told her what he'd written during the week. He knew she wasn't intrigued by the story, but she encouraged him, told him to keep at it, that it sounded interesting.

Donnie finished the novel, pulled the final page – numbered 324 – from his typewriter and added it to the stack. He put the stack in a brown folder and went to where Melissa was folding clothes in the bedroom. He tossed the manuscript onto the bed and slid his hands around her waist.

"I finished it," he whispered into her hair.

She grunted a response that was no comment.

Donnie burrowed his face through her hair and kissed her neck. His hands tightened on her, moved up, toward her breasts. She squirmed to the side and pushed away from him.

"Stop it," she said. "I'm busy."

"I just finished a novel," Donnie told her. "I finished my first novel."

"Good." She picked it up and handed it back to him, then folded the towel that had been under it.

Donnie looked at her dumbly for a moment, then turned away and left her with the clean clothes. He went back to his desk and sat in his metal folding chair, feeling the weight of the manuscript in his hands, wondering why he'd bothered doing it.

Tick ... tick ... tick

Ice pellets hit the tent and rolled down the sides unseen in the night. Donnie remembered how he'd felt that day, sitting alone in the little living room, holding the pages of a stillborn novel that never sold. But it had been his first, and he'd wanted his wife to be proud of him, to say something nice, to celebrate by making love to him.

She'd let him take her that night after commenting at dinner that he was sulking. But she'd just lain there while he rutted on her. She didn't even pretend to enjoy it. Donnie had rolled off her when he finished, turned off the lamp, and felt hot tears rolling from his eyes.

Melissa got pregnant that night and Brian was born the following January.

Donnie loved Brian from the beginning, but he knew he wasn't a good dad. He tried. He remembered crawling around on his hands and knees, pretending to be a bear or mountain lion, hunting the baby, then he was a horse and the toddler was riding him. But there was never a connection between him and his son like there was between Brian and Melissa.

There was always the desire to write. Sometimes he couldn't wait to put the baby to bed and get to his writing, done on a computer then, a used one with a twenty-megabyte hard drive and a green monochrome display. Melissa would give him dirty looks when he said he needed to write and handed Brian off to her.

Then one day Melissa found a timesheet Donnie used to keep track of how much time he spent writing. It had just been a curiosity for him based on an article he'd read in a magazine for writers. She mocked him.

"What? Are you gonna pay yourself? You sure aren't getting any money for what you do at that desk all the time," she said. Donnie tried to explain about the article, but she didn't care.

Melissa got pregnant again. They moved into a bigger house with a garage that had been converted to a large master bedroom. Donnie walled off one end of the long room with bookshelves and made it his office. Melissa accused him of hiding from her and Brian.

"I'm not hiding," he argued. "I just need my work space."

"That's not work," she told him.

"Your dad has a workshop," he countered. "You don't say anything about that. Why can't I have my space?"

"Dad makes useful things and sells them for actual money," she said.

Always, Mrs. Wilder was there. He complained to her that he was feeling trapped by responsibility, that nobody understood his need to write.

"People who don't write, don't understand," she told him. "It's the same with teaching. People who don't do it don't understand what it means to be part of the lives of your students. But if you believe in it, Donnie, if you believe in yourself, you keep at it. You do it no matter what."

He kept at it. He placed another story here and there. Sometimes for a tiny bit of money. More often for free copies of the magazine his story appeared in. Melissa shook her head and told him the payment wasn't worth the effort. She said her dad would teach him woodworking if he absolutely had to have a hobby.

"It's not a hobby," he shouted at her, a copy of a digest-sized magazine in his hand. The publication was cheap, shabby, unprofessional, but he was proud of the story he had in it. "You just don't understand," he told his wife, then he threw his old green tent into his beat-up Ford pickup and drove away.

He spent two nights at the lake, fishing a little, but mostly sitting and watching the wind on the water or the dancing flames of his campfire, wondering where his life was going. It was the evening of the second night when he was joined at the fire by the bounty hunter who changed his life.

Bolkar the Death Merchant seemed to step from the shadows into the circle of orange light and glower down at Donnie where he sat whittling a point on an oak stick. The man was about six feet tall and broad shouldered, wearing wolf pelts and leather pants. His eyes were black pits under heavy brows, his hair long and black, hanging loose around a hard face. As Donnie envisioned the man standing there, everything about him fell into place, his backstory, his ongoing quest, his regrets and the determination to never let them catch up to him. His strength. His willingness to do what others couldn't or wouldn't do.

Listening to the sound of sleet on his newer tent, Donnie remembered that long ago night. He didn't have his computer. Laptops weren't a thing yet. He had a spiral notebook and a couple of pens. He sat in the firelight and wrote frantically, outlining on one page, recording a snatch of dialogue playing in his head on another, writing down a description of Bolkar's physical aspects and a list of his most notable deeds. The man's childhood, his adolescence, his first kill, his first love, his first betrayal. The fever of creation kept Donnie up most of the night, throwing wood on the fire to keep enough light to see the pages as they turned under his pen.

When dawn came, he crawled into the tent, exhausted, and slept for a few hours, then broke camp and went back to town, but he didn't go home. He went to Mrs. Wilder's house, a nice stone structure in the old, wealthy part of town. As he rang the doorbell, he realized he hadn't showered in two days and didn't smell very good. He'd worn the same clothes, too. There was dirt on his hands and he could smell fish and worms. It was too late to turn away, though. The front door opened and his old teacher welcomed him inside.

Mrs. Wilder sat him at her dining room table of rich maple, gave him lemonade, and listened with a smile on her face as he told her about the bounty hunter and his binge writing. He pulled the notebook from his backpack and showed her the pages covered in blue ink.

"You have definitely hit on something that inspires you," she told him. "You need to keep after this. Write about your death merchant. See where he'll take you. Can you bring me twenty pages by Saturday?"

Donnie knew Melissa had been mad at him when he got home, but he couldn't remember what she said. He showered and went to his work space and started typing the first volume in the Death Merchant Chronicle. The words flowed as if he was only the faucet, running from his brain through his fingers, onto the green monitor, and then onto the printed page like water moving through pipes.

"It's so bloody," Mrs. Wilder said. "But that's how it has to be, I think. Your rules for magic are logical and believable. I like that the wizard can't just use an unlimited supply of spells without it taxing him."

She always encouraged him.

The first book was a hit. The check for his advance against royalties was equal to two years of his old salary. The paperback sale a few months later was *four* years of his salary. The foreign rights sales added up, and then the contract for the second book was staggering. There was a movie option from a major studio.

"You really need your own office," Melissa told him one day, baby LizBeth held against her bare breast. "We should buy a bigger house."

Donnie was tired. Despite the cold, he felt himself drifting off, carried on a cloud of memory. He thought of Mrs. Wilder beaming at him as she worked her way up the line of fans at his first book signing. How she'd leaned over the table and kissed his cheek, wrapping him in a scented cocoon of powder, perfume, and sugar cookies.

"I knew you would do it," she said, her hands on his cheeks, tears in her own eyes magnified by her big glasses. "I knew it."

"I miss you," Donnie whispered to the falling sleet. "I'll come see you. I have to. I have to say good-bye."

Chapter Five

E very blade of the brown grass was encased in a sleeve of glittering ice that crunched as Donnie moved about his camp, building up the fire and putting a skillet of bacon and eggs on a rack over the flames. Soon, the camp smelled of breakfast and coffee. He sat in a folding chair to eat from a sectioned maroon plastic plate and drink steaming coffee from a matching tiny cup.

He would break camp, go home, clean up, and get a good night's sleep before tomorrow's funeral, Donnie told himself. He was definitely going.

The drive back was slow. The highway under a cold, leaden sky still had patches of ice here and there and Donnie was afraid to drive too fast. Once home, he opened the shop just minutes before Sherry Brown started across the street from the bank. Donnie let out a little laugh as he settled into his usual chair and watched the woman cross the street, one gloved hand holding her coat closed, the other swinging briskly at her side.

"I didn't expect you to be back," the woman said as she came in and closed the door behind her.

"I actually just got back," Donnie said. "I haven't had time to shower. So, you know, sorry if I smell ripe."

She waved his concern away and pulled yesterday's book from her coat pocket. "This was so good!" she exclaimed. "I'm going to see if you have others by her." She hurried off into the shelves and a few minutes later Donnie heard her, "Whoo-eee!" and he guessed she'd found gold.

Mrs. Brown came back and showed him another thick novel with the typical perfect couple in medieval garb on the cover. "So?" she asked. "Did your trip to the wilderness provide the answers you needed?"

Donnie grinned. "It usually does," he said. "I'm going to Lawton tomorrow for the funeral. So, if you need another book, go ahead. I'll be home late tomorrow, but I don't think I'll open the shop."

"I don't blame you," she said. "I think I will get another book, but this cold weather and all the pumpkins on porches has put me in the mood for something scary." She wandered away again and came back with a beaten-up copy of Stephen King's *The Shining*.

"That's my favorite of his books," Donnie told her.

"The movie scared me to death, with the elevator opening and all that blood," Mrs. Brown said. "I was afraid to read the book, but I think I'll do it now."

"It's a lot different than the Stanley Kubrik movie," Donnie promised.

"Scarier?" she asked.

Donnie shrugged and grinned. "I thought so. Your mileage may vary."

She stacked her books up and looked at him earnestly. "Did you eat? I didn't think you'd be here, so I didn't bring anything."

He smiled at her and nodded. "I made a big breakfast at camp. I'm fine. Thank you, though."

"Donnie, you be careful driving tomorrow," she said. "I don't like that new weatherman on Channel 9, but he says tomorrow should be sunny. I'd trust Gary England more, but maybe this guy will be right and the roads will be in good shape. You drive careful," she repeated.

"I will, Mrs. Brown," Donnie promised. "Thank you."

"When the preacher asks people to stand up and share a memory about the deceased, don't you let that chance pass you by," she said, and he was struck by the earnestness in her voice. Her eyes were hard, but then softened into something wistful as she continued. "I hate to think that someday I'll be laying there in that box and people either won't have anything nice to say or they'll be too shy to say it."

Donnie looked at the woman for a long moment, his face slack. "What if the memories are just too personal to talk about?" he finally asked.

"Nonsense." Her gloved fingers flicked the thought away as if it was dust on the counter. "You pay your respects." She stopped herself suddenly and shook her head.

"Lord. I'm acting like I'm your mother and you're a little boy. I'm sure you'll do the right thing."

"My mother's gone," Donnie said softly. "I miss her. I ... I wasn't myself when she died and I don't even remember much about her funeral." He paused, then offered a weak smile. "It's nice to be mothered sometimes."

She reached across the counter and patted his wrist. "It is," she agreed. She squeezed his wrist once, lightly, then pulled her hand away. "Be careful, Donnie. You may not know it, but you're a part of this town and we'd miss you."

Donnie watched her leave the store and walk back to the bank. He shook his head and wiped a hand over the stubble around his mouth. She was a remarkable woman.

A good part of the rest of the afternoon was spent unpacking boxes and sorting books into stacks according to their genres, with one pile in a corner of the stockroom reserved for the poor copies that were too damaged to be worth shelf space. It still hurt a little to relegate a book to the trash pile, despite his years in the business and his own history, especially if it was a title he'd read and enjoyed. Donnie found himself with a copy of *Watership Down* in his hands, turning it over and over, caressing the broken paperback spine with one thumb while the other flipped the uneven edges of pages that had come unglued and stuck out from the book. The bottom quarter of the cover was torn away and there were water stains on what was left. He smiled, remembering how he'd first read about Hazel and Bigwig and their friends and enemies when he was in junior high. This copy, though, was beyond repair. With a sigh, he tossed it aside and pulled more books from the box.

At about four o'clock, the bell over the door sounded. Donnie looked into the store and saw Omar Sanchez looking around. Omar was fifteen, often carried an acoustic guitar in a black nylon case, and had a voracious appetite for fantasy fiction.

"I'll be right there," Donnie called. He pushed himself off the floor and stretched until his back popped. He started to leave the stockroom, then hesitated and grabbed the crippled copy of *Watership Down* before going out to greet his customer.

"Omar," Donnie said. "Is it still freezing out there?"

"It's pretty cold, Mr. Nelson," the boy answered.

Donnie smiled. He'd told the boy repeatedly that it was okay to call him Donnie, but Omar couldn't allow himself to call an adult by his first name. "No guitar today?"

"No, not today. Bertin's mom found out he's failing his English class, so he's making up all his missing work," Omar said.

"English homework," Donnie said, nodding. Bertin was another high school sophomore and the drummer for the little three-piece band Omar was in. "I haven't had any of that in a while."

Omar looked confused, then said, "No, sir, I guess not."

"Did you finish *The Prydain Chronicles*?" Donnie asked.

"Yes! I loved all the books. That black cauldron that would bring bodies back to life was pretty cool," he said. "I like how the author made Taran grow up a little more in every book, too."

"It was one of my favorites when I was a teenager," Donnie said. "I thought you'd like it." He saw that, despite his enthusiasm, the boy was shifting from foot to foot nervously, not used to extended conversations with adults. Donnie put the book he was holding on the counter and pretended to wipe away some dust. "So, what's next?"

"What would you recommend?" Omar asked.

Donnie looked at the floor as if he was deep in thought and tried to hide his grin. Omar reminded him a lot of himself at that age. He thought of all the great fantasy books he'd read as a teenager. The boy had already gone through Tolkien and C.S. Lewis, Christopher Paolini, Rick Riordan, and of course J.K. Rowling, the gateway to fantasy nowadays.

"There's Robert E. Howard," Donnie suggested. "He wrote the original Conan the Barbarian stories, plus a lot of other great characters. You might like Patricia A. McKillips' *Riddlemaster of Hed* series, or Ursula K. LeGuin's *Earthsea* books." He thought for a moment about George R.R. Martin, but decided against such a grim series.

"I saw the movie *Conan the Barbarian*," Omar said. "Jason Momoa was cool in it."

"Umhmm," Donnie agreed. "Back in the '80s there was a better movie with Arnold Schwarzenegger as Conan. You should give it a try sometime. Skip the sequel, though." He looked toward the fantasy shelves. "I have all the Conan books together, even if they're by different authors. Go all the way to the right, third shelf from the top."

"Okay. Thanks, Mr. Nelson," Omar said and started toward the shelves.

Donnie went around the counter and took his usual chair and looked out the window at the sleepy little town he'd chosen to call home. The clouds were breaking up, letting some fading sunlight wash over the streets. Shadows became long and dark, hungry harbingers of the coming night. A few people moved here and there. Wilson Pepper, the editor of *The Sagebrush Democrat* newspaper, stood in front of his office, smoking a cigarette, his sheepskin suede coat hanging open. He liked true crime and horror novels and was a binge reader, sometimes going months without a book, then reading six or seven a week for half a year. Wilson took a final drag from his smoke before throwing the butt at the gutter in a dramatic John Wayne-type of move, then went back into the office of his weekly paper.

Omar stepped out of the shelves carrying three thin paperbacks. He put them on the counter and stood expectantly. Donnie looked down and saw the top book was the first in the Ace series of Conan paperbacks. The muscular barbarian hero, knife in one hand, a grimace on his face, battled a primitive monster. Donnie nodded with the memory of his first time reading the pulp book. He picked it up, expecting to see the second volume in the Ace series below it.

He froze, then recovered himself and wrote down the ISBN from the Howard book. He picked up the second book, *Bolkar, the Death Merchant,* and recorded the ISBN without comment, putting it back down on the counter and covering it with the Conan novel. The third book was another Conan story, but written by Robert Jordan.

"Is that other one any good?" Omar asked. "The one about the death merchant?"

"It's okay," Donnie answered.

"Isn't that guy's name the same as yours? Or almost?" Omar asked. "Donald L. Nelson. You're Donnie Nelson."

"Yeah, it's almost the same," Donnie agreed. The first four or five years he'd had the bookshop, he hadn't allowed any of his titles to make their way to the shelves. If they came into the store, he'd thrown them in the trash. It had just been the past few years, when he felt the chances were slim anyone would connect them to him, that he'd almost secretly put a few on the shelves, almost like he was hiding the fact from part of himself.

"Mr. Nelson, can I ask you something?" Omar asked. "It's not about books."

"Sure, Omar. What's up?" Donnie asked, a little surprised.

The boy hesitated, his fingers caressing the edges of his new books as he searched for words of his own. "You don't have a girlfriend, do you?" Omar asked, then flushed. "I mean, I don't, either. I want one, but ... I don't know how to get one and I think I might end up living alone."

"Like me?" Donnie asked. He managed to smile, but inside, his words echoed through a deep empty chamber in his chest.

"I'm sorry," Omar offered. "My dad, well, he tells me to just fu-- to go to bed with a lot of girls until I get one pregnant, then learn to love her. That doesn't seem right to me."

Donnie shook his head. "Your dad said that?" The boy nodded. "Well, that's not the way I'd go about it. You're too young for that. You have a bright future ahead of you and you don't want a baby and wife, or baby mama, or whatever, in your life just yet. It's okay to hold out for love. I thought guitar players and singers got lots of girls."

"Just the good ones, I guess," Omar said, and smiled a little.

Donnie thought back to himself as a teenager. "There's time, Omar. Figure out who you are and what you want out of life. Go to college. Get out of this little town and you'll find there's a world of opportunities, and girls, out there waiting for you."

"Why did you come here, Mr. Nelson? Where did you live before?" Omar asked.

Donnie sucked in a deep breath and held it, then let it out in a slow sigh. "I made a mess of my life, Omar. I came here to leave it all behind."

The boy nodded. "This is a bad place to start over. I haven't been to other places very much, but this seems like a town that's dying. It's taking a long time, but I think it's dying."

"It's definitely a town stuck in time," Donnie agreed. "Isolated. That's why I picked it. But enough of that. Keep reading. Keep playing that guitar. You're a good-looking young fella and you'll be fighting the girls off before you know it."

Omar gave up a real grin and his face transformed into one Donnie knew girls would soon find attractive. "Thank you, Mr. Nelson," he said. "For the books and for talking to me."

Donnie nodded and smiled. "You're welcome," he said. "Well, I hope you like them." He looked at the battered copy of *Watership Down*. "I want to give you this one. I was about to toss it out when you came in. It's ... not really fantasy, but I think you might like it. I did when I was your age." He put the copy on top of the three the boy had paid for.

Omar's eyes lit up despite the condition of the book. "Thanks, Mr. Nelson. I can really have it for free?"

"Yeah," Donnie said. "It's in pretty bad shape. I couldn't sell it. I'd rather give it to someone who might like it than throw it away."

Omar picked up the book and started reading the back cover. "They're rabbits?" he asked skeptically.

Donnie chuckled. "Yes, they're rabbits. But they travel to a new home and have to go to war. Give it a try."

"Okay. I will. Thanks again, Mr. Nelson." Omar scooped up his four books and tucked them into pockets of his coat.

"See you later, Omar," Donnie said, waving as the teenager left the store. Donnie watched him turn right and walk past the picture window, then disappear from sight, toward the mobile home park where most of the town's Hispanic residents had settled, or settled for a while before moving into more permanent housing, if they stayed to work at the local fertilizer factory.

Omar in the fertilizer factory, with a wife and kid before he was eighteen, Donnie mused. He shook his head again. What father would want that for his kid?

Donnie sat and stared blankly at the window as night settled over the town. Headlights cruised by as people left offices and went home. The bank went dark. The café emptied. The clothing store, hardware store, and dollar store all closed for the night. Soon, his light and the light in the newspaper office were the only ones he could see were still on, not that he really noticed them.

Bolkar …

Donnie remembered the letter accepting the novel for publication. Somewhere in the boxes he refused to open, it was still in its frame where he'd preserved it so long ago. He'd submitted it hesitantly after a three-minute pitch session with the fantasy editor at the state's biggest writers' conference. His wife had been against him going, saying they couldn't afford the cost and that he was just trying to make friends who wouldn't like her because she didn't like to write or read. But he'd remained steadfast and bore the arguments until she gave in and he sent the check for his fee. The editor, Ed Warner, had been telling people all weekend that their projects weren't right for him, according to the gossip Donnie heard in the panel sessions. When his time came, he expected the same. Ed had seemed bored as Donnie sat down, offering a half-hearted handshake.

"Tell me about your project," the heavyset editor invited.

"It's kind of a Conan the barbarian in a grim Middle Earth," Donnie began. He'd heard it was good to compare his work to something the editor would already know.

Ed Warner offered an indulgent smile and rotated his plastic water cup on the table. "Tell me about your protagonist," he suggested.

"He's a bounty hunter called Bolkar the Death Merchant. He's a big guy, muscular, dresses in black," Donnie said, feeling his throat dry as he talked. "His village was massacred when he was a boy. We only see that in flashbacks. He'll work for anyone if the price is right. He doesn't care if they're guilty or not. And he never brings anyone back alive. But his conscience is finally starting to bother him, especially when he gets sent to kill a woman said to be a powerful witch."

The editor nodded. "How is your story told? Third person?"

"Yes, sir," Donnie said. "Third person, past tense, but limited to Bolkar's point of view."

"Why?"

Donnie stumbled mentally. He hadn't expected that question. "Well, I think it adds suspense for this kind of story. He can be surprised by events he didn't expect, and the reader will be surprised, too. But the narrative voice takes the reader through his thoughts without him actually having to articulate it, like in first person," Donnie said, feeling the rush of words. "I think completely omniscient becomes too distant. That's just my opinion, though."

Ed pursed his lips and nodded again. "Have you published anything before?"

"A few short stories and poems," Donnie answered.

"You've finished your book?"

"Yes, sir. It's told in four parts. Four long stories in chronological order, each with its own objective."

"How long is it?"

"It's eighty-two thousand words."

Ed Warner shifted his bulk in his chair and took a sip of water, then fixed his blue eyes on Donnie. "Send me a full synopsis and the first three chapters. The fantasy market is pretty hot right now. Yours might be a little too much like the Conan property, but that isn't our property, so I'm willing to take a look. No promises, you understand?"

Donnie nodded, not trusting himself to speak. Ed Warner had just asked to see his work! It wasn't an acceptance, but it was so much more than he'd dared hope for. "Yes, sir," he finally croaked out.

The editor smiled at him and seemed to suddenly relax. "You don't have to call me sir. But I like that you did. Do you have an agent, Donnie?"

"No, sir. Umm ... No, Mr. Warner. I don't. Do I need one?"

"Not necessarily," he said. "If I accept your book -- and again, I haven't even seen it, so it's still less than a maybe -- but if I did, you'd want to find an agent to deal with the contract. If you have an offer, getting an agent will be a lot easier. This book, it's the first in a series?"

"Yes," Donnie said. "I have the story arc for the first five books. It could end there. I'm not sure yet."

"That's fine," Ed said. "When you send that submission, give me a real brief summary of the series arc."

"Okay," Donnie said, suddenly wanting to slip away before this man changed his mind. He wanted to run to the bank of payphones in the lobby and call home to share the news. "Thank you so much, Mr. Warner. I'll get that in the mail Monday."

"That's fine, Donnie. It was nice to meet you." Ed held out his clammy, meaty hand again and Donnie gave it a fast pump, then hurried away from the pitch room.

In the lobby, he went to the cubby on the far end of the line of seven pay phones and dropped some change into the slot. He dialed home. Melissa picked up on the second ring.

"Ed Warner just asked to see my book!" Donnie gushed. "The first chapters, I mean. Ed Warner!"

"Who's that?" Melissa asked.

"The editor I told you about," Donnie said, his voice losing some enthusiasm. "With Obelisk Publishing. One of the big companies."

"Oh," she said. "Is he paying you?"

"Not yet. He just agreed to look at a partial. The synopsis and first three chapters," Donnie said.

"Is that all? He didn't even ask for the whole book?" she asked.

"No. That's not how it works. He asks for the beginning to see if he likes it, and if he does, he asks for the rest," Donnie explained. "This is the first step."

"Oh. Well, that's nice," she said. In the background, Donnie heard the baby start to cry. "I need to feed him," Melissa said. Then she was gone.

Donnie hung up the phone and turned away, his head down, his brow furrowed.

"Don't let it get you down."

Donnie looked up to find a plump elderly woman in plum-colored pants and a white blouse with yellow polka dots on it looking at him. Her powdery cheeks had too much rouge on them and her bright red mouth smiled at him.

"What?" he asked.

"I heard," she said. "I'm waiting on my ride. I didn't mean to eavesdrop, but the excitement in your voice caught my attention." She smiled and reached over and put a papery hand on his wrist. "You had a good pitch. That's a big deal. I'm sorry the person you were talking to didn't understand that. Good luck to you." She patted his arm and withdrew her hand.

Donnie smiled at her, appreciating her kindness. "Thank you," he said. "It was my wife."

"She's not a writer, is she?"

"No, ma'am," he said.

She smiled and nodded. "People who don't write just don't understand." She looked through the glass doors to a creamy Cadillac that had just pulled up. "That's my ride. You keep your chin up, young man." She pushed through the door before Donnie could think to open it for her, got into the luxury car, and drove away.

Donnie went to more panels at the conference, but he could never remember what they were about. He left before the banquet to go home and read over his first three chapters again.

Donnie shut off the lights and locked the doors to Lost Pages Bookstore. He went to his back room and microwaved a can of chunky beef stew that he ate with half a sleeve of saltine crackers and a can of Diet Coke. He read a few pages from a novel about a depressed married woman who jumped into a river in France and was saved by a homeless man, but his eyelids wouldn't stay up and he soon put the book aside and slept within minutes of turning out the light.

Chapter Six

F riday dawned clear and cool under a Technicolor blue sky made all the more brilliant by the gossamer wisps of puffy white cloud drifting beneath the azure dome. There was a light breeze that made the air seem colder than it was, but Donnie left his coat open as he walked from the closed store to his truck, carrying his suit jacket and tie in a garment bag that he hung in the back seat.

Sagebrush was coming to life around him. The café was open, but only a couple of pickup trucks were parked out front. Jerry Blanton, the owner of the little jewelry store down the street, was sweeping the sidewalk in front of his business and the dress shop his wife ran next door. Duwayne Keller, the chief of police, sat on the park bench in front of the police station, sipping coffee that sent curls of steam rising from his thick white ceramic mug.

Donnie got into his truck and started the engine, letting it run for a minute before backing out of the spot he'd taken in front of Lost Pages yesterday instead of his usual place in the alley behind the row of buildings. He waved at the men outside as he crept through the little, almost antiquated downtown area, speeding up as Main Street reverted into the two-lane state highway that would take him to the four-lane highway, through Woodward, and on south to Lawton. It was almost a four-hour drive, but he had a good audiobook loaded on his phone and playing through the truck's Bluetooth connection.

Donnie stopped in Woodward for breakfast at McDonald's, and again in Weatherford to relieve himself of the coffee he'd had with breakfast. It was after noon when he rolled into Lawton. Even after so many years, the streets, buildings, and natural landmarks were as familiar as if he'd just left yesterday. There were changes, of course. The town had sprawled into what used to be fields of wheat, and a few businesses had come or gone, but the city still had that feeling of home.

Donnie shook it off. This place was not home. It had been once, but it wasn't now. It was a little city of broken promises, broken dreams, despair, and so many things he'd rather not think about.

He found the church where Mrs. Wilder's body would be laid out in her coffin. He was almost an hour early. Donnie considered leaving and getting a quick lunch, but the biscuit from breakfast was still sitting heavy in his stomach and he wasn't hungry. There were other cars and trucks parked around the church. A few more pulled in as Donnie sat with his engine idling. He watched as elderly people got out of the vehicles and slowly made their way to the front door of the tall red brick church, all wearing their best dark clothes. He didn't recognize any of them, and he was glad for that.

Stay anonymous, he told himself.

Donnie shut off the engine and got out. He left his overcoat in the truck, taking his black sport coat and tie from the garment bag and carrying them over his arm as he made his way to the church, enduring the chill in the air as he hurried his steps.

The church foyer was warm and sterile, filled with racks of pamphlets and a small table of books and mints. A young Hispanic lady with a smile that was somehow both radiant and sad greeted him.

"Thank you for coming," she said. "I'm Shelby, from the funeral home. Would you please sign the guest book for the family?" She motioned with small hands devoid of jewelry toward an oblong open book on the table.

Donnie nodded and moved to the book. The signatures above the first line were cursive, shaky from aged hands. Donnie studied the blank line, considering using a fake name – a pseudonym since he was a writer – but somehow that didn't seem right. Not for Mrs. Wilder. As much as he wanted to come and go without being noticed, he couldn't use a fake name at her funeral. He signed Donnie Nelson, compromising with himself by not signing like he used to do when he autographed books.

"You can go into the sanctuary and view Mrs. Wilder, if you'd like," Shelby told him.

"Is there a restroom?" Donnie asked. "A mirror? I need to put on this tie."

"Of course," the young woman said. She motioned down a narrow corridor and told him to open the second door on his left.

His tie on, his collar straight, and the top button of his sport coat fastened, Donnie smiled back at Shelby as he passed her and entered the church's sanctuary. His nose was assaulted by the smells of cologne, hair spray, new carpet, and old hymnals. And death. Or maybe he just imagined that odor as his eyes picked out the shiny black box at the front of the room. The split lid was open on one end, showing gleaming, puffy white satin. Knots of people, mostly old people, sat around the large room, whispering. All heads turned when Donnie entered. He was evaluated, then eyes moved away, but attention remained on him as he made his way up the center aisle to the waiting casket.

Donnie took a deep breath and stepped up next to the raised box. He steeled himself and looked down.

Mrs. Wilder lay there in a dark blue blouse with a white collar. Her liver-spotted hands were crossed over her chest, one over the other, her nails perfectly manicured. Her hair, thinner than he remembered, was styled in her typical bouffant, still dyed the same golden-red he remembered from high school. Her thick, large-lensed glasses were gone, making her face look naked, but younger than Donnie expected. The skin of her face was pale, almost translucent, and seemed as thin as dried parchment. Her eyes were closed and for a moment Donnie imagined them opening, rolling to the side to look at him, her red lips parting to ask, "Why aren't you writing, Donnie?"

Behind him, Donnie felt other people waiting to see the empty husk of the woman who had been so inspiring to him. He lowered his head, closed his eyes, and mouthed, "Good-bye, and thank you, Mrs. Wilder." He moved away, found a seat in the back of the sanctuary, on the edge of the row, and sat down.

His eyes scanned the people in the church, and found a set of eyes staring back at him. The eyes belonged to a girl, young, probably mid to late teens, possibly early twenties, turned in her pew to look at him curiously. He offered a half-smile and nodded in greeting, then looked away. She did not look away. She sat alone, in the center of the three sections of pews. Her hair was dyed sky blue and silvery white. Her skin was very white, so that the scattering of freckles on her cheeks and nose stood out. The black shirt and black jeans she wore seemed out of the ordinary for her. Donnie suspected she typically wore loose, flowing clothes, like a gypsy or bohemian. Their eyes met again and he smiled and nodded once more. She nodded back and turned away at last.

More and more people entered the sanctuary. Most went to the front and viewed the body. Some did not. Most came in couples or small groups. Donnie tried to guess how each person had known his old teacher. Some, the older ones, were probably friends from Mrs. Wilder's life outside the school. A few he thought he recognized as other teachers from the high school. Donnie lowered his eyes to look at the memorial pamphlet he'd found in the pew whenever he thought one of the other teachers might look his way. Other, younger people, were former students like him, he suspected. Mrs. Wilder had been loved by her pupils. Soon, the sanctuary was nearly full. An elderly woman who smelled of talcum powder and roses sat next to Donnie; her husband, who seemed to have Parkinson's Disease, sat trembling on the other side of her.

After what seemed a very long wait, a somber minister who appeared to be in his early forties stepped onto the stage and went to the podium. He looked at the packed sanctuary and his shaved, shiny face broke into a smile.

"I feel the love," he said in a voice that carried without booming. "My name is David Yarbrough. I'm the lead minister. Welcome to our church. Wanda Wilder was a loved woman. I know she would be so pleased to see the turnout here today. She lived a long life, a rich life, touching and improving the lives of thousands. She outlived all her siblings, her husband, and, tragically, her one daughter. She is survived by her granddaughter, Josey, who she was so proud of." He paused and smiled into the gathering, his eyes picking out someone Donnie couldn't identify in the crowd. He'd known Mrs. Wilder had a daughter, but wasn't aware she'd died.

"There's a video that Josey put together with photos from Wanda's life," Rev. Yarbrough said. "It's about seven minutes long, with music and captions by Josey. She did a great job."

A white screen descended from the ceiling above the stage. The lights dimmed and a projector sent a beam of light from a booth in the back and above the sanctuary. Melancholy instrumental music began playing and images rolled across the screen, showing Wanda Wilder as Wanda Fitzgerald when she was a child with her brothers and sisters, as a high school graduate, a college graduate, her first faculty photo as a teacher, as the winner of the state's Teacher of the Year award, many photos of her in the classroom with students.

Suddenly, Donnie felt his heart skip and goosebumps break out on his arms as he saw himself as a teenager on the screen, shaking hands with Mrs. Wilder as the winner of her poetry contest so long ago. His name and the year were in the picture. He looked around surreptitiously to see if anyone was looking back at him, but no one he could see was.

More pictures, more poetry winners, other students, a few Donnie recognized, then pictures of Mrs. Wilder speaking at conferences for writers, in casual settings with the poetry group Donnie remembered attending, volunteering at a Thanksgiving dinner.

And then Donnie was on the screen again, posing with his former teacher as she held a copy of his first novel in a local bookstore, both of them smiling. *With Donald L. Nelson at his first book signing,* the caption said.

His eyes wide and his throat dry, Donnie quickly looked around the big room. No one was looking at him. All eyes were on the screen or down at cell phones. Except …

The teenager with the slivery-blue hair was looking at him again. She smiled and nodded once, then turned back to the screen.

She knows …

Who was she?

Was that Josey? The granddaughter?

It had to be.

The music ended without Donnie noticing the last several photos. The lights came on and the screen ascended and vanished. The minister returned to the podium and beamed at his audience.

"What a wonderful life," he said. "Wanda was truly a blessing to so, so many of us. Praise God for her. She was a longstanding member of our congregation, a Sunday school teacher for many years." He paused and smiled. "She was my Sunday school teacher when I was in third and fourth grade. I'll never forget her lesson on the plagues of Egypt." He paused again as a ripple of happy murmurs went through the crowd.

"As her health failed over the past few months, I spent a lot of time with Wanda, mostly in the hospital," Rev. Yarbrough said. "Her spirits were always high. She was happy with her life, with what she'd accomplished, and was ready to move on to her reward. She had a few Bible verses she wanted me to share with you, plus a poem she was working on for this occasion."

He read from Psalms and Ecclesiastes, his voice rising and falling in a cadence that seemed to be unique to ministers. Donnie's attention drifted and he found himself scanning the crowd again, picking out people he recognized, or thought he did, and devising strategies for avoiding them if they tried to approach him.

"On the back of your memorial, you'll find the text of Wanda's final poem," the minister said. "If you want to follow along, I'll read it to you."

Donnie looked at the back page of the little rectangular brochure. There were thirteen lines in fancy script.

Farewell

Our paths have forked;

I journey on a different road,

But I carry thoughts of friends --

Of students and colleagues --

As I journey on.

Don't cry for me.

Don't weep!

If I touched you in some helpful way

I did what I was put here to do.

Farewell! Farewell!

We'll meet again

On the far side of the mists.

He smiled, thinking of how Mrs. Wilder had once talked to him about how somber his poetry always was. It was no surprise that, as she lay dying, she continued to write optimistic verse about living life to the fullest.

"At this time, would anyone like to stand where you are and share a memory about Wanda?" the minister asked.

Dozens of people rose to their feet. Donnie looked around, panicked, remembering his promise to Sherry Brown. He hadn't expected there to be so many people. What if he was recognized? He'd already been on the screen twice. Mrs. Brown's words came back to him. *Regret.* He would regret it if he didn't speak now. Reluctantly, slowly, he stood up. The minister started on the other side of the sanctuary, choosing people to speak.

" ... she was the nicest teacher ... "

" ... she helped me when I couldn't understand what other teachers were saying ... "

" ... Mrs. Wilder talked to me at the shelter and helped me through rehab ... "

" ... Wanda was the kindest person and my best friend for fifty-three years ... "

" ... I remember her reading poetry in the park ... "

" ... she made Sunday school interesting ... "

" ... she inspired me to keep a journal and that's kept me sane ... "

" ... she made the best pumpkin pie ... "

" ... talked to me when my own daughter died the same way hers did ... "

Then the minister pointed at Donnie and asked what he'd like to share. Donnie felt his mouth go dry and his throat close up. He hadn't thought out what he wanted to say. He looked around and saw hundreds of eyes looking back at him.

"Mrs. Wilder was a huge inspiration to me, both professionally and personally," Donnie said, forcing enough air through his throat to make the appropriate sounds. "She was a wonderful woman and I'm a better person for knowing her."

He sat down quickly as the crowd murmured assent. Another man spoke, then a woman, and then the minister said, "And finally, Josey, would you like to speak?"

The girl with the silvery-blue hair stood up slowly and looked around at the crowd. She cleared her throat loudly. "Grandma loved you all," she said. "She told me she hoped people didn't have to interrupt their schedules to come to her funeral. I told her there would be a lot of people here. She laughed and said she didn't think many would come." Here the girl reached up and knuckled away a tear from one eye. She smiled and her voice broke a little as she said, "I knew she would be wrong. Thank you." She swiped at the other eye, wiping the tear away on her black jeans. "When my mom decided she couldn't raise me, Grandma took me in. She was already living alone because Grandpa had died. She treated me so good." Her voice broke again. "She set rules, but she let me be me with my crazy hair and torn jeans and loud music. I – I just love her so much."

She practically fell back into her seat. Hands reached over and rubbed and patted her. A swell of voices showed appreciation.

"And now, if you'd like to say a final good-bye to Wanda Wilder, you're welcome to pass by the casket," the minister said. "We'll move to the gravesite for those who want to come." He named a cemetery and gave brief directions.

People stood and moved toward the open casket, filing by slowly, some crying, many smiling at memories. Donnie considered slipping out of the church, but he was surrounded by people shuffling toward the front of the sanctuary and found himself pushed along with them.

At the casket, he lowered his head and took one more look at his old teacher, then moved on. Outside, people lingered by cars, waiting for the procession that would go to the cemetery. The long, shiny black hearse waited with the back door gaping open. Two police cruisers were parked nearby to lead and end the procession.

Donnie went to his truck and slid into the driver's seat. He inserted his key, but didn't start the engine yet. To go to the grave or not? No, he'd done enough. He reached for the key.

There was a tapping at the passenger window.

Donnie looked over, fearing a reporter, expecting someone who'd ask for directions to the graveyard. Neither was the case.

"Open the fucking door!"

Instinctively, Donnie's hand moved and hit the door lock. The doors clicked and the passenger door swung open. An elderly man in a black suit climbed in beside him.

"Dad?"

Chapter Seven

"Didn't think you'd see me, did you?" Mike Nelson glared at his son and Donnie felt as if he was nine years old and had broken the neighbor's window with his slingshot again. "Probably thought you wouldn't see me again until you came to *my* funeral, if you'd even bother to bring your sorry ass home for it."

"What are you doing, Dad?" Donnie asked. "Why are you here?"

"I knew you'd be here, Donnie. I knew if you were going to come home for anything, it would be your favorite teacher's funeral. And I was right."

"Okay," Donnie said. "But what are *you* doing here? Why aren't you ... home?"

Mike snorted. His thin gray hair was combed over a bigger bald spot than Donnie remembered. His ears seemed bigger, too. But otherwise he didn't look seven years older. He also didn't look like a man suffering from dementia. "The old folks' home? Is that what you mean, Donnie? That place where you and your sisters put me after your mom died?"

"I ... " Donnie lowered his head, unable to hold the gaze of his father's blazing, very clear blue eyes. He nodded.

"Lighten up, kid," Mike said. "Your life was a mess with the divorce, then Mom dying. Maggie ramrodded that operation. She wanted the house. You were out of it, Katelyn never would stand up for anything, and let's face it, I probably *acted* like an old man with Alzheimer's. Losing your mom fucked me up. I loved that woman."

Donnie nodded again. "I know that. But still, I just let Maggie take over. I didn't ... I had doubts, but I never acted on them."

All around them, car engines were starting and vehicles were moving, getting into line, following the police car and the hearse pulling out of the church parking lot.

"We'll talk about it later. Let's go to the gravesite," Mike said. "I want to visit a couple of other graves while we're there."

"Can you go?" Donnie asked. "I mean, well, are you supposed to be here?"

"I got myself checked out to attend this funeral," Mike said. "They know I'm not actually crazy. It's a game we play at the home. I've got nowhere else to live now. I checked myself out and used one of those phone apps where people drive their own car like a taxi. Some long-haired guy who talks too much drove me here. We were late."

"Oh," Donnie said. He started his truck and pulled into line behind a cream-colored Lincoln Town Car. "You just checked out?"

"The nurses like me," Mike answered.

"So, do I take you back after the service?" Donnie asked.

"We'll talk about that later, too."

"Dad, this doesn't seem right. Did you just *leave*?"

"Don't worry about it, Donnie. Just watch out so you don't rear end that Lincoln."

Donnie saw he'd gotten too close to the car in front of him and hit his brakes. The truck slowed, the gap between vehicles widened. They went through traffic, moving in a long line toward the cemetery. Donnie tried to think of things to say to the father he hadn't seen in years.

"How have you been, Dad?"

Mike snorted again and gave a brief bark of laughter. "You mean other than being locked up in a home for old people who shit themselves and eat baby food and watch HGTV all fucking day? I've been great, Donnie. Great."

"I'm sorry, Dad," Donnie said. "I should have known better. I shouldn't have let Maggie do that to you. I just didn't know. I wasn't myself."

"We've covered that already."

"Yeah." Donnie drove, navigating a couple of turns, glancing at the cars pulled over to let the procession pass. "Is it bad?"

Mike took a moment before answering. "It wasn't horrible at first," he said. "I was pretty out of it. I didn't mind being taken care of. But as I got used to the idea of Faye being gone, I realized where I was and what was going on. By that time, Maggie had taken the house. I signed it over to her. I apparently signed a lot of stuff when I wasn't in my right mind."

"Can we fix that?" Donnie asked. "I mean, if you don't want to live there anymore?"

"Am I gonna kick my daughter out of the house she's living in?" Mike asked angrily.

"It's your house."

"It's her home. My grandkids live there," Mike answered. "She was a bitch for taking it the way she did, but I'm not gonna be the asshole that kicks her and her family out on the street."

"So you're just going back to the nursing home?"

"Assisted living center," Mike corrected. "There's a difference. I'm not going back. I'm going to Bum Fuck Egypt, or wherever the hell you live now."

Donnie felt his hands tighten on the steering wheel. "You're ... coming with me?"

"You got a problem with that? Do I need to lay the guilt on a little thicker?" Mike asked, his voice hard. "Almost eight years I've been living in that home, having my sleep interrupted every fucking night by nurses wanting to check to see if I'm still breathing because if I stop breathing the checks stop coming. I think you owe me a visit."

Donnie didn't answer. He followed the cars through the wrought iron cemetery gates and found a place to park under an elm tree clinging to its summer leaves like an old person holding memories of childhood.

"No comment, huh?" Mike asked. "Trying to think of a way to convince me to go back to the home? It's not gonna happen, Donnie. I'm going to visit my son."

"Dad, I don't even live in a house. I run a little bookstore. I sleep in the back room," Donnie argued.

"If you can, I can. I slept on the ground in the rain in Vietnam. I think I can make do in a bookstore stockroom," Mike said.

Donnie looked at his father but couldn't hold the intense gaze. He turned back and looked through the windshield. Men in suits were moving the coffin to a gaping hole in the earth. "For how long?" he asked.

"Not as long as she'll be where they're putting her," Mike answered. "I'm going to visit my buddies. You see your teacher into the ground." He threw open his door and slid out of the truck. Donnie had no choice but to do the same.

The minister was more somber this time and didn't talk about Mrs. Wilder's life. He stuck to scriptures about the meaning of life and death and service to the Almighty. He stood between the closed casket and a wall of flowers that had been erected in a semi-circle around the foot of the grave. A large gray polished stone stood at the other end of the open hole. People cried quietly despite Mrs. Wilder's poem.

Donnie stood awkwardly, staring at the shiny box, thinking of his own mortality, remembering times in Mrs. Wilder's class, and thinking of his father. It was another aspect of the guilt he carried. He'd been depressed, his marriage broken, his kids blaming him, not wanting to visit him or talk to him on the phone. His wife calling and texting daily to tell him what a horrible person he was, how he'd ruined the family, how the kids would need years of therapy, how he wasn't a good person who'd made a mistake, he was simply a bad person who'd thrown away years of marriage.

And then his mom died. She called the family together for dinner on a Sunday afternoon in April to announce that she had cancer, that it was terminal, and that the doctors said she had about three months left. She lasted almost two. Even her husband hadn't known how severe her illness was. "I knew he'd just fret about it," she'd said when Mike raged out of the room during the family meeting.

The memory of Maggie coming to him the day after Mom's funeral and talking about having Dad committed to a home was fuzzy and distorted to Donnie. He'd been drinking a lot at the time to drown the grief and depression.

"You really think he's got dementia?" Donnie remembered asking.

"Don't you?" Maggie countered. "Have you listened to him? Watched him? He's walking around in a daze, talking like Mom's still with us, like she's out for groceries or whatever. His mind is gone."

"I don't know," Donnie remembered being hesitant, unsure, trying to remember something that would help him evaluate his father's recent behavior.

"I do," Maggie insisted. "I can't take care of him and my kids. Do you want to take on that responsibility? You're in no condition for it. You're barely functioning as it is."

And so it had gone. Maggie had started the process. Donnie, as the oldest child, had signed off on the paperwork. Mike had signed it, too, obviously not fully understanding what it was.

Could they get out of it? Could he get released from the home? Did a doctor have to sign off on it? Donnie didn't know.

He realized suddenly that most of the people had moved away from the grave. He'd watched the coffin descend into the hole, but hadn't actually seen it happen. He stood alone, his eyes boring into the open grave.

"Donnie?"

He looked around and found a man in a suit watching him. The man was about his age and seemed vaguely familiar. The man stepped forward and extended a hand. Donnie shook it warily. "You look familiar," he said.

"Eric Francis," the man said. His hairline had receded toward the bald spot at the back of his head. "We went to school together."

"Oh. Yeah," Donnie said.

"I called you and told you about Mrs. Wilder's passing," Eric prompted.

"Oh," Donnie said. Then it clicked. "The reporter."

"Yeah. Can I ask you some questions about Mrs. Wilder?" Eric asked.

"I'd really rather not," Donnie said. He turned quickly and made for his pickup.

"Donnie!" Eric called, coming after him. Donnie hurried his steps. "Man, you wouldn't even have known about this if I hadn't searched high and low to find your number. Just give me a minute. Just one quote about what she meant to you and where you've been."

"I said my piece at the church," Donnie said, not even looking over his shoulder.

"I could expose you, dammit," Eric said. "Donnie! I'll include where you live in my article about the funeral if you don't give me just one fucking quote."

Donnie pulled his keys from his pocket. His father was waiting at the passenger side of the truck and he didn't know whether to be happy or upset that the man was there. He pushed the button to unlock the doors and watched as his father gave him a smirk before getting into the cab of the truck.

"Just answer one question," Eric called. "One question and I'll keep your secret."

Donnie hesitated, one hand on the door handle. He looked at his old classmate. "What?" he asked.

"Why aren't you writing anymore?" Eric asked.

"Writer's block," Donnie answered.

"Why?" Eric asked.

"You said one question," Donnie told him. "I answered one."

"Please, Donnie. No one has heard anything from you in years. Give me this, man. Please." Eric's face was earnest, his cheeks red from the cold. "Come on, man."

Donnie took a deep breath. "Pride," Donnie said at last. "I thought I was better than I was and I did stupid stuff when I was on top. My life fell apart and I went ... away, and now I just can't write anymore."

"The divorce?" Eric prompted. "The affair?"

"That's all I'm saying," Donnie said. "I appreciate you letting me know about Mrs. Wilder." He pulled open his door and jumped into the truck, slamming it on the reporter's final words.

"Gotcha, didn't he?" Mike quipped.

Donnie started the truck and put it in reverse. He backed out, cranked the wheel around, and barely kept himself from spinning the back wheels as he took off out of the cemetery.

"I'm hungry," Mike said as they passed a strip of restaurants just before the entrance to the highway.

"We're not stopping anywhere in this town," Donnie said.

"At least you gave up the idea of not taking me with you," Mike said, grinning.

Donnie sighed. "I should take you back," he said. "But ... I'm tired of the guilt. You can come visit for a while. I'll figure something out. You can have my bed. I'll sleep on the cot I take camping sometimes."

"Damn decent of you, son," Mike said. Donnie shot him a sour look and focused on the highway unspooling ahead of them.

They drove in silence for several miles. Finally, the anger Donnie felt toward Eric drained away a little. He glanced over at his father, who was watching the early winter scenery slip past them. "You ever hear from the girls?" he asked.

"Christmas cards. Birthday cards. A phone call every once in a while," Mike answered.

"They never visit you?"

"Did you?" Mike countered.

"But they both live right there in town," Donnie argued. "They really never visited?"

"They put me away like an old pair of shoes they'd outgrown but couldn't bring themselves to throw away," Mike answered.

"I'm sorry, Dad," Donnie said. "I'm really sorry."

"Words," Mike told him. "Those are just words. You're good with them. But you better show me you're sorry. Show me a good time."

"Show, don't tell," Donnie said softly. "Mrs. Wilder used to preach that all the time. You know, Sagebrush, Oklahoma, isn't exactly a happening place. There are no strip clubs, casinos, amusement parks, or anything like that. There are a couple of bars."

"Good ones?"

"I don't know, Dad. I don't drink like that anymore," Donnie said.

"Hmm," Mike grunted. "I guess I can see that. You spent that last year in Lawton drunker than almost anyone I've ever seen."

"Yeah," Donnie agreed. "I mostly gave it up when I left town. New start." He didn't add, *But I never really started anything new.* He thought of the laptop computer and the cursor blinking at him as he tried to think of new adventures for his bounty hunter.

"You run a bookstore?"

"Yeah."

"It does okay?"

"No. It doesn't make hardly any money," Donnie admitted. "I'm still able to pay my bills with royalties from the books, but sales are drying up. The checks are getting smaller. I don't know how much longer they'll last, or what I'll do after that. Close the store and move again. Become a factory worker or something."

"Can't you just get unblocked?" Donnie felt his father looking at him. He kept his eyes on the road. "I never understood how you wrote all those stories or where the ideas came from, but they came from somewhere. Can't you find new ones?"

"I haven't found any for a long time," Donnie said. "I didn't even try to write for that year after we separated and divorced. For seven years since, I've sat down at the counter in Lost Pages and turned on a computer and opened the word processor but have written nothing. No fiction, no blog posts. I only answer the most urgent email. I quit updating any social media sites years ago. I don't know why I even bother turning the machine on every day."

"It's what you do, Donnie," Mike said. "You're a writer. Always have been. Maybe it'll come back to you. I hope it does. I never really told you, but I kinda liked those stories of yours. Your bounty hunter didn't take any shit from anyone. I like that."

"He was an arrogant son of a bitch," Donnie said. "Just like I was. And when he gets in a tight spot, he just kills someone."

"Did you ever want to kill her?"

"Who?" Donnie asked, then stopped himself. "No. I never wanted to kill anyone. I was the guilty party."

"She raked you over the coals, though," Mike said. "She didn't have to do that. It's not like you're the first man who ever – "

"I know what I did, Dad. We don't have to talk about it," Donnie interrupted.

"Whatever," Mike said. He pointed to a dead female deer laying on the shoulder of the highway. "I bet that fucked up somebody's car."

"Probably," Donnie agreed, casting a glance at the bloated carcass as they whizzed past it. He remembered an insurance salesman who came to the house once, not long after he and Melissa had been married. He'd claimed his wife died when they'd hit a deer in their car. His appeal to pathos had not been enough to convince the young couple to buy insurance from him.

"I looked up this town you live in," Mike said. "You were right to say there isn't much to it."

"Nope."

"It snowed there a couple of days ago."

"We had ice, too. It was all melted away this morning," Donnie said. "That close to the panhandle gets more weather than the southern part of the state."

"Not much in the way of businesses or entertainment," Mike prompted.

"No. I guess there's a dance most Saturday nights," Donnie said. "I've never been. I pretty much keep to myself."

"Did they accept you? The stranger and all?"

Donnie shrugged and squinted at the road, remembering Sherry telling him he was part of the town whether he knew it or not. "I guess they have. They think I'm some kind of shy recluse who spends all his time reading."

"Are they wrong?"

Donnie felt a sad smile twitch at his lips. "No."

"You always went to your books when you got in trouble or if a girl broke up with you or when your dog died," Mike said.

Donnie nodded, remembering how he'd reread the entire *Lord of the Rings* story after his Cocker Spaniel mix Bilbo had died. Books had always been his retreat from reality.

Reading them at first, then writing them, and now it was just back to reading them and wishing he could write them.

They pulled over in a little town that had a McDonald's and ordered from the drive-thru. Donnie dipped chicken McNuggets into barbecue sauce and ate while they drove. Mike ate a Quarter Pounder, smacking loudly as he did.

"Do you get much fast food in the home?" Donnie asked.

"Not unless somebody brings it when they visit," Mike said. "And since none of my family visited me, never."

"Oh," Donnie said, and went back to eating and driving.

He stole glances at his father as they traveled. They'd never been that close. Mike Nelson had worked hard during the day and came home expecting dinner to be ready. After he ate, he showered and sat in his favorite recliner to watch the evening news, whatever sitcoms or dramas were on that night, then the late news, then he went to bed. He talked to his kids when they asked questions. It was rare for him to suggest going outside to play catch or any kid games. Donnie remembered there had been a time when they'd played board games as a family, but that had died out after a while. When Dad went to his recliner, Mom cleaned up from dinner, then read or worked on crochet or knitting until it was time to get the kids ready for bed. In the summer, when the daylight lingered, she'd often read on the porch. Donnie recalled seeing her in the porch swing, rocking and reading, sometimes smiling, the soft orange and red light of sunset filling her face as he rode around the neighborhood on his bicycle.

As if reading his thoughts, Mike said, "Your mom was a reader. I guess she had to be. I was never able to give her much adventure. I was always putting money away. Never wanted to spend it, knowing we'd need it for retirement. If I'd known then what I know now, we would have gone to Disney World, or on a cruise. She always wanted to go on a cruise."

Donnie gave his father a long look, then turned back to the highway. "Hindsight is always better," he said. "But we can't go back."

"No," Mike agreed, and bit into his sandwich.

They rode in silence for a while and the afternoon sun moved toward the horizon, casting long shadows back at them. Between the sun and the ground, Donnie noted that there were more dark clouds moving in from the west. More rain? Another cold front?

He wished he'd watched the weather forecast. Soon, the tall, narrow grain elevator on the eastern edge of Sagebrush came into view.

"There's home," Donnie said, flicking a finger toward the structure.

"About time," Mike said. "I have to pee like a racehorse."

Donnie grinned. "Prostate doing okay?"

There was a long silence, then Mike answered gruffly, "Fuck you."

Donnie gave his father a quick glance before navigating a curve in the road. "Sorry," he said. "But now I really want to know. Is everything okay?"

"I'm fine," Mike answered, but his voice was still edged.

Donnie let his speed drop as they entered the city limits. He didn't speak again as they crawled along Main Street, past the Lost Pages Bookstore, and around a corner and into the alley that ran behind the row of buildings that contained his shop. He pulled the truck into the space beside his wide stockroom doors.

"This is dreary," Mike said.

"It's an alley," Donnie pointed out.

"The whole town. I only saw a few lights on in buildings."

Donnie shut off the ignition and shrugged. "It's Friday afternoon. A lot of places close early. Let's go inside so you can pee."

He opened the door and got out, stretching his back as he did. He slammed his door closed and took one step, then froze. Something moved in the bed of his truck.

"What the fuck?" he breathed as he caught a glimpse of disheveled blue-and-silver hair around a pale white face. The girl sat wrapped in a blanket that she was pushing off her torso as Donnie watched.

"Are we finally at your house?" Mrs. Wilder's granddaughter asked as she rubbed at a blanket crease along her cheek.

Chapter Eight

"What the hell is this?" Donnie asked. "What ... what are you doing in there?"

The girl sat up uncomfortably and rubbed at her shoulder with one slender, white hand.

"How long has she been back there?" Mike asked from his side of the truck. "Do you know her?"

"Josey, right?" Donnie asked. "Mrs. Wilder's granddaughter."

"She's been in there since Lawton? And you didn't know?" Mike asked, then gave a bark of laughter. "That reporter really fucked with your head."

"You were standing beside the truck and didn't see her in there, either," Donnie snapped at him.

"It ain't my damn truck. Why would I know if a rolled up blanket isn't supposed to be there?" Mike said.

"I'm right here," Josey said. "Stop talking about me like I'm not."

"Okay," Donnie said, his voice taking on an edge he hadn't used since the days when he was able to scold his own kids. "What the hell are you doing in the back of my truck?"

"Obviously, I was sneaking out of Lawton," she said, dropping her hand from her shoulder. "I'm cold and I'm hungry and my whole body hurts from laying back here. Can we go inside?"

Mike laughed again. "A stowaway with an attitude."

"Two of you," Donnie mumbled. "What the fuck? Yeah," he said louder. "Let's go inside."

The girl pushed the rest of the blanket off herself. She was still wearing her black jeans and black ankle boots with tall chunky heels. She picked up the blanket, then stood up, rubbing at the hip she'd been laying on. She walked to the end of the pickup bed and hesitated. Sighing, Donnie went around and lowered the tailgate, took the blanket, and helped her step onto the asphalt of the alley.

"I never should have gone back there," Donnie muttered as he selected the key to the store's back door and put it into the lock. He opened the door and reached inside, flicking on the light switch to reveal stacks of cardboard boxes spilling paperback books onto the cement floor, and his little living area off in one corner. Mike and Josey pushed past him, then Donnie went inside and closed the door.

"What's this?" Mike asked, looking toward the narrow bed, the table with the hot plate and microwave, and a thrift store dresser of clothes. "Don't tell me this is where you live. I thought that was a fucking joke or something you said to keep me from coming with you."

"This is it, Dad. This is home and work, all in one," Donnie said.

"You really live here? What is this place?" Josey asked.

"It's the stockroom of the bookstore I run," Donnie told her.

"It's pathetic. You lived in a damned nice house back in the day," Mike reminded him.

"That was before the divorce, Dad."

"Surely you can afford some kind of house or apartment or something," Mike said.

"There's not much around here to rent, and no, I probably couldn't afford it."

"You have food, right?" Josey asked.

Donnie thought about the packages of Ramen noodles, the loaf of bread, and a few frozen dinners he had. "Maybe we should go across the street to the café," he suggested.

"You don't have food?" Josey asked.

"Not much," Donnie answered defensively. "I wasn't expecting guests, ya know? If you want Ramen, we're covered. You want something else, we have to go to the café. Either way, you're going to explain why you were in the back of my truck, a hundred and fifty miles from home."

"Jesus. Grandma never told me you were such an ass," Josey said. "When is grocery day?"

"Come on," Donnie said, and led them through the stockroom and onto the floor of the shop. They went through the rows of books to the front of the store, where he unlocked the door and led the little parade onto the sidewalk. A cool wind was blowing down the street ahead of the clouds approaching town. He looked across to the café and saw that it wasn't too crowded. Most people went home for dinner on Fridays.

Inside the café, he took a table in the corner and they sat down. Debbie the waitress gave him a curious look but didn't ask about his guests. Instead, she addressed Josey.

"I just love your hair," Debbie said. "You didn't get that done 'round here, did ya?"

Josey gave her a winning smile. "No. It was in Lawton. I've only been here for less than an hour."

"Well, I love it," Debbie said, then lowered her voice. "Some of the folks 'round here'll give ya queer looks because of it, but don't you pay them no mind." She winked at Josey. "What can I get y'all to eat tonight?"

Donnie and Mike ordered lighter meals, but Josey ordered the largest portion of chicken strips and fries. She handed back her menu and looked around the restaurant.

"It's really like time just stood still right here," she said, reminding Donnie of his talk with Omar. "This stuff is vintage, not recreations like in some places that try to have an old-timey feel."

"Josey, why are you here?" Donnie asked, ignoring her wonder at the décor.

"Grandma was my guardian after Mom died. I don't know my dad." She shrugged. "She left me everything, but I thought I'd get away for a while. Grandma talked about you a lot. You were her favorite student. She was so proud of you, like if you were her own kid or something. When I saw you at the funeral, I decided I wanted to meet you and, you know, hang out."

"So you hid in the back of my truck?" Donnie asked. He looked to his dad for help, but Mike was pretending to be engrossed in the week-old newspaper he'd found on the empty table beside them. Donnie saw the older man smiling, though.

"Yeah," Josey said, as if what she'd done was perfectly natural.

"Most people would have come up and introduced themselves," Donnie said. "Maybe ask if they could come visit."

"What if you'd said no?" she asked. "Then it would have been really rude for me to do it anyway."

"You don't think hiding in my truck and coming uninvited was rude?"

"Not as rude as if I'd asked and you said no." She smiled at him and sipped from the Dr Pepper Debbie had brought her.

"Good God," Donnie said, and drank from his sweet tea.

"She's got you there," Mike said without looking up from the newspaper.

"Thanks, Dad," Donnie said.

"I wondered if this was your dad. Does he live here with you?" she asked, then scrunched up her face. "No. Otherwise he would have known you live in your shop. You really live back there?"

"Yes, I do," Donnie said. "And my dad basically forced himself on me, just like you did." He studied the girl for a moment. She had dark circles under her eyes that looked even darker than they should have because of her pale skin. "How old are you?" Donnie demanded.

"I'm eighteen," she said.

"How do I know you're eighteen? How do I know you haven't run away from somebody and I could get in trouble for having you around?"

"Sheesh, Mr. Nelson," she said. "Why are you so rude and paranoid? I'm eighteen. I just graduated in May. It's cool. Nobody's looking for me."

The food arrived. Donnie looked at his fried catfish nuggets and fries he'd ordered off the kid portion of the menu. He wasn't hungry, though the food smelled good. Josey dipped a chicken strip in a bowl of cream gravy, several French fries already in her mouth. Mike bit into his cheeseburger and pretended he was alone.

"This isn't over," Donnie said. "Not for either of you." He forked a fish nugget into his mouth. "Damn," he cursed. "I never should have left town. I never should have gone back. This is all Sherry Brown's fault."

"Who's Sherry Brown?" Mike asked. "You dating her?"

"No! She's the wife of the bank president. An older lady who reads a lot," Donnie answered. "She told me I'd regret it if I didn't go to Mrs. Wilder's funeral."

"Would you have?" Josey asked with her mouth full. A drop of cream gravy clung to her chin. She chewed hurriedly and stared at him with intense green eyes.

Donnie sighed and looked at his plate. "Yes. It was ... Not good to see her. Not like that. But ... I'm glad I went." He looked at Josey, then at his dad. "I just don't know why I had to bring home stragglers."

"Stragglers?" Mike said. He looked to Josey. "His own father and the granddaughter of the teacher who inspired his career. Stragglers!" He shoved a tater tot into his mouth and glared at Donnie.

"I didn't mean it like that," Donnie said. He put a hand over his eyes. "I've lived alone for a really long time. I don't know how to deal with all of this."

"Deal with it like a decent human being," Mike snapped. "You have guests. Be polite. Southern hospitality. You've heard of it. What would your mother do if people dropped in unexpectedly?"

Donnie couldn't look at them. He looked at his plate, but couldn't eat. He knew Mom would have welcomed anybody and treated them like family, offering food and a place to sleep and anything else they needed or wanted. She would have scolded him good if she heard how he talked to his guests, then given him that look that said she was disappointed in him.

"I'm sorry," he said. "You're right. You're right." He took a deep breath. "I wasn't too polite about it, but I'm making sure you have food. I need to figure out where everyone's going to sleep. Dad, you'll take my bed. Josey, you can have the camping cot. I'll push a couple of chairs together to sleep in the main part of the store. You can put the cot wherever you want," he told Josey. "I have some tarps we can hang up to give you some privacy."

"Are either of you creeps?" she asked.

Donnie and Mike looked at each other, then both looked at Josey and said, "No," together.

She laughed at them. "You are definitely father and son. If you're not gonna be creepy, I don't need tarps."

Donnie nodded and looked at his dad. "You didn't bring anything? Either of you? Clothes Toothbrush?"

"Nope. The folks at the home would have guessed I wasn't coming back if I'd packed a bag," Mike said.

Josey shook her head. "It was spur of the moment," she said.

"I guess you can sleep in something of mine. We can get you some clothes tomorrow," Donnie said. Accepting the fact the two would be staying with him was actually a little bit of a relief. Better than fighting it.

"Can I work in your store?" Josey asked.

"Uhhh," Donnie began, unsure what to say. "I don't really make enough money to pay an employee."

"Feed me and let me sleep under your roof and that's payment enough," Josey said.

Donnie shrugged. "Okay."

"I'm retired," Mike said. "I ain't doin' shit to earn my keep. I brought you up. You owe me. You *really* owe me."

"Yeah, Dad, I get it," Donnie said. "I don't know what you'll do all day. I think some of the older guys in town play dominoes in the evening."

"I'd be offended, but I like dominoes," Mike said. "And mature company. Where do they play?"

"I don't know," Donnie answered. "I'll have to ask around."

They turned their attention to the food before it got cold. Outside the café windows, darkness moved in with the cloud cover. Leaves and wisps of trash blew down the street. A stray dog the size of a golden retriever sniffed at the café door, wagging his tail hopefully.

"There's Jasper," Debbie said to nobody in particular.

"Pretty dog," Mike commented.

Debbie looked over at him and smiled. "Chigger'd probably give him to you if you asked," she said. "He can't keep Jasper in the yard. Probably because he forgets to feed him."

"A dog gets hungry," Mike agreed.

"Let's take him in," Josey said.

"No!" Donnie said, setting his tea down hard on the table. "I think I've taken in enough strays for one day."

"You probably have a cat already," Josey said.

Donnie thought of Sherry Brown's playful nagging about a bookstore cat. He smiled. "No, I don't have a cat."

"So, let's make Jasper the Lost Pages pet," Josey said.

"Sounds good to me," Mike agreed.

"The dog has an owner already," Donnie argued.

"If y'all are serious, I can call Chigger and ask him if y'all can buy the dog," Debbie said. "He'll prob'ly tell you you can have him if you can keep him home."

"No, it's okay," Donnie said.

Debbie shrugged and smiled at him. She had a nice smile, and her eyes twinkled. They were blue. "How's business, Mr. Bookworm?"

That caught him off guard. He had always been Mr. Nelson to her. She wouldn't even call him Donnie. Now she'd called him Mr. Bookworm. Like a pet name. Or was she mocking him? Her eyes said she wasn't teasing. "Slow," Donnie said. "Do you need something to read?"

Debbie laughed. "Maybe. Maybe I could take up readin' those trashy romances. You got any of those?"

"Tons of them," Donnie said.

"I don't know your dad and daughter. They just visitin'?" she asked.

Donnie pointed at his dad. "This is Mike Nelson, my dad." He pointed at Josey. "Josey is the granddaughter of an old friend. They'll be staying with me for a while, I guess."

"Welcome to Sagebrush," the waitress said. "I'm Debbie. We're a little town, but pretty friendly."

"It's nice to meet you, Debbie," Mike said. "I look forward to seeing you often. My son here doesn't seem to cook."

"He needs a wife," Debbie said. "Every man does."

"Hmm," Mike said, grinning. "Has he dated anyone in town?"

"Not that I know of, and I hear about most everything," she answered. "Course, I've only been back in town a couple of months."

"Any women shown any interest?" Mike asked.

"Dad. That's enough," Donnie said. He felt his face reddening. "Debbie, can I get the check?"

"Not that he's noticed," she said. Grinning, she took her receipt pad from her apron pocket and tore off a page and handed it to Donnie. "I'll get ya at the register on your way out," she said. She nodded at the front door. "Jasper's still out there." She winked and moved away.

"I think she might like you," Mike stage-whispered to Donnie.

"Let's go," Donnie said, getting up and pulling his wallet from his pocket with one hand and picking up the check with the other. He didn't pause to see if his companions were following him, but went to the cash register at the front of the restaurant. Debbie met him there.

"Everything okay today?" she asked.

"It was good," Donnie answered. He paid the bill with his Visa card and left Debbie a tip. Mike and Josey joined him at the register, each taking a free mint from a bowl. He led his little procession out the door. The dog was gone, but only for a moment.

"Jasper!" Josey called. The dog was at the corner. Its brown head lifted from the stain it had been sniffing and his floppy ears perked forward as he looked at the three humans.

"Stop," Donnie warned. Josey ignored him.

"Come on, boy!" Josey urged. She bent at her knees and patted the thighs of her black jeans.

"Please don't do this," Donnie said, his tone already showing his defeat.

The dog came trotting toward them, wary but eager. Donnie noted that Debbie was watching them from the window of the restaurant. She was smiling. Donnie wished she'd call the dog's owner and the irresponsible man would come and collect his animal. But she wasn't moving toward a phone and the dog was tentatively sniffing at Josey's extended hand.

"He'll pee in the store," Donnie complained.

"He might be housebroken already," Josey said. "If he's not, we can train him. I'll take full responsibility."

"You ... " Donnie bit off his response. He wanted to complain that no one was even responsible for Josey, or his father, but that would be rude. He shook his head. "When Chigger comes looking for his dog, we give him back."

"Yeah. Okay," Josey agreed. She scratched the dog behind one ear, then the other. "Do you want to come home with us, boy? It'll be warmer. I don't know if Uncle Donald has any dog food."

"Of course I don't," Donnie said. "And I'm not that dog's uncle."

"I always thought I'd be the cranky old man of the family," Mike said.

A colder gust of wind brought the first fat drops of rain. "Let's go inside," Donnie said. He started across the deserted street toward his store, feeling the others falling in behind him. Josey continued to talk to the dog in that high, singsong voice people used with animals and babies.

The dog followed them inside and promptly shook the water from his coat. Donnie watched with pursed lips, grateful the animal had done it early, before getting deeper into the store where the water would have landed on his inventory.

"I keep thinking you're going to say this is all a joke and you actually have a cozy house on a few acres on the edge of town," Mike said. "But you really live here, don't you?"

"Yes, Dad. I live here. Alone. This is all I've needed," Donnie said.

"You need more now," Mike said.

"I need to fill the truck up with gas and take you both home tomorrow," Donnie grumbled under his breath, knowing the battle was lost.

"Do you have anything Jasper can eat?" Josey asked. She was crouched beside the dog, scratching his neck and shoulders, causing the beast to wriggle all over, his tail going wild and a look of canine ecstasy on his furry face.

Donnie sighed. "No," he said. "I'll go to the store. Y'all can come, or you can explore my vast empire, or whatever. I guess I'll need more groceries, anyway."

"I can cook breakfast in the morning," Josey offered.

Donnie looked at her for a moment, then nodded. "That would be nice."

"Then I'm coming to the store with you," she said. She looked to Mike. "Can you watch over Jasper?"

"I'd be glad to," Mike said, giving Donnie an amused look.

Donnie rolled his eyes and hung his head in defeat. "Let's go," he said, and led Josey through the store and out the back to the truck.

"Wow, it's so much more comfortable in the cab," Josey joked as she buckled her seat belt.

"Definitely," Donnie agreed. He backed up, cranked the steering wheel, and drove out of the alley.

The local IGA store was small and the prices were considerably higher than at the bigger stores in cities. Most residents of Sagebrush under the age of seventy considered the store a stop-gap, a place to get a few things they ran out of between trips to the mega-stores in Woodward. Older people shopped locally for everything, saying they were supporting the local economy as an excuse to cover up the fact they simply didn't like traveling. The store was clean, though, and the people friendly. The owner, Roger Perry, was a short man in his late fifties who oiled the remnants of his black hair and combed it over the shiny dome of his head. He wore a green apron, white shirt, black tie, and black pants every day, and knew every customer by name.

"Donnie, you're out late tonight," Roger called from where he was chatting with an elderly customer over her cart of bagged groceries. He gave Josey a curious look but tried not to stare. Donnie knew the man wanted to ask who she was and why her hair looked like it had been colored by a gnome, but to his credit, he didn't. "And a couple of days early. But it's good to see you."

"You, too, Roger," Donnie answered.

Josey pulled out a cart and started toward the produce section of the store, where she chose apples, oranges, bananas, grapes, and strawberries.

"You like your fruit, huh?" Donnie commented.

"Love it!" she answered enthusiastically. "Do you like smoothies? Do you even have a blender? I love smoothies for breakfast."

"I don't have a blender," Donnie said.

She gave him an incredulous look and shook her head. "Do they sell blenders here?" She looked around the store as if she'd see small appliances shelved with the celery and turnips. "Not likely. We'll have to get a blender."

Donnie couldn't completely repress the sigh that escaped his mouth. Josey gave him a look that bordered somewhere between annoyance and pity.

"I'll pay for it, if that's what you're worried about. Grandma made sure I had money before she died," Josey said.

Donnie felt his cheeks burning with shame that this girl had figured out he was worried about the cost of a blender. Or that he was so backward as to not already have one. He thought of his pathetic home in the back of the store and felt even more embarrassed. He shook his head and said, "It's okay," he said. "No fresh vegetables?"

"Nope," she said, letting the issue go. "Canned or frozen. I don't make smoothies out of those."

Josey pushed the cart on and around a corner. Donnie let her collect cans and bags and packages of food without saying a word about the cost of the filling cart.

"I was glad to hear Mrs. Wilder – your grandma – kept writing," he said.

"Right up to the end," Josey answered, pausing in her comparison of name brand and store brand macaroni and cheese. "Mostly poetry. That was her passion. But she wrote some short stories, too. I tried to get her to write a novel but she said she knew she didn't have the time to finish it."

"Oh," Donnie said. "She knew the end was coming way ahead of time?"

Josey chose the name brand mac and cheese, then added two more boxes to the cart as she gave him a mischievous smile. "She used that excuse for like ten years. Maybe it takes ten years to write a novel. I mean, you're the expert. I don't know. But I've heard about that thing where thousands of people write a whole novel in the month of November, so I kind of doubt it takes ten years."

Donnie smiled and nodded. "I always associated her with poetry," he said. "That's mostly what she had us write in class. We wrote a short story, and mine was pretty bad. She gave me a B. But it was always poetry for Mrs. Wilder."

"She loved poems," Josey said as she put three large packages of spaghetti in the cart. "What kind of sauce do you like?"

"Traditional," Donnie answered.

"Of course," Josey said. "You're a pretty plain guy, aren't you? Meat and potatoes and a piece of bread. That's your usual meal, I bet."

Donnie shrugged and added cans of spaghetti sauce to the cart. "Pretty much," he said. "Usually microwavable."

"We'll have to work on that," Josey promised.

They moved on. Donnie groped for something to talk about. They passed a few other shoppers, most of whom Donnie knew. They nodded at each other and exchanged quick greetings until Josey turned the cart into the frozen food aisle and they came face-to-face with Sherry Brown.

"Donnie!" the elderly woman exclaimed. "How was the funeral? And who is this beautiful young lady? I love that hair!"

"Oh, hi, Mrs. Brown," Donnie said, desperately thinking how to answer. What would the town think of him having this much younger woman living with him? "The funeral was good, I guess. You know, it was a funeral. How good could it be?"

"I understand," she cooed. "But I bet you're glad you went."

Donnie wasn't sure how to answer that. He didn't get a chance to, anyway.

"I'm Sherry Brown," the woman said, extending an age-spotted hand to Josey. "I visit Donnie's store almost every day."

"I'm Josey, Uncle Donnie's niece," the girl said, taking the hand and shaking it twice. "Me and Grandpa came to stay with him for a while."

Donnie gaped at the girl, but before he could say anything, Mrs. Brown was on him. "Donnie Nelson! You never told me you had a niece. And I just assumed both your folks had passed on."

"Only my mom," Donnie said quietly. "Dad was in a home. He kind of busted out. Him and Josey here sprung this visit on me."

"Don't be so glum about it," Mrs. Brown said. "A visit from family is always good. Unless they're just wanting money." She laughed and Josey laughed with her.

"Can I have a quarter for the gumball machine, Uncle Donnie?" Josey asked teasingly.

"No," he answered.

"She is adorable," Mrs. Brown said. She reached up and touched Josey's blue-and-silver hair. "I just love what you've done here. I wish I could have been so bold when I was your age."

"It's never too late," Josey said.

"Oh child, my old lady hair is too thin these days," she said. She turned her attention to Donnie and used her eyes to pin him to the freezer door behind him. "Where are these people staying? You're not making them live in the back of that store, are you?"

"Uhh ... Well ... " Donnie stammered. "It's all I have, and I didn't know – "

"It's okay, Mrs. Brown," Josey said. "We're figuring it out. We just had to buy food. You know all he had was Ramen noodles? I don't know how he's been surviving."

Mrs. Brown clucked her tongue. "I've been doing what I can, bringing him lunch sometimes. It's going to be so good for him to have you around." She looked at Donnie again. "I look forward to meeting your father, too."

Donnie tried to imagine his foul-mouthed dad in the company of Mrs. Brown. It was cringe-worthy.

"I'll let you two finish your shopping," Mrs. Brown said. "It was lovely to meet you, Josey. I'll see you tomorrow when I come to the store, I hope."

"I'll be there," Josey said. "I'm going to work for Uncle Donnie so he can get back to writing."

"Writing?" Mrs. Brown let her cart roll to a stop again. "Are you writing a book, Donnie?"

"No," he said quickly, giving Josey a look that was half panic, half pleading. "No," he said again, more calmly. "I just need to write some letters to business friends." He was very aware of the confused look Josey was giving him. "It was good seeing you, Mrs. Brown. I'll see you after the bank closes tomorrow."

They parted and moved on, picking up some frozen tater tots and mixed vegetables and, with Donnie's grumbling, some dog food before heading to the checkout. Roger and the cashier both greeted Donnie by name and asked about the young lady with him. Not knowing what else to do but continue the lie she'd started, he introduced Josey as his niece.

"It's nice to have you in town," Roger told her. "I hope you'll make your uncle get out of his own store a little more."

Donnie couldn't help but snort and grin despite his souring mood. "You're a fine one to talk, Roger," he said. "I don't think I've ever been in this store and not seen you working."

"Touché, Donnie. Touché," Roger agreed. "The grocery business is a harsh mistress. Did you get a dog?"

Donnie sighed. "Chigger's dog is staying with us for a while, I guess."

Roger shook his head and clucked his tongue. "Jasper's a good dog. He deserves more attention than Chigger can give him."

"He'll get it now," Josey promised.

Donnie paid the bill, the largest grocery bill he'd had since he and his wife separated, and Roger pushed the cart of groceries out to their car, carrying on some mundane conversation about the town with Josey the whole time. Donnie helped move the bags to the bed of his truck to hurry the process along.

"Everyone is so nice here," Josey said as they drove back to the bookstore.

"It's a small town," Donnie said. "Everyone knows everyone and everyone wants to know everyone's business." He pulled into the mouth of the alley and couldn't hide a grin. "By tomorrow, everyone in town will know about my niece with the blue-and-silver hair."

"Is that bad?" she asked.

Donnie parked the truck and shrugged. "It might actually be good for business for a few days," he said ironically. "I bet every guy under twenty-five will have the urge to read for a while."

Josey laughed. "They'll be disappointed."

Donnie shook his head. "You're not one of those girls with self-esteem problems, are you?"

"I'm a realist," she said as they both grabbed plastic bags and started for the back door of the shop.

"Well, if it isn't weird for an old man to tell you this, you're not an ugly girl. The guys won't be disappointed there," he told her.

Josey stopped at the door and whirled around to face him. "Why, Mr. Nelson, I think that's the nicest thing you've said to me so far." She grinned, and in the yellow glow of the nearby light, she seemed every bit the playful elf, despite her mourning clothes.

Mike opened the back door as Donnie was fumbling for his keys. "We got food!" Josey announced. "Will you help us bring it in?" The older man laughed at her and moved to the back of the truck to grab some bags.

There was more food than Donnie had space to hold. His tiny refrigerator would barely close and he had to stack cans on the little table where his toaster stood. Josey gave the dog a bowl of food. The three of them stood there in the Spartan living quarters and looked at the area while Jasper noisily crunched the dry food.

"This is pretty sad," Mike said.

"It never seemed that way before," Donnie argued, though he knew it was a lie. It had been plenty sad, but in a different way.

"Because you've been living in self-pity for so fucking long."

"Dad!" Donnie looked from his father to Josey. "There's a young lady here. Can't you please watch the language?"

Mike's face wrinkled in disgust, then he turned his attention to Josey. "Does my language offend you?" he asked.

"No, Mike, it doesn't," Josey said. "Sometimes you just have to throw out a fuck to make your point."

"Fuck yeah," he said, giving his son a satisfied look.

Donnie sighed, then turned away. "What the fuck ever," he said. Everyone laughed. "It's been a helluva fucking day. Let's get some fucking sleeping arrangements laid the fuck out."

Mike slapped a hand down on his son's shoulder. "That's my fucking boy," he said.

Mike tried to change the arrangement they'd discussed and insisted Josey take the only real bed, but the girl refused.

"It's because you think I'm too damn old to sleep on a cot," Mike growled.

"You are the patriarch here," Josey said. "I usually would not honor the patriarchy, but I like you. You take the bed."

Mike lost the argument. Donnie wondered if anybody ever won an argument with Josey.

The camping cot was pulled from where Donnie had left it just yesterday. He marveled that so much had happened since his return from camping. Josey insisted it wasn't necessary, but finally helped hang a crinkly blue tarp from the ceiling in the corner where the cot was to give her some privacy. Donnie went to the floor of the store and pulled the cushions off the Queen Anne chairs, laying them out on the tiles to create a padded surface to sleep on. They took turns in the tiny bathroom, showering and brushing their teeth, then everyone settled into their places for the night.

There was a foreign clicking sound and Donnie turned his head to see Jasper, the new store mascot, walking toward him. The dog stopped beside him and studied the man on the chair cushions for a moment, then turned in three circles, lay down, sighed, and closed his eyes.

"Josey is most definitely giving you a bath tomorrow," Donnie whispered. The dog ignored him.

Donnie lay on his makeshift bed and stared up at the ceiling in the pale yellowish illumination from Sagebrush's street lamps coming through the plate glass at the front of his shop. The chair cushions moved and began to separate if he shifted his position, so he tried to lie still. When he realized he was lying flat on his back with his hands crossed over his chest, like Mrs. Wilder in her coffin, he unfolded his hands and put them at his sides.

What the hell happened today?

Of all the possibilities he had considered before setting out for Lawton, coming home with his escaped father and Mrs. Wilder's orphaned granddaughter were never even in the universe of things he thought about. And now there was a dog, too.

He replayed and sorted the events, trying to make sense of how it had all happened, from finding his father waiting at his truck, to being pushed into the procession going to the gravesite, the reporter hassling him for an interview, and then finding Josey in the bed of his truck.

It was the reporter, he decided. From beginning to end, it was Eric Francis. He'd had to search relentlessly to even find a way to contact Donnie to tell him about Mrs. Wilder's death. Then his insistence on asking questions had made Donnie feel anxious and caused him to rush his exit from the cemetery. If he hadn't been distracted by the reporter, he would have seen the strange blanket roll where Josey was hiding in the bed of his truck.

He would have kicked Josey out of his truck and driven his father back to the home, or back to the house he used to live in and leave him with Margaret.

"Fucking reporters," he muttered into the still night of his store.

Once upon a time, he had been terribly excited to talk to reporters. He'd sent an advance reader copy of the first Bolkar book to the Lawton newspaper, and several others, but the local paper was first to contact him. It hadn't been Eric that time. Tim Feely was the entertainment reporter. He'd come to Donnie's house, the old one, before he made enough money to move into a bigger house. He met the family. They talked about writing. The story that ran the following Sunday raved about the local boy who had gotten his big break and was potentially on the brink of fame. A follow-up story that was equally enthusiastic ran a couple of months later when the book was released and Donnie did his first book signing at a local store.

Melissa was with him at that book signing, sitting beside him, smiling, answering questions from fans about what it was like to live with an author, as if she had been supportive of her husband all along. Donnie remembered well gritting his teeth and smiling and joking during the signing, all the while thinking how Melissa had called his writing a waste of time until that advance-against-royalty check arrived in the mail. The signing was a success, with a long line. The store sold all but nine of the copies they'd bought for the event.

Melissa had wanted to quit her job. Donnie argued that it made more sense for him to quit his job and focus on writing since that's where the big money came from. It had become an argument that lasted for a few years until his writing provided enough income for them both to stay home. In those first years, though, she finally gave in to his logic and Donnie quit his regular job in the machine shop and stayed home to write. But then Melissa complained that he didn't also do the dishes and laundry and clean up around the house while he was there all day.

She wanted a new car. Donnie argued that the money wasn't enough for him to quit his job and spend so much on a new car. She pouted. She wanted to overspend on Christmas. When Donnie again told her there wasn't enough money for that, she told him he could at least work part-time somewhere. In the end, he agreed, working part-time at a convenience store for almost two years, pulling evening shifts so he would be gone when Melissa was home.

Conventions came calling as Bolkar rose up the best-seller lists. He was asked to speak, to be on panels, to be the guest of honor at various conventions in different states. The organizers put him up in the hotels where the events were held. His readings and signings were packed. People dressed as Bolkar and walked around the convention posing for photos with other members of fandom. It was surreal.

He'd been in Dallas the first time a fan propositioned him.

She'd been dressed as some kind of barbarian woman, wearing an outfit that looked like she'd sewn together several chamois cloths meant for drying cars. She wore a plastic sword on her round hip and had fur from a fabric store wrapped around her shins with leather shoelaces. She looked to be about twenty-one, with deep brown eyes, blonde hair swept back and held in a leather string. She was tanned and fit, her legs long, her arms slender, and her smile open and inviting.

"I loved your book," she said as she handed over an already well-worn hardcover of the novel.

"Thank you," Donnie said from his seat at the autograph table. "Who do I make this out to?"

She pointed to a name tag sticker on her left breast. "Brittany," she said, then she held out her slim hand. "It's so good to meet you."

Donnie shook her hand. It was small, warm, and soft. "It's good to meet you, too, Brittany. Are you having a good time here?"

"It could be better," she said. Donnie paused in his signing, wondering if he really detected a note of coyness in her reply. He glanced up at her and she smiled down at him.

"How's that?" he asked.

Her smile widened. "I'll be in the bar this evening at six," she said. "Maybe I'll see you there."

Donnie remembered he tried to smile at her, but was so shaken that it probably looked as broken as a jack-o-lantern in December. "Maybe," he said. He finished his signature and handed the book back to the young woman. "Thank you, Brittany."

"I'll see you later, Mr. Nelson," she said, taking the book, making sure her delicate fingers brushed meaningfully over his hand. She turned and walked away, her leather-clad ass wiggling provocatively as she went.

Donnie avoided the bar that evening. But he saw Brittany in every panel he did for the rest of the weekend. In his last panel, she came to the table after the discussion was over and made conversation until the room cleared.

"Where did you get the idea for Bolkar?" she asked. Donnie told her the story about camping. "When will the next book be out? How many books do you think there'll be in the series? Where did you get the idea for the creatures in the lost jungle city?" Donnie answered her questions, watching as people left the room. It was the last event of the day. No other authors or artists were coming in to replace the last panel. Closing ceremonies were due to start in a few minutes and he had to be there.

"Will Bolkar find a strong woman to love him?" Brittany asked, stepping closer and putting one hand on his forearm while her other hand went lower and cupped his genitals through his jeans.

Donnie almost jumped away from her touch. He pulled his arm free and looked at her, his mind warring between coming off as a prude and afraid someone might have seen what happened. He knew a lot of other writers and artists slept around at conventions. They weren't at the level of rock stars or anything, but there were women like Brittany … fangirls. She was beautiful. She was smiling at him, amused.

"I'm sorry," he said. "I'm married. I've got kids."

She stepped closer. "I'm not looking for a ring," she said playfully. "Just a good time. Something more than an autograph."

"I … " Donnie looked again toward the open door. "You're beautiful and all. If I was single, definitely. But I just can't."

"Are you sure?" she asked, reaching for his crotch again.

Donnie sidestepped her. He laughed nervously. "I probably seem like a scared teenager or something. But I just can't."

"It's okay, Mr. Nelson," Brittany said, withdrawing her hand. "It's actually kind of nice to know you're so loyal." Before he could respond, she stepped close, rose to her tiptoes, and kissed him lightly on the cheek. "I'll see you next year." She turned and he watched her hips sway toward the door and out.

She hadn't been the last. She hadn't even been the one …

Donnie stopped himself. He closed his eyes and breathed deeply.

She hadn't even been the one to break through his defenses. He hadn't felt low enough that first time. He'd still held on to the belief that he and Melissa could fix their problems. He hadn't given up yet. Not then.

That came later.

Chapter Nine

Donnie woke up stiff and achy, his butt on the floor, hanging between the cushions that had parted for him during the night. The shop was still dark, but there was a gray tint to the air. He groaned and shifted, trying to right the cushions beneath him, but it was useless. His back hurt where his body dropped off the edge of the chair cushion. He wriggled off the cushions and lay flat on the floor, pulling his blanket up to his chin, but the floor was too hard, the air was too cold, and he suddenly had to pee. Jasper watched him get to his feet, but made no move to get up himself.

Keeping the blanket around him, huddled within it, Donnie made his way to the restroom and relieved himself. He knew he wouldn't be able to sleep again, so he went to the coffee machine and started the brewing process, standing over the dribbling device with his cup in hand like a beggar on the street.

Steaming coffee cup in hand, he went to his worn leather desk chair behind the counter and sat down, staring out at the dawn creeping over the little town he now called home. Donnie sipped and thought. What should he do about his two guests? His father was one thing. Family. His sister was likely to be upset with him, but he figured he could deal with that. She'd demand he bring Dad back to the home, and ... he would. Maybe in a few days. Donnie had to admit he kind of liked the idea of having his dad with him. Sure, it would have been nice if the visit had been planned, but still, the man was his father and he and his sisters had done him wrong.

Josey, on the other hand, he just didn't know what to do with. If what she said was true, and she had no family now that Mrs. Wilder was dead, there would be nobody to wonder where she was, or even care. Did the girl have no friends she could have stayed with? Why stowaway in the pickup truck of a total stranger she'd only heard her grandmother talk about? There was a lot that didn't seem right about Josey.

"That isn't much of a view."

Donnie jumped in his chair, nearly sloshing coffee from his mug. Fortunately, he'd drunk enough of it that the warm liquid didn't come over the edge. He looked to his left and shook his head. "You scared the shit out of me, Dad. How long have you been standing there?"

"A while," Mike answered. He sipped from a mug of steaming coffee and looked knowingly at his son. "Your mind was far, far away. Like usual."

"Hmm," Donnie said without committing. He looked back toward the rear of the shop. "Was Josey up yet?"

"Didn't hear her moving around," Mike answered.

"What do you think of her, Dad?"

"She's too young, Donnie. Get your mind off that."

Donnie stared, trying to understand, then the meaning hit him. "Dad! Not that. Shit. She's a kid. Does her story add up to you?"

Mike shrugged. "I don't know. You know her family better than me. You ever meet her mom?"

"No."

"Her grandmother ever talk about her?"

"Not to me," Donnie answered.

"You doubt she is who she says she is, or what?" Mike asked.

"No, I think she is who she says she is," Donnie answered slowly. He took another drink, then explained about the minister at the funeral acknowledging Josey. "But is she as old as she says? Is there somebody looking for her? Another relative, a boyfriend, debt collectors? I don't know."

"We could check her license," Mike suggested.

"We could," Donnie agreed. "But that would make her mad, I bet." He stared into his coffee cup, thinking.

"Donnie, you gotta ask yourself why you're wondering these things," Mike broke into Donnie's thoughts. "Are you really concerned someone is looking for her? Or are you worried she's going to be another interruption to your life? Like me."

"She's not family, Dad," Donnie protested. "We don't know her."

Mike sighed and sipped and looked at his son. "I'm not the best judge of women. I never would have believed your sister would toss me in a home and forget about me. But anyway, in this case, I want to trust Josey. I like her spunk. It took a lot of balls to do what she did."

Donnie couldn't disagree with that. He chuckled. "I bet that was a cold, bumpy ride in the bed of the truck."

"Yep." Mike sipped his coffee. "You gonna let her work here in the store?" He settled his elbows onto the counter and Donnie wished there was another chair close by.

Donnie shrugged. "I guess so. There isn't much work. I don't know what I'll do if she takes all the work."

"You could write," Mike suggested.

Donnie looked at his father sharply, then looked away. "I can't," he said.

"Why not?"

"Writer's block," Donnie answered dismissively. He drank his own coffee, hoping his dad would let it go. He didn't.

"I'm no psychologist," Mike said. "But a guy gets bored living in an old folks' home before his time, so I did some reading. I knew you weren't publishing anything. At least, not under your real name. I figured you were blocked. Like that time as a kid when you ate the whole block of cheese." He paused and grinned at Donnie, who only shook his head and rolled his eyes. "Anyway, writer's block is a psychological issue. It's usually brought on by some traumatic event. Well, you had two back-to-back traumatic events. Is it your mother's death that did it?"

Donnie slowly turned his coffee mug, his eyes fixed on the steaming black liquid inside, his fingers hungry for the warmth. "No," he said quietly. "I was already blocked when Mom died."

"Um-hmm," Mike said knowingly. "That's what I thought. It's the divorce."

"Yes, Dad, it's the divorce," Donnie said, his voice calm but angry.

"You cheated on your wife with a young fan," Mike said bluntly, just throwing the truth down on the counter like the skinless carcass of a rabbit.

"Jesus, Dad," Donnie complained. "I know what I did."

"You think you're the first writer to do that?" Mike asked.

"Of course not."

"Hell no. You did it. It was wrong, sure, but you did it. It was a long time ago," Mike said.

"I destroyed my family," Donnie countered. "My kids won't talk to me. Melissa told me ... " he trailed off.

"Told you what?"

Donnie fought it, but felt the lump thicken his throat, then his eyes blurred with warm tears. He shook his head, ashamed and angry.

"Tell me, son," Mike said. He reached across the sales counter and put his hard, rough hand on Donnie's wrist. His voice was more gentle than Donnie could ever remember. "Tell me what she said."

"She told me ... she told me I'm not a good man who made a mistake," Donnie choked out. "She told me I'm a bad person. She called me a ... monster." He lifted his free hand and rubbed hard at his eyes. "I've never told anybody that."

"You believe it, don't you?" Mike asked, his voice soft, his hand remaining on his son's wrist, not judging, but not letting go, either.

Donnie lifted his eyes and looked into his father's. "I lied to Melissa for months while I sneaked around with a girl half my age. I made my wife think she was going crazy because I'm a good liar and she trusted me. Yeah, I believe what she said."

"So you gave up writing, moved to the middle of nowhere, probably haven't dated in eight years, and I'll bet you pretty much stay right here in this building all day, every day, not participating in whatever goes on in this little town." Mike's blue eyes bored into Donnie's face, gently demanding an answer.

Donnie gave a half-smile. "When did you get so smart?" he asked.

"I'm old, Donnie. Old people know shit." Mike gave Donnie's wrist a final squeeze and pulled his hand away. Donnie missed the contact. "You're miserable, aren't you?"

"It's not so bad," Donnie lied.

Mike snorted. "Bullshit, Donnie. That's bullshit. Maybe you've convinced yourself it's true, but I'm here to tell you it's not. You always had friends. Sure, you were an introvert, but it was like you were charging your batteries. You'd go out with your friends, but you always had a part of the day you kept to yourself, did your own thing. You used to play that board game, *Risk*, by yourself. And the shit you built with those Legos ... " He shook his head and smiled.

Donnie looked down, ashamed again. "I thought you never noticed. You always seemed to work, then go to your shop or watch TV. I didn't think you paid much attention to what I was doing."

"I didn't show you enough," Mike admitted. He raised his cup and drank thoughtfully, his eyes looking into the past. "You're not the only guy in this store with regrets. I didn't know much about how to get along with kids, so I just didn't. But I knew what you were doing. Me and your mom talked about you kids late into the night, after you went to bed. She was always telling me to go in and play with you, help you build your little houses and forts, ask what you were reading. But, well, I figured you were okay and probably didn't want your old man butting into your business."

Donnie smiled. "You were probably right. I was pretty dumb. I didn't know what was important. I guess I never did learn that."

"You were a kid," Mike corrected. "Kids are supposed to take family for granted. And I'm here to tell you, Don, Melissa is wrong about you. You're a good man. I know that. You made a mistake, like a lot of men do. Like a lot of *people* do. You're not a fuckin' monster. She could have forgiven you. A lot of spouses do and the marriage moves on."

Donnie shook his head. "The lying ... " he said. "I looked her in the face and lied to her over and over again. The mother of my children, Dad. Why?" He looked away, into the gray dawn outside the window and shook his head. "Ego. I'd made it and she hadn't supported me and I thought I was the shit."

"This is your punishment?" Mike asked, indicating the store and the whole little town with a slow wave of his coffee mug. "Or are you just hiding like a kid in his bedroom?"

Donnie looked into his own cup. "At first, it was hiding. Sulking. Then it became a penance. Being alone and poor gives you perspective."

Mike snorted. "That's bullshit, Donnie. Utter fucking bullshit. We've only been together a day, but I can tell you've sat alone up here, all wrapped up in your misery, making it worse than it really is. You're wearing it like a metal suit, like one of those knights." His voice took on a mocking falsetto. "'Look at me. I'm a bad person. My ex-wife called me a monster so I'm making myself sad and alone.' It's bullshit."

"Stop it, Dad," Donnie said, feeling a twinge of anger. His hand tightened on his coffee cup handle. "You don't know. Not this time. You never hurt Mom like I hurt Melissa. She ... she told the kids I chose to live separate from them when I moved up here. She said – "

"It doesn't matter what she said," Mike interrupted. "What did you tell your kids?"

Donnie looked up at his dad, then back down. "I apologized," he said weakly. "At first, you know, I wanted to try to explain myself to them. I'm glad I didn't. It was bad enough. They were on Melissa's side from the beginning. I don't blame them. I had nothing to say and they didn't want to talk to me or see me. That's why I didn't fight for custody. Then I came up here."

"And you quit trying," Mike said.

"I texted pretty often at first. They ignored me. They wouldn't pick up when I called. Wouldn't answer letters," Donnie said.

"That's on them," Mike said, his voice low and sympathetic again. "Perspective, Donnie. You've built yourself up to be the villain like in one of your stories, but you're not. There are other sides to you. You can't judge a whole diamond by a single flaw."

Donnie smiled briefly. "Actually, Dad, I think you can. And even if you can't, once someone finds the flaw, it's all they're going to see."

"Whatever," Mike said, grinning and sipping his coffee. "I'm not going back to the old fart's home until you realize I'm right," Mike said.

Donnie laughed for real. "Is that a fact?"

"Goddamn right it is," he said. "Are you going to cook breakfast?"

"I'm not much of a cook," Donnie said. "Good enough for me, but I don't know about making anyone else eat what I cook."

A female voice behind them said, "If you leave me some of that coffee, I'll cook breakfast."

Chapter Ten

The men turned to look at her and Josey smiled. Her blue-silver hair was crazy from a restless night and she looked like a kid in her sweats and a big Oklahoma Sooners T-shirt that hung to mid-thigh. The sight stirred memories and Donnie couldn't help but grin. He saw a grin split his father's grizzled face and guessed they were both remembering their own daughters standing in kitchen doorways, rumpled and sleepy.

"You cook?" Mike asked.

"I cooked for Grandma all the time," she answered. "I'm not bad. I've never been limited to a hotplate and a microwave, but I think I can handle it."

Donnie laughed. "My kitchen, with all of its conveniences, is yours," he said. "You know what we bought last night."

"What time does the store open?" she asked.

"Ten o'clock on Saturday," Donnie answered.

"It's 8:30 and you look like you didn't sleep," Josey said. "You should shower and look presentable."

Mike chuckled. "She's a bossy little thing."

Donnie sighed. "She ain't wrong," he admitted. He hadn't even realized the sun had come up while he and his father talked. Somewhere, deep down inside, he thought he felt a tiny bit better for the talk.

"Go shower," Mike said. "I'll take our chef some coffee, then make some more. You get many customers on Saturday?"

"A few. There'll be some teenagers, mostly boys, coming in after lunch to play a game back there," Donnie said.

"Anyone ever buy anything?"

Donnie grinned. "Not much. Most of my sales are online."

"You play games with those kids?"

"Every once in a while," Donnie said, pushing himself up from the chair, which suddenly seemed more comfortable than it ever had before. He briefly considered going to his now-empty bed and getting a quick nap, but gave up that idea as rude to his guests. He made his way toward the back of his store.

"Let the dog out," Josey called just before Donnie went through the door into the living area.

Jasper still lay curled up beside the cushions Donnie had slept on. "Jasper," he called. The dog's head popped up and his ears pricked forward. "You need outside?" Jasper scrambled to his feet and came to Donnie in a trot. Donnie led the dog to the back door and opened it to the cold morning air and watched as Jasper quickly explored the alley and decided the best place to piss was on three tires of Donnie's truck.

"You sure you don't want to hop up on the hood and take your morning dump?" Donnie asked as the dog slipped past his knees and back inside. Jasper gave no answer but went back into the store.

When he came out of his tiny bathroom, the stockroom area was filled with the smell of bacon and the popping sound of frying potatoes. He went to the kitchen area and found Josey holding a white ceramic coffee mug in one hand, stirring something in the skillet on the hot plate. He looked into the skillet and saw slices of browning potatoes mixed with shredded bacon.

"Butter that toast that just popped up, will ya?" Josey asked. She turned her face toward him and offered a quick smile. She was a pretty girl with skin like ivory seasoned with a sprinkling of light freckles. Her eyes were green and her lips thin and she had about her the air of an elf or pixie.

Donnie looked to the toaster and saw two golden slices poking from the slots. Four more pieces already glowed with butter on a plate in front of the toaster. Donnie sighed playfully. "You're gonna be running this place, aren't you?"

"Probably," she agreed. Her eyes twinkled over the rim of the cup as she sipped. Donnie saw that her coffee was brown and wondered how much milk and sugar she added. And, in general, why women didn't just drink black coffee anymore. Josey lowered the drink and smiled at him. "Grandma always told me I was a take-charge kind of gal. She didn't raise me to wait on a man to do anything."

"Feminist, too," Donnie said. "Great."

"You'll get used to it," she said. "I'm not the big-boobed damsel in distress Bolkar always gets to rescue."

"I have a feeling you'd scare that old bastard off," Donnie joked.

Josey started scooping the meat and potatoes out of the skillet and into a big bowl. "Hand me three eggs," she said. "Scrambled okay?"

"Sure," Donnie said, licking butter from one thumb while taking the carton from the little refrigerator with the other hand.

"And the milk. I like to add milk. Makes them fluffier," Josey said.

"Yes, ma'am." Donnie did as he was told, then stood back and watched the girl crack the eggs into the skillet, add milk, and scramble the whole mess, stirring it constantly as the eggs turned a solid yellow. She used a potholder to lift the skillet and scrape the eggs into a smaller bowl.

"We eat at that little table in the store?" she asked.

"Yeah," Donnie said sheepishly.

"Carry stuff." She put the bowls of food in his hands. "I'll bring plates and silverware."

"There's ... not much," Donnie confessed. "I have some plastic forks and knives from a party I had here a while back. A few years, I guess."

"Seriously?" Josey asked. "Okay. Get in there. I'll bring them."

Donnie did as he was told, putting the bowls on the table where his father sat reading a mystery novel. "Made you a waiter, didn't she?" Mike asked.

"Bossiest girl I've ever seen," Donnie said.

Mike looked at the food. "Any toast? I like to put my eggs on toast."

"I know. And yes, there's toast."

Josey came out of the back with Styrofoam plates and plasticware in one hand and the plate of toast in the other. They all sat around the low table and Josey passed out the plates. They dug into the food and it was good.

"Helluva breakfast," Mike commented as he rolled the last of his egg into a piece of toast. He bit into it and chewed while he smiled at Josey.

"It was good," Donnie agreed, looking at his empty plate.

"Thank you, gentlemen," Josey said. She got up and collected the plates, stacked the bowls, and started away with them.

"Josey, you don't have to do that," Donnie called.

She paused and turned back to look at him over her shoulder. "I have to earn my keep."

"You said you'd work in the store. You don't have to be a maid, too," Donnie told her.

"Fine. You do it tomorrow," she said and went on her way.

"Now you've done it," Mike said. "You didn't learn to keep your mouth shut while you were married, did you? If she wanted to cook breakfast every morning and clean up after us, you should have let her. Dammit, now I have to eat your cooking tomorrow." He shook his head as if truly disgusted. "I'm not taking a turn. I'm retired. And I'm a horrible cook."

Donnie went to the front of the store, flicked on the rest of the lights, and unlocked the door. Outside, Sagebrush looked cold and empty. John Barnes, a farmer west of town, got out of his rusty old Chevy pickup and hurried into the post office, clutching his work-stained coat around him as he did. Donnie considered how he had never spoken to Mr. Barnes and was only able to put a name to the man based on Sherry Brown's gossip. The marquee over the bank said it was 9:55 and the temperature was 31 degrees Fahrenheit. The sky was gray and overcast. Leaves and bits of trash skittered along the street in the wind.

"Gonna be a cold one. Maybe more snow," Mike said, coming to stand beside Donnie.

"Yeah. Maybe so. What are you going to do today?" Donnie asked.

"I'm going back to that restaurant and see if I can find out where an old feller can find a domino or card game today." Mike laughed softly. "Kinda got addicted to that stuff in the home."

"Old man," Donnie teased. "I was out of sorts yesterday and couldn't remember which was which. The Saturday dances are at the Elks' Lodge. It's the Veterans of Foreign Wars building where the old timers hang out during the day. From here, you turn right, then turn right at the corner and go to the end of the block. Last building. I hear the coffee's good but there's a lot of farting." Again, Sherry Brown's gossip.

"Perfect!" Mike said. "I'll get my coat and leave you and the boss to run this place. How late you stay open on Saturday?"

"Three o'clock. I close early if it's slow and the gamers don't show up. They might not come today if the weather gets worse," Donnie mused.

"What kind of games?" Mike asked, looking toward the area where they'd eaten breakfast. "There's no TV back there. Don't kids just play video games these days?"

"These are uber-nerds," Donnie said. "Dungeons and Dragons."

Mike shook his head. "They still play that?" he asked. "I remember you and that fat kid and the one with a nose like a pelican's beak and a couple of others sitting around playing that. No board or anything. I never understood it."

"Some kids still play," Donnie said. "There are a lot of role-playing games now. It's not just D and D anymore. Now, go on and play your Old Maid or whatever ancient games old farts play."

Mike huffed, but went to the stockroom to get his coat. Donnie looked at his laptop on the low counter behind the register. He didn't turn it on. A few minutes later, he noticed Josey wandering around the store. She saw him looking at her and called out to him.

"I'm just getting the lay of the land," she said.

"That's fine." Donnie wondered how she'd be at entering the titles he needed to add to the online inventory. Could she use a computer? Probably. What kid these days couldn't?

When Donnie turned back, he was just in time to see Sherry Brown reaching for the door. She came in with a blast of cold air and exaggerated shivering in her fur coat. Her cheeks were rosy and her eyes twinkled. She was like an elf with gray hair under a black knit cap.

"Mrs. Brown," Donnie said in greeting. "I guess it's cold out there?"

She leaned toward him in a conspiratorial manner. "Like a witch's breast in a brass bra," she said. "That's what my husband would say. But he wouldn't say breast."

Donnie laughed. "I didn't expect to see you until after the bank closes at noon."

"I've had a busy morning," she said. "You were on my mind all night."

"Why, Mrs. Brown, what a thing for you to say," Donnie teased.

She blushed, her wind-chapped cheeks coloring a deeper red. "I meant your situation now with your visitors," she gushed.

Before she could continue, Mike returned with his coat and hat on. He was pulling on black leather gloves as he approached the front of the store.

"This man must be your father," Mrs. Brown said. "You have his nose and cheekbones."

"He better give them back when he's done charming you with them," Mike said, pushing his fingers into the gloves.

Sherry Brown laughed heartily. "Your sense of humor, too."

"Uh-huh," Donnie said. He introduced them. "Dad was just going over to the VFW to try some dominoes with the other guys."

"Those gossiping old men," Mrs. Brown said playfully. "You go on, Mike. The doughnuts will be gone if you don't hurry."

"It was a pleasure to meet you, Mrs. Brown," Mike said.

"Just call me Sherry. Your son won't learn that," she said.

Mike left, but in his place was Josey. She was bouncing on the balls of her feet and had a mischievous smile on her lips. "Hello, Mrs. Brown," she said.

"Please, it's Sherry. Even for a youngster like you," the older woman said.

"Hi, Sherry," Josey tried again.

"Good morning, Josey," Sherry said. "How are you?"

"I'm good," Josey said, then turned her attention to Donnie. "Where's the Halloween display?"

Donnie shook his head. "I don't really do that kind of thing."

"Why not?" she demanded. "You've got to engage your customers. You have a big horror section."

Donnie shrugged. "I don't know. I just never have."

"Can I build one?" Her face beamed with happiness. Donnie couldn't resist her enthusiasm. But Sherry Brown spoke up before he could answer.

"That's a lovely idea!" she exclaimed. "Do it, Josey. Donnie won't mind."

"Can I?" Josey asked.

"Sure," Donnie said. "Knock yourself out."

"I'm gonna go pick out the books!" She dashed away. Donnie and Sherry watched her go.

"She's going to be good for you," Sherry said. "Good for business, too. So much energy! Whew! To be young again."

"Yeah. So, my situation kept you up?" Donnie prompted.

"Yes! Oh, my goodness." Sherry pulled off her gloves and dropped them on the counter, then fixed Donnie with a serious eye. "Where did you sleep last night?"

Donnie gaped at her for a moment, wondering what she was implying. "I pulled the cushions off the chairs and slept on those."

"Comfortable?"

"No," Donnie admitted.

"Where did that young lady sleep?"

"On my camping cot."

"Gave your father your bed?" Sherry asked, her voice saying she approved. Donnie nodded. "Well, that was fine for a night or two, but I bet you, especially, didn't get much sleep."

"Well, no," he admitted.

"Hmm." She plunged one age-spotted hand into her big purse and pulled out a small notebook. She opened it on the counter and jabbed a finger at some writing at the top of the page. "This one is two bedrooms. You and your father could share. It's the least expensive rental I could find in town that isn't a total dump." Her finger moved down to the next block of text. "This one is three bedrooms with two baths. It's $75 per month more than the other one, but you'd get your own bedroom." Her finger moved to the last block. "This is a two-bedroom, but it has a detached garage apartment, in case Josey wants that much privacy." She looked up at him triumphantly.

"Uhhh ... "

"Donnie Nelson, you can't keep sleeping on chair cushions, and you need a decent kitchen and bathroom," Mrs. Brown scolded. "That young lady is going to have needs you men don't and she'll want privacy."

"I understand that," Donnie said. "But I didn't invite her. I didn't invite either one of them. And honestly, I just don't have the money to pay rent on a house. I'm fine here."

"*You're* fine here," she agreed. "But it isn't just you now." She paused and her voice became more sympathetic. "Are your finances really so tight that you can't afford a place to live?"

"The stockroom was a major selling point of the store," Donnie admitted. "I wouldn't need a house or apartment."

"There are no apartment houses in Sagebrush. This is what's available." She tapped her finger on the notebook.

"How much?" Donnie looked at the prices Sherry had written in her insanely neat handwriting. He shook his head. "I'm sure those are all reasonable, but I just can't afford it."

"I'm going to leave these here," Sherry said. She tore the page from her notebook and pressed it into Donnie's hand. "You talk it over with your father and Josey. They may have some ideas. If it doesn't work out, well, we will just have to come up with some other ideas."

"You're very kind," Donnie said humbly. "I don't know what to do." He looked over to where Josey was stacking horror novels on a cart near the front door. "I had no idea I would be bringing anyone back with me."

"What was your relationship like with your father?" Sherry asked.

Donnie shook his head. "Not so good. After my own divorce, about eight years ago now, then my mom died a year later, and I wasn't right in the head. I let my sister talk me into believing Dad had Alzheimer's or something and signed off to get him into a home. He obviously didn't belong there. I've only talked to him a couple of times in those seven years until yesterday."

"And Josey?"

"I didn't even know she existed," Donnie admitted. "I knew Mrs. Wilder had a daughter, but that's all I knew."

Sherry Brown cocked her head at him, almost like a dog that had heard a strange sound. "Didn't she say she's your niece?"

Donnie rolled his eyes. "I have no idea why she said that."

Sherry looked toward the girl, who had put a set of wireless earphones in and was bobbing her head as she sorted the books she'd selected. "The Good Lord works in mysterious ways," Sherry said. "You're reunited with your father and this young lady has come into your life for some reason. You'll figure out what it is when you're supposed to."

Donnie chuckled. "I figured you'd be more of a free-will kind of person, but here you are talking about fate and predestination," he said.

She smiled and patted the hand that held the rental information. "God knows what we all need. Sometimes He just lets us think we're running the show."

"A road map or sign here and there would sure be nice," Donnie said.

"You just have to recognize the signs," Sherry told him, looking at Josey again with real interest. "She's a special girl. There's a light in her eyes. She'll be good for you. She'll wake you up."

"She makes me think of my own daughter," Donnie said, his voice soft and sad. "Except LizBeth doesn't talk to me."

Sherry gave him a hard look. "When was the last time you spoke to her?"

"On her birthday, back in June. She sounded annoyed for the whole two minutes we spoke," Donnie said.

"Leave it to God to fix," Sherry said. "Now, I need another smutty romance novel. There's another winter storm coming in and I don't want to be caught without a book. Do you mind?"

Donnie laughed. "Of course not. Help yourself."

She fished the two paperbacks she'd recently borrowed from her bag and said she'd return them to the shelves. Then she shook her head and said, "That Stephen King book was too much for me. When that old woman came out of the bathtub ... " She stopped and did a theatrical shiver, then went into the stacks, returning a few minutes later with a thick Johanna Lindsey novel. She showed it to Donnie, saying, "I think we'll go with pirates this weekend." She put the book in her purse and began pulling on her gloves. "A lot of romances feature women working in little restaurants swept off their feet by men with troubled pasts," she remarked.

"That's oddly specific," Donnie said dryly.

She smiled and shrugged her shoulders. "All I'm saying is that there might be a waitress at Annie's who gets a bigger smile on her face when you come in."

"That's ridiculous," Donnie said, thinking of the waitress, Debbie.

"It's just my unprofessional opinion, Mr. Nelson," Sherry said, "But I think you've taken yourself out of the game for so long that you don't even know when you're being called off the bench." She gave him a wink, then added, "You have a good day." Donnie watched as the matron made her way to Josey and stopped.

"Are you leaving, Sherry?" Josey asked, standing up from her stack of books and popping out only one earphone.

"I am, sweetie," Sherry answered. She reached out and put a hand on the younger woman's arm and leaned in. Donnie could just barely make out her whispered words. "These are good men, but they need you, honey. Donnie especially. Drag him out of that cocoon he's built around himself. You let me know if you need anything. Anything at all." She straightened and then said out loud, "I look forward to seeing your Halloween display when I come in next time."

"Thank you, Sherry," Josey said.

Sherry Brown left without giving Donnie another look. There was a blast of cold air as she opened and closed the door and Donnie watched her short, sharp steps as she crossed the street to the bank.

"Was she talking about the waitress from last night?"

Donnie turned away from the window to find Josey standing at the end of a bookshelf, both hands clutching books but hanging at her sides. There was a light in her eyes, he noted. So much ... life. She was a blue-and-silver forest fire of energy. She smiled at him.

"Hello?" she said. "Earth to Donnie. Are you there?"

He grinned back at her. "Sorry," he said. "I guess she's talking about Debbie. I don't know. Did you ... ?" He suddenly felt embarrassed to be asking.

"What?"

"Did you think she was flirting with me?"

Josey shrugged one shoulder. "I don't know her personality. She was friendly with you. She tried to get you to talk more and you wouldn't. But is that just her? Is she like that with everyone?"

Donnie shook his head. "I really don't know."

"Ask her out."

He gave one quick snort of laughter, then shook his head again. "I don't think so."

"Take her a book you think she might like," Josey suggested. "She mentioned wanting to read a romance, which was such a clue that she wanted to talk."

Donnie shook his head again. "I don't know. How's the horror display coming along?"

"You're scared to ask her out," Josey challenged.

Donnie felt himself rolling both his lips into his mouth, something he did when he didn't want to give a true answer. He forced himself to stop. "Okay," he conceded. "We'll go with that. How's the display?"

"You need small shelves for the ends," she said. "But I can make do with some of the cardboard boxes you have in the back if you have some colored butcher paper to cover them."

"Sorry," he said. "No butcher paper."

"We used miles of colored butcher paper in student council," Josey said. "I bet there's no office or school supply store in this town, huh? Just the Wal-Mart?"

Donnie laughed softly. "We don't have a Wal-Mart," he said. "There's a Dollar General store at Broadway and Fifth."

"Where's that? How far? How do you exist without a Wal-Mart?"

"About five blocks," he said, pointing west. "Two blocks that way, turn left, go a few more blocks. Too small for a Wal-Mart."

"Can I take the truck?" She stacked her fistfuls of books on top of the shelf she was standing beside and turned to face him.

"Do you have a driver's license?" he asked.

"Of course," she said. "I just never owned a car of my own."

Donnie saw an opening and mulled over whether or not to seize it. "Show me," he challenged.

"Are you serious?" she asked. Her tone said she was offended, but not truly upset.

Donnie shrugged. "It's a small town. If one of our two police officers see a stranger driving my truck, they might decide to investigate."

She pursed her lips and looked away for just a moment, then faced him. "Fine. I don't have a license. Well, I do, but I didn't bring it. You know I stole that blanket from the church where Grandma's funeral was, right?"

"What?" Donnie felt a little revulsion at first, relating the blanket to a dead body. He decided that couldn't be the case.

"Yeah. It was a spur-of-the-moment thing, stowing away in your truck. My purse is in the limo that took me to the cemetery. Or was. That's where I left it. Do you think I wear black every day? I'm not goth or emo."

Donnie realized with shame that he hadn't even realized the girl was wearing her funeral clothes again today. There'd been a time when that kind of detail would have jumped out at him. "We need to get you some clothes," he said quietly.

She tilted her head and raised one light brown eyebrow. Yes, Donnie thought. Light brown. Her natural hair color.

He reached into the pocket of his jeans and pulled out his ring of keys. He tossed them to her. "Let me give you some money."

"I'll pay you back," she promised. "I do have money. Just not with me. I ... I'll need to figure that one out. Do you have Midfirst Bank here?"

Donnie laughed. "Nope. First National, right across the street," he said. "Sagebrush doesn't offer much, and what it does offer, doesn't come in much variety. Sherry Brown's husband is the bank president."

"I'll get the money," Josey promised.

Donnie pulled out his wallet and selected his credit card. He tried to hide his reluctance as he handed it over, but had to add sheepishly, "I'm not rich. Dollar General doesn't have much, but they do have clothes. Get a few outfits. We'll figure out something better later. Bring the receipt so I can keep track of what we spend for the store."

"Gotcha, Donnie," she said, taking hold of the card.

Donnie didn't let go of the card yet. "Did you hear everything we talked about?"

Josey blushed a very pretty pink. "Maybe."

"She'll stick to the story of you being my niece if that's what we're going with," Donnie said. "But next time you get the urge to say something like that, talk to me first."

"Okay, Uncle Donnie," she agreed with a smile. Holding his over-used credit card in one hand and the keys to everything he owned in the other, she spun on her bare heel and bounced toward the back of the store. Just before she disappeared, she turned and said, "Look over those rentals Sherry brought. I have enough money to pay the rent. I'm serious. Grandma left me everything."

Donnie looked at the paper Sherry had left. Living in a house? After so long in the back of the store, the idea seemed almost alien to him. What would he do with all that space? What about furniture? And appliances? And the bills associated with another building? He folded the paper and slipped it beneath the cash register. It was just too much.

Donnie heard a strange noise and realized it was the panting of a dog the moment before Jasper rounded the end of the front counter. The dog came over and sat beside him, looking up at him with eyes the color of sunlit honey. He wagged his tail a couple of times and opened his mouth to show his pink tongue. Donnie reached out and patted the dog's head, then let his fingers scratch behind a soft, floppy ear.

"I'm not as alone as I thought, am I?" he asked the dog. "I guess those days are over for a while." He paused, then confessed, "I've missed having a dog. I couldn't take Duke with me when I left. Not after everything else I'd done. I haven't had a dog since."

Duke was dead now. Melissa had informed him of that in a cold text message about three years ago. *Duke died last night. Heart disease. He'd been coughing for weeks.* Knowing how much his daughter, especially, had loved the dog, Donnie called LizBeth. It was all silences and sniffles until she said, "At least he didn't leave me." Donnie apologized, told his daughter he loved her, and hung up. All Brian would say was that Duke had been sick, so he'd expected it, then excused himself.

"I couldn't even be there for Duke," Donnie said. "He was a Husky. Big guy. Looked so much like a wolf. I paid out the ass for him as a puppy." He gave Jasper a sad grin. "I haven't always been the destitute bookseller you see before you. Wealth, like happiness, was fleeting."

Jasper seemed to understand the tone, if not the words. He turned his head and gave Donnie's hand a few slow, sympathetic licks, then looked back up at him, giving permission for the ear scratching to resume. Donnie obliged.

The door of the shop opened with the obligatory rush of cold air and Donnie looked up to see the editor of the *Sagebrush Democrat* newspaper come in. The man stood in the doorway a moment, the wind flapping the bottom of his worn suede coat while he took the last drag from a cigarette and flicked the butt toward the curb. He came in and closed the door.

"Wilson, how are you?" Donnie asked. "Time for another crime novel?"

"It is," the man answered. He was a tall guy in his early forties, just starting to get soft around the middle. His dark hair showed the beginning of gray at his temples, but it helped soften his otherwise rather hard features. His face was sharp and angular, ravaged by acne scars, and his lips were without color and blended with his face. He'd grown up in New York and sometimes that Eastern attitude came out in his editorials. Wilson didn't immediately move toward the shelves of books.

"Anything else I can help you with?" Donnie asked.

"I heard you went out of town and came home with company," the editor said.

"That's true enough," Donnie admitted. "Not really newsworthy, though."

Wilson cocked his head at Donnie and grinned, showing his small, nicotine-stained teeth. "Community journalism, Donnie. I know you've seen the local gossip section of the paper where we run a paragraph about dear Mrs. Lois Dunnagan entertaining her sister and brother-in-law from Elk City for a week and things like that."

Donnie smiled and nodded. "I have," he said. "That's some old-school stuff. I remember my grandma's local paper running a piece like that way, way back and hadn't seen it again until I came here."

Wilson grunted. "I think half my circulation is thanks to that piece. Small-town folks love gossip."

Still scratching the dog's ear, Donnie shrugged. "I think everyone does, regardless of location."

"Isn't that Chigger Jurnigan's dog?"

"Yeah. He spent the night here," Donnie said. "He was wandering the streets."

"He wanders the streets all the time," Wilson said, coming over to the counter to watch Donnie pet the dog. "You've never taken him in before."

"No," Donnie admitted. "It was Josey's idea."

"That's the silver-haired girl you brought home?"

Donnie chuckled. "Is this an interview?"

"I'm interested," the newspaperman said. "She's altered your behavior already. Who is she to you?"

"I'd be willing to bet a cup of coffee you already know the answer to that," Donnie challenged.

Wilson grinned at him again. "How's business, Mr. Nelson?"

"Slow. Like always."

"How long have you lived here? Ten years?"

"Seven."

"Most people still don't know you," Wilson said, fixing Donnie with a dark, probing eye. "You're the guy who lives alone in the back of your store and you spend all day sitting by the window with an open computer but you never seem to do anything on it. You're nice enough when people come in, but you don't make an effort to come out. If you did, it might be good for business."

Donnie looked at the man, then back at the dog. He thought of how he'd just been considering how he didn't really know hardly anyone in town. Now the newspaper editor was pointing out his foreignness to him. Why right now? Like he'd read Donnie's mind or something.

Wilson leaned over the counter and his voice was low, but not threatening. "I know who you really are, Donald Nelson. Bestselling author, divorced, in hiding from the world."

Donnie's head snapped up and he stared at the newspaper editor. His throat was dry and his mind raced with questions. "How ... how long have you known?"

"The day after I interviewed you when you took over this store," Wilson admitted.

"And you never told?"

Wilson shook his head. "There was a time, Donnie, back in my youth, when I would have seen that as a huge story and would have defied anyone to stop me breaking the news.

I've never had your fame, but I've had a messy divorce. You're not the first writer to come to Sagebrush to hide from his past."

Wilson waved at the dog. "But there's a sudden change in your pattern of behavior. You make a very rare trip out of town to attend a funeral and you come home with your sharp-eyed father and an elf of a girl with hair unlike anything this town has ever seen. Then you're taking in stray dogs. And what's this?" He pointed casually at the cart and stacks of horror novels between the front door and the shelves of books.

Donnie sighed. "Josey is going to build a Halloween display."

"In seven years, have you ever had a holiday display in this store, Mr. Nelson?"

"No," Donnie admitted.

"Your patterns are changing," Wilson repeated. "What else will change? I like you, Donnie. I think I'm one of the few people who knows you at all. You're a good guy. Let me help you."

"Help me?"

"Let's get you in the gossip column," Wilson said. "We can do that this week. Next week, a little piece with a picture of you, your guests, and this Halloween display. See if people will come in. It's free advertising."

"Free?" Donnie asked, his voice sounding more suspicious than he'd intended.

"Quid pro quo, as Hannibal Lector would say," Wilson answered with a grin. "If business picks up and you find yourself with a few extra dollars, maybe you'll run an ad in the paper."

Donnie laughed. He nodded. "That sounds more than fair."

"And if, someday, you ever want to reveal who you really are, you'll let *The Sagebrush Democrat* break the story."

Donnie sobered up. "That's not likely to happen."

"Patterns are changing, and that's when news happens," Wilson said. "A stone has been dropped in the pond of your life, Mr. Nelson, and you don't know how big those ripples will get before they make it to shore."

"You're just full of metaphors today," Donnie said. "No wonder that rag of yours is just yellow journalism."

Wilson feigned heartbreak. "The Pulitzer alludes me, sir."

"I'm joking," Donnie said. "I enjoy the paper. Especially the gossip column."

"So, you ready to talk about your visitors?"

"Ask away," Donnie said.

Wilson reached into the inside pocket of his coat and pulled out a battered notebook. He flipped open the cover and thumbed through several pages of writing to a blank one. "Tell me about them," he invited.

"Mike is my dad," Donnie said. "Josey is my niece. I have two sisters. I bet you knew that much." Donnie found himself biting his lips again, wondering if Wilson knew his sisters' names and the names of his actual nieces and nephews.

"I did. You picked them up in Lawton, your hometown, right?"

"Yes."

"What's the girl's last name?"

"Wil ... " Donnie caught himself, then lied. "Josey Walker."

"How old is she?"

Donnie hesitated for a heartbeat. "She's eighteen," he said, adding mentally, *Or so she claims.*

"And your dad?"

Donnie had to think. His father was twenty-three when he was born, so he added that to his own age. "He's seventy-seven." He paused, letting that sink in. "Wow. He really is seventy-seven."

"Did you guys make plans for this visit?" Wilson asked.

Donnie laughed. "No," he said, then stopped, unwilling to tell how his guests had come to be with him. "It wasn't planned at all."

"Where are they staying?"

"Here," Donnie said, sighing and looking around the shop. "This is all I have."

"That can't be very comfortable," Wilson said, cocking an eye at him over his notebook.

"We're working on some arrangements," Donnie said. "Dad took my bed. Josey was on my camping cot, and I made a pallet out of chair cushions."

Wilson gave a short, distracted laugh as his pen scratched over the paper. "That doesn't sound fun for you."

"No," Donnie agreed.

"How long are they staying?"

"I'm not sure," Donnie said. "It was all very spontaneous."

"I guess your dad is retired," Wilson said. "What did he do?"

"He worked at a grain elevator in Lawton. He was there for years. Assistant superintendent when he retired," Donnie said.

"He's a widower?" The newspaper man's tone said he knew the answer. Donnie nodded. "The girl graduated from Lawton High School?"

"Yeah," Donnie said, and realized his voice had been too flat. "Just this past May."

"What else can you tell me about either of them?"

Donnie shrugged. "Dad is out looking for people his age to play dominoes or cards with. I sent him to the VFW. Josey is going to work in the store a little. She thinks she needs to earn her keep."

"Sounds like they plan to stay for a while?" Again, he cocked an eye over the notebook.

"Yeah, it does," Donnie admitted. "And they're welcome," he added, and for the first time, he really meant it. Jasper had lain down behind the counter. He wasn't asleep, but was just relaxed as if he was home. Donnie grinned down at him.

"And the dog?"

Donnie looked back up. "I don't know. We all know the dog has an owner. But he's a good boy and welcome here anytime."

"The funeral you went to was an old teacher?" Wilson asked.

"Yes. Wanda Wilder," Donnie answered. "Creative writing. She was great."

"Part of my job is to notice things, Donnie," Wilson said, closing his notebook and putting it away. "I already see a change in you. Something different about your personality. Next thing you know, you'll be asking out that waitress who, rumor says, has her eye on you."

"Good Lord, man!" Donnie exclaimed. "How do you hear these things?"

"My sources are confidential," Wilson told him with a grin and a wink. "Now I'll get that book. With this early cold weather, people aren't doing anything and I don't have much to report on. I'm mostly running AP stories and looking for local angles. That isn't much fun." With that, he wandered off toward the crime section and came back with a couple of thrillers and a biography of a little known serial killer from Texas.

"Do you want to talk to Dad or Josey?" Donnie asked as he recorded the sale of the books and totaled up the amount due with sales tax.

"Not this time," Wilson said, handing over a few limp bills to pay for the books. "For the gossip column, it all needs to be your perspective. You're the resident. But when I come back for the story about your display, yes, definitely then."

"I'll let them know. I'm not sure Dad will talk much."

"I get that. The girl, though, she's the one who'll shake this place up," Wilson said. He picked up his books and headed for the door. "Read about yourself on Thursday."

Chapter Eleven

Josey returned with a bouquet of yellow plastic bags clutched in one hand. She had Donnie's keys and credit card in the other and she placed those on the counter and smiled at him. "They had some really cool stuff," she said. Then she hesitated, her face scrunching up just a bit, a thin line appearing between her pale eyebrows as she looked past Donnie to his open computer. As he watched, her face lit up. "Are you writing a new book?"

Donnie glanced quickly at his laptop screen, at the few words that had been there for so long, waiting for a succession of more and more words, then he gently closed the laptop and shook his head. "Old, dead dreams," he said as he turned back toward the girl. "What did you get?"

"Uh-uh," she said. "You'll see what's in the bags as the display takes shape. I've got the image in my head. I think it'll be super cute."

"Super cute," Donnie echoed, smiling.

"That was definitely a word processing program and it looked like a book," Josey said, nodding at the closed laptop.

Donnie shook his head. "Don't worry about it. It's nothing."

"Your fan-fic group would be really happy if Bolkar returned," Josey said. "I mean, they're making up stories about him, but they want you to come back."

"My what group?" Donnie asked.

"Fan-fic," Josey said, her tone telling him this was a term he should know. He guessed his blank look told her he didn't have a clue what she meant. She rolled her green eyes and sighed. "Boomers just don't get it," she said.

"Boomers? My dad is a Boomer. I'm Generation X," Donnie told her, grinning. "The one that's always overlooked, but we don't give a shit."

"Whatever," Josey said, smiling. "Fan-fic is where other people take the characters and setting and plot or whatever from famous works and write their own stories using those things."

"But ... " Donnie began. He felt his face scrunching in confusion. "That's not legal. It's a copyright violation. That's going on?"

"Duh," Josey said. "Haven't you heard of *Fifty Shades of Grey*? It started off as *Twilight* fanfiction."

"Where is this stuff published?" Donnie asked. "No publisher would open themselves up to the lawsuits of copyright violation like that."

"It's all online, Donnie," Josey said patiently. "Nobody gets paid. It's all done out of love."

"And people are doing this with my stories?"

"Oh yeah," she said. "You have a pretty big group. Some of the stories are decent. Most are pure crap."

"You've read it?" He tried not to gape at her.

"Yes," she said, some attitude slipping into her tone. "How would I know otherwise?"

"Will you show me?"

"Later," she said. "These bags are getting heavy and I want to finish my display."

Donnie sighed. "Okay. But you have to show me later." He paused and watched as she moved over to her endcap display and put her bags on the floor. "We should talk about what Sherry proposed, too. My dad will need to be in on that one."

Josey turned and looked at him, her face thoughtful. "Yeah," she said. She looked back at her yellow bags splashed on the floor, then out the windows. "That's the bank across the street, right?" Donnie nodded. "Sherry is the bank president's wife?"

"Yes," Donnie said. "Why?"

"I'm gonna go talk to her real quick," Josey said.

She didn't wait for Donnie to ask her why, she just whisked herself out the front door, letting in another blast of cold air as she left. He watched through the windows as she hurried across the street, her coat held closed in front of her and her blue-silver hair bouncing with her steps. She pulled open the bank door and disappeared into the darkness within.

"Every time," Donne mused, looking from his closed laptop to the bright yellow bags in front of the fledgling book display. "She just blows in, shakes things up, and moves on. Fanfiction? Of Bolkar?" He shook his head. He considered going over and looking through her bags, but grinning, he shook his head and decided not to. Let her have her surprise.

There were about half a dozen books he needed to package for mailing, so Donnie turned to that job, printed labels, and was putting the third on a padded brown envelope when his cell phone rang. The ringtone was familiar, but one he seldom heard. He inhaled deeply and blew the breath out with a whoosh as he lifted his phone and hit the green button to answer the call.

"Hello, Maggie," he said.

"Is he with you?" Her voice was cold and demanding.

"Who?" he asked, playing dumb.

"Our father, Donald. Is. He. With. You?"

"You mean he's not in the old folks' home you stuck him in?"

"You agreed to that," Margaret snapped at him. "Now answer me. Is he with you? I swear to God, we're about to put out a silver alert on him."

"Don't do that," Donnie told her. "He's with me."

"How the hell did he get way the fuck up there?" she demanded.

"Such language, Maggie. Mom would not approve," Donnie teased.

"Fuck you, Donald," she said. "Do you realize the problems this has caused? He just disappeared. No one has seen him in two days."

"And they just told you he was missing today?" Donnie asked. "That's pretty irresponsible of them."

"Damn it, Donnie," Margaret said, her voice softer, relieved. "How did he get up there?"

"I came to Lawton for a funeral and he met me and insisted he come with me," Donnie said. "There was a reporter and things got all weird and next thing I knew, we were on the road."

"He's okay?" she asked.

"He's fine."

"Are you going to bring him home soon?"

Donnie thought about it, remembering his earlier plan to get his dad back in the home as soon as possible. "I don't know," he said. "Maggie, Dad does not have Alzheimer's. I'm sure of that. He's been coherent every minute. We were wrong to put him in there."

"That's ridiculous," Maggie said, the hard edge back in her voice. "I went to see him last month and he didn't even know who I was."

Donnie looked out the window, wondering what was taking Josey so long. "Yeah, well, I think it was an act. He's pretty mad at you. He knows you were the leader in putting him in that home."

"Are you bringing him home, Donnie, or do I have to drive up there and get him?" she asked, her voice full of acid. Donnie felt his resolve harden.

"I'll bring him back," he said. "But not until he's damn good and ready. Do you understand that, Margaret? He's a grown man. He's of sound mind. And dammit, I like having him here."

"You *always* got your way, Donald," she said.

He laughed at her. "This isn't what I want. It's what *he* wants. He's been rotting away in that home where he never should have been in the first place. If he wants to live up here with me for the rest of his life, that's what he'll do." Donnie stopped. The words were out. He hadn't thought about them. Did he mean them? There was no turning back now.

"But – "

"He doesn't want the house, Maggie," Donnie said, sticking the knife in. "He knows that's why you shipped him off to the nursing home."

Silence. "It's an assisted living center," she said meekly.

"It's not his home," Donnie said. He counted off a few silent heartbeats, then let her off the hook. "How are Joel and the kids?"

"They're good," she said dully. "Ben is a starter for the football team. Defensive back. Brooklynn is at OU, majoring in nursing."

"That's good," Donnie said. "Tell them hi for me. How's Katelyn?"

"She's okay. She's dating again."

Donnie thought about that. He'd forgotten his youngest sister had divorced her first husband, an alcoholic pill-popper, because of his addictions and all the problems that came with it. "Good," he said. "I hope she finds someone better this time."

"How are you, Donnie?" she asked, and he couldn't tell if she was being polite or really cared.

"I'm doing okay," he said. "Not rolling in money, but doing okay."

"Are you seeing anyone? Are there even single women in that town?"

He chuckled. "I guess there are," he admitted, thinking momentarily about a certain waitress. "But I'm not seeing anyone."

"You should," Maggie told him.

"Have you seen Melissa?" Donnie asked. "Brian? LizBeth?"

"I have," she said. "Melissa is ... Donnie ... she's getting married next month."

Donnie was quiet. He knew he shouldn't be surprised. He had never asked if she was seeing anyone. On one level, he knew she probably was, but consciously, he had never allowed himself to admit it. Now she was getting married. "Oh," he said. "The kids?"

"They're okay, Donnie. I saw them at a McDonald's a few weeks ago. They're doing good," she said.

There was a lump in his throat and his eyes burned. Donnie struggled with the words. "Did they ask ... "

"No, Donnie," she said softly. "I'm sorry."

He shook his head, then realized she couldn't see that. "It's okay," he said, his voice thick and forced. There was a long awkward silence. Finally, Donnie broke it. "We're good with Dad?"

"Can you handle him, Donnie? He's an old man."

"He's fine. We've been catching up. It's been nice," he said.

"Who died?" Maggie asked. "Whose funeral did you come to?"

"Mrs. Wilder," he said.

"From high school?"

"Yeah," he said. Then he had an idea. "She had a granddaughter who lived with her. Have you ever heard anything about her? Josey, I think her name is."

"No, I didn't know," Maggie said.

So, Josey wasn't on the news as a missing person. That was good.

"Why didn't you come see me? Or at least call?" Maggie asked.

Donnie hesitated, then tried to wing a reasonable answer. "There was the reporter harassing me, and Dad showing up confused everything. He demanded I bring him home with me. I just ran, I guess."

"You wouldn't have called," Maggie accused.

Donnie didn't answer. She was right. He knew it. She knew it. There was nothing to say. "Sorry," he mumbled.

"I am sorry the family is so … dysfunctional," Maggie said. "It's my fault. I know that. I regret how it went down. I just couldn't bear the thought of the family losing the house where we grew up. Dad wasn't in any condition to keep up with the bills and everything."

"He wasn't," Donnie agreed. "But it was grief, and the fact Mom always did everything with paying the bills and stuff. It wasn't because he was senile."

"If you say so," she said. "He always acted like he didn't know me. Will … If you get a chance, will you tell him I love him?"

"Of course," Donnie said. "I'll tell him. We've been expecting to hear from you."

"Sorry I was so rude at first. I was scared," she said. "I thought he just wandered away."

"I understand. He's fine. He's out playing dominoes or something with the other old guys up here," Donnie said.

"If he's really not coming back, we'll need to do some paperwork with the home," Maggie said. "I'll take care of it. I guess it should be my responsibility."

"Okay," Donnie said, wanting to agree but suspecting he'd sound like an asshole if he did.

"His retirement and Social Security checks have been going there to pay for his … Well, to pay for everything. He'll want those forwarded to your house, I guess." She paused, then asked, "Donnie, are you living in a house? Tell me you're not still living in the back of the store."

Donnie sighed. "It's a work in progress. A friend at the bank is helping me find a more suitable place."

"Thank goodness for that," she said. "Okay, well, I need to go. I'm glad Dad is okay. I'll talk to you later."

They hung up. Donnie looked at the phone for a moment, then returned his attention to the books he had been packaging. He had expected more anger. Accusations. Fear that their father was going to try to kick Maggie and her family out of the ancestral home. She had seemed genuinely glad to hear their father was safe. And there had even been contrition.

"I guess people can change," he said as he taped the last envelope closed. He compartmentalized the news about his ex-wife remarrying to work over at some later point. It wasn't something to examine yet.

Movement caught his eye and he looked out the store window to see the afternoon light flash again on the glass door of the bank as it swung closed. Josey was there, her vibrant hair blowing in the wind. She looked toward him in the store, but instead of crossing Main Street and coming back, she crossed Broadway Avenue, going east, and went into the cafe. Donnie thought it was odd she would go eat without asking anyone to go with her, or seeing if he wanted anything, but, maybe that's how kids acted now, he reasoned. He stacked his packages of books on the counter to take to the post office Monday and looked at a cardboard box of books behind the counter. They needed to be put into the inventory, but he just wasn't feeling it at the moment.

Donnie sat at his computer and closed the open manuscript. It was a relief to not see the blinking cursor mocking his blocked brain. He opened the Chrome browser and typed in "bolkar death merchant fan fiction" and hit the Enter key. The first few options were links to his books on Amazon, a personal webpage he had begun just before the first book was published and had ignored for almost a decade, but then there was a link to a site called *Fantasy Fan Fic* and then his character's name was highlighted in the text sample. He clicked the link.

What came up was a list of hyperlinked phrases he soon learned were story titles. He clicked one and found three single-spaced pages about his bounty hunter having gay sex with a "swarthy-skinned desert-dweller" he met while hunting for a stolen horse. The piece was full of misspellings, typos, showed a complete lack of grammatical understanding, and ended with Bolkar killing his lover to protect his reputation.

"What the actual fuck?" Donnie said quietly as he closed the link and returned to the main page.

He considered stopping there, but instead scrolled down until one link named "The Moon Beast" caught his attention. He suspected it would be something about Bolkar having sex with a crazy woman on her period. The first paragraph was surprisingly well written and interesting, describing a corner of Bolkar's world Donnie had never elaborated on in his own stories. The author, C. Bollinger, showed an understanding of the complexity of Bolkar's character and why he acted the way he did. The story itself was about a village shaman who came to Bolkar in a tavern and offered him all the wealth his people had mustered in exchange for Bolkar's services in killing the "Moon Beast" of the title. Bolkar took the money, killed the werewolf terrorizing the village, and made love to the chieftain's daughter before riding away in a misty dawn.

"Damn." Donnie sat back and looked at his computer screen. The story was good. It was well written, with very few typos, and showed a real knack for narrative structure. There was a time stamp near the top of the story and he saw that it had been submitted just about three months ago. "People are still reading it. And writing their own stories about him."

Donnie went back to the main page of Bolkar stories and scrolled down, looking for more written by C. Bollinger. The front door of the store opened and a blast of cold air swirled in around Josey as she spun around and pushed the door closed. She turned to face him, her cheeks flushed red with cold and a mischievous look in her eyes.

"What are you up to?" Donnie asked suspiciously as she shrugged out of her coat. "You've got the devil's light in your eyes."

"The devil's light?" she asked, laughing.

"That's what my grandma called it when she knew I was up to no good," Donnie answered.

She laughed again in a way that told him his suspicions were right, but she denied it. "I'm not up to anything. Just back to finish my Halloween display."

"I guess you already had lunch?" Donnie asked. "I saw you go to the diner."

Josey squatted beside her cluster of yellow bags. "I just got some fries and a Coke. I'm good until dinner," she said without turning to face him.

Donnie watched her, wondering if her pale neck was really reddening from a blush or from bending over or if he'd just imagined it. Whatever. He shook his head. "I read a couple of those fan fiction things," he said.

Now she turned to face him, a brown Styrofoam human skull in one hand. "Oh yeah? What did you think?" Her eyes studied him intently.

"One was absolute crap," he said. "They made Bolkar gay just to write some of the worst sex scenes I've ever read. Couldn't spell or anything. The second one I read, though, was really good. I mean, really good. I wish I'd written it."

"That's cool," she said. "Most of it is like the first one you read. Most fan-fic is just there to make popular characters have sex. You should see what they've done with the *Star Trek* characters."

Donnie shook his head and grinned. "I don't even want to think about Mr. Spock and Captain Kirk."

"Yep, that's a popular one," she said, turning back to her work. She placed the skull on one of the paper-wrapped boxes she was using as a shelf, then carefully stacked a hardcover of the collected works of Edgar Allan Poe as a base, with Lovecraft's *Bloodcurdling Tales of Horror and the Macabre* angled differently on top of that, and then a green paperback of an anthology edited by Isaac Asimov called *13 Horrors of Halloween*. On the front of the box she glued a humped-up black cat showing its fangs.

"That looks good," Donnie commented.

"Thanks," she said. "But are you going to sit there and watch me the whole time? What do you usually do during your work day?"

Donnie chuckled. "Very little," he answered. "I've already packed the books to mail. I have boxes of books to inventory. I guess I could do that. It's just so tedious."

"How do you do it?" she asked as she pulled a small scarecrow from her Dollar General bags and sat it on another box, its back resting against the fixture behind it.

"I keep a spreadsheet. I write the title and author and edition, along with the ISBN and book's condition," he said.

Josey stopped what she was doing and looked at him, her head tilted a little to one side like a curious puppy. "You type all that yourself?"

"Well, yeah," he said. "Until today I've never had anybody working with me."

"Why don't you just scan the bar code?" she asked.

"What do you mean?"

"Really, Donnie?" She put down the handful of books she was holding and stood up. "There are apps you can put on your phone that will let you just scan the bar code and put the titles, authors, editions, and original retail price into a database or spreadsheet. All you'd have to add is the book's condition. I used one for mine and Grandma's personal libraries."

"There's an app for that?" he asked, incredulous. "Am I really so far behind the times?"

She stood before him at the counter and regarded him as if he was a pathetic relic of the past, not quite useless, but outdated by modern appliances that could do his functions more quickly and cleanly. "You're not hopeless," she said. "I can show you. But I want to finish my display first. The app is ... " She stopped, looking over his shoulder out the window. "I think we have customers coming," she stage-whispered.

107

The door opened and Omar came in with another boy about his age. Donnie recognized him as Austin Pierce, the son of the town's only cop other than Chief Henderson. Neither Austin nor his father were regulars. As he was about to greet them, Donnie saw both boys' eyes widen as they took in the sight of Josey. He could almost feel their tongues tying themselves into knots.

"Good afternoon, boys," Donnie said as if he had noticed nothing. "What brings you in?"

Austin was first to recover. He punched Omar in the arm, just above his elbow, then gave him a look when his friend turned. It was all Donnie could do to keep a straight face as both boys turned to look at him. For her part, Josey acted like nothing weird was going on as she leaned with an elbow on the counter.

"I showed Austin the books I bought," Omar said. "He's into that stuff, too, so I told him he should come."

"We're glad to have you visit, Austin," Donnie said, noting how the boy's eyes kept sliding toward Josey. Now she was twirling a silver lock of hair and he knew she was doing it to deliberately tease the younger boys. Donnie motioned toward her. "This is Josey. My niece. She's helping out in the store."

It seemed both boys were fighting a battle within their skins, trying to speak without embarrassing themselves. Finally Omar spoke in a stiff voice, "It's nice to meet you," he said.

"Yeah," Austin echoed.

"It's good to meet you, too," Josey bubbled, letting go of her hair and reaching for Omar with her slender, milky hand. Donnie had to cough to stifle the laugh that came up as he watched the boy's eyes widen in terror, but Omar manned up and gave Josey's hand a very quick shake. Austin did the same, but blushed from his collar to his scalp as he did it. "Can I show you anything?" Josey asked.

"N-no," Omar answered. "I know my way around pretty well."

"Josey, this is Omar," Donnie said before the boys could slip away into the stacks. "He and some of his friends play Dungeons and Dragons here once a week. His friend is Austin. I don't get to see him in here much, but maybe that'll change."

"I hope so," Josey said, turning her brilliant smile on the boy, who blushed to his hairline again while his eyes widened.

Austin pulled at Omar's sleeve and they slipped away, but stopped at the nearly finished display of horror books. "Cool," Austin said as he picked up a paperback copy of Stephen King's *Night Shift* with the bandaged hand covered in eyeballs. He flipped through the pages then paused and read a little. "How much is it?" he asked Omar.

"Half the cover price unless there's a sticker on it," Omar said.

"I want this," Austin said. "Let's go look at the fantasy books."

They made their way deeper into the stacks. Josey turned to Donnie with a grin on her elfish face. Donnie rolled his eyes, but smiled back.

"I told you that you'd bring in the boys," he whispered.

"And I told you that displays would sell books," she whispered back.

"Touche," he answered, still grinning.

From the far end of the store they could hear the boys still talking over the merits of book covers and summaries. They were animated and direct in the way of young boys on the brink of becoming men, arguing over details and making comparisons to other books they'd read. Josey went back to her display and Donnie returned to his computer, but he didn't read any more fan fiction based in the world he'd created. He bookmarked the website and closed the browser.

Donnie opened an inventory spreadsheet and pulled over a box of books he'd recently acquired from a young lady who had to clean out her parents' estate after they'd gone to live in a retirement home in Enid. He typed in the ISBN, title, author, and condition of each book, stacking them on the counter as he finished. There were only a few books left in the box when he was startled by Josey's voice right behind him.

"Whatcha doin'?" she asked.

Donnie jumped a little in his chair, then turned to face her. "You're as quiet as a ghost," he admonished. She only smiled at him. He sighed. "I'm inventorying these books," he said.

"Seriously?" Her eyes squinted at him as if she was studying some strange bug pressed under glass. "You really do it that way. We need to get you that app."

"Is it really easier?" Donnie asked.

"Gimme your phone." Josey rolled her eyes and stuck a hand toward his face.

Donnie handed over his cell phone and watched as she slid and tapped on his screen. She watched for a minute, then handed it back to him. He looked at the screen, which was showing a moving image from his forward-facing camera. At the moment, it was Josey's jeans. He looked up at her.

"Now what?" he asked, looking up at her expectant face.

She blinked at him, unbelieving, and Donnie felt like a dinosaur asked to drive a car. "It's an app that scans the bar codes on books," she explained. "It'll save them in an online database, with the title, author, ISBN, year of publication, and then you can add notes. I told you, Grandma used it for her personal library."

"Mrs. Wilder knew about this?" Donnie asked, really feeling out of the loop now.

Josey shrugged, then winked at him. "I had to show her, too. I scanned most of her books. You can use it to remove books, too. So, like, when those boys buy their books, if those books were already in your database, you could scan them again and take them out."

Donnie looked at his phone and thought about how he used to have to set the clock on his parents' video cassette recorder because they couldn't figure it out. "This is pretty amazing," he admitted. "I had no idea I could do that. Can I merge the online database with the spreadsheet I already have, or do I have to scan everything already on the shelves?"

"Hmm. I'll look into that," Josey said. "There should be a way to do it." She paused as they heard the voices of the customers coming closer. The boys fell into an almost reverent silence as they came to the counter and into the presence of the town's newest female resident. "Did you gentlemen find what you wanted?" she asked them.

Omar cleared his throat and nodded. "Yes, ma'am," he said, putting a thin novel with blue-edged pages on the counter.

"Yeah," Austin agreed, trying to sound bolder despite the tremor in his voice. He put the King collection and a Michael Moorecock Elric novel on the counter.

Josey looked at Donnie, then her eyes swept the area behind the counter. "Oh my gosh. You don't even have a cash register," she said.

"I've never needed one," Donnie said. "I just keep track of the sales in a notebook."

"Do you seriously write down the titles and how much for each transaction?" she asked. Donnie nodded sheepishly. Josey turned back to the boys. "Guys, come back soon to see how we're about to modernize some things here at Lost Pages Bookstore," she said, laughing.

They boys laughed with her as Donnie tallied up the totals with sales tax on an adding machine. She had bonded with them, bringing them in as part of the younger generation pitying the old man who didn't understand technology. It was okay, though. It would make them come back. Not that these two would need much encouragement; they were already so wrapped up in Josey's spell. Donnie took the boys' money and watched them leave.

"Bye, Josey," Austin called before the door closed. Donnie saw Omar congratulating his friend on that particular boldness as they hurried up the street.

"You'll have every male between the ages of thirteen and thirty-nine eating from the palm of your hand within a week," Donnie said. "And everyone will think I'm some kind of Luddite afraid of technology."

"Scan the last books in that box with your new app, Grandpa," Josey teased.

Donnie pulled out the last books, found the bar code of the first one, and held his phone over it. The app automatically recognized the bar code, snapped a picture, and showed him all the relevant information for the book. "I'll be damned," he said. A box for notes was highlighted and he typed in the book's condition, hit the Save button, then Scan Another and repeated the process.

"Welcome to the twenty-first century," Josey joked as he put the last of the books on his stack.

"Did your grandma take a switch to you very often?" Donnie asked, putting his phone aside.

"Grandma never touched me in anger," Josey laughed. "I'm a saint. Look at my display now."

Donnie looked at the display, which walked the line between actual scary decorations in the form of skeletal hands and spiderwebs and the cuteness of smiling jack-o-lanterns. The books were stacked in a pleasing way that showed either the covers or at least the spines so customers could see all the titles. In all, he guessed there were about twenty-five titles on the display, with most of those faced out.

"It's really amazing," he admitted. "And we've already seen how effective it is, even before it was finished."

"This is true," Josey said. "I'm a marketing, design, and sales genius." She smiled and her eyes twinkled.

"And a saint," Donnie reminded her.

"Oh, of course!" She laughed and it was the most musical sound Donnie could ever remember hearing inside his shop. He couldn't help but smile in response. "So, what's next?" she asked after her laugh.

Donnie shrugged. "I mean, these books need to be put away now that they're inventoried. I can do it, though."

"I'll do it," Josey said, reaching for the stack.

"How about if you take the pilot's seat here and see if you can figure out how to combine the books I scanned with your fancy app to the clunky old spreadsheet I've been using for years?" Donnie suggested.

"Ooo, the pilot's seat," she said in mock awe. "Are we on the Millennium Falcon? Are you Han Solo?"

Donnie cocked his head at her. "Wouldn't that make you Chewbacca?"

"Mmm," she said, putting a long, slender finger to her lips. "Mike is more like Chewy. I'm kind of R2-D2. And really, you need a bit more swagger to be Han."

"A bit?"

"I didn't want to be rude," she said.

Donnie chuckled. "I'm pretty sure our customers from earlier today would say you are definitely Princess Leia. Or, more likely Rey."

"Nope. I'm a pacifist," she said. "I hate violence."

"Okay, Ghandi, here's my phone. The spreadsheet is open," Donnie said, leaving his chair and handing over his phone. "Work your R2-D2 magic and fix the flux capacitor before Voldemort finds the One Ring and puts us all in the Hunger Games."

Josey flopped down in the office chair and shook her head. "I won't even acknowledge your obvious attempt to gauge my level of geekdom," she said. "Go forth and shelf the books so they can be purchased, sir."

Donnie picked up half the books he'd checked in, smiling and feeling a warm sensation he hadn't known in many years. He turned away, then stopped and turned back. "Josey?" She looked up at him, her small, elfish face curious. Donnie shook his head. "Nothing," he said.

"What?" she asked as he turned away again. "You can't tease me like that. You were about to say something serious."

Donnie stopped and lowered his head, his eyes fixed on the top book in his stack, *The Shepherd of the Hills*. His own mother had owned a copy of that and let him read it in his early teens and he'd loved the sense of mystery despite a pretty didactic message. "It's good to have you here," Donnie said quickly, then walked away before Josey could respond.

Chapter Twelve

J osey showed her genius by linking the bar code-reading app to his existing spreadsheet and working out the few glitches that came up. Donnie felt as if a new world had opened to him, one where his job would be easier. But then, he reasoned, he had never felt any pressure to be more efficient. Typing in the book information was one of the things that had kept his mind from roaming into dark places where he really didn't want to go.

In the early afternoon, he and Josey began working on dusting shelves and lining up book spines with the front edge of the shelf so every book had an equal chance to catch the reader's eye. After they had worked for about an hour, Donnie noticed that Josey often looked over at the cheap analogue clock hanging on the wall in the back of the shop, near the area with the Queen Anne chairs. He started to tease her about having a date, but then decided not to. Maybe she was bored. Already regretting her commitment to help in the store. Maybe she didn't like the mundane tasks like cleaning and only wanted to do fun things like build displays. Then he saw her glance at the clock and try to suppress a grin.

It was three o'clock in the afternoon. The Dungeons and Dragons group hadn't materialized today.

Donnie wondered what there was to smile about at three in the afternoon of a cold, blustery October day in the flatlands of northwest Oklahoma. Then the front door opened and before he turned to see who it was, he caught Josey grinning like the proverbial cat that had swallowed the canary. She winked at him and turned away, dusting like she was clearing a pathway to Heaven. Donnie turned toward the front of the store.

It was Debbie, the waitress from Annie's Café across the street. Donnie's mind flashed back to watching Josey go into the diner after her visit at the bank. What had that girl done now?

"Hi, Debbie," he called as he walked toward the front of the store. "Is it getting colder out there?"

"It sure is, Mr. Nelson," she said, rubbing her hands together. She had delicate, tapered fingers. He wondered why she wasn't wearing gloves.

"You have to call me Donnie," he said. "I wish you would at the café, but now you're in my store, so I insist."

She grinned and her cheeks were red, either with the cold or a blush. "Donnie it is," she agreed. She wore a camel-colored wool coat that came down to her thighs. Beneath the coat, Donnie saw her waitressing apron over a blue-and-yellow striped flannel shirt and faded blue jeans.

"What brings you in?" Donnie asked.

"Books," Debbie said, as if it was the silliest question she'd ever heard, but Donnie saw how her eyes flicked quickly to where Josey was pretending to dust but was actually listening very intently. "What else would bring a girl to a bookstore?"

"Very true," Donnie agreed. "I mean, we have coffee, but you don't have to come here for that." They both laughed politely at his lame joke. "You haven't been in before. Would you like for my new assistant to give you a tour?"

"I'm busy here," Josey called before Debbie could answer.

"Uh-huh," Donnie said sardonically. He caught Debbie hiding a grin behind a hand. "Well, what kind of books do you like?"

"To be honest, I haven't read a book in years," Debbie said in her country drawl. "But it's somethin' I want to get back into, ya know? A girl gets lonely in the evenings around here."

"No better company than a book," Donnie said. "Even better than a dog." He looked over to where Jasper had been sleeping near the table with the coffee pot for several hours.

"Isn't every bookstore s'posed to have a pet?" Debbie asked. "Like a mascot or something? Ain't it s'posed to be a cat?"

Donnie chuckled. "So I've heard. But we have a dog instead. I think you've met Jasper."

"I like romance books," Debbie said. "The trashy ones with half-naked people on the cover. My mama used to read those and I'd sneak looks in them, tryin' to find the sex scenes." She laughed and Donnie smiled. "I like mysteries, too. Where you gotta try to figure out who the killer is."

"You're in luck. We have lots of both of those," Donnie said. "The romance books are over here." He began walking toward that section, still talking. "I've separated them into contemporary and historical. You're wanting the historical, I think."

"Oh yeah. You got any with hot cowboys on the cover?" Debbie asked.

Donnie stopped and looked at her to see if she was joking. He didn't think she was. He caught a faint snicker from Josey. "Yeah, I think so," he said. "A lot of the ones with hot cowboys on the covers are actually contemporary."

"That means set in our time, right?" she asked.

"That's right," Donnie agreed. He pulled a copy of Sarah McCarty's *Promises Linger* from a shelf and handed it to Debbie. "It's the first in a series."

She looked at the cover and nodded, then scanned the summary on the back. "Okay. I'll get this one," she said.

"Do you want to see the mysteries, too? Or is one enough for now?" Donnie asked.

She smiled, and it was a nice smile. Her eyes were a soft brown with a twinkle that seemed very deep, like a light at the bottom of a well. There were wrinkles around her eyes, and the old acne scars and too much makeup, but she was an attractive woman and Donnie seemed to sense now that they were outside the busy atmosphere of the diner, that she shared his sense of sadness. He wondered what had happened to her. Why was she here in Sagebrush? "I think one is enough for now," she said.

They walked back to the counter, Donnie struggling for something to say. He finally went with the cliche about the weather. "I guess there's another storm coming in," he offered.

"Yep. S'posed to get really cold tonight. Maybe sleet," she agreed as they came to the counter and Donnie went around to his side.

"Josey has me all set up with this fancy new app and database thing," Donnie explained as he took his phone and scanned the barcode on the back of the book. He tapped to remove the book from his inventory, secretly marveling at the ease of the task, then rang up her total on the adding machine.

She handed him the money. "So, umm, Donnie, I was wondering if you'd like to come to dinner sometime."

It was like a blow to the head. Donnie had not seen it coming, despite being sure Josey had arranged for Debbie to come to the store. He said the stupidest thing he could have said. "At the café?"

She laughed, but it was a high, nervous laugh. "No. I meant at my house. I'll cook and then maybe we can watch a movie and get to know each other better. There's not a lot else to do around here."

"There's not," he agreed. From the corner of his eye, he caught Josey glaring at him. He nodded and smiled. "I would like that. Yes. Thank you. When?"

"That storm ain't comin' in until around midnight and I'm off work," Debbie said. "How about this evening?"

"Oh," Donnie said, even more shocked. "I was going to talk to Dad and Josey about something," he said, thinking of Sherry Brown's notes about available houses. But he saw a look of defeat cloud Debbie's soft eyes and made up his mind. "It can wait until tomorrow. We're not likely to have any customers to distract us if the roads are icy."

She smiled and the soft light came back to her eyes. "Good," she said. "Would about six-thirty work for you?"

"Yes," Donnie agreed.

"I know from your visits to the diner you ain't vegetarian or anything like that," she said, her smile bigger now. "Anything you don't really like?"

"Brussel sprouts?" Donnie suggested.

She laughed, a lower laugh that was real and comforting. "Nobody likes those nasty things. You gotta scrap of paper I can write my address on?" Donnie gave her a strip of paper from the calculator and she wrote her address and phone number. "There ya go, hon," she said as she passed it to him.

"What can I bring?" Donnie asked.

"Just yourself," she said.

"I have to bring something. I'll bring wine. People do that, right? I haven't ... Well ... I haven't spent an evening with a woman in a long time," Donnie finished lamely.

She laughed again, and it was a sound Donnie was starting to like. "Okay. Bring wine."

"Red or white?"

"Red," Debbie said. "I'll see you at six-thirty."

"Bye," Donnie said as she walked out the door. When the door closed, he turned to the store's interior. "Josey?" he called. The girl was nowhere to be seen. He called her name again. Her blue-and-silver head popped up from behind a shelf. She was trying hard not to grin, but her eyes gave her away.

"You called?" she asked.

"You think you're pretty slick, huh?"

"What do you mean?" Still, only her head was visible above the low shelf.

Donnie shook his head. "You set that whole thing up."

Josey stood up and came to the front counter, where she leaned on the surface, her arms crossed and her pointy chin on her folded hands. "She was already interested. I just explained about you being shy and made a suggestion she take up reading. You two worked out the rest."

"My life was quiet and peaceful and very ordinary before you got here, young lady," Donnie said.

"Your life was boring, sad, and lonely, Mr. Nelson," she shot back.

"Maybe I liked it that way," he said, but even he heard the lack of conviction in his voice.

"Your dad is right about you hiding up here," Josey said. "It's not good for you. Even if you and Debbie don't date, you need a friend. And I think she needs somebody, too."

"You felt that?" Donnie asked. "She's sad?"

"Yeah," Josey said.

Donnie looked out the windows at the gray afternoon. "I need to go get a bottle of wine," he said. "I think I'll pick up Dad, too. We need to talk about the living arrangements."

"We do," Josey agreed.

"I can't believe you haven't been here even a full day yet and you've turned my life upside down and inside out," Donnie said.

"Grandma always said I was a tornado of creative energy," Josey said. "Go get the wine. I'll watch the store."

Donnie drove to the Veterans of Foreign Wars building first. He had never been inside the place. It was a low, squatty, square building painted dark blue. Only a white plywood sign with red lettering told the passerby what the building housed. Donnie opened the door and was hit with the smell of age and old cigars and stale beer. The lighting was surprisingly dim. Inside, he saw several round tables where men sat playing cards, dominos, or checkers. One corner was boxed off with old brown sofas so men could sit and watch a large TV mounted on the wall. Donnie knew before the law was passed banning smoking in public buildings this one would have been so smoky he probably would not have been able to see across the main room.

"You're the bookstore guy." A short man with a protruding belly and bald head had appeared beside Donnie. He wore a cream-colored button-down shirt and dark brown pants. There was a wisp of hair in the ear Donnie could see.

"I am," Donnie said. He offered his hand. "Donnie Nelson."

"Vic Rowland," the man said, giving him a shake. "You're looking for your dad, aren't you? He's over there." Vic pointed to one of the tables where four men sat. "He's a helluva domino player."

"Is he?" Donnie asked, looking at the table. His dad was in profile and, as he watched, Mike must have won a game or made a good move. He laughed and smiled and the other men joined his mirth. Donnie felt kind of bad to intrude. He started to excuse himself and leave, but Vic didn't give him the chance.

"Mike! Mike Nelson!" he shouted. "Your son's here," he added when Mike looked over. Donnie watched his dad excuse himself to the other men and come toward him, still grinning.

"Donnie," Mike said. "I didn't expect to see you here. What's going on?"

"I'm going to the store. I thought I'd see if you want to ride along," Donnie told him. "Also, we need to talk with Josey about the living arrangements. Sherry Brown had some ideas."

"Can't we do that over dinner?" Mike asked.

Donnie felt his face reddening and tried hard to stop the rise of blood to his cheeks. "I kind of have plans. Something came up," he said.

"Plans?" Mike looked from him to Vic. Vic shrugged. Mike turned back to Donnie. "What plans?"

Donnie cleared his throat. "I've been invited to someone's house for dinner."

"Someone?" Mike asked, catching on. "Could that someone have blonde hair and brown bedroom eyes and give people food for a living?"

"Dad, do you want to ride to the store with me or not?"

Mike laughed at him, then told Vic he'd be back the next time Donnie let him go out. He shrugged into his coat and followed Donnie to the truck. "How'd this all come about?" Mike asked as Donnie left the parking lot.

"That stowaway girl," Donnie said, feigning irritation.

Mike laughed. "She is something else," he commented. "She'll shake you up from root to leaf." There was a moment of silence, then, "What's this about the living conditions?"

"Sherry Brown thinks we need a house and she found three places for rent," Donnie said. "I can't afford them, but I promised her I would talk to you and Josey about them. I thought I would just get another cot. Not a whole house."

"I get a monthly pension check, Donnie," Mike said. "It's been going to the home for my room and board. It might as well go to you now that *you're* providing room and board."

Donnie looked over at his father. "I know. Maggie called. She was worried. She says she loves you."

Mike gave him a look, but only grunted.

"She said she'd take care of the paperwork at the home if you want to stay here," Donnie said. "She'll have your checks sent here. But I won't take all your money. You'll need some money. We'll see about a budget. If you're interested. Both of you," he said.

"I'll be honest, I think we all need beds," Mike said. "You sure can't keep trying to sleep on those chair cushions."

Donnie pulled into the grocery store parking lot and found a spot. He shut off the engine. "We'll talk about it when we get back to the store," he said.

Mike shrugged. "What are we here for?"

"Wine," Donnie answered.

"Oo-la-la," Mike said with a laugh, then he got serious. "I thought you gave up drinking."

Donnie sighed. "Yeah. Mostly. I don't keep any alcohol in the store. I don't drink hard liquor anymore. I can have a glass of wine without going back to where I was."

Mike's voice was low and sincere as he asked, "Are you sure, son?"

Donnie looked at his dad and was moved by the real love he saw in the man's blue eyes. "Yeah, Dad," he said. "I've tested it. Had a beer every once in a while, usually while watching football. The old wish to obliterate my ability to think was gone. I'll be okay."

Mike nodded, then they went into the grocery story. Like always, Roger was working and he greeting Donnie, who introduced his father before they went to the shelves.

Back at Lost Pages Bookstore, the occupants gathered in the reading corner, a dark green bottle of red wine on the low table. Jasper, the newly ordained store pet, sat at

Donnie's knee and he rubbed behind the dog's short, floppy ears and listened to his tail thump against the leg of the chair.

"Well, Donnie, you wanted to talk to us," Mike said at last.

"Yeah," Donnie agreed. He looked up from the dog, but kept scratching him idly. "It's about our living conditions."

"You're kicking us out," Mike interjected. "Except the dog. It looks like you actually like him."

"Dad," Donnie said as if he was about to contradict, but then he saw the twinkle in Mike's eye. He sighed. "I didn't expect to have guests. Or roommates. Or a dog. But here we are and … " He paused and looked at both humans quickly, then back at the dog, keeping his eyes on Jasper's nose. "I'm not sorry you're here."

"He's melting my heart," Josey joked with Mike.

"He's never said kinder words to his old man," Mike agreed.

"You're both insufferable," Donnie said. "The sleeping arrangements last night weren't great. Mrs. Brown went to the trouble of finding some rental properties she thinks would give us more room." He paused and sighed. "I think you both know by now that the store barely pays for itself. In slow months, I supplement with money from a savings account that is running out. Book royalties have pretty much dried up. My income is limited. I can't pay the rent on a house."

"I've offered you my pension and Social Security checks," Mike reminded him..

Donnie nodded. "Yes, you have. I'm not taking all of your money, though."

"Grandma left me a lot of money," Josey said. "And her house will go up for sale soon and I'll get that money, too. I went to the bank and talked to Sherry today about transferring some of my money to her bank. I'm totally in on getting a house. A girl needs a real bathroom and an actual mirror."

Donnie pulled his hand away from Jasper's head, causing the dog to give him a reproachful look, and took the folded paper Sherry had given him that morning. He read off the information about the three available properties. "The cheapest is a two-bedroom, so Dad, you'd have to share a room with me. Then there's a three-bedroom, two-bath house, and another that has two bedrooms and a detached garage apartment. Sherry thought Josey might want more privacy."

"She's so sweet," Josey said, smiling.

"She is," Donnie agreed.

"I don't need my own apartment," Josey said. "We'll be like family."

Donnie grinned, but it was tinged with sadness as he thought about his own estranged family. He reached down and rubbed the dog's head again. "Right down to the family dog," he said softly.

"You two seem to have taken to each other," Mike commented. "But you always did take up with dogs. Remember the Bryants' mutt?"

"Yes, Dad," Donnie said. It was a story his parents had repeated often.

"What?" Josey asked. "Family secret? You have to share."

"We had neighbors named Bryant," Mike began. "Jerry and Ruby Bryant. He was a mailman. They had this old dog, just some kind of mutt that had some beagle in it. That was the meanest dog I've ever seen. Jerry was the only one who could do anything with it. It would bark and growl at the neighbor kids and snarl at people when Jerry walked him. It got out one day and you could hear the commotion all up and down the street as kids ran or pedaled to get away, with that mutt chasing them and barking and snapping. The Bryants weren't home. Donnie here went out on the front porch and sat down and that dog ran by chasing the little Abbott girl. Donnie clicked his tongue and called the dog and it stopped, stared at him for a minute like it couldn't believe somebody had dared to interrupt him. Donnie said something else, and I'll be damned, but that dog trotted up to him like they were old friends and Donnie sat there petting the thing. Other kids tried to come up, thinking he'd tamed the monster, and it would show its teeth until they went away."

Josey studied Donnie for a minute, then asked, "Why didn't you have a pet before now?"

Donnie couldn't hold her gaze. He shrugged half-heartedly and said, "I don't know."

"Donnie put himself in exile," Mike said. "He couldn't have a pet because it would have interrupted his self-hate."

"Dad, did you do anything in that old folks' home other than watch Dr. Phil or whatever other TV quack doctor you got this psychobabble from?"

"Tell me I'm wrong," Mike challenged.

Donnie couldn't and he knew it. He looked at the note in his hand and changed the subject. "What about the houses?"

"I think we've decided on the three-bedroom one," Mike said.

"Can we go see it?" Josey asked.

Donnie looked again at the paper in his hand, then rubbed at his neck. He could feel his face reddening. "I just … This is hard to say. I don't know that I can cover even my third of the rent."

There was a moment of silence in which Josey and Mike looked at each other. Mike cleared his throat. "Donnie, we both kind of imposed on you. You didn't invite us here. For myself, I don't plan to be a burden. If you two want this house, my checks will cover the rent plus some. I'm fine with that."

"He's right," Josey said. "I can buy groceries and pay utilities. You just keep up with the store like you have been, but you'll have a real house to come home to."

Donnie fought it as much as he could as he felt his throat thicken and his eyes sting. "Why?" he asked at last. "Why do you want to do this?" The first tear broke free and ran down his cheek and he wiped at it furiously. "I don't deserve it."

Mike stood up and clamped a hand down on his shoulder, squeezed, and said, "You're not the villain you think you are. You're my son and I want to spend time with you." He released Donnie's shoulder and turned away, heading for the back room. "I'm gonna fry baloney for a sandwich," he said.

"I don't have anywhere else to go, Donnie," Josey said. "Grandma always talked about you. She was so proud of you. She knew about the divorce and said she knew in high school you shouldn't have married that girl. I felt like I knew you. Grandma would be proud of the nice person you are, but she always thought you should write more."

Donnie nodded, unable to speak.

Josey looked after Mike. "We are *not* having fried baloney sandwiches for dinner," she said before turning back to Donnie.. "And you are not wearing that T-shirt to your date. Go shower and change clothes."

Donnie did what he was told, changing shirts until he got to a scarlet button-down with long sleeves that met with Josey's approval.

Chapter Thirteen

Debbie lived in a standard, older mobile home in the park on the south end of town. There were a few dozen trailers in the park with blacktop lanes and pecan trees and little kids playing in tiny yards. Donnie pulled into the driveway and parked his truck. He carried the bottle of wine, his grip tight and sweaty as he made his way up the narrow wooden steps to the porch. The door opened before he had to knock.

Debbie was wearing dark blue jeans and a powder blue sweatshirt. She had on white socks, but no shoes, and her face was somehow different, but Donnie couldn't put his finger on what the difference was. Her hair was pulled back in a ponytail. She looked younger than she did at work.

"Did a cat get your tongue?" she asked, tilting her head a little and smiling at him.

Donnie felt his face reddening. "I'm sorry," he said quickly. "You just … " He trailed off, unsure what to say.

"What?" she asked, still smiling.

"I've never seen you out of uniform," he offered.

She laughed, and her eyes danced with light. "I can change if you want," she said.

"No," he said, and realized he said it way too quickly. His face burned hotter. "You look fine. Good. You look … really nice."

"Are you planning to get me drunk?" Debbie asked, nodding at his right hand.

"On one bottle?" Donnie asked.

"She laughed a little, then asked, "You comin' in?"

The inside of the mobile home was moderately furnished with a new but off-brand recliner and an old sofa that was outdated but still in good shape. A medium-sized flatscreen TV was on a tiered wooden table with an old gray VCR/DVD player and there was a cable box on the shelf below. An oil painting of a golden sea, the foaming waves crashing on the cliffs below a white lighthouse, hung on the white wall behind the sofa. The aroma of cooking meat came from the kitchen and, looking over, Donnie saw a big silver pot with steam coming from a vent in the lid. Beside it, ground beef was browning in its own grease.

"It's just spaghetti," Debbie said apologetically. "If I'd'a planned ahead more, I woulda had a bigger meal."

"I love spaghetti," Donnie said.

She threw a smile over her shoulder as she returned to the kitchen to stir the meat. "How was your day at the bookshop?" she asked.

Donnie put the bottle of red wine on the small dining table. "It was good," he said. "Josey is revolutionizing the store with databases and displays and energy. And pulling star-struck teenage boys out of the cracks and crevices of this little town."

Debbie laughed her rich, musical laugh. "That girl is a ball of energy and just as pretty as she can be," she said. "I wish I'd'a been bold enough to dye my hair like that back in the days when I was young and pretty."

Donnie laughed. "You're still ... " He realized what he was about to say and the words died in his mouth, leaving an ashy taste, as his face reddened again.

"What's that?" Debbie asked teasingly, a wooden spatula hovering over the ground beef.

Donnie swallowed, then shrugged mentally. He admitted, "You're still pretty. And young."

She laughed. "Thank you," she said. "You're not used to giving out compliments, are ya?"

"No, I guess I'm not," Donnie agreed.

"You can go ahead and sit down," she said, nodding at the dining table. "I'll have this here ready in just a minute."

Donnie sat. He watched Debbie at the stove, her back to him for a moment. She did still have a nice figure and graceful movements. She wasn't hurrying, wasn't trying to please multiple customers in a café. She was relaxed and confident, and Donnie couldn't help but be impressed by her as he sat wondering what to do with his hands, where to look, what to say. He could feel his heart hammering in his chest. Was he like this when he was married, he wondered? When the affair began? "You have a nice home," he offered.

"Thank you," she said, giving him another smile. "I heard you're lookin' for a place to live now that your family's here."

Donnie chuckled. "Small town news travels fast," he said. "Yes, I am. We can't all live in the store's back room."

"Of course not," she said. She took the skillet off the stove and, holding the lid on, drained the grease into an empty spaghetti sauce can. She put the drained meat back on the stove, the burner turned low, then poured the spaghetti sauce from a bowl over the meat. She stirred it all together, then left the meat and took the steaming pot of boiling noodles from its burner and poured the contents into a colander. She shook the colander to get the last of the water out of the noodles, then poured the noodles into a big red plastic bowl. She then poured the meat and sauce into another bowl, and brought them to the table. "Give me just a few minutes for the garlic bread."

She went back to the counter and cut off slices of bread from a loaf of French bread. She buttered it on one side, sprinkled garlic on it, then put it in a clean skillet. She lifted the pieces out a few minutes later, toasted, and put them on a plate that she brought to the table.

"I feel bad just sitting here watching you work," Donnie said. "You serve people all day at the café. You shouldn't have to do it at home."

She laughed. "Ain't you sweet? It's okay. I like cooking."

"Well, next time, I'm taking you to a restaurant," Donnie promised.

"Already talking about a second date," Debbie teased.

Donnie reddened again. "That was presumptive of me," he apologized.

"I like it," she said. "I'd love to go to a restaurant with you. If you wanna take me. I feel like I'm bein' awful forward with you. I keep making you blush."

"I haven't dated much," Donne admitted. "It's all pretty new to me and I don't know what to do and, as my dad would tell me, I've been living like a hermit for the past seven years."

"You don't get out much," she said. "I've heard that about you from the first day I moved back here." She scooped spaghetti noodles from the red bowl to his plate, then to hers. "I forgot the wine glasses," she said, and popped out of her chair.

Donnie added sauce to his spaghetti and added some parmesan cheese from a plastic shaker bottle while Debbie put two stemmed glasses on the table.

"Would you like to open the bottle?" she asked, offering him a corkscrew.

Donnie opened the bottle, something he wasn't especially good at, and poured them each an equal amount of wine, then sat down again. He took a bite of his spaghetti, swallowed, and told her how good it was.

"You gonna tell me about yourself, Donnie?" she asked.

"What would you like to know?" he asked.

"I know you haven't always worked in a bookstore in Sagebrush, Oklahoma," she said. "What did you do before that?"

Donnie slowly twirled spaghetti around his fork, thinking. He raised his eyes and looked at Debbie. Her large brown eyes were watching him, shining, her face relaxed but expectant. "I usually just tell people I worked in a machine shop," he said. "And that's true. I did do that for quite a while. But that's not what I was doing before I came here." He put the spaghetti into his mouth and chewed. She also chewed, but watched him, waiting. She spoke first.

"I get the feeling I'm about to learn a big, dark secret," she teased.

Donnie fidgeted with his fork on his plate. He sighed and faced her. "I was a writer. A best-selling author," he said.

He saw her lips stretch into a smile, but then falter over his tone. She tilted her head just a little, like a curious puppy. "I can feel a 'but' comin'," she said.

"Yeah." He took a bite, chewed, swallowed, and took a sip of wine. He forced himself not to grimace over the alcohol. It wasn't that the wine was bad, the sharp bite of alcohol brought back memories of the year he lost control. "I wasn't happy at home. Things just weren't good. I had an affair. Got caught. Then my mom died. I couldn't write, so I moved up here and bought the store, then kept to myself."

"You don't write anymore?"

He shook his head. "No. I ... I try, but nothing comes."

"Writer's block," she said. "I've heard of that. In a movie, I think."

He smiled, but it died quickly. "Yeah."

"Are you happy?" she asked softly.

STEVEN E. WEDEL

Donnie studied her. He shrugged. "What I've learned today is that I've been numb. Happy? Sad? I don't know. I've just been doing one day after another until Dad and Josey showed up."

"And now?" she prompted.

He sighed and couldn't help a smile. "I guess I realized I've been missing out on some things," he admitted.

"Did you do anything for fun before they came?" Debbie asked.

"I'd go camping sometimes," Donnie said.

"I like camping. And fishing," she said.

Donnie grinned. "Okay. Tell me more. It's your turn." He pulled more spaghetti off his fork and chewed while he watched her.

"Typical story," she said. "All I wanted was to get out of this little town. I dated a boy from over in Buffalo. After high school, we moved to Woodward. We both worked at Wal-Mart. He cheated on me. I moved in with an older woman I worked with, met someone else. That stuff just kept repeating until I ended up in Oklahoma City. I got married once. He's in prison. My last boyfriend beat me up pretty often. Finally, one day, I got tired of it and wanted to come home, so I did."

"They say you can never go home again," Donnie said. "That it's never the same place. How has it been for you?"

She smiled and swallowed before answering. "Surprisingly good. People haven't asked a bunch of questions. Lots of folks remember me and we talk in the café about old times. I was afraid people'd be all in my business. 'Why'd she come back here?' and all of that, but it really hasn't been that way. I appreciate this town a lot more than I did when I was growing up in it."

Donnie nodded, impressed. "It's always seemed like a nice place," he agreed.

"You gotta get out more," she chided. "People that know you like you, but most folks don't know anything about you. Sherry Brown just loves you to death, but most people only know you run the bookstore and keep to yourself."

"I have kept to myself," Donnie said. "Not to brag, but I was still kind of famous when I moved here, and I just wanted to disappear. I didn't want fans stopping by to ask about the new book. I didn't want invitations to conventions or to be asked to speak to writers' clubs or college classes."

"I understand," Debbie said. She nibbled at her toast, her brow furrowed in thought. She put the bread down. "I know you're divorced. Sherry told me that. Josey told me you have kids."

"Did she?" Donnie asked. He felt as though his privacy had been violated. "What else did she say?"

"Don't you be mad at that girl," Debbie said, her voice almost scolding. "She told me she ain't really your niece. And she told me about her grandma and how you were her favorite student and she feels like she's known you most of her life even though she only just met you. She said your relationship with your kids ain't very good."

"It's not," Donnie admitted with a sigh. "They barely talk to me because of the divorce. Because of ... the affair."

"I ain't gonna ask you about that, Donnie," Debbie said firmly. "I can tell by your face that whatever happened there shames you and it ain't who you really are. Sometimes we do things we shouldn't. Sometimes we know they're wrong, but sometimes, I think, we do the wrong thing for the right reasons."

Donnie studied her face for a moment, then nodded his head twice, more in acknowledgment than agreement.

"Tell me about your dad," Debbie prompted.

Donnie twirled spaghetti around his fork. "I let my sister bully me into signing papers to put him in an assisted living center about seven years ago. She claimed he had Alzheimer's and couldn't live alone. I was reeling from the divorce and Mom dying and just went along with it. I was drinking quite a bit then."

Debbie put her silverware down and reached over and put her hand on top of Donnie's left hand on the table. She squeezed. "You have to stop answering questions through your guilt," she said. "I asked about your dad and you told me what you think you did to him. That ain't what I asked."

Donnie looked at her hand on his. It seemed small, and felt softer than he expected, warm and comforting. He wanted to turn his hand over and hold hers. Would that be too forward? Donnie considered, and then thought about her pulling her hand away. Without letting himself consider the matter further, he twisted his hand under hers and gripped her, thought he was holding too tight, and relaxed, letting his thumb gently stroke the back of her hand. He looked up and saw that she was smiling at him.

"You had to think about that," she said.

Donnie felt himself blushing. "I did," he admitted. He allowed a moment for the flush to leave his face. "I'm learning a lot about my dad. He's a lot wiser than I gave him credit for. A lot. And apparently he loves to play dominoes. He's smaller than I remember, and his eyes twinkle like ... " He gave a wistful motion with his forkful of spaghetti. "Like he's having a really good time."

"I think he is," she said. She chewed her food for a moment, her eyes on him. "Are you sorry they're here?"

Donnie watched his thumb stroke the back of her small hand with the chipped red nail polish. "No," he admitted. "I'm not. I know I was in a rut. I know they'll knock me out of it. They already have." He looked up to face her. "I'm glad I'm here now, with you."

This time, it was her face that flushed red. Her hand squeezed his. "I am, too," she said.

They finished eating and Donnie helped her load the dishes into the home's small dishwasher, then they went to the dim living room and sat on the sofa with their wine glasses, the bottle on the coffee table before them. They talked about the town for a while, people they'd known, how it changed in the years Debbie was away, and then she raised her wine glass and asked, "What is it you want from life now, Donnie? To be a famous author again? To get rich selling used books?" She sipped her wine, her eyes fixed on him over the rim of her glass.

Donnie was taken aback. He didn't know how to answer. He stared at the red wine in his own glass. He held the glass more like a brandy snifter and swirled the wine as if it was brandy. The wine warmed, but he didn't realize it. Donnie thought about his life, about how he had felt for so long. "I just want to be happy," he said at last, then drained his glass in one long drink. He looked into the empty glass and said it again. "I just want to be happy."

"What would make you happy?" she asked.

He sighed. "That's the hard part. I don't even know."

Debbie poured more wine into his glass and hers, then made him hold his glass by the stem. "Your hand warms it up. So does that swirling thing you do."

"Oh. I ... usually just did shots or had bourbon on the rocks," he admitted. He took a drink. "What about you? What do you want out of life?"

"Same," she said. "I want to be happy. I think that's what everybody wants, ain't it?"

"How do you get there?" he asked.

"Baby steps," she answered. "I quit my old life that wasn't making me happy."

"Are you happy now?" he asked.

"I'm happier now than I was before I came back here," Debbie answered. "I'm happier tonight than I was last night."

"You just get a little happier every day?" Donnie asked.

She laughed at him. "You weren't sittin' on my couch drinkin' wine and talkin' to me yesterday, Donnie," she said.

"Oh." Donnie gave an embarrassed laugh. "That's true."

Debbie leaned toward him and gently shoulder checked him, rocking him to the side a little. The arm he'd had over the back of the couch slipped down and fell over her shoulders. "Oh," Debbie teased. "Now you're making some moves." When Donnie began to lift his arm and sputter an apology, Debbie grabbed his wrist in her free hand and kept the arm over her shoulders, nestling in closer to him.

"I really didn't mean – "

"Stop talking, Donnie," she said softly. She put her head on his chest.

Donnie let his hand settle onto her shoulder. The smell of her hair filled his nostrils. It was the scent of coconuts and something fruity, maybe apricot. Her body was warm against his and he was aware of her steady breathing. It was a good feeling. A feeling he hadn't experienced in years. It was exciting and scary and foreign but familiar and he pushed those thoughts away and lowered his cheek to the top of her head and rested it there for a moment.

"You're remembering," Debbie said softly.

Donnie grinned. "Some things just seem natural."

"It feels nice," she agreed. "You're not trying to grope me. I haven't been with a gentleman in a helluva long time."

They sat quietly for a while, savoring the moment, perhaps both trying to think of what to say next. Outside, the winter wind whispered around the mobile home and somewhere far off a dog barked. Another answered.

"How's Jasper?" Debbie asked.

Donnie grinned. "He's fine. He has the run of the store. Josey takes him out. He lets us know when he needs out."

"He's a sweet dog. Tommy, our cook, used to give him scraps out the back door of the café," Debbie said.

"He seems like a good dog. I always had a dog before ... Before the divorce."

"Now you have another one." Debbie's voice vibrated against his chest. "Did you always want to be a writer? When you were a kid? You didn't want to be a cowboy or anything like that?"

"I wanted to be a rock star first," Donnie admitted. "But I could never sit down and focus long enough to learn the guitar." He remembered the dark wood of the acoustic guitar his dad had passed down to him when he was about eleven years old. Where was that now? "What about you?"

"I wanted to be a dancer," Debbie said. "I wanted to be Madonna first, but I can't sing, so I thought maybe I could be one of her dancers. I thought I was pretty good, but I pro'ly wasn't."

"You don't dance anymore?" he asked.

She laughed softly. "Nope. Now I sing, but I don't dance, and I know the singing is bad, but nobody hears it 'cept me."

They sat quietly for a few minutes. Outside, the wind blew. Inside, the central heat unit clicked on, the motor revved up, and warm air wafted down from ceiling vents. The living room light was off, so the only illumination came from the kitchen and dining area behind them. Debbie's blonde hair shone like gold in the soft light. Hesitantly, his fingers trembling just a little, Donnie moved his hand and lightly stroked her hair.

"Mmm," she moaned softly against him. "Do you really sleep in your store?"

Donnie smiled. "Yes. There's a back room I have set up. Dad and Josey have it partitioned off and sleep there now."

"Where did you sleep last night?"

"On chair cushions on the floor," he said.

"That sounds awful," she said.

Donnie took a lock of hair between his fingers and let it flow out like strands of burnished thread. "It was," he said. "The cushions wouldn't stay together."

"I have an extra bed," Debbie said. "You're welcome to it tonight."

"I don't know ... " Donnie began to object, thinking about being away from the store all night.

"There's also my bed," she said.

Donnie was silent. His fingers, half-buried in her hair, became motionless. Debbie sat up and looked him in the face. His hand slipped from her hair and down her back.

"You know what's the best thing about dating at our age?" she asked.

"No," Donnie confessed.

"We don't have to pretend about anything," she said. "Going to bed together doesn't have to be such a big deal. Maybe we'll have sex. Maybe not. It's just about bein' together. You know, not alone in the night."

Donnie couldn't speak at first. So many nights crowded into his memory, nights alone in the back of the shop, the silence and loneliness pressing him into the bed, squeezing the moisture from his eyes as he longed for companionship. The smell. The sound of another person breathing. The solid feel of a fellow human being close in the dark. He knew what Debbie meant. He knew exactly.

"I know," he whispered.

"You can stay," she whispered back. "If you want."

His hand still trembling, Donnie put his palm on her cheek and leaned in and kissed her. Debbie's lips were soft, inviting, tasting of the wine while her breath still had the warm smell of garlic. They put their glasses on the coffee table and the kiss intensified. Donnie's mind rebelled, told him this was wrong, that he was cheating again, that he didn't deserve this, that … that … He kissed her harder, held her tighter, until finally Debbie stood up and, taking Donnie's hand, pulled him up and led him through the dim trailer to a small master bedroom.

Chapter Fourteen

He was in a cave. No, that wasn't it. It was a chamber made from stone blocks. Each block was at least three feet long and high and, Donnie guessed, just as thick. They were gray, rough-hewn, and stained with the soot from the torches spaced along the walls. He was alone, but there was a corridor leading away and down at a slight angle. More torches lit the way and Donnie moved down the shaft, knowing he was supposed to. Knowing, somehow, that this had once been a silver mine, but that now it was used for something else. A sharp crack, like a gunshot, split the air of the corridor and Donnie stopped.

On a deep level, Donnie knew he was dreaming. He knew he was actually lying naked in the bed of Debbie's mobile home. He even sensed that she was no longer in the bed with him. Her weight beside him was an absence, her fragrant skin, steady breathing, and comfortable warmth were noticeably gone and he knew he should pull himself to consciousness and investigate.

But the stone chamber was important. There was something at the end of the corridor he had to see. Had to know.

He let himself sink back into the dream or vision or omen or whatever it was, and he moved forward.

There were voices. "Where is your god? He hasn't shown himself. You will bow to us," a thin, reedy voice rose above the din.

The corridor ended and Donnie shrank against the wall. The room held a few dozen people standing in a ring several bodies deep, surrounding something. Some wore long, flowing robes, clean or stained from travel or toil. Others wore armor, swords, maces, bows with quivers of arrows, or other weapons.

"Why are you silent?" another voice screamed.

Donnie couldn't help it. He edged toward a red-robed figure, hoping to see over his shoulder to the center of the circle. As he stepped behind the figure, a white-haired man with jaundiced skin, another man stepped back and sideways. Donnie flinched. They should have bumped into one another, but the man's shoulder passed through him.

I'm not real here, he realized.

Donnie pushed through the crowd like a ghost, eliciting no response from the men of the circle. They couldn't even feel him pass through them like a spirit through the forest.

Emerging from the ring, Donnie saw what they were looking at and he froze. He felt his eyes widen and he almost stepped back, but with a force of will, he held his ground.

He remembered the first time he'd seen this man, so many years ago, stepping from the swirling snow and smoke of his campfire to direct him in his career. He had been in his prime then, dressed for battle, a smirk on his face as he stood and began telling his story.

But now he was naked, his skin covered in more scars, his muscles nearly gone, his hair gray at the temples and his face thin and bearded. His eyes, though, still smoldered with an inner fire that had not yet been quenched.

Bolker the Death Merchant was stretched and bound on a rack, his arms and legs strapped to cross pieces and geared away from the center so that he was stretched nearly to the breaking point. Once powerful sinews shone with a sheen of sweat despite the dirt and grime and blood. As Donnie watched, a man wearing only a loincloth and leather mask standing on the other side of the torture device made his whip whisper and crack over the mercenary's body again.

Bolkar didn't cry out ... but Donnie did.

"No! You can't have him!" Donnie screamed.

No one heard him. No one but the captive.

Bolkar turned his head and those black, probing eyes found Donnie. He nodded. "You come at last," he said.

A sudden, startled murmur went around the ring as the captors asked who the bound man was speaking to.

"I'm sorry," Donnie offered.

Bolkar ignored the apology. He grinned. "If today is the day I must die, let it be with a sword in my hand, a song on my lips, a woman to mourn me, and a son who will find glory greater than my own," he said.

"Who's there?" someone asked.

"What demon does he address?" another demanded.

"We should have killed him years ago," another said.

Donnie tried to respond, but his mind was foggy, distracted. There was something else happening here. Bolkar opened his mouth to speak again, but his voice was soft and feminine.

"How do you like your eggs?" he asked, but it was Debbie's voice. "Donnie? It's getting late and I'm making breakfast. How do you like your eggs?"

The dream broke apart, and Donnie let it go. He opened his eyes and found that he was on his back and Debbie was leaning over him, her unbound blonde hair inches from his face. She smiled down at him. "You were having a real struggle in your dream, mister," she said.

Bolkar is back! Donnie's mind sizzled with joy. The Death Merchant was back!

He lifted a hand and cupped Debbie's cheek. She smiled and let him pull her face down for a kiss, but then pushed herself away.

"The bacon will burn," she said.

"Scrambled, please," he answered. "But you didn't have to make breakfast. I could have taken you out ... " He realized the absurdity of the statement as soon as he said it.

Debbie paused in the bedroom doorway and gave him a sardonic look. "We have one café in town and I work there, buddy. After what we did last night, we'll have breakfast here before I have to go back to being your waitress."

She was wearing the shirt Donnie had shown up in for their dinner date. It hung a few inches below her butt and he watched it swish seductively as she went back down the hallway to the kitchen where he could hear the crackle of bacon and smell its aroma mixing with strong coffee. He got up and found his underwear and jeans and the faded T-shirt he'd worn under the dress shirt Debbie had commandeered. He followed her to the kitchen.

"Sit down," Debbie ordered from the stove where she scrambled eggs in a cast iron skillet. "Pour some juice and tell me what you were dreaming about. You yelled 'No' real loud at one point and I had to go check on you."

Donnie felt his face redden a little as he poured cold orange juice into a former jelly jar. "You know writers are pretty weird, right?" He put the plastic jug of juice down and lifted the glass to look at her.

Debbie shrugged, and Donnie couldn't help but notice how his stolen shirt slipped up, then down on her thighs. "I think I saw something about that in a meme." She took the skillet off the stove and scooped fluffy yellow eggs onto a platter with bacon and pancakes. She put the platter on the table and went for the coffee pot.

"I've had writer's block for years," Donnie said. "The character I used to write about, his name is Bolkar, he first appeared to me when I was camping in the snow. He just – "

"You mean like a ghost or something?" she asked, pausing just before filling his coffee cup.

"It was in my head. I imagined him coming out of the snow and smoke of my fire and he started talking to me," Donnie explained hurriedly, wanting to get to this morning's dream.

"But you didn't really see him there?" she asked as she moved to her own coffee mug, then sat down.

"No," Donnie said. "I was trying to think of something to write that I thought people might want to read. I was staring into the fire, thinking about what I liked to read, and as I watched the smoke and sparks rise, the idea came to me and I pictured him and could hear what his voice would be like and started filling in his back story in his voice."

She studied him for a long moment, then smiled a deep, radiant smile. "You're really cute when you get excited like this," she said. "Eat while it's hot."

Donnie chuckled at her. "Yes, Mom," he said. They both scooped food onto their plates. He buttered and poured syrup over his pancakes, sipped coffee, then began eating.

"But what made you yell like that this morning?" Debbie finally asked.

Donnie couldn't suppress the huge grin as he looked across the table at her, a piece of bacon in one hand and his empty fork in the other. "He's back," he said, his voice low and triumphant. "I found him in my dream. Tied to a rack with all these people around him, torturing him. He's older and thinner, but it was him. His eyes were still black pits of fire, like Clint Eastwood's in *The Outlaw Josey Wales*. That's what I've always thought of when it comes to Bolkar's eyes."

Debbie was still smiling at him, her own eyes like honey as the morning sun hit them from a window over the kitchen sink. "Go on," she urged.

"None of the people torturing him could see me, but he could," Donnie explained. "He looked at me and spoke to me just like he used to, but this time it wasn't about his past. It was about his future." He told her what the warrior had said about dying. "I can't leave him there."

"This'll be a new book?" she asked between blows over her hot coffee.

Donnie nodded. "Every day for seven years, I've opened my computer and stared at the end of about thirty pages I wrote just before everything fell apart," he said thoughtfully. "I have to let that go. It's not relevant anymore. I have to ... let it go."

"You said that, Elsa," Debbie teased.

"Elsa?"

"The Disney ice princess," Debbie explained. "The movie *Frozen*?"

Donnie shrugged. "I haven't watched a Disney movie in years."

Debbie shook her head as if there was just no hope for him. "You said you have to let it go like there was some other meaning to that. What'd you mean?"

"Something my dad told me," Donnie said slowly. "I've been living in my past, holding on to my great sin. He told me to let it go." He took the last bite of his pancake and chewed thoughtfully as his brow furrowed.

"Uh-oh. Thunder on the head," Debbie said.

"Huh?" Donnie looked up at her, confused.

"You got those lines in your forehead. My dad used to get those. Mom called them thunderheads."

"Oh," Donnie said. "I was just thinking about how Dad and Josey have just completely turned my life upside down. And now you, too. But ... I like it. I feel like I've been living in a hole and you all are pulling me out and showing me the sun still shines."

Debbie laughed. "The difference is pretty plain," she said. "Especially right now." She paused, then leaned forward and lowered her voice to a husky whisper. "If you'd looked this excited the day we first met, I would have dragged you home right then."

Donnie laughed. "They're going to give me hell at the store for coming in like this," he said.

"All you needed was sex," Debbie said.

Donnie started to laugh, then stopped. He looked hard at her, trying to read her expression, but she was deliberately hiding her thoughts. "You don't think that's all it was, do you?" he asked. "I mean ... Is that all it was?"

THE LOST PAGES BOOKSTORE

She fixed her eyes on him and they were still filled with morning sunlight with deep specks in the center and her face was solemn as she held him pinned with her gaze across the table. "Tell me what you think it was, Donnie," she challenged.

"Not just sex," he answered softly, desperately. "I'm not going to be the guy who says I love you right after the first date, but I do like you. Last night was incredible. Not just the sex! All of it. Dinner, talking, holding you after, falling asleep next to you. I hope it was the first time, but not the last."

"Friends with benefits?" she asked, her voice still without emotion.

Donnie shook his head slowly. "No," he answered.

She shrugged. "We're adults. We like doing it. Wanna be fuck buddies?"

Donnie was confused to the point of panic. He felt the thunderheads returning above his eyes as his mind raced with what she was saying. What had happened? Had he said something wrong? He reached across the table and caught her hand in his and squeezed it. She let him, but didn't return the pressure.

"Did I say something wrong?" he asked softly. "I didn't mean to. Last night was the best night I've had in a decade. I hope I haven't ruined it."

"Tell me what you want, Donnie," she said.

"I want ... " he began, then fumbled. "Hell, if this was junior high, I'd ask you to go with me. To be my girlfriend."

"Why can't you ask it now?"

"Is that how it works at our age?" he asked. "Just like when we were kids?"

Her face broke and she laughed at him and now she did squeeze his hand. "It really has been a long time for you," she said. "But yes, Donnie, it still works the same way."

Donnie felt his body almost sag with relief that he hadn't ruined this beautiful new thing in his life. He shook his head, then faced her and spoke in a voice like the teenage boys who came to the bookstore. "Debbie, would you, umm, you know, wanna, like, be my girlfriend?"

She shook her head. "No. Just fuck buddies," she said.

Donnie felt his jaw drop open. A moment later, Debbie burst into laughter.

"We gotta toughen you up or you'll never survive me," she said. "I'm fluent in sarcasm." She stopped and held his hand again. "I guess that was mean of me, you being almost as new as a virgin and all," she apologized.

"I may rescind my invitation," Donnie pretended haughtiness.

"Too late," she said. "You asked, and my answer is yes. You don't think a simple fuck buddy would get to stay all night and get breakfast, do you?"

"I wouldn't know," Donnie confessed.

"Of course you wouldn't," she said, grinning. "Aren't you supposed to go look at a house this morning?"

"Not until ten," he said.

"What time do you think it is?"

Donnie shrugged. He hadn't worn a watch and his phone was still on the coffee table as far as he knew. He looked around for a clock.

"It's 9:40," Debbie said.

Donnie gaped at her. "No way."

"You better go," she said. "And no, you don't get the shirt. It's mine now. A trophy."

Donnie laughed, but he did so as he pushed away from the table and began looking for his shoes and socks.

"Don't worry," Debbie called after him. "I made breakfast and I'll clean it all up and do the dishes."

Donnie came halfway back down the hall, two socks and one shoe in his hands. "I'm so sorry," he said. "I'll call Dad and tell him I'll be late so I can help."

"No, you won't," she told him. "You'll just promise to do all this for me after you move into a real house like a civilized person."

"I swear it," he said.

"Go!" she said, waving him away.

Chapter Fifteen

Donnie called his father as he hurried the pickup through Sagebrush's streets to the alley behind the bookstore. "I know I'm late," he said. "But I'll be there in just a minute. Can you both be waiting out back?"

"Did she make you breakfast?" Mike asked, laughing.

"Dad ... " Donnie started to protest, then let it go. "Yes, and I'm pulling into the alley now."

Mike and Josey got into the truck. It was a cold, windy day and they were both wearing jeans with their coats. Mike took the passenger seat while Josey sat in the middle. They managed to hold out for as long as it took Donnie to put the truck into reverse before they both burst out laughing.

"You slept with her on the first date?" Josey asked.

"A gentleman doesn't discuss those things," Donnie answered.

"I knew she liked you, but wowzers!" Josey laughed.

"Us Nelson men have a long history of being irresistible," Mike said. He and Josey laughed, and Donnie allowed himself to smile.

"Debbie is a nice girl," he said. "Don't say mean things about her."

"Ooooo," Josey said appreciatively. "I think he likes her."

"I do like her," Donnie said when the laughter died down a little. "I have something else to tell you, though."

"There's a wedding coming!" Josey shrilled.

"No!" Donnie said, cutting off another round of mirth. "I had a dream. I have a story idea. I want to write again."

The cab of the truck was silent for a moment. "That's great," Mike said at last.

"I'm happy for you, Donnie," Josey said. "What's it about?"

Donnie parked the truck in front of a little gray house with a decent porch and a big yard. There was a car parked in the driveway, engine running. A woman bundled in a red cloth coat and white stocking cap got out as he pulled to the curb. "It's Bolkar again," Donnie said. "I'll tell you the rest later."

The owner of the house had driven over from Alva to show it. Donnie had doubts from the beginning. He and Mike had both expressed reluctance at sharing a room, but had agreed to look at the smaller house. The living room was small; the kitchen and dining area combined were smaller. One bedroom was average and the other tiny and one had to pass through the tiny bedroom to get to the bathroom. Donnie thanked the owner and apologized that she'd had to drive all the way from Alva, then they left.

"That was disappointing," Josey said as they got back into the pickup.

"My room at the old folks' home was bigger than that second bedroom," Mike said.

"That one's definitely out of the running," Donnie agreed. "The one with the detached garage room is next."

"I don't like the idea of being separated," Josey said. "We're kind of like a family now."

Donnie glanced over at her and saw that Mike was looking at her, too, and they were all smiling. "You're damn right we are," Mike said.

"Damn right," Donnie agreed. "But we made the appointment."

The house belonged to an older couple who had moved to Kansas a month earlier. It was shown by their neighbor, a doddering man who sucked his dentures as he talked. The kitchen had avocado green appliances and the living room, hallway, and bedrooms were carpeted in worn rust-colored shag. All the walls were paneled. The garage room, the man explained, had been converted for the couple's son in the 1980s and it was only a little better, with a small white refrigerator, space heater, window air conditioner, and a cramped bathroom with a shower stall.

Donnie thanked the man and said they'd let him know, then they all piled back into his pickup truck and talked about the house being a museum to the age of disco.

"That's the BeeGees and Donna Summer and Club 54, right?" Josey asked. "Polyester suits and wedges with goldfish in them?"

"Dad, you want to answer that?" Donnie asked.

"It was after my time," he said.

The last house was obviously the best of the lot. It was in a neighborhood of older houses with maintained lawns and mature trees. The house was painted white with black trim. A massive oak tree shaded the front yard. A red-haired woman got out of a silver SUV as Donnie parked. She wore a knee-length black leather coat, black gloves, and a red cap. She smiled as they approached.

"Donnie?" she asked, extending her hand. "I"m Darci."

Donnie introduced himself and his companions. "This looks nice," he said, waving toward the house.

"I grew up here," Darci said. "My dad planted that tree the spring after I was born." She led them to the porch and unlocked the white front door.

"Your parents moved?" Josey asked.

"Mom passed on a couple of months ago," Darci answered quietly. "Dad died about ten years ago. Jack and I, he's my brother, we both moved, but we don't want to sell the house yet, so we decided to rent it out."

The house smelled like vanilla and lace and co-mingled aromas of years of home cooking. The living room was polished hardwood floors with a fireplace at one end and a picture window that looked out on the front yard.

"The master bedroom is downstairs, with a bathroom," Darci explained, leading them into a large bedroom. "Mine and Jack's bedrooms and bathroom are upstairs. The kitchen is a little dated, but we got rid of the 1970s gold refrigerator and stove a long time ago."

Donnie and Josey both burst into laughter and Mike smiled. "We just left a shrine to the fashions of the Carter Administration," Mike explained.

Donnie couldn't help but notice that Josey was bouncing on her toes by the time they started up the stairs. He was impressed with the house, too, but still concerned about how to pay for it. The upstairs rooms were moderately-sized, but the bathroom was comfortable. Josey was grinning like a fox in a henhouse.

"How much is the rent?" Donnie asked as they started back down the stairs. Darci told him. "And deposit? Do you need first and last months' rent in advance?"

"Just the deposit and first month's rent," Darci said. "Do you have pets?"

"Yes," Josey piped up. "A dog. He's so sweet. We just got him."

143

"We always had a dog," Darci said. Donnie expected her to add a pet deposit, but she didn't.

"Can we have just a minute to discuss this?" Donnie asked. Darci excused herself and left them in the living room. Donnie watched her go outside and lay a hand on the trunk of the oak tree as if reading her own history in the tree's bark.

"I love it!" Josey said, her face beaming and her hands clasped at her chest.

"How – " Donnie began.

"Mike and I already figured it out," Josey said. "While you were getting laid, we were talking finances. With his pension and my inheritance, we can make the payments."

"My monthly paychecks will start going into your friend's bank next month," Mike said.

"You don't really even need me here," Donnie said. He wasn't sure how he felt about that.

"You've taken us in, Donnie," Josey said. "You'll contribute to groceries and the bills. And you've got the only vehicle among us. Plus a business to run, and now you've got writing to do, too."

Donnie shook his head again, but then shrugged. "I guess we're renting a house."

"Yes!" Josey cheered, jumping up a little.

"Let's tell Darci," Mike said. "I think she's done communing with her tree."

Papers were signed on the kitchen counter and keys exchanged. "No background check?" Donnie asked.

Darci smiled. "Sherry Brown has already vouched for you," she said. "Her word is as good as gold."

"That woman," Donnie said, shaking his head.

"She's an angel," Josey agreed.

"The furniture stays," Darci said. "Unless you don't want it. In that case, I'll have it removed. The beds are covered, but no sheets, and I'll be taking the covers with me. You'll have to get your own linens."

"That's fine. Thank you," Donnie said. "I think we'd like to keep the furniture. None of us really have anything to replace it."

"I'll take care of those bedcovers now, then, and you can start moving in whenever you're ready," Darci said.

On the way back to the store, Josey began laying out plans. "I think Donnie should have the big room downstairs so he can use it for an office, too. He has a book to write."

"No," Donnie interrupted. "I think Dad should have that one. He doesn't need the stairs."

There was a moment of silence, then Mike spoke. "Ordinarily, I'd argue with you, but in this case, I'm going to agree. My knees aren't what they used to be."

"Okay," Josey went on, unbothered. She told Donnie he could choose which of the two upstairs rooms he wanted and that she wanted to buy a big flat screen TV and a gaming console for the living room. "But you do need an office space," she finished.

"I write on a laptop," Donnie said. "I can do that anywhere. And, if I need a quiet space, I'll have the whole area I've been living in at the back of the store. It's only a few minutes away," he said as he parked the truck behind the store.

"I think me and Mike should start taking the food and whatever stuff from the store to the house and get some sheets and stuff while you run the store and start on that book," Josey continued.

Mike threw open his pickup door and laughed. "She's a bossy little thing," he said as he got out.

"Amen to that," Donnie added.

The late October air whipped around them, blowing locks of silver and blue into Josey's face as she went on. "With you not living back there, we can really spread out those boxes and get that stuff inventoried and shelved," she said.

"Yeah," Donnie said as they entered the storeroom. He looked at his twin bed, the little refrigerator, hotplate, and tiny table that had been his home for seven years. He couldn't hold back a stab of nostalgia. They had not been good years, but it felt strange to suddenly have all that familiarity ripped away. He felt as if he was unmoored, drifting on the wind of Josey's enthusiasm and his father's recrimination.

"There are plenty of boxes," Josey was saying. "Not that we're taking much with us. No offense, Donnie, but that bed is crap. It should go in the trash. It sags in the middle."

Donnie nodded. "I know. It was like it was hugging me."

"That's the saddest thing I've ever heard," Josey said, pausing, her hands in the air like birds stopped in flight.

"Pathetic," Mike agreed.

"It can go," Donnie conceded.

"Go open the store. Start writing," Josey ordered. "Gimme the keys, though."

Donnie did as he was told, passing her the keys and unlocking the front door of the store. He went to his usual place behind the counter, turned on the laptop computer and waited for it to boot up. He opened his word processor and almost automatically opened the saved, stalled document, then stopped himself. He opened a new document and looked at the blinking cursor on the fresh, blank, white page.

He asked himself, *Can I do this?*

Gently, he placed his fingertips on the home row of the keyboard.

Why was Bolkar in that dungeon? Donnie didn't have the answer. Why was he on the rack? Who were those men around him? How had he been caught?

No answer.

Donnie cleared his mind and closed his eyes. Outside, the cold wind blew down the little town's main street. It was cold. It was windy. Just like that night Bolkar first appeared. He had been so strong, so confident. He just took control and told his story. It had been so simple.

Donnie was aware his fingers were moving but he ignored the sensation. He felt the keys beneath his fingertips. He thought of the bounty hunter. Over six feet tall, wearing a horned helmet, carrying a heavy broadsword with a battleaxe strapped to his back, a long straight dagger on his belt. His knee-high boots were wet from snow and the furs he wore bristled in the wind, catching white flecks. Bolkar's black horse stood nearby, stamping and blowing. There was a fire in front of Bolkar, but he had not built it. Slumped near the fire was a headless man.

Donnie opened his eyes and looked at the screen.

Bolkar knew he had been tricked. Tricked and trapped. He had killed the wrong man. This was no raving murderer dressed in wolfskins terrorizing villages and farmers, taking the shape of a great wolf to ravage the local women and steal children. The face looking up at him from the bloody snow belonged to Edric, nephew of King Rathulf. He heard the wizard's cackling laughter a moment before he was blinded by a blast like the noon sun exploding before his face.

It wasn't great. It needed work, but it was a start, and Donnie could see the next scene and the next scene coming forward in his mind like tarot cards being turned over by a gypsy fortune teller. Bolkar captured, a bounty on the bounty hunter, not just for the death of the king's nephew, but to prevent him from fulfilling other jobs he had been contracted to complete. Held. Tortured. His captors believing he held a treasury of gold earned over his career. But more ... They wanted to know the whereabouts of a baby he had taken in payment many years ago.

Donnie didn't realize he was smiling as he bowed his head over the glowing computer and let his fingers dance over the keys in a way they had not done in a very long time.

Chapter Sixteen

"This is the real deal," Donnie said into his cell phone.

Some two thousand miles away, Gene Adkins took a deep breath and held it, then blew it out. "What have ya got, Donnie? Don't get me wrong, I want this. I want you back. I want your book. I want us to both be filthy fuckin' rich. It's been a long time. Can you really finish it?"

"I've written fifty-three pages in five days," Donnie answered. "It was a slow start. It took me over a week to write the first twenty pages, but I'm back into it now. My life has changed since the last time we talked. Did I tell you my creative writing teacher from high school died?"

"No, you didn't mention – "

"She did. Her granddaughter and my father are living with me now. And, get this, I have a girlfriend," Donnie added. He looked around at the empty store to be sure he wouldn't be heard. "I got laid the night before I started writing. First time in like eight years, and I dreamed of a scene for this book, and I've been writing like a wildfire this past week."

Donnie felt the tension break on the New York end of the line. Gene chuckled. "That's all it took, huh? Just some pussy? Shit, I woulda sent a dozen hookers to see you seven years ago if I'd known that."

"It was more than that," Donnie said. "It was ... everything. The timing, the people. Mrs. Wilder dying. All of it. But it's back. That's what I'm telling you. You said you thought there was still a market. Did you know there is Bolkar fanfiction on the internet? I had no idea that stuff existed."

"I hadn't looked for it, but I'm not surprised," Gene answered.

"Anyway, the book," Donnie returned to the subject, his eyes fixed on the diner across the street. Every once in a while, he could get a glimpse of Debbie moving around in there. "Do you think you can sell it?"

"You know they've changed editors a dozen times at your old publisher," Gene said. "But they still have first refusal rights to anything you do in that universe. I can't make any promises."

"You said I should be where George R.R. Martin is. That everyone is looking for the new *Game of Thrones*," Donnie argued. His laptop was open and he looked down at it, at the black words on the white background.

"Of course I told you that. I wanted you to fuckin' write something," Gene said. "Look, Donnie, send me what you've already written and an outline of the whole book. And tell me how it picks up from the last book. Send me that and I'll see what I can do."

"They'll be in your email tomorrow morning," Donnie promised.

"One more thing there, Donnie."

"What's that?"

"You tell whatever girl you're shagging in that little speck on the map thank you for me," Gene said. "Even if this book is absolute shit, it's good to hear you have some life in you again."

Donnie laughed and ended the call. He was hungry, having left the house before sunrise to walk through the tiny town to his store. He had been revising the first four chapters of his book instead of writing new material because his anxiety had begun to eat at him that the writing was no good. He had almost convinced himself he had lost whatever gift or talent or skill he had once possessed, but after reading through what he had written, he was happy with it. There had been tweaks to make, of course, but he had always found that work to be easy. The story had more depth, more gravitas, than the previous volumes, but still had a lot of action. He liked what he was doing.

Mike and Josey would be along soon. It was the first week of November. Josey's Halloween display was gone and she was working on a Thanksgiving theme, mixing books about colonial America with cookbooks and histories of American Indians. She had insisted that she, Donnie, and Mike all make turkeys from tracing their hands and list four staff picks on the four tail feathers. The memory made Donnie smile. All over the store, one could see Josey's hand at work in simple ways, doing things he never would have thought of with bits of dried corn husk, cheap antique housewares she picked up at one of the three junk shops in town, and always with a few thematically-matched books. She was good.

Donnie saved his work yet again and closed the laptop to go across the street and order breakfast.

"Hey Debbie, your boyfriend's here," someone called as soon as Donnie opened the door. There was general, friendly laughter as Donnie stepped in and let the door close behind him. It was the usual crowd of mostly older men, a few with their wives. Lots of denim and flannel and canvas clothing. The smell of coffee was strong, with hash browns and bacon beneath it. Donnie's stomach rumbled, and then Debbie was beside him, her hand on his arm and her smile lighting up her face.

"Nothing stays a secret in a small town, huh?" he joked.

"Nope. Nothin'," she agreed. "Come on, there's an empty table over here." Her hand still possessively on his arm, she led him across to an empty table. Donnie could smell her perfume trailing her and he felt several pairs of eyes and smiles moving across the diner with them. They were good people, he thought, and wished he'd gotten friendlier with them earlier in his time here. "Here ya go," Debbie said, placing a menu on the table.

Donnie sat and Debbie stood looking down at him. "Busy morning?" he asked.

"It's just like every other mornin'," she said. "I saw you over there in the store. Why didn't you turn on the light?"

"I didn't want people to think the store was open early. I got up early and was writing. Then I called my agent."

"Agent, huh?" she said, smiling. She was wearing red lipstick and Donnie just realized she only wore it at work. "Mr. Bigtime." Someone called for her and she waved at a group of thick farmers at another table. "You'll have to tell me how that agenting works later. You want the usual, or are we gonna play that game where you look at the menu for a while first?"

Donnie grinned and felt himself flushing a little. "The usual," he agreed. She took the menu and swept toward the other table.

"Oh, now, you just hush," she told the laughing farmers. Three of the four were bald, all clean-shaven, all with merry eyes in chubby faces. "He's just a customer when he's in here, same as you or anyone else."

"You didn't lead me to this table with a hand on my arm," one of the men teased her. They all laughed and she swatted at the farmer with the menu.

"I'll be right back with more coffee, you old coots," she promised and moved away.

One of the farmers facing Donnie caught his eye and the man winked. "She hasn't been this happy since she was in high school," he called over. "It's good to see it on her."

Donnie wasn't sure how to respond. He smiled and said, "Thanks. I'll do what I can."

"I bet he will," one of the men with his back to Donnie joked. The men laughed, but in a way that made it known to all that the conversation had reached an end and no one was the butt of the good-natured ribbing. Debbie came back and refilled their coffee mugs and they thanked her with no more teasing.

Debbie made her way to Donnie's table and put down a fresh white ceramic mug that she filled with steaming black coffee. She slipped into the booth opposite him and sighed. "My feet're already killing me. I need some new shoes, but I gotta go to Alva to get 'em."

"As it happens, I'll be heading to Alva this afternoon," Donnie said. "I guess the air fryer Josey wanted was cheaper through Wal-Mart than Amazon if it was shipped to the closest store. And she says we need better towels than the ones I bought at Dollar General. You are more than welcome to come along."

"It wouldn't be a bother?" she asked, and he wondered if she was exaggerating her country twang, but decided it was still just part of her natural speech. He liked it. A lot.

"No bother, ma'am. I'd be pleased with your comp'ny."

"You're makin' fun of the way I talk," she accused, but she was smiling. "I gotta git. I'm off at one. I'll just come across the street." She pushed away from the table and weaved through others, pouring coffee and smiling and putting a couple of checks on tables of customers ready to leave.

Donnie thought about the outline he needed to put together for Gene. He didn't like outlining. Once committed to paper — or pixels — he felt like he'd nailed a story down and it couldn't grow organically anymore. He always put it off, to the frustration of his agent and editors, until he felt he had the ending of the book pretty well in mind. There were still a few slippery details in this latest story about Bolkar, but Donnie felt he could commit to enough to make Gene happy.

Could Gene sell the book? Donnie didn't know, but Josey had subscribed them to HBO and he'd begun watching *Game of Thrones* and was hooked, hoping the audience of the show would also be readers of gritty sword-and-sorcery fantasy that fell somewhere between Martin's complex politics and Robert E. Howard's brutal tales of Conan the Barbarian.

Debbie brought his food and Donnie dug into the biscuits and gravy and bacon as the restaurant patrons began to thin out and the murmur of voices died down. Without staring, Donnie watched as Debbie bussed tables and pocketed tips and cleaned and continued to chat with other customers. Then she came back and sat with him again.

"An air fryer?" she asked, as if their conversation had never been interrupted.

"Yep," Donnie said before swallowing. "The way she sells it, this thing will gather the stuff out of the refrigerator and have dinner cooked when we get home from the store."

Debbie laughed, an uninhibited, musical sound that turned every head toward them for a moment. "Don't let Annie hear about those or we'll all be outta work here," she said.

Donnie grinned. "Perhaps you'd let me buy you dinner in the big town of Alva," he suggested. "They have a fine McDonald's across from the university."

She cocked an eyebrow at him. "McDonald's?"

He shrugged. "Maybe we can find something else," he said, and winked. "That reminds me, I have very strict orders to make sure you will join us for Sunday dinner at the new homeplace."

"And who gave you those orders?"

Donnie sighed. "The boss lady. I tell you, for being so young, she really has no problem taking charge. But ... I can't argue with the results. She's good at everything she does."

"She's quite a girl," Debbie agreed. "She gonna cook in that new air fryer?"

"She said we're having old-fashioned pot roast," Donnie said. "To me, old fashioned means made in the oven. But this younger generation, well, you never know. But I'm not going to doubt her skill. Somehow she made the best French toast I've ever eaten yesterday and she won't tell me what she did. She just said her grandma taught her."

"That was your teacher," Debbie said, proud that she remembered. "The one that taught you to write stories."

"Yeah," Donnie said, happy she recalled that detail. Something caught his eye and he looked up. Across the street, the lights were on in his store. "Speak of the devil, she just showed up for work. She's making Thanksgiving displays. Lord help us all next month when she gets to decorate for Christmas," he said.

"You like her a lot," Debbie said. There was no jealousy there, just admiration.

Donnie nodded slowly. "I do. I just wish ... " He trailed off and looked away.

"What is it, hon?" Debbie reached over and touched his arm. "Your own daughter?"

"Yeah," he said. "I wish I could have this kind of relationship with her." He shrugged and thought about LizBeth, wondered what class she was in right now, what she'd do for lunch and after school. "It is what it is, I guess."

Debbie's hand tightened sympathetically on his arm for a moment. "You tell her I'll be there for Sunday dinner, but she has to let me help with the cooking or bring something."

"No," Donnie said. "She won't allow it. She said you deal with feeding people five days a week and you're not going to do it on Sunday. You're to come over as early as you want and we'll play games, watch movies, or sit around and talk until the food is ready."

Debbie laughed softly. "She is an assertive little woman. I like that. I wish I'd been like that when I was young. Woulda saved me a lot of heartache." She looked around, then back at him and said, "I gotta clean the rest of those tables. Don't worry about your check. I got it. Don't argue, mister." She winked. "I'm gonna learn from Josey how to boss you around." She slipped away.

Donnie finished his meal and slid a ten and a five dollar bill under his empty coffee cup, then scooted for the door. He heard Debbie's voice behind him.

"I told you – "

"I'll see you at one," he called over his shoulder, slipping into his coat and out of the café.

Across the street, he found Josey and Jasper in the store. Josey was dusting bookshelves while the dog roamed around the store, sniffing as if to make sure no other animal had invaded his space during the night.

"Good morning," the girl said as Donnie entered.

"Good morning," he answered. "Did you eat?"

"Waffles," she said. "I made them while Mike made the coffee."

"Where is Dad?" Donnie asked.

"He asked me to drop him at the VFW," Josey said. "Does this town have any homeless people?"

Donnie settled into his chair and swiveled to face her. "None that I know of. Too small. One of the churches would pick them up and take care of them. And everyone knows everyone, so ... It's not really a problem."

"Oh," she said.

"You sound disappointed," Donnie said.

"I thought we could do a Thanksgiving dinner for the homeless," she said.

Donnie shook his head. "Sorry."

"You're still okay with the craft day?" she asked.

Donnie nodded. He'd forgotten she asked about having a day for kids the Saturday before Thanksgiving Day, where they'd do more of the same stuff they did in school, like making the hand-turkeys. He reminded her of that.

"We'll do more than that," she said. "We'll have a costume contest and they'll dress like Native Americans or pilgrims and we'll play games and have candy and story time."

Donnie grinned. "You are such an organizer. Have you already talked to Wilson at the newspaper?"

She looked away from him, but he caught her smile. "Maaaaybe," she admitted.

Donnie laughed. "You're practically running this place," he said. "You know sales were up for October, right?"

Josey stopped dusting and faced him, her face lit up. "Really?"

"Almost ten percent over September and about seven percent over last October," Donnie said. "I know that was all you. Thank you."

The girl blushed deeply and tried to laugh it away. "I love being here," she said. "It isn't even work."

"Oh, it's work, but you do it well and make it fun," Donnie said. "Speaking of working, I guess you'll be in charge this afternoon."

"Air fryer!" Josey said triumphantly.

Donnie chuckled. "Yes, I'm going to pick that up. I'm also meeting a friend who scours garage sales and thrift stores for books for me."

"In Alva?" she asked.

"He lives in Wichita and is going to Woodward to visit family," Donnie explained. "He found a mint set of Karl Edward Wagner's Kane books, plus some vintage horror paperbacks from the 1980s."

"I've never heard of Kane or that author," Josey said.

"They're hard to find, and even harder to find in decent condition."

"Why does he give them to you?"

"Oh, I pay him for them, and for his time," Donnie said. "He already has the Kane books or he would have kept them for himself and never even told me about them. He loves his fantasy fiction."

"Okay. Well, I hope you have a good trip," she said, and turned back to her dusting. Over her shoulder she added, "And don't forget to pick up my air fryer, buddy. I know you think it's weird, but you're going to love it."

Donnie chuckled. "I won't forget," he promised. "Umm, Debbie is going with me and we're going to have dinner in Alva and get her some new shoes before we come back," Donnie added.

Josey gave him a devilish smile, but only said, "Okay."

Donnie suddenly thought of something. "Crap. How are you and Dad going to get back to the house?"

"We'll be okay," Josey said, still dusting.

"It's too cold to walk," he argued.

"How'd you get here this morning?" she asked.

"I didn't say it was too cold for *me* to walk," he argued.

She straightened up and faced him. "Because I'm a girl?"

Donnie laughed. "No. I'm sure you'd be fine, and I can't imagine you not being safe on the streets of this town, but Dad ... Have you noticed he's been moving kind of slow the past few days?"

"No," Josey said, but there was something about her tone that tweaked Donnie's mind.

"He has. He says it's just adjusting to the new bed," Donnie said. "I don't know. Maybe he's right. But I don't think he should make the walk."

"I bet he can get one of his VFW buddies to drive him home," she said.

"Maybe," Donnie agreed.

"If not, we'll just hang out here until you get back," she said. "You're just getting dinner, right? You're not getting a hotel room and making a night of it?"

"No," Donnie said, a little embarrassed. "I guess you're right."

"I usually am," she said in a sing-song voice that made Donnie grin. "Did you talk to your agent yet? You were supposed to do that days ago."

Donnie made a childish face at her, then chuckled. "I did. He wants to see what I've written, and he wants an outline of the whole book. He wouldn't make any promises, of course."

"He'll love it," Josey assured him. She took another swipe at the shelf, then gave up dusting and came over to lean on the counter. Jasper, who had lain down on his big pillow near the first shelf of books, tracked her with his eyes, then lost interest when she proved to not be doing anything too interesting. "Have you written the outline?"

"No. I was going to do that now," Donnie said. "Debbie gets off at one. I can have it done before then."

"You better get to work," Josey said. "Since you're up here, I'm going to scan books in those boxes in the back until you leave, then I'll stay up front."

"Okay. Thank you," Donnie told her, and watched as she moved away, pausing to ruffle up the hair on Jasper's head as she passed him. The dog watched her, too, but didn't get up to follow her. He looked back at Donnie. "You're kinda lazy," he told the dog. Jasper yawned and put his head on his paws.

Donnie turned back to his computer screen.

Two hours later, he took a deep breath and pulled his hands off the keyboard. What he'd written was more a synopsis than an outline, but it got across his plan for a novel in which the bounty hunter was tricked and captured by a wizard who wanted a piece of treasure Bolkar had accidentally acquired in a job. The wizard and various allies held Bolkar captive for months before he was able to escape, weak and naked, into a barren landscape of ice and wind. Rescued by a hunter and taken to a village, Bolkar recovers, sees the value of family and community, and decides to be more selective in the jobs he takes, pursuing only those accused of severe crimes. Healthy again, he returns to the wizard's castle and takes his revenge, finds his armor, and sets out for new adventures.

It wasn't high literature. There would be no Pulitzer or Nobel prizes for the work, but he knew the writing and the overall storyline were more mature and nuanced than his early novels, while maintaining the key elements of quest and violence. Donnie composed an e-mail to his agent and attached the synopsis and what he'd written so far and was about to hit the send button when Josey startled him by saying his name.

"Huh?" he asked, turning in his chair, his heart racing. Josey was grinning from ear to ear.

"I didn't mean to sneak up on you," she said, and giggled like a little girl.

"But you're not sorry you did, ya little brat," Donnie teased.

"It was pretty funny how you jumped," she said. "Like I caught you watching porn or something."

"I was focused," he said defensively. He saw she was holding something yellowish-brown in her hands. "What do you have there?"

She put it on the counter and turned it toward him. "I found it at the bottom of a box that was mostly old *Reader's Digest* condensed books. I think it might be valuable."

It was a copy of John Steinbeck's short novel *The Red Pony* in a cardboard slipcase that might have been white or cream-colored when it was new but was now yellowed to the point it was more gray and brown, though still with reasonably sharp corners and the picture on the front was pretty vibrant.

"You could be right," Donnie said thoughtfully. He picked the package up and slid the book from its case. The cover showed age, but the two blue borders, one near the edge and another around a watercolor of a red pony, were still bright and the watercolor was in very good shape. "Let's see what edition it is." He opened the cover.

Donnie turned to the page with the publisher information on it. "Viking Press of New York. Published in 1945." He paused. "I'm not a Steinbeck expert, but I think he published this book earlier than that. But ... This seems to be some kind of special edition. He wasn't famous enough to have a slipcovered book when this story was first published. I think. This ... " He trailed off, studying the page.

"It is a first edition, isn't it?" Josey asked, her voice brimming with excitement.

Donnie looked up. "It is," he agreed. "Did you already look it up?"

"No," she said. "I should have."

"It's okay," he said. "There's time. It might be worth thousands of dollars, but it might only be worth twenty bucks. If it was signed," he said and winked at her. "If it was signed, we could all go on a very nice vacation." He looked down at the book. "It's not signed, is it?"

"No," she said. "But it does have nice pictures."

Donnie flipped through the pages and agreed with her. He had not read this book; he had only read four Steinbeck novels in his life. He closed the volume and put it back in its slipcase. "I didn't know this was in the store. Or in that box. I probably thought it was all *Reader's Digest* books. Whatever it's worth is probably more than I paid for the box."

"What do I do with the *Reader's Digest* books?" Josey asked.

Donnie considered a moment. "For now, set them aside. Just leave them and mark the box and push them out of the way. There are more back there. And boxes of old encyclopedias, dictionaries, and other reference books nobody would buy on their own, but I sell those books by the yard."

"By the yard?" she asked, her nose wrinkling.

"Yeah. People buy them more for decoration," Donnie said. "Some think it makes them look smart to have all these matching hardcover books on a shelf in their house. Sometimes it's realtors, furniture stores, bed-and-breakfast owners who buy them to decorate their space. They don't care what the books are, as long as they look good. Or old. So I sell them by the yard. Three feet of books for thirty dollars."

"That's a waste," Josey said. "They're books, not throw pillows."

Donnie chuckled. "Have you ever bothered to read a *Reader's Digest* condensed book?"

"No," she admitted.

"Most real readers don't," he said. "And who uses a print encyclopedia in the age of the internet? Even I know that, missy."

"What about the Steinbeck?" she asked. "What do you want me to do with it?"

"Put it somewhere safe, somewhere your fresh young mind will remember, and we'll look into its worth later," he said. "I'm about to send my proposal off to Gene."

"Oooo," she cooed. "I got here in time to witness history in the making." She smiled a genuine smile and leaned over the counter, her blue-and-silver hair slipping off her shoulders to make a curtain around her pale oval of a face. Donnie shook his head and returned to his seat.

He read over the e-mail one more time, then looked at Josey. "Here goes nothing." He pushed the Send button. "Done."

"It's about time for your big date," Josey teased, batting her eyes at him.

"It's not a big date. Not really," he said.

"One to ten, how much do you like her?" Josey asked.

"I don't know. It's too early to tell," he argued.

"But you like her."

"I do like her, yes."

"Do you love her?"

"Josey, we've only been dating for, what? About a week?" Donnie said.

"It wasn't love at first sight?" she asked, her chin on her fists.

"We'd kind of known each other for a few months," he said.

"Love at first ... Well ... you've slept together," she said.

Donnie felt his face warming. He cleared his throat. "That's, umm ... private stuff."

"So it wasn't innocent," she said and grinned. "Mike told me he thought you two passed out on the sofa watching a movie. I had faith in you, though."

"Josey! What ... " Donnie let it go and shook his head. "Anyway, it's not love. Maybe later. Old people do things differently."

"Old people bring all their baggage into a new relationship," Josey countered.

Donnie stared hard at her. She met his gaze with her clear, innocent green eyes. "How do you know things like that?"

"Grandma had book clubs and poetry groups and women of all ages, friends and former students who became friends, at the house all the time and I listened," she said. "Can I ask you the real question?"

Donnie hesitated, half afraid of what she'd ask. Finally, he nodded. "Okay. Just don't be offended if I don't answer."

"Are you afraid to fall in love?" Josey asked.

"My God," Donnie breathed, and swiveled his chair away. He looked out the store's window to the bank's digital clock. The gold dots said it was 12:32 and 43 degrees Fahrenheit. "I'm afraid," he said, his voice little more than a whisper.

"Mike says your guilt will eat at you," Josey said. "Guilt about the affair you had while you were married."

Donnie nodded. "There's that," he admitted. "But it isn't that. I think I'm over that. I think knowing that Melissa is happy and getting married again helped me get past that. Plus, you know, you and Dad telling me to let it all go."

"Then what is it?" Josey asked, her own voice soft, sincere, neither pleading nor prying. Just asking, one friend to another. Donnie wondered what his life had come to when his best friend was a teenager he hadn't known existed a month ago.

"It's been so long," he said, his eyes still on the bank clock. It was 12:35 now. "What if ... Well, with the affair, you know, I was at a really low point and I fell for the first person who was nice to me." He made himself turn to face Josey and he saw the sympathy in her eyes. "What if I do that again and it isn't right?"

"How does it feel, Donnie?" she asked. "How do you feel when you're with her?"

"I feel good," he said. "In a lot of ways, I feel more alive than I have in a long time."

"Do you both laugh a lot? Women love men who make them laugh," she said.

Donnie thought about it and finally nodded. "Yeah, I think so. We laugh."

"You're a good man, Donnie," Josey said. "You took me in, and your dad, without inviting either of us. You let us talk you into getting a real house and moving out of your storeroom. You adopted Jasper over there." She nodded toward the dog, whose ears pricked up at the mention of his name, but he neither opened his eyes nor raised his head. "People in town like you, even though most don't know you very well. You love your family even though they never call you. You deserve to be happy."

"People keep telling me that," he interrupted.

"Because it's true. We all deserve to be happy," she said. "Here comes Sherry." Josey's eyes flicked up to the window. Donnie turned and saw the bank president's wife making her way across the street, holding her fur coat closed against the wind. "Before she gets here, I'll add that Debbie is a good person, too. Time will tell if she's the right one for you, but she won't hurt you. I feel sure about that."

Donnie wanted to hug her, but instead he reached out and took one of her hands and squeezed it in his own. Her skin was soft and smooth and warm with young life. "Thank you," he said. The door of the store opened and Sherry Brown entered. "Thank you for stowing away in my truck that day. I needed you more than I ever knew."

Josey returned the pressure of his hand and smiled her radiant smile at him. "All three of us needed each other more than we knew," she agreed. "Now, we have a customer." She looked at Sherry as she released Donnie's hand. "Hi, Mrs. Brown," she chirped. "More literary sex today?"

"Josey," Donnie said again. Then he laughed. "You know, I'm getting on to you like you're my own daughter." The women laughed and Donnie shook his head. "Good afternoon, Mrs. Brown."

"I'm not coming another step into my favorite store until you both call me Sherry," the woman said, and she stamped a foot, the heel of her green pump making a sharp rap on the tile floor.

"Sorry, Sherry," Donnie and Josey said together.

"That's better." Sherry stepped up and deposited an old Sara Orwig paperback on the counter. "What's this?" she asked, turning the slipcased Steinbeck novel so she could see it.

160

Josey explained what it was and how she'd found it. "We don't know what it's worth yet," she said. "Oh, and Donnie sent his new book to his agent just now."

"You finished it?" Sherry said, her face beaming.

"No," Donnie said. "He asked to see what I've written and he wanted an outline, so I sent those. We'll see how it goes."

"It's going to be a bestseller," Josey said confidently. "*A Song of Ice and Fire* and *The Lord of the Rings* all wrapped up in one."

"It's hardly all that," Donnie said.

"And he's taking Debbie to Alva for a big date, but he'll say it's a business trip," Josey gushed.

Sherry turned her merry, twinkling eyes on Donnie and smiled. She had just a tiny bit of red lipstick on a front top tooth. "Who is this man and where did the old Donnie Nelson go?" Sherry asked, then waved her gloved hands. "Never mind. I like this one better. He smiles so much more."

"I have to pick up some books," Donnie said. "I asked Debbie if she wanted to come along and have dinner. I owe her a dinner."

"Mmm," Sherry said. "You must pay your debts."

"I unpacked and scanned a whole box of romance books this morning," Josey said. "Most of them look brand new. They're still in the back. Do you want to be the first to see them?"

"Absolutely!" Sherry said, and held out her hand. Josey took the fingers in the black leather glove and together they started toward the storeroom, chatting about the Thanksgiving displays as they went.

"I hope that Donnie is gone, too," Donnie said as he closed his laptop. A few minutes later, he saw Debbie come out of the cafe's front door and start across the street. She was wearing jeans and a black leather motorcycle jacket and the wind whipped her hair around her face like yellow flames. It was a mess when she finally made it into the store, but Donnie didn't laugh as she used her hands to try to fix it. He took his coat off his chair and came around the counter. Josey had taken the Steinbeck and the Orwig novels with her.

"Did you have a good shift?" he asked Debbie.

"It was the usual, except for the grease fire, but Connor got that put out before there was any damage," she said, still trying to straighten her hair.

Donnie chuckled. "Okay then." He slipped into his coat and checked the pocket for his keys. "Are you ready to roll?"

"I am," she said. "Do you sing when you drive?"

"Not when there's anybody with me," Donnie said.

"That's about to change," she promised as they made their way to the back of the store.

"I wouldn't bet on that," Donnie said. They entered the storeroom, where Josey and Sherry were sorting through a folding table full of paperbacks. "Josey, I'm leaving. You're in charge. Bye, Mrs. Brow-- Bye, Sherry."

Sherry cocked an eye at him, but grinned. "You're a slow learner, but you're getting there," she said.

Chapter Seventeen

Donnie hesitated as he was about to turn onto Main Street. "I should tell my dad I'm going out of town."

"Do you want to call him?" Debbie asked.

Donnie considered. "No, let's just hop over to the VFW and I'll tell him in person."

Debbie acknowledged many of the old men by name as they shouted greetings at the couple. Donnie knew a few of them and called them by name and waved at the others and shook a few hands. He didn't see his father in the main room of the building.

"I'm looking for my dad," Donnie said.

The room got very quiet and a few men looked at each other and avoided eye contact with Donnie.

A man to Donnie's left cleared his throat and stepped forward. He held out a hand and Donnie shook it. "I'm Jack Schwartz," the man said. "Major Schwartz, US Army, retired."

"It's nice to meet you, Mister ... Major Schwartz," Donnie said. "But, what's going on? Where's my dad?"

"Oh, he and Lester Mitchell went down to Woodward for the day," the Major replied. "They got to talking about wanting a road trip. Probably gonna hit a couple of bars. Maybe some pawn shops. I think I heard them talking about military souvenirs and army surplus stuff. They'll likely be gone most of the day."

"He didn't tell me he was going," Donnie said, confused.

"It was a spur-of-the moment thing," Major Schwartz said. The older man grinned at Donnie in a friendly manner. "He's a full-grown man, you know."

Donnie scowled. "Yeah, I know. He still could have sent a text or something."

"Folks our age don't always think about using those cellular phones to check in with people," Major Schwartz said. "Sometimes I have mine in my pocket and still look for a pay phone."

A few other men laughed at this and Donnie smiled. He knew his dad wasn't the best at using the smartphone, and it could be he got caught up in the moment and forgot to let him or Josey know he was leaving. *Did* Josey know? Donnie wondered.

"Alright, well, Debbie and I are going to Alva," Donnie said. "I have to pick up some merchandise and we're going to have dinner. I'll just call him. When did they leave?"

"It was just a little after that pretty girl with the blue hair dropped him off," the major said. "He sat in a round or two of dominoes, then they left. He tells me you have a good selection of war books. Novels and nonfiction."

"Oh, yeah," Donnie said. He felt like the man was trying to draw him away from the subject of his dad and he didn't like it. There was something fishy going on here. "I know I just shelved a copy of General Patton's *War as I Knew It*. And the novelization of *Rambo Two*."

"God, I love those Rambo movies," the Major said, smiling like a happy child.

Debbie had wandered to a table and was leaning over between two elderly men, talking and laughing with them as they laid out their dominoes. She patted one on the shoulder as he played a piece that stumped the other players.

"I guess we better go on," Donnie said. "I hope you'll come over and look those books over. Josey's minding the store this afternoon. She'll talk your ear off, though."

"Pretty young girl like that wouldn't have anything to say to an old fart with shrapnel in his leg from a war that happened before her mama was born," Major Schwartz said and laughed.

"You'd be surprised," Donnie said, then called to Debbie. "Are you ready to go?"

Debbie said good-bye to several men, then put her hand on the crook of Donnie's arm and, together, they left the VFW. As Donnie fastened his seatbelt, he said, "Something is really weird about this. Dad hardly ever drinks, so he's not going to Woodward to go to bars. He did like pawn shops and military stuff, but ... " He got the pickup onto the road and they started out of town.

"I couldn't get anything, either," Debbie said. "But Major Lester Schwartz did feed you a line of bull. I asked Freddie and Jack where Mike really went. Every man at that table shifted their eyes at Lester and went quiet. Finally, Freddie just said, 'I can't tell you that.' And he wouldn't tell me anything else."

Donnie puckered his lips in frustration. He looked to Debbie. Her blonde hair was thick and full and beautiful, even with the few strands of gray she probably hadn't realized were there. Her brown eyes were soft and watching him. She smiled. "I'm sure it's okay," she said. "He is a grown man, like Lester said."

"I know," Donnie said. "But still." He pushed a button on the steering wheel and a computerized voice asked for his command. He told it to call Josey. She answered after a few rings.

"Did you already get lost?" the girl asked.

"No, we're not lost," Donnie said while Debbie laughed. "Everything okay there?"

"Yeah. You literally just left, Donnie," Josey said. "Sherry took her daily book and now I'm shelving some of the other romances."

"Okay. Well, I actually called to ask if Dad said anything to you about going out of town today," Donnie said.

The hesitation was barely noticeable, but it was there. Donnie was sure of it. "No, he didn't mention it," Josey said. "Did he go somewhere?"

"Yeah. Woodward," he said.

"Why?" Josey asked.

"Josey, seriously, did he say anything about it?" Donnie asked. "Is everything okay?"

"As far as I know, everything's A-okay," she said. "Did you call him?"

"Not yet," Donnie said.

"Let him have his fun," Josey said. "He has to be bored of playing dominoes with those old guys."

"He's an old guy," Donnie reminded her.

"Not like they are," she said.

"Promise me there's nothing I need to know about," Donnie said.

Again, there was a split second of hesitation. "I promise," she said, and her voice was lower than before, missing her usual cheerfulness.

"You're not going to tell me," Donnie said, and his voice sounded more accusing than he'd intended.

"I can't," she said, very quiet now. "I promised."

Donnie drove in silence for several seconds. He felt a warm, soft touch on his right hand and looked over to find Debbie pulling it toward her and squeezing it gently, reassuringly. "Josey," Debbie said, her voice almost as twangy as a Texan's on the word. "You'd tell us if there was something wrong, wouldn't you, honey?"

"Yeah," Josey said.

"Mike trusted you with some secret," Debbie said. "That's fine. Just you don't keep it if somebody's gonna get hurt, okay?"

"Okay," the girl said.

"You want us to bring you anything from Alva?" Debbie asked.

Josey's voice was perkier as she said, "If the restaurant you go to has a really good dessert, you could get me one to-go. And don't let Donnie forget the air fryer."

"Okay," Debbie promised. "You have a good day."

"Thanks," Josey said. Then she added, "Donnie, I'm sorry I can't tell."

"It's okay," he said, but in his heart it was not okay. Why would his dad keep a secret from him? Why would he tell Josey and not him? And those guys at the VFW obviously knew more than he did. Why? He wondered if it was about a gift. That didn't seem like his father's style. If he wanted to give Donnie something, he'd just do it. There wouldn't be any sneaking around about it.

"Josey, honey," Debbie said. "Donnie here hasn't asked me over for Thanksgiving dinner yet. Maybe he's expecting me to ask him to my trailer. But I was wondering if maybe you and me could work together and make dinner at your new house."

"I'd love that," Josey said enthusiastically. "I was going to talk to Donnie about hosting dinner, but I knew he'd get all weird about money."

Debbie laughed while Donnie scowled again. "I'm not *that* cheap," he argued.

"I didn't say you were cheap," Josey said. "But you're used to living on a very tight budget and that shows when you go shopping."

Donnie remembered Josey's wrinkled little nose as she'd unpacked groceries the last time he went. He bought generic store brands of everything in boxes and cans. He'd argued that they were just as good and a lot cheaper and she'd countered with the fact her grandma always bought the real stuff.

"We don't want a dry old Great Value turkey," Josey teased.

"You and Debbie can handle the shopping," Donnie conceded. "The important thing is watching the Dallas Cowboys take a beating."

166

"The important thing is the food, dummy," Josey laughed at him.

"I'll make Donnie drive me to the house when we get home so I can deliver that dessert," Debbie said. "You turn your music back on and have a good day."

"How did you know?" she asked, surprise in her tone.

"Oh, honey, I was a teenager once upon a time," Debbie said. "Bye now." Debbie pushed the button on the dashboard screen to end the call.

"What the hell?" Donnie asked. "Something's going on and he tells her but not me?"

"Whatever it is, I'm sure he'll tell you when he's ready," Debbie said. She still held his right hand. It was between both of her hands now. She traced circles around one of his knuckles with her index finger. "You can't ask him about this. You know that, right?"

"What do you mean?" Donnie asked.

"He didn't want you to know," she answered. "Whatever it is, it's private to him until he's ready to tell you."

"You think it's okay for them to have secrets?" Donnie asked, giving her a quick glance before navigating a curve on the two-lane highway.

"Not really," Debbie said. "But I don't know what it is, so I can't really say. When's your birthday?"

"May eleventh," he answered.

"Well, Christmas is next month," Debbie said.

"I doubt he went Christmas shopping," Donnie said.

"But you don't know. Just tell yourself that's what it is until you find out something different. You can't let it eat at you," she urged.

"He's pretty old," Donnie said.

"He seems to be in pretty good health."

Donnie chewed at his lower lip. "We gave him the master bedroom downstairs so he wouldn't have to use the stairs," he said. "I've noticed he's walking ... funny sometimes. Kind of shuffling and he'll, like, steady himself on furniture. And he goes to the bathroom a lot."

"Old men just do that," Debbie said. "Stop fussin' over it. Tell me how your book is goin'. What's that barbarian doin' now? And when are you goin' to give me the copies of the books you already published?"

"Do you really want to read those?"

"My boyfriend is a famous writer," Debbie said in mock exasperation. "Of course I want to read his books."

He liked being called her boyfriend. He liked having her sitting next to him. Liked how she was holding his hand, her body turned in the seat to face him, her eyes and full attention on him. It felt nice. He thought about the conversation with Josey that morning and how he'd said he was afraid of falling for the first woman who was nice to him. He remembered the guilt and pain of his marriage ending and, as much as he hated to admit it, the sharper, deeper heartache of Addison breaking up with him after ... He shook that thought away. He didn't like bringing that up. He didn't talk about it and didn't think about it. It was shameful.

"I need to get my girlfriend some books," he said.

"Tell me about your agent. He's a New Yorker? I bet he talks funny," Debbie said.

Donnie bit down on his grin. He knew his own voice had a twangy country accent, but it was pretty mild compared to Debbie's. He loved how she talked, but it was funny to think of her accusing somebody else of talking differently.

"He does," Donnie agreed. "He sounds kind of like a mobster and he cusses like a sailor and doesn't care who's around to hear it. Ladies, men in tuxedos, kids, he doesn't care. 'If they don't wanna hear it, they can get the fuck away'," he said, trying to imitate Gene's tone. Then he got serious, thinking. "You know, he never really gave up on me. He'd call and check on me a couple of times a year and encourage me to keep writing. He really is a good man. I hadn't thought of that before. He was just a nag and a reminder of my failure."

There was so much he hadn't thought of before his life was turned upside down. It was hard to fathom that just a month ago he'd been living in a fog, taking one day at a time, not really caring if he died in his sleep because there was nothing to live for. Now, everything was different. He cared, and he saw things with new eyes. He liked his life.

"Maybe I'll get to meet him someday," Debbie said. She smiled when Donnie looked over at her.

"Maybe so," he agreed. "I've only met him in person I think ... three times. Most of the business is done over the phone and email."

"Tell me about the book," Debbie prompted. "Last time, Bolkar was looking for a way to die honorably instead of letting them torture him anymore."

"Well, he's realized that the people holding him don't actually like each other," Donnie said. "His plan is to turn them against each other. He wove some of his sleeping straw into the shape of an amulet he saw one of the wizards wearing, and when his guard caught him, he said that the wizard had whispered to him that the shape was a spell that would give him strength."

He went on recounting the escape plan of his fantasy bounty hunter as the gray highway stretched on between dark, fallow fields toward a gray horizon of lowering winter clouds. Giant white windmills rotated lazily on both sides of the highway and sometimes a few stray snowflakes slammed against the truck's windshield. There wasn't much traffic on the lonely road and the couple drove on, Debbie still holding his right hand, until the little city of Alva came into sight.

"This was the place to go back when I was in high school," Debbie said. "We'd drive over and try to hang out with the college kids in the evening after we shopped during the day. We thought it was actually a big city. We were so dumb." She laughed softly and her hand stroked Donnie's as her eyes looked into her past.

"It's all a matter of perspective," Donnie said.

"I'm no better off now than I was back then," Debbie said. Her voice was wistful and sad. "I coulda gone to college here. I was smart enough. But I made so many stupid decisions, and now I'm just a waitress in the town where I grew up, livin' paycheck to paycheck, nothin' in savings and nowhere to go."

Donnie squeezed her hand. "You're wiser than you were."

She gave a short, sardonic laugh. "Wisdom and a dollar'll buy you a cup of coffee at Annie's Cafe," she said.

"What do you want out of life?" Donnie asked as they made their way into the town.

"I don't even know anymore," she said. "I gave up on all them dreams. I just wanna be happy. Be able to rest once in a while. Know I'll be able to retire someday. Find somebody to get old with."

The highway became the town's main street and they passed the university and drove under a traffic light. Donnie thought about what she'd said. Up ahead, the Wal-Mart sign loomed above them. "We're going to talk about this some more," he promised. "Over dinner. But I want you to know I believe in you. You're not just a waitress."

She smiled at him, but it was a sad smile. Donnie turned the pickup in at the department store parking lot, found a spot to park, then called Mark Finley on his phone. The man answered after several rings and Donnie could barely hear him.

"Donnie? That you?" The man's voice boomed through the Ford's speakers via the phone's Bluetooth connection.

"I'm in the Wal-Mart parking lot," Donnie said, trying to be heard over the background noise on Mark's end.

"You're in the parking lot? The Wal-Mart in Alva, right?" the other man asked.

"Yes," Donnie answered. "Where are you?"

"I'm in the store. Gimme ten minutes and I'll call you back from my car." The connection ended.

"He sounds interesting," Debbie said.

"Hardcore fantasy nerds are always interesting," Donnie said. "The first time I met this guy, he was dressed as Cesar Romero's Joker. You know, from the old *Batman* TV show?"

Debbie gave him a concerned look. "Why?"

"It was a sci-fi convention. Lots of people dress up as characters from movies and TV," he explained. "That was Kansas City. The next time, he was dressed as Lando Calrissian from *Star Wars*. That was in Wichita. The third time – "

"Wasn't Lando a black guy?" she asked.

"Yeah."

"He didn't paint his face black, did he?" she asked, her own expression shocked.

Donnie laughed. "No. Mark is black."

"So he was a black Joker?"

"No, he wore white face paint like the TV Joker. Purple gloves. Died his hair green. Or maybe it was a wig."

Debbie laughed her musical laugh. "You have got to take me to one of these conventions so I can see all this for myself. It sounds pretty weird, but I bet it's fun."

"It can be," Donnie agreed. "Mark is a fun guy, but if you engage him in any of his favorite topics, it is full-on Nerdvana and you're not getting away for a while. He knows his stuff, too. He does one of those internet shows on YouTube where he talks to people in the field and reviews books and movies."

"I've heard some people doing that make a lot of money," Debbie said.

"Yeah, that's what I've heard," Donnie said. "Brian used to talk about it. He wanted to be a YouTuber. We were talking about what his show would be about when ... you know."

"Did he ever do it?" Debbie asked.

Donnie shrugged. "Not that I know of. I search his name every once in a while and never find anything. Maybe he blames me for ruining that, too."

Donnie's phone rang and he answered it through the pickup. "I'm in my car," Mark said. "Where are you?" Donnie explained where they were parked. "I got you. You see me getting close, you flash your lights or toot your horn or something."

Donnie looked at Debbie. "He drives a boat of an Oldsmobile. It's from the late '70s or early '80s and is purple with a white vinyl top. He calls it the USS Apollo Creed."

"There it is," Debbie said, pointing to a car approaching them. "Why that name? I call my car Betsy."

"USS indicates it's a United States vessel. Apollo Creed was Rocky Balboa's opponent in the first two *Rocky* movies, then his friend."

"This guy is really interesting," Debbie laughed.

The long purple car pulled in beside them and stopped. Donnie got out of the truck and was surprised when Debbie got out, too, and came around to stand with him. The trunk of the Oldsmobile Delta 88 popped open, then Mark got out. He was wearing faded jeans and a thick brown coat, open to show off a blue T-shirt with Harrison Ford as Han Solo holding his blaster and the words, "I fired the only shot."

"Nice shirt," Donnie said as they shook hands. Mark Finley was a short man at only about five-eight. His curly hair was cut short and there were flecks of gray around the temples.

"Han is the man," Mark said, grinning. His eyes moved to Debbie. "Who is the beautiful damsel?" Donnie introduced them and Mark raised an eyebrow. "When you get back in the game, you aim high, sir."

Beside him, Debbie laughed and blushed and Donnie couldn't help a chuckle. Unlike most sci-fi/fantasy enthusiasts, Mark Finley was not an introvert and could be absolutely gregarious. "She's got brains and can cook, too," Donnie said, trying to play along.

"A Renaissance lady," Mark said, nodding. "Can she swing a sword?"

"Oh, we haven't really gotten to that point yet," Donnie said.

"'Stab them with the pointy end'," Debbie said, quoting Arya Stark from *Game of Thrones*. "I learned that much."

"She's a keeper, Donnie," Mark said. "But it's colder than the plains of Hoth out here, so let's transfer some books and some cash."

They went to the trunk of Mark's car, where four sturdy bank boxes were nestled in the deep well. "This one here is all fantasy," Mark said, pulling the lid off one box. "Those Kane books are in here. There's also a full set of the Ace Conan books. I haven't seen a full set for a while. There's lots of good stuff." He put the lid on the box and tapped another without opening it. "We got science fiction in here. Now, this lady that was running the garage sale where I got the Kane and Conan books. She was a widow, see? Her husband was the reader and had all these books. So, in here there's a full set of Burroughs' Tarzan books in a set published in the '50s, and all the John Carter books."

"The full sets? From the 1950s?" Donnie asked.

"Yeah, man. Good stuff," Mark said. He moved his hand to the next box.

"You guys sound like you're making a drug deal," Debbie joked. "'Good stuff, man'." She laughed and Donnie grinned, but Mark didn't share the humor.

"I'll take good books over drugs any day," he said. "Books don't make orphans."

"I'm so sorry," Debbie said, her eyes wide and a hand over her mouth. "I didn't mean anything. I was just trying to make a joke."

Donnie put an arm around her waist and gave her a reassuring hug. Mark waved it away. "It's cool. This next box is romance novels, but they're mostly pretty old, I guess. And the last one is horror and western novels and a few of the classics. Charles Dickens, Theodore Dreisser, and some other dead white guys. All the boxes are full. You can check them."

Donnie smiled. "You've never shorted me, Mark. You're a good man to do business with. Did you find anything you decided to keep? Just curious."

Mark's smile could have lit up the small city of Alva. "You won't believe it if I tell you."

Intrigued, Donnie urged him on. "Tell me."

"It's from 1965," Mark said. "Take a guess."

Donnie couldn't guess. "Tell me more."

"Printed illegally. In a fucking slipcase and – " He cut himself off and turned to Debbie. "I'm sorry about that. My mouth got away from me."

Debbie laughed. "It's fine."

"Illegally printed in the '60s?" Donnie asked. "You've got to be kidding me."

"Say it, man," Mark coaxed.

"The Ace Books *Lord of the Rings*?" Donnie asked.

"Right there on a table in a garage sale in Arkansas City, Kansas, with a piece of masking tape on them saying the little old lady wanted two dollars for it," Mark gushed.

"Two dollars?" Donnie said. "You robbed her."

Mark cocked his head and looked up at the taller man. "I'm not a thief," he said. "I explained to her that they were worth more than she was asking for and I gave her twenty dollars for them."

Donnie shook his head. "You still got a helluva deal." He paused and then asked, "Any chance you have them? I've never even seen that set."

"I knew you'd ask," Mark said and tapped Donnie's chest. He went to the back seat of his immense car and came back with a medium-sized brown cardboard box. He opened it and Donnie saw the black cardboard slipcase holding the three volumes, one orange, one yellow, and one sky blue. Printed on the sides of the slipcover in gold were images of Sauron's eye and the ring of power. The boxed set of books were held in a nest of plastic bubble wrap.

"Wow," Donnie breathed. "You sure you wouldn't take another forty just for those? Double your money."

"No, sir," Mark said, closing the lid on the box. "These will stay in my private collection until I die." Mark put the box back in his car and closed the door. "Now let's get your merchandise moved to your truck so I can go on to Woodward."

Together, the three of them moved the four bank boxes to the bed of Donnie's truck, then Donnie counted out the money for Mark and handed it over. "Sixty for the Hobbits?" he asked.

"No way," he said. "I might trade them for the authentic captain's chair from the *Star Trek* original series."

"Yeah, well, I don't exactly have that," Donnie said. They shook hands and Mark got into his car, gave a final wave, and drove away as Debbie pushed herself into Donnie's side. Instinctively, he put an arm around her, realized what he'd done and tensed, then relaxed. It felt good.

"Are you ready to eat?" he asked her.

"You're forgetting something," she said.

He turned his head and kissed her on the forehead. She smiled and snuggled closer as the wind whipped around them, bringing a few more swirling snowflakes.

"That was nice, but not what you're forgetting," she said. "Do I need to call Josey?"

"Air fryer," Donnie said, and they both laughed.

Chapter Eighteen

Based on a search of local restaurants via their smartphones, they chose a place called The Bull Smokehouse and Saloon, and drove to it with Josey's new air fryer secured in the truck's back seat. It was a little early for dinner and the place wasn't too crowded yet. The walls were covered in classic beer signs and there was a long bar where a few people sat and ate. The middle of the place held a couple of pool tables shielded by low walls, with some booths on the other side. Donnie requested a booth, and a perky young brunette with a very long ponytail took them to their table and left them with menus.

"Sure puts Annie's to shame," Debbie said.

Donnie looked around, then shrugged. "It's a different kind of place. Annie's has its charms. Small, everyone knows everyone, good food that's cheap, and a pretty waitress." He winked at her.

"Look at Mr. Hermit learning how to flirt," Debbie grinned, then turned to her menu.

A waitress with curly red hair and a freckled nose came and asked if they were ready to order. They both ordered steaks, Debbie with hers medium rare while Donnie went with medium well, with baked potatoes and salads.

"You might as well have ordered shoe leather," Debbie teased when the waitress had left.

"And you might as well wait until the drive home and go take a bite from a steer in a pasture," Donnie said.

Debbie stuck out her tongue, then said, "It was pretty cute, listening to you talk to your nerd friend today. Almost like another language or something. Like, I don't know, some kind of tribe that has books instead of golden idols."

"I can't believe he got that set of Tolkien books," Donnie said, shaking his head and adjusting his silverware by tiny increments. "And did you see the condition? Near mint, at least."

"Oooga booga," Debbie said, grinning at him. "When I read a paperback book, I bend it up all kinds of ways and fold down pages and leave it face down on the table."

Donnie looked at her very seriously and said in a flat, even voice. "Ma'am, this relationship is over. I hope you find your way home." He made as if to leave the table, but the shocked look and hanging mouth of Debbie made him stop. He settled back into his seat. "I'm joking," he said quickly.

"I don't know," she said. "Not after the way you and Mark carried on."

"You do whatever you like with your books. God will deal with you," Donnie joked.

She laughed at him. "Did you bend down pages when you were a kid?"

"Nope. But, I guess I was always very careful with my stuff. Most of it," he said. "You know, somewhere, I still have my old electronic football game. The one where the players are just red dots on a little screen? From the late '70s."

"I remember the ones that were big metal fields that vibrated and the players moved because of the vibrations," Debbie said.

Donnie nodded. "I have one of those, too. I got it after Super Bowl Twelve, so it came with the Dallas Cowboys and the Denver Broncos, and Santa included the AFC Central teams."

"That was nice of him," Debbie said, grinning.

Their salads were brought to the table. As she was pouring the little cup of ranch dressing over her salad, Debbie said, "You said you took care of most of your stuff. I think there's a story there."

"Oh, as I was saying, I took care of my stuff, I just flashed back to my white Winchester rifle I wanted so bad one Christmas," he said wistfully. "I got it, and it was so cool. Lever action. Shot caps, of course. Me and a friend were playing cowboys and Indians in front yards when his older brother jumped into the game and got the drop on me. He told me to drop my gun or he'd shoot. Something possessed me to toss my new toy rifle all the way across the yard to him, where it hit the ground and the hollow stock broke. I was really upset, but I knew there was no one to blame but me."

Debbie chewed, nodding, and swallowed. "I cut Baby Alive's hair off," she confessed. "She ate and pooped her diaper like a real baby, so I was just sure her hair would grow back. It didn't, though. My mom whipped my butt for that. Did you get in trouble over your gun?"

"No. Dad just told me I shouldn't have thrown it," Donnie said. He pushed a cherry tomato around in his salad. "I should call him, make sure he got back okay."

"No," Debbie said. "He's fine. You would have heard if something went wrong."

"I wonder how Josey will get home," he said.

"That's right, she doesn't have a car," Debbie said. "She coulda taken mine. Oh, I wish I'd thought of that."

"I'll text her and ask."

"No," Debbie said. "You'll ask about your dad. Josey is a smart girl and she'll figure it out."

Donnie sighed, but he smiled. "You're kind of bossy. Not quite Josey level, but close."

"You need it," she said.

Their meals came and they focused on eating for a while. The steaks were good, cooked just as they'd asked, and Donnie found himself secretly watching how Debbie cut and chewed her food. She really did have a pretty mouth, and her eyes were dark and soft in the restaurant light.

"Your ex-wife is getting married," Debbie said at last. "How do you really feel about that?"

Donnie chewed, wondering if he was being set up for a trap. In the old days, if Melissa had asked him about some other woman, it was always a trap. Debbie's face was open and innocent. He answered her honestly. "I did her wrong. I'm glad she's found someone and I hope he treats her better than I did."

"You're takin' all the blame," Debbie said.

Donnie shrugged.

"It takes two to tango, mister," she said.

"Yeah, but I let somebody else into the dance," he said.

"Be honest with me, Donnie," Debbie said, her voice serious and all trace of her usual smile gone. "Do you still feel anything for her?"

Donnie smiled, but it was a sad smile. He had asked himself this same question many times over the years. "She's more like an old friend that I've lost touch with," he said. "She's the mother of my children, so for that, I do still have some affection. Is it love? Not a romantic love, but ... I still care about her and want the best for her."

"If she called you and asked you to come home, would you?"

Donnie shook his head. "That isn't my home anymore," he said. "She'll never do that, but if she did, I wouldn't go. That relationship is in the past." He put a forkful of baked potato in his mouth, but didn't really taste it as he chewed.

"I don't hafta worry about you leaving me to go back to her?" Debbie asked.

The grin spread slowly across Donnie's face. "Is that what you were worried about?"

Debbie shrugged. "I guess a girl has to think about things like that. It wouldn't be the first time I was thrown away for a toxic ex." She took a drink of her tea but kept her eyes on him.

"You don't have to worry about that," he promised. "Even if she wasn't getting married. We hardly ever talk. I call to ask about the kids because they don't really tell me anything."

They ate for a while, then Donnie remembered their early conversation. "My dad," he began. "He thinks he was a bad father when I was growing up because he went to work, then came home and either worked in his shop or watched TV, then went to bed most days. He says he regrets not spending more time with me and my sisters."

Debbie looked at him, clearly wondering where this conversation came from and where it was going. "I guess that's pretty common," she said.

"He wasn't a bad father, of course," Donnie said. "There might have been times I wished he was more involved, but he was there for the big stuff. But he thinks he was a bad father. That's probably one of the reasons he made me bring him up here, so he could fix all that, at least in his mind." He took another bite of steak and watched Debbie chew and study him.

"I can feel that you're workin' up to something," she said.

"Perception," Donnie said. "His perception is that he was a bad father. It isn't true, but he believes it, so he's acting like it is true."

"Okay," she said.

"I know this woman who thinks she's only a waitress and can't be anything more," Donnie said.

178

Debbie laughed loud enough that a few other people looked over at them. "You were building up to *that*?" she asked.

"It's perception," Donnie said. "Dad believes he was bad, so he's acting on that. You believe you're only a waitress and so you act on that. But you can be whatever you want to be. Tell me what you wanted to be when you grew up."

"Nah, it's dumb," Debbie said, and she ducked her head to face her plate and put more steak in her mouth.

"I bet it was a veterinarian," he said.

She looked up, her cheek bulging with meat that she wasn't chewing. "How'd you know?" she asked around the food.

"Most girls want that at some point," he said. "Or teacher or nurse. It's kind of funny how girls gravitate toward fields where they help others. Natural nurturers."

"Are you bein' sexist?" she asked.

"I don't think so," Donnie said. "Anyway, it's never too late. A lot of people go to school when they're ... " He stopped, knowing the next word was dangerous with women.

"When they're what, Mr. Writer-man?" Debbie asked, smiling again.

"You know, when they're non-traditional students," he offered.

"You mean old," she said. "You're callin' me old."

"I'm just saying you're not right out of high school," he said defensively. "And you're off topic. I'm saying you could go to school. I hear most colleges have online classes now. You wouldn't even have to leave Sagebrush."

"Maybe I wanna leave and go live in a dorm," she argued.

Donnie thought about the words that almost popped out of his mouth, wondering if he meant them, then decided he did. "I would rather you stayed," he said.

The smile was different this time. It spread slower and lit up her face, even her eyes. She reached across the table for his hand and he took hers. "Donnie Nelson, are you sayin' you kinda like me?"

"Kinda," he said, and squeezed her hand. "Kinda a lot, really."

She held his gaze for a while, then said, "I'll think about school, but I just don't know. It's been a long time since I was in the classroom, and I don't really feel like bein' a veterinarian anymore. I just want a nest egg for when I'm too old to wait tables."

"I understand," he said. "But don't you ever think you're just a waitress. You're a lot more than that."

"Should we talk about your perception of you?" she asked.

Donnie laughed and released her hand when she gently pulled away to finish her dinner. "I don't think that's necessary. Josey, and especially Dad, have been going over that."

"What's Josey's perception of herself?" Debbie asked.

Donnie shook his head. "I don't know," he said. "There's a lot about her I don't know. Everyone loved her grandmother. From what I gather, Josey's mom, Mrs. Wilder's daughter, was a drug addict and that led to her death. Josey, I think, lives in both those shadows. That could be why she works so hard."

"To show she's her own person?" Debbie asked.

"Yeah." Donnie nodded. "Yeah. To show she can stand on her own. She's not her mom and can be as valuable as everyone saw her grandmother." He thought about that, comparing his theory to Josey's relentless activity at the store and even in the house, where she was always cleaning or arranging something.

"You like her quite a bit," Debbie said.

"I do," Donnie said as he sipped sweet tea.

They finished their meal and Donnie paid the check. The sun had set and the wind was blowing. Above them, the clouds were tattered and drifting away, showing flecks of starlight and a tiny crescent of moon. The lights of the parking lot and surrounding buildings and street lights seemed somehow muted and soft as Donnie and Debbie walked toward his pickup holding hands.

"How about you let me drive back?" Debbie asked.

"Why?" Donnie asked.

"'Cause I want to," she said. "I might have a surprise for my city-boy boyfriend."

"Oh yeah?" Donnie asked as he handed over the keys.

About halfway between Alva and Sagebrush, Debbie slowed the truck and turned onto a county line road that was only dirt. When Donnie asked where she was taking them, she told him to be quiet and enjoy the ride. There was nothing but plowed fields and stretched barbed wire on either side of them. Soon, the highway was out of sight behind them, but Debbie kept driving until she came to a turnoff for an oil pump.

"There didn't use to be a gate here," she said as she parked the truck in front of a long metal gate. The pump jack inside the fenced area was still and quiet beside a faded white tank. Debbie killed the truck's engine and after a moment, the headlights went out and the pump and tank were only darker shapes in the dark night. "Get that blanket off your back seat," Debbie ordered, then threw open her door, hopped out of the truck, and left Donnie sitting there.

He looked to the truck's back seat where there was a faded dark blue quilt he kept just in case he was ever stranded in the cold. It was folded and tucked under the end of the seat. With some effort, he reached it and pulled it to himself, holding it against his chest as he got out of the truck.

Debbie had the tailgate down and was shoving aside the boxes of books as Donnie came around to her. Realizing what she had in mind, he grinned and asked, "Isn't it a little cold for stargazing?"

"Nope," she said. "Help me make room in the middle."

Together, they moved the boxes to the sides of the truck's bed. Debbie took the blanket and spread it out. "We're gonna lay on half of it and cover up with the other half," she said. Then she lay down in the bed of the truck, looking up at him expectantly.

Donnie looked around them. There was nothing to see. Darkness. Plowed fields. A couple of leafless trees within the closure with the pump jack. There were no lights from cars or houses anywhere to be seen.

"Come on," she urged.

Donnie lay beside her and she pulled the blanket over them and cuddled close against him as he put an arm under her head.

"What do you see?" she asked.

Donnie looked up. The sky was clear now and filled with stars. More stars than he could ever remember seeing. They twinkled and shimmered above him like glitter spilled on black felt. "There are so many," he said in a whisper, as if he were in church.

"Certain times of the year, you can see the Milky Way out here," Debbie said.

"Your high school boyfriends brought you here?" Donnie asked.

"No." Her hand rested on his chest, her finger making circles there. "I've never brought nobody here. I found it a while after I got my driver's license. I had a fight with my mom and went drivin'. It was dark. I just turned off the highway and drove until I found this place. I pulled in right next to that oil pump. It was pumpin' that night. It was summer. I lay on the hood of my car, a big old Cutlass. I was in shorts and a halter top and the metal was warm and there was the sound of the pump, kinda like a giant heartbeat, ya know? And all those stars. I cried, and then I fell asleep for a while. After that, I always thought of this as my own special place. I used to come here a lot, and after I moved back, I started comin' here again."

"It's beautiful," Donnie said.

"I used to think out here there wasn't nothin' between me and God except the stars, and they were just like chips of broken glass," she said. "It's peaceful."

"It is," he agreed, and it was perfectly natural when he turned his head and kissed her forehead.

"You know, girls love forehead kisses," she said.

"I didn't know that," Donnie said, and he kissed her again.

She giggled, snuggled closer, and her hand moved down his chest to find the fly of his jeans.

"Isn't God watching?" Donnie asked as he felt his body responding.

"I hope so," she whispered.

Chapter Nineteen

Within two hours of Josey putting the Karl Edward Wagner books into the store's online database, they were purchased through the Alibris website. That one sale more than paid for what Donnie had given Mark for the boxes of books. He couldn't help but smile as he packaged the books in preparation for mailing them. The old Steinbeck novel Josey had discovered had also sold for a handsome price. Sales numbers and income for November were the best they'd ever been and Donnie knew who he had to thank for that. On his own, that Steinbeck might have languished under the *Readers Digest* books for years, and might have eventually been thrown out. The Wagner books would have gathered dust while he continued to sit by the window with an open laptop and a heart full of despair.

Donnie finished labeling the package and set it aside to return to his seat to finish the chapter he was working on. The writing was going well. He had added nearly fifty pages since he e-mailed the first set to his agent. So far, he had not heard back from Gene, but he knew the gears of publishing were incredibly slow, and as they neared the holidays, those gears would move even slower.

Outside, the world was gray. Thin clouds hung low and, at just after four in the afternoon, it was already getting dark. The wind, as always, blasted down the street, sending dust, old Styrofoam cups, scraps of paper, bits of straw, and other trash tumbling before it. Annie's Cafe across the street was lit up and invitingly warm looking, but Donnie knew Debbie's shift had already ended.

Donnie put his hands on the keyboard, took a breath, and the words flowed from his fingertips into the lettered keys and onto the harsh white screen. Within a couple of minutes, he was in the zone and the words came quickly, faster than he could actually think them in his mind, almost as if someone else was using him to tell the story. It had been years since he'd experienced writing like this and he relished it.

A tinkling noise broke through to him and he was aware it had been going on for a while. He turned his head to find Josey sitting cross-legged on the store's floor, running her hands in circles through the thick winter fur of Jasper's throat, making his rabies and ID tags jingle like little bells. The dog had his head lifted, his eyes blissfully closed, and his tail swished back and forth happily as Josey told him he was the best doggy-woggy to ever work in a bookstore. Donnie couldn't help but grin.

"He's a lazy old mutt," Donnie teased. "He hasn't sold a book in weeks."

A light went on in Josey's eyes as she looked back at him. "We need to put pictures of Jasper in the pet section with captions about some of the books," she said.

Donnie laughed. "Why not?" he agreed.

"I'll take some pictures of him at home on Thanksgiving," Josey said.

"Are you all ready for that?" Donnie asked. The big feast day was only two days away now. There had been multiple calls between Josey and Debbie as they made plans, and Josey had gone to the grocery store more times than Donnie could count.

"I'm ready," she said, and gave him a big thumbs up that caused Jasper to look at her questioningly until she got both hands back into his neck fur.

Donnie returned to his writing, but after a few minutes he was interrupted by a familiar but seldom heard ringtone on his cell phone. He picked it up and stared at it for a minute before answering it. "LizBeth," he said. "How are you?"

"I'm good," his daughter answered. "How are you?"

"I'm doing okay," he said, then risked adding, "I miss you."

There was a long moment of silence, and then, "I miss you, too, Dad. I've been meaning to call. Well, I was gonna text, but I thought I should call, but ... I didn't know if you'd want to talk."

A lump formed in Donnie's throat. He couldn't remember the last time she had said that she missed him. His eyes stung and he knew there would be tears. Quietly, Josey got up and left the front of the store and he was grateful to her for the privacy. "I always want to talk to you, LizBeth," Donnie said. "Are you okay?"

"Yeah. It's just ... I think I was really hard on you," LizBeth said.

"It was a bad thing I did. I don't blame you," Donnie told her.

"Mom isn't the easiest person to live with. I kind of realize that now," she said.

"I'm sorry," Donnie said, not knowing what else to say. "Are you okay?"

"Yeah, I'm okay. You know she's getting married, right?"

"Yes," Donnie said. "Is he good to you?"

"He's okay. But Mom spends all her time with him now. She treats him different than she did you," LizBeth said. "She was never real affectionate with you, was she?"

"I've never bad-mouthed your mother to you or your brother," Donnie said. "I'm not going to now."

"I know you haven't, Dad. I've been thinking about that. Mom said you did what you did because you got too big for your britches. That's how she used to say it. It's different now. She says you had a mid-life crisis and that you just wanted some younger ... well, a younger woman. That wasn't it, though, was it?"

"No." Donnie couldn't get out more than a whisper. He licked his lips and swallowed and tried again. "No. That wasn't it."

"I think I understand more now," LizBeth said. "You were still wrong to cheat on her, though."

"I know."

"I wish you could be here for Thanksgiving," she said.

"I do, too," Donnie said.

"I don't think Brian and Mom are ready for that."

"What are you doing for the holiday?" Donnie asked.

"Mom's cooking. Alan and his kids are coming over," LizBeth said.

"Alan?" Donnie asked, then realized who it must be.

"Mom's fiancé," LizBeth confirmed.

"You don't like them?"

"They're okay," she said. "Are you coming back to Lawton anytime soon?"

"I hadn't planned on it, but if you want me to, I can come spend a day with you," Donnie said. "I'd like that."

"Me, too," she said. "What have you been doing?"

"Well, selling books. Business has picked up. And I'm writing again. I think I'm about halfway through a new book," he told her.

"Mom said you don't do that anymore."

"I haven't for a really long time. Some things have changed, though," Donnie said. "Did you know your grandpa lives with me now?"

"I thought he was in a nursing home," she said. Her voice was more relaxed now, not nervous and hesitant like it had been.

"He busted out," Donnie said, and allowed a little laugh. "I was in town for a funeral and he made me bring him home with me."

"You were here?" she said, and her voice gave away her hurt.

"I was," Donnie said. "I … I didn't think you wanted to see me, and then things got all crazy after the funeral. A reporter kind of chased me in the cemetery and then Dad was at my truck. If I had any idea you wanted to talk to me, I would have called you, picked you up, crawled to you."

"Don't be dramatic, Dad," she said. "But that's fair. I haven't been very nice to you. Who died?"

"My high school creative writing teacher," Donnie said.

"Oh, yeah," LizBeth said, and now her voice was excited. "Did you hear about her granddaughter?"

Donnie felt his heart begin to hammer in his chest. "No," he said, not trusting himself to say more. "What about her?"

"She disappeared after the funeral," LizBeth said.

"She did?" Donnie remembered his talk with his sister and Margaret saying she had not heard anything about Mrs. Wilder's granddaughter. "How do you know?"

"Duh. She went to school with me. She was in my English class," LizBeth said.

"Really?" Donnie said. He turned his head to make sure Josey wasn't close by. "I thought she was older."

"Nope. A junior," LizBeth said.

Donnie put a hand to his forehead and massaged just over his eyebrows. His mind screamed at him that Josey could only be sixteen, maybe seventeen years old. She was a runaway. "Are they looking for her?" he asked.

"That's what's so weird," LizBeth said. "She was a straight-A student, but the word is she dropped out after the funeral."

"What about the police? Amber alerts and all that?" Donnie asked.

"No, not that I've heard."

"Maybe she transferred. Went to live with other relatives," he suggested.

"Maybe." He could hear the shrug in her voice. She wanted to think there was a scandal. She wasn't wrong, he thought. "It's just weird."

"It is," Donnie agreed. He wanted more information, but wasn't sure how to ask for it and was worried about Josey catching him at it. "How's Brian?"

"He's a brat, like always," she said. "But he's okay."

"Do you really want me to come down?" Donnie asked.

"Yes. Please?"

"Okay. I could come Sunday. Would that work?"

"Yeah, Sunday is good," she said.

His computer screen had gone dark as he talked on the phone. Donnie looked through the gloom to the bank's sign and saw that it was nearly five o'clock. The post office would close soon. "I'll leave here Sunday morning and be there in time to take you to lunch. Then we'll do whatever you want and have dinner."

"Can we go to Chickasha and see the Christmas lights?" she asked.

"Anything you want," he promised, and he felt the fullness of his heart. His little girl wanted to be with him. The joy was indescribable.

"Thanks, Dad. And ... I'm sorry I've been such a brat," LizBeth said.

"We all needed time to heal," he said. "I love you."

His heart truly melted as she said, "I love you, too."

They said their good-byes and hung up. Donnie put his phone down and stared at the black screen, warring emotions filling his mind. LizBeth forgave him. She wanted to see him. Josey lied to him. She was underage, and he was keeping her. But nobody was looking for her.

"Josey," he called, but he knew he couldn't confront her about it. Not now. He had to think, had to process what was going on. The girl with blue and silver hair came bouncing in from the back room.

"That was your daughter?" she asked, smiling.

"Yep," he said. "She actually wants to spend time with me."

"That's great!" Josey's face lit up and her enthusiasm seemed genuine.

"She's a sweet girl," Donnie said. "Maybe you'll get to meet her. Or maybe you already know her. You lived in the same town and you can't be too far apart in age."

"I didn't know anybody with the last name Nelson," Josey said. "That would have stood out because of how crazy Grandma was about you. I think your daughter is younger than me."

Donnie nodded, but averted his eyes, focusing on the package to mail. She was really going to stand there and lie right to his face? What would she do if he brought LizBeth up to stay with them for a weekend?

"These books need to be mailed," he said. "Do you want to do it, or should I?"

"I'll do it," she said, her voice as bubbly as ever. "Mr. Blevins always flirts with me."

"He's a hundred years old," Donnie said, managing a small smile.

"He's cute and harmless," Josey said. "I'll go get my coat." She came back a moment later bundled in her coat, gloves, knit cap, and a scarf around her neck. She scooped up the box and took the store debit card from Donnie and went through the door. The wind blew her hair out behind her like some kind of mermaid flag as she went up the street toward the post office.

Donnie sat down. There was still the mystery of his dad's trip to Woodward. Josey refused to discuss it and Debbie had told him to just leave it alone, that if it was anything serious, Mike would tell them when he was ready. Whatever it was, it hadn't been discussed at the Sunday dinner after Mike went to Woodward and Donnie and Debbie to Alva. Donnie had sat at the table with his dad and the two women and listened to him tell stories of when Donnie was a boy building with Legos, Lincoln Logs, and a Fort Apache western set or green and yellow army men that he'd then shoot down with rubber bands. They watched football, played board games, and talked some more, but no trip to Woodward was ever mentioned.

And now Donnie knew that Josey was definitely keeping more secrets than just his father's. He wondered if his dad knew about her age. Could he ask him about that?

Donnie snatched up his phone and sent a text message to Debbie, asking if he could drop by for a little bit after he took Josey home. She said he could and that she would save him some dinner.

Satisfied that he had at least one person he could talk to, Donnie brought his laptop computer back to life, but his concentration was gone and writing was over for the day. He saved his work and shut it down.

Donnie went over to a shelf of books and pretended to line up the spines with the edge of the shelf, but he was really just thinking. When the door of the shop opened, he turned, expecting Josey, but instead found Omar Sanchez coming in and pushing the door closed behind him. Cold air swirled around the front of the shop. Jasper lumbered up from his nap and went to Omar, his long tail wagging happily. When the boy leaned over to pet the dog, Jasper pushed his flank into Omar's shins, his tail fanning the air while his brown eyes looked up adoringly at the boy.

"Hello, Omar," Donnie said. "How are you today?"

"I'm doing good, Mr. Nelson," the boy said, still rubbing on the dog while his dark eyes scanned the store.

"She's not here," Donnie said.

"Who?" Omar asked, his brown face taking on a red tinge.

Donnie laughed softly. "I was a teenager once, Omar. Josey will be back soon. She went to the post office."

Omar gave Jasper a final triple pat and straightened up. The dog stayed for a moment, tail slowing while he continued to look up, hoping for more attention, then he yawned and went back to curl up and resume his nap. "She's so pretty," Omar said.

And closer to your age than I thought, Donnie almost said, but didn't. "She is that," he agreed. "Did you come in just to see her?"

"I wanted to ask you a question, Mr. Nelson, and I hope you'll be honest with me," he said.

Intrigued, Donnie turned away from the shelf and gave the boy his full attention. "What is it?" He fully expected the boy to ask him for more dating advice.

"You wrote that book, *Bolkar, the Death Merchant*, didn't you?" Omar asked, his voice almost accusing.

Donnie had forgotten about Omar buying that used book along with a couple of Conan books last month. "Why do you think that?" he asked, stalling.

"In the back of the book, it talks about the author," Omar said. "It says he lives in Oklahoma with his wife and two kids. I looked up Donald L. Nelson on the internet and found pictures of you. You're signing copies of the book and talking at conventions. And there are other books in the series. I saw the covers."

Donnie sighed. Omar's tone was disappointed and accusatory, but also hopeful. He saw Josey on the sidewalk outside a moment before she pushed her way into the store. Omar turned and Donnie saw him stand a little straighter and puff out his chest.

"He's a famous author," Omar said to the red-cheeked girl. "He's been here all this time and nobody knew."

Josey stopped in her tracks, looking from Omar to Donnie, then a grin spread across her face. "I knew," she said.

"You're his niece. Of course you knew," Omar said.

"Listen, Omar," Donnie began, and the boy turned back to him. "When you bought that book, I was having a writer's block that had lasted for about eight years. I didn't think I would ever write again. I thought that part of my life, like living with my wife and kids, was over. So I didn't admit it was me."

"Why would you hide that?" he asked. "That was one of the best books I've ever read. And you know I read a lot."

Donnie smiled and nodded. "I know you do. And thank you."

"Do you have the other books in the series?" he asked.

Donnie hesitated. He sighed again and looked up at the ceiling as if hoping for divine intervention, then faced his new fan. "Not here. I have some new copies in a box at home."

Omar's face showed his confusion. "Don't you live here?" he asked.

Josey laughed, then covered her mouth and looked away.

"Not anymore," Donnie said. "I rented a house with my dad and my ... niece. I'll bring you some books and you can pick them up after the holiday."

"Will you autograph them? And the one I already have?" He unslung the dark blue backpack from his shoulders and ripped open the zipper before Donnie could say anything. His hand darted in and came out with the battered paperback. He held it out like an offering to a god.

Something deep in Donnie's mind shrank away from the book. He heard a voice say, *It's starting again. The adoring fans. Pretty soon you'll be in bed with some pretty little girl young enough to be your daughter.* Donnie tried to silence the voice, to push it back, to tell it that this time would be different because he is a different man now.

"Please?" Omar asked.

Donnie took the book, hoping Omar didn't notice that his hand trembled a little. He went over to the counter and found a black ink pen, then opened the book's front cover and began writing on the title page. *"To Detective Omar, You found me. Your friend, Donald L. Nelson."*

"He's writing a new book," Josey said. She and Omar had also drifted to the counter and stood leaning on it from the other side.

"About Bolkar?" Omar asked incredulously.

"Yeah. He got a girlfriend and it inspired him," she said.

"You have a girlfriend, Mr. Nelson?" Omar asked, wide-eyed and again looking at Donnie as if he'd just come down from Heaven. "Who is she?"

"It's Debbie," Josey said. "The waitress across the street."

"I want a girlfriend," Omar said, and then remembered he was talking to Josey and his face burned with embarrassment, but she pretended not to notice.

"Donnie has an agent in New York who's going to sell his new book for a ton of money and he'll be famous again," Josey said.

"I don't know about any of that," Donnie said. He pulled his eyes off his signature in the book. It had been so long since he'd signed his author name. It looked like alien writing to him. He closed the book and pushed it toward Omar.

"Can I tell my friends?" Omar asked.

"Let's keep it our secret," Donnie said. "At least for a while. See if the new book finds a publisher."

Omar looked at him for a moment as if he wanted to say something else, but then he said, "Okay, Mr. Nelson. What's it about? The new book?"

"You'll have to wait and see," Donnie said.

"I can't believe I know a famous author," he said to Josey.

"It's exciting, isn't it?" she said, playing along.

"Don't forget to lock up the debit card and file the post office receipt," Donnie said to Josey. "Taxes, ya know."

"I know," Josey said. "We can scan all of those, too. Save all your tax records, record the amount and category and all that. I think you have to pay for the app to do it."

"Maybe next year," Donnie said. He sat down in his chair and lifted the screen of his laptop.

"Is that the computer you're writing the book on?" Omar asked breathlessly.

"Yes," Donnie answered, and had to make a real effort not to be short with the kid. "It does all kinds of stuff."

"I should go, Mr. Nelson," Omar said. "I have band practice tonight." He paused, then turned to Josey. "I'm in a band. I play guitar and sing."

Donnie pretended to be deep in thought and pressed a hand to his lower face to hide his grin. He remembered telling Omar that girls loved musicians.

"That's really cool," Josey said. "What kind of music do you play?"

"Mostly blues and Mexican music and some country," he said.

"Cool," Josey said, nodding and smiling.

"You could come listen to us practice sometime. If you want to," Omar added.

"I might do that," Josey said. "But today, I have work to do around here." She pulled off her knit cap and gloves as if to emphasize she needed to get busy.

"Okay. Well, it was nice talking to you. Bye, Mr. Nelson," he said.

Donnie and Josey watched him leave the store, pull up the collar of his jacket, and make his way up the sidewalk.

"Somebody has a fan," Josey said.

"And somebody has an admirer," Donnie returned.

"He's a cute kid," Josey said.

Donnie almost literally bit his tongue to hold back his response. "When we close, I'm going to take you home, then go by Debbie's for a little while," he said.

Josey gave him a knowing look and grinned. "Need a little wow-chicky-wow-wow in the middle of the week?" she asked.

Donnie groaned and shook his head. "If your grandmother could hear you now."

Josey just laughed. "It's about time," she said. "I'll go turn off the heater in the back and straighten up a little bit. I'll be ready when you are." She patted her leg for Jasper to follow her and went off toward the back of the store, chatting at the happy dog.

Donnie checked the store email one more time to make sure there were no new orders, then powered off the laptop and folded it up to take home with him. He locked the front doors and turned off the lights and made his way to the back to put on his coat.

With Josey, the dog, and the laptop safely deposited at home with his father, who sat in a recliner watching one of those shows where judges look for talent, Donnie set off for Debbie's trailer. She was watching the same show and offered him a hamburger and chips on a plate, with a glass of sweet iced tea. Donnie sat on the sofa and ate while she watched the show.

"My dad is watching this," he said between bites.

"It's so good," Debbie said.

Donnie didn't say anything, just took another bite. He had never been a fan of pop music and that's what the show seemed focused on. Why couldn't they bring on aspiring bands? Find the new Rolling Stones or AC/DC. He kept that to himself, though.

"Something's on your mind," Debbie said during a commercial break.

"Yeah," Donnie agreed. "But it'll wait until your show's over and I'm done eating. This burger is great."

She chuckled. "I'm not a bad cook. You just wait 'til me and Josey team up on Thursday. We'll cook your socks right off."

The show came back on. People hit big buttons. Confetti flew. A young woman on stage cried and hyperventilated. Credits rolled. Debbie turned off the television as Donnie chewed the last bite and turned to sit cross-legged and facing him on the sofa. She fixed him with her soft brown eyes and waited for him to swallow. When he plucked another barbecue chip from the plate, she took the plate away from him and put it on the coffee table and took his hands in hers.

"What's up?" she asked.

Donnie swallowed. He considered how to say it. To tell the whole story about LizBeth calling, how they really talked, how she wanted to see him, and then getting to Josey. Debbie would want to know all that. But he could have told her that over the phone, or on Thursday. He squeezed her hands in his. "Josey is lying to me," he said. "She's probably only sixteen."

Debbie was quiet. She blinked a few times, studying his face, her hands steady in his. "She's so mature. Yeah, she's got the energy of a kid, but she's so ... mature."

"Maybe being raised by an elderly grandmother makes her act that way," Donnie said. "I don't know. But she's been missing from one of my daughter's classes at Lawton High School since the funeral."

Debbie's head tilted a little, like a curious puppy. "You talked to your daughter?"

"Yeah."

She let go of his hands and scooted over next to him, snuggling against him, putting one of her arms under his and hugging it against her. She was warm and soft and smelled like heaven and for a moment Donnie just wanted to hold on to her and cry because life didn't make any sense.

"Dad is keeping secrets and Josey is lying to me," he said quietly through a lump in his throat. "Everything was going so good, and now it's like it was all built on sand and the tide is going to wash it away."

"That's pretty dramatic," Debbie said, unknowingly echoing LizBeth. "I want you to tell me about this conversation with LizBeth. Tell me everything, just like she said it to you."

Donnie took a deep breath, then began to recount the conversation. "After, I even asked Josey if she knew LizBeth and she told me no. I thought about confronting her right then and there, but ... I just don't know if I can handle it."

"I'm glad you didn't," Debbie said. "She's a smart girl. She's gotta have her reasons for doin' this."

"Debbie, I'm harboring a runaway. A minor runaway. A female minor runaway," Donnie said. "Do you know how bad that'll be when somebody finds out?"

"You said there ain't nobody lookin' for her," Debbie argued. "Why is that?"

"I don't know," he admitted.

"And she got that money to help get y'all's house from somewhere," Debbie went on. "She didn't bring it with her, so she had to call somebody to get it."

"You're right," he agreed. He rested his cheek on the top of her head and she hugged his arm tighter. "Sherry Brown probably knows. I could ask her."

"Nuh-uh," Debbie said. "You can't invade that girl's privacy like that."

"But if the police – "

"The police ain't lookin' for her," Debbie said. "If there was some kinda Amber alert on her or she was reported missing, Duwayne would have already come and got her. Everybody in town knows about her and she stands out with the blue-and-silver hair."

Donnie was quiet. Duwayne Keller was the police chief of Sagebrush. It was a small force, with just the chief and one officer named Alejandro Banuelos and an elderly woman named Betty Duvall as dispatcher and secretary. Still, Donnie reasoned, if there had been a missing persons report made, they would have seen it. They would have come, like Debbie said.

"I guess you're right," Donnie said at last.

"I usually am," she said, her breath warm against his arm.

"Why would she lie to me?"

"She's a smart girl. I've never met a girl her age so smart. I'm sure she's got a good reason for it," Debbie said.

"Did she think I'd never find out?" he asked. "What am I going to tell LizBeth?"

"You didn't tell her Josey was here?" Debbie asked.

"No. I just ... It didn't seem right," he fumbled for the words.

"Like you're cheatin' on your daughter?" Debbie asked.

"Oh God," Donnie whispered. "That's exactly what it felt like."

"You're gonna see LizBeth on Sunday, right?"

"Yes," Donnie said.

"Are you gonna tell her then?"

"I don't know. Should I?" he asked.

Debbie was quiet for a little while. "Do you trust your daughter?"

Donnie almost immediately answered in the affirmative, then stopped. "I barely know her anymore," he admitted.

"It's a sticky situation," Debbie agreed. "If you tell her, she might get mad you didn't tell her when y'all talked on the phone. She might get mad that a girl her age is livin' with you. She might tell people and that might get stuff stirred up that ain't gettin' stirred right now. If you don't tell her now, it'll just be worse if she finds out later on." Debbie paused and kissed his shoulder as she thought. "If you tell her now and explain the situation and ask her not to tell, then she knows and you have a shared secret. But you gotta be able to trust her."

"This is what I mean about the tide coming in and washing everything away," Donnie said. "There's no right way."

"Go see LizBeth on Sunday," Debbie said. "Trust your gut. Tell her if it feels right. You'll know."

Donnie sat quietly, thinking about his past. "I have a history of making the wrong decisions," he said softly.

"You've been makin' pretty good decisions here lately," Debbie corrected.

"Should I talk to Chief Keller, just to be sure everything is okay?" Donnie asked.

"No," Debbie answered. "You don't stir things up. And you don't harass Josey about it, either."

"She's only sixteen. Maybe seventeen," Donnie argued. "She should at least be going to school."

"You gotta point there," Debbie said. "She's old enough to drop out, if that's what she wants to do."

"No," Donnie said emphatically, then stopped himself.

Debbie giggled. "You already think of her as another daughter," she said. "Look at you gettin' all Papa Bear about her droppin' out."

"It's so complicated," Donnie said, and he knew full well his voice sounded like a whine.

"Life ain't easy," Debbie agreed.

"I lied to Melissa for a long time," Donnie said quietly. "I had her thinking she was going crazy. Now two of the people closest to me are lying and hiding things. I guess karma is real."

"Baby, you can't be so negative," Debbie said, nestling her face into his bicep. "It ain't all about you. Mike and Josey are livin' their lives the best they know how. For right now, they're just overlappin' with yours."

Donnie smiled, and the smile widened until, finally, he laughed. He put his arm around Debbie's shoulders and pulled her closer. He kissed her forehead, then pressed his own against hers and stared into her brown eyes. "That was the wisest bit of southern-fried country philosophy I've ever heard," he told her.

"I think yer makin' fun of me, mister," she said back.

Donnie started to laugh, but it died in his throat. He stared into her eyes and she stared back at him. They were both quiet. Words came, slow and halting. "You make me feel so good," Donnie said. "You make me feel ... like I matter."

"Of course you matter," she said.

"I haven't felt like I matter in a long time," he said. "I ... I promise I'll never lie to you or hurt you. I'll always be honest with you."

Tears formed in the corners of Debbie's eyes, but they had their arms around each other and there was nothing she could do about it. One of them broke free and slid down her cheek. "I promise the same," she said. "I'll never lie to or hurt you."

"I've been scared of falling for you. Of falling for the first person who was nice to me," Donnie said. "But ... I have. I've fallen for you. Completely. And I'm scared of that. I'm scared I can't be good enough because I wasn't before."

"We've all made mistakes and done stuff we wish we could take back," Debbie said. More tears were coming and running down her cheeks and Donnie could feel his own eyes watering.

Donnie took a deep, shaky breath and held it for a moment. "I love you," he said as the breath whispered out of his lungs.

Debbie's lip was quivering. "You're a good man, Donnie Nelson. A good man. Better'n I deserve," she said. "I love you, too."

Donnie pulled her closer and they hugged desperately, clinging to each other, both sobbing softly onto the other's shoulder. It went on for several minutes before Donnie relaxed his hold and they sat up straight and looked at each other. They both wiped their eyes.

"That has to be the saddest first admission of love in the history of love," he said, trying to joke.

"It was like right out of a Hallmark Christmas movie," she agreed. They laughed. Debbie asked, "Are you staying the night?"

Donnie considered, then shook his head. "Not tonight. I should go home. Josey thinks I came over for some mid-week sex. Or, as she put it, some 'wow-chicky-wow-wow'."

Debbie laughed. "Well, that is available if you want it."

"I want it," Donnie admitted. "Mostly, I want to hold you against me all night and breathe the smell of your hair and skin and feel your heart beating. But I've hardly talked to Dad the past couple of days and I didn't tell them I'd be staying. I should go home before he goes to bed."

"I understand," she said.

"Maybe Thursday, after the feast?" he suggested. "Or you could stay at my place."

"And have Mike and Josey hear your sex noises and tease me about it? I don't think so," she said in pretend horror.

Donnie laughed and kissed her and she kissed him back, pushing her warm, probing tongue into his mouth and for a moment his resolve faded and he reconsidered staying. She broke the kiss off and pushed him away.

"Go home," she said. "I've got a toy I can pretend is you. Again."

"What?" Donnie asked, startled.

She laughed at him. "Maybe I'll send you a video."

Donnie sat and blinked at her. She laughed again and got up from the sofa, taking his empty plate and glass to the kitchen, then coming back with his coat.

"Go home," she said. "Tell Mike and Josey I said hi and I'll see them on Thursday."

"Yes, ma'am," Donnie said, and got up and put on his coat. She followed him to the front porch, where she wrapped her arms over her chest and shivered in the biting night wind. Donnie pulled her to him, holding her tight, and kissed her warmly. "I love you," he whispered into her ear after the kiss.

"I love you, too," she said, and nipped at his ear. He swatted her bottom and she laughed. "Don't get fresh. I don't need to be the scandal of the trailer park," she told him.

"Go inside and stay warm," he said and kissed her one more time before she turned and went inside. She watched from the closed storm door as he got into his truck and backed away. They waved one final time, and he drove toward home.

Josey was sitting alone on the couch with a giant bowl of popcorn and a can of Dr Pepper, watching a horror movie when he came into the house. He took off his coat and sat on the couch with her.

"You don't smell like sex," she said.

"My gosh, what kind of greeting is that?" Donnie asked.

She threw a piece of popcorn at him, then returned her attention to the screen. "You smell like her perfume, though."

He didn't have a response for that. "Where's Dad?"

"He went to bed about a half hour ago," Josey said.

"He's been going to bed so early," Donnie said. "Is he okay?"

"Yeah. He said it getting dark so early makes him tired," she said, then ate several pieces of the popcorn. Jasper appeared and lapped up the fallen piece of popcorn, sniffed toward Josey, then returned to his dog bed when no more popcorn was offered.

"I was hoping to talk to him," Donnie said.

"There's always tomorrow," Josey said. "Want some popcorn?" She offered him the bowl. Donnie took a handful and started eating one piece at a time, watching the television.

"What is this?" he asked.

"I don't remember the name of it," Josey said. She was wearing an oversize white T-shirt with the Cup o' Noodles logo on it and pink-and-black plaid fuzzy pajama pants. She pulled her bare feet up under her and offered Donnie more popcorn. "It has 'moon' in the title and somebody is a werewolf. It's pretty cheesy, but the kill scenes are cool."

"Well, that's the important thing," Donnie said in mock seriousness.

"You should write a horror story." Her eyes never left the screen, where some growling presence stalked two teenagers making out on a blanket under the moonlight near a pond.

"Not tonight," Donnie said. "I think I'll go to bed."

"Good night," she said, her gaze still on the TV.

Donnie went upstairs and showered. When he came back to his bedroom, he saw the light flashing on his phone to indicate he had a message. He opened it and found that Debbie had, indeed, sent him a video. Grinning, he sat down on the bed to watch it.

Chapter Twenty

T hanksgiving Day dawned overcast and windy, with temperatures hovering around the freezing mark with no intention of going any higher. Naked tree limbs rattled and slashed at each other along the street while orphan leaves spun and somersaulted through yards and over sidewalks. Chimney smoke rose from several houses, the gray wisps torn to shreds and gone as soon as it left the brick structures.

Inside his home, Donnie sat on the sofa with his stockinged feet propped up on the coffee table. He was sipping coffee and watching the Detroit Lions battle with the Chicago Bears. Mike sat in the recliner, with his feet up and his head back, his own cup of coffee on an end table. They both wore blue jeans and flannel shirts, Donnie's gray and black while Mike's was red and black.

"The best thing about this game is not having to listen to Troy Aikman and Joe Buck blather between plays," Donnie said. Mike grunted. He had always been a Dallas Cowboys fan and thought Aikman was the best quarterback to ever wear the uniform. He would undoubtedly say so later in the afternoon when Dallas hosted the Washington Redskins and the former quarterback and his weasley partner did the commentary. Donnie had never forgiven Joe Buck for making such a big deal about Randy Moss of the Vikings fake mooning the Green Bay Packer fans. He was sure that had played a part in the Vikings' decision to trade the gifted but troublesome wide receiver.

Mike still had not mentioned his trip to Woodward.

Behind the men, in the kitchen, Debbie and Josey could be heard chattering non-stop about recipes, mothers and grandmothers, favorite candles, and other domestic things.

The house was filled with the smell of roasting turkey and baking bread and various other dishes.

Donnie thought about the cold outside, the warm interior of the house, the aromas of cooking food, and the feeling of being together with people he loved. He had known he missed being with people for holidays, but he hadn't realized just how deep that ache was, and now, he promised, he would savor every moment of this day. And, he decided, he would pitch in one hundred percent with Josey and deck the house out for Christmas.

Maybe LizBeth would even come to visit during the winter break from school ...

Maybe. He didn't want to think about it too much. It still felt surreal that she had called him. He'd texted her yesterday and asked how she was doing and she replied promptly and said she was doing good and asked how he was. They carried on a conversation for a few messages and it had been good. She was with her mom and brother and Melissa's new almost-husband at his parents' house for the day. LizBeth hadn't wanted to go, but Donnie told her it would be okay.

Debbie poked her head into the living room and asked over the sound of the television, "Which one of you alpha males wanna carve the turkey?"

Donnie looked at Mike. "You're the patriarch," he said.

Mike smiled but shook his head. "You do it," he said.

Donnie left his coffee cup on a coaster on the coffee table and went to the kitchen. There was so much steam rising from the dining table that he was worried the smoke alarms might go off. There were bowls of corn on the cob, mashed potatoes, dressing, gravy, green beans, a plate of fresh bread, cranberries, sweet potatoes, and a few other things still covered. And there at the end of the table was the huge golden turkey on a giant white platter.

"You ladies have outdone yourselves," he said in awe.

They both had their hair up in buns. Debbie wore black jeans and a red sweater with bangle bracelets. Josey had on black yoga pants and an oversized University of Oklahoma sweatshirt. Josey hadn't bothered with makeup and her face was flushed and youthful and shining with joy. Debbie had put on a little makeup, trying to cover the old acne scars she was self-conscious about. They were beautiful and their happiness seemed to radiate out of them.

"Here you go, mister," Debbie said, and handed over a carving knife and a big three-tined fork with a black handle. "Josey wants a drumstick and she's earned it."

"Indeed she has," Donnie agreed. He went to the head of the table and cut off both legs, then cut slices from the white breast meat. "This smells amazing," he said. "And look how juicy it is."

Josey bounced to the living room and called, "Mike, come and get it before Donnie eats it all."

"I'm coming," Mike replied.

Donnie carved off several slices, arranging them around the bottom of the bird. He glanced up after a few minutes and saw his dad standing in the doorway, one arm propped against the door frame, leaning on it, a forced smile on his face. He started to ask if he was okay, but then Josey was there, directing Mike into the chair at the other end of the table, pulling it out for him and fussing with his napkin.

"I've got it," Mike said, waving her away. He smiled for real. "Flutter somewhere else, little bluebird."

Josey slapped at his shoulder playfully, then stood with Debbie and the two women surveyed their work. "Are we forgetting anything?" the younger one asked.

"We just need to serve the tea," Debbie answered. "I think that's all."

Glasses of sweet iced tea were put at each place setting, and then the women sat down. Donnie took his seat, and everyone looked expectantly at the food.

"Should somebody say grace?" Debbie asked. "It is Thanksgivin' and all."

After a moment of silence in which nobody volunteered, Donnie said, "Dad, I carved the turkey. This one's yours."

Mike fixed him with a steely glare.

"Mom made you go to church a lot longer than I had to," Donnie said.

Mike grunted. "Okay," he said. "I'm not very damn good at this kind of thing, though."

"You'll do just fine," Debbie said. "Just talk from the heart." She smiled and Donnie knew she was trying to be encouraging, and he wondered what her religious beliefs were. He knew this was something his dad would rather not do, however, Mike lowered his head and began to speak.

"Lord, we thank you for this food," he began. There were a few heartbeats of silence and Donnie was about to look up, but then Mike's voice went on in a different tone, more somber. "We thank you, too, for the fellowship. I remember once some preacher read to us, 'My soul clings to the dust.' I didn't know what it meant back then, but now I do. Dust is material things and the past, and they don't mean anything. All of us here have let go of the past in some way, and we'll have more to let go of later, but here we are together today, and we thank you. Amen."

Echoes of "Amen" went around the table and everyone raised their heads and stared at Mike Nelson. Debbie had tears in her eyes and Donnie felt a lump in his throat. Josey reached over and took one of Mike's hands in her own and squeezed it.

"That was beautiful," Josey said. "We know where the author in the family gets his way with words."

Mike gave a crooked grin. "I guess I can rip one off every once in a while," he said.

Donnie swallowed the lump in his throat while Debbie dabbed her eyes with a napkin, then she said, "Let's eat."

Plates and dishes were passed around with compliments dished out almost as often as helpings of food. Debbie and Josey seemed intent on making sure the other one got more credit for the meal. Silverware rang against plates and conversation jumped from topic to topic, mostly about people in town. Donnie told them how last Thanksgiving Day, he had heated up a microwavable tray of thin turkey slices in brown gravy and ate that with slices of Wonder bread. Everyone laughed at him.

There was pumpkin pie with whipped cream for dessert, and when Donnie finally put his fork down for the last time, he thought he might explode.

"I can't remember the last time I was so full," he complained.

"You ain't too full to help clean up," Debbie assured him.

The food put away and the dishes in the dishwasher, Donnie, Debbie, and Josey went to the living room, where they found Mike asleep in his recliner, his head turned to the side and his mouth open while he snored softly. The Redskins were leading the Cowboys and the commentators were as annoying as Donnie expected.

"Isn't he cute," Josey said, grinning.

"I'm afraid that'll be me pretty soon," Donnie said.

"Another twenty years?" Debbie teased.

"I was thinking like twenty minutes," Donnie said. They all laughed. Donnie took his place on the sofa and Debbie settled down beside him with his arm around her shoulder.

"I'm going upstairs to play games," Josey said. She had bought herself a TV and gaming console for her bedroom. "No sex on the sofa, okay?"

"I can't make any promises," Debbie said. "He's an animal."

"That's so gross," Josey said, and went to the stairs.

"She's a good kid," Debbie said.

Donnie grunted. "Yeah. Heavy on the kid part."

Debbie punched him lightly in his full belly. "Are you still hung up on that?"

"A little, yeah," he admitted.

"Let it go," she said.

They watched as the Redskins scored another touchdown and listened to Troy Aickman lament Dallas's porous defense.

"That dinner was really amazing," Donnie said again, then yawned.

"You really are gonna go to sleep, ain't ya?"

"Of course not," he said. But within minutes he felt sleep, like a lead blanket, settling over him, making him feel heavy and slow. The sounds of the television faded in and out and Debbie's body became a heavy, pulsing thing on his chest, her breathing a rhythm synched to his own heartbeat. He realized she was asleep and it occurred to him to tease her about it, but then his chin settled onto his chest, his nose close to her hair that smelled of her, of shampoo, and of roasted turkey. He slept.

Donnie awoke to the voice of God telling Clarence Oddbody, Angel Second Class, to watch closely, followed by the sound of George Bailey rushing to save his little brother who had fallen through the ice. Donnie lifted his head and blinked as his eyes focused on the black and white images on the television screen.

"You old people can't handle your tryptophan," Josey said. She was settled on the sofa on the other side of Debbie, her knees pulled up under her chin, her mismatched socks on the cushion, and the remote control for the TV held loosely in her hand. She gave Donnie a quick glance, then focused on the movie. "This was Grandma's favorite movie," she said.

"I know," Donnie said quietly so he wouldn't disturb Debbie. Mike still snored in the recliner, but had turned his head to face the other direction.

Josey wiped at her eye and Donnie realized she was wiping away a tear. "We'd watch it on TV every Thanksgiving, even though I bought her the DVD." She paused and wiped at the other eye. "I've never watched this movie without her. I started to watch it upstairs, but I couldn't do it alone, so I came down here. I'm sorry I turned off the football game."

"It's okay," Donnie said. With the arm around Debbie's shoulder, he reached over and squeezed Josey's arm. "I would rather watch this movie any day. It's one of my favorites, too."

"It's so cheesy," Josey said, and she smiled, but it was a sad smile punctuated by a tear that got past her finger to run down her cheek. "Grandma loved happy endings."

"She did," Donnie agreed. He remembered her chastising him for his angsty teenage poetry and early short stories where almost everyone died.

"I miss her," Josey whispered. She didn't look at him. She stared doggedly at the television as if determined to hide her human weakness.

"She was a great woman," Donnie said. "And I know she was very proud of the person you are."

Still staring at the television, Josey whispered, "I was so scared she would die before I was old enough and they'd put me in an orphanage."

Donnie watched the girl, his chin just above Debbie's head, and he saw her wipe at more tears and grit her teeth in frustration at herself. And he understood at last why she had lied to him, why she had stowed away in the back of his pickup. There were still questions, like how was she getting her money, but now he understood her motive.

"It's okay to cry," Donnie told her quietly.

She turned her face to him at last and her green eyes had an otherworldly shine to them behind their veils of tears. "I'm trying so hard," she said, her voice choking at the end. "It isn't easy to make myself be happy all the time. I miss her so much. She didn't have to take me in. She was an old lady, but she felt guilty for what Mom was and she took me and gave me a h-h-home."

Josey put her face against her crossed arms over her knees and her shoulders shook with sobs. Donnie called out to her and reached for her again, but his voice and movement woke Debbie and she sat up with a start, heard the sobbing, and turned to find Josey crying.

"Josey?" she asked. "Josey? Honey, what's wrong?" She shot a look back at Donnie. "Did you – "

"No," Donnie said, cutting her off. "The movie got her thinking about her grandmother and we were talking about her."

"Oh, honey," Debbie said, and she leaned away from Donnie to wrap Josey up in her arms. She pulled the girl against her and rocked her back and forth, one hand patting her shoulder.

Donnie wanted to help, to offer his own comfort, but he didn't know what to do. Josey's crying got louder and Debbie squeezed her tighter. Finally, Donnie thought of tissues, and he got up to fetch the box his father kept on a night table in his room. He heard Josey talking through her sobs.

"I cried right after she died, but I haven't cried over her since then," the girl said. "We always made a big Thanksgiving dinner and she had friends who would come over. They were mostly other old people whose husbands or wives had died. This was the first one without her, and now the movie we always watched, and pretty soon it'll be Christmas without her."

Donnie pulled several tissues from the box and offered them, but Josey didn't see them with her face still in her arms. Debbie took them and gave him a thankful smile. He put the box on the coffee table and sat back down.

"It gets easier," Donnie said. "Maybe that sounds bad, but it does. The first everything is horrible. Holidays. Places you used to go together. And then you divide your memories and you have the things that happened before and the things that happened after. Eventually you have enough stuff in the after column that it makes the before hurt less. But it'll never go away completely."

Donnie found that he was staring at the television as he spoke, watching the druggist slap young George Bailey for refusing to deliver a prescription that was actually poison. He turned to face the women and found they were both looking at him. Debbie had a sad look on her face, but Josey, still tear-streaked with glassy eyes, smiled at him.

"Are you talking about your ex-wife or your mom?" she asked.

Donnie nodded slowly. "Both," he said. "Mom loved to bake and she'd have multiple desserts for Thanksgiving dinner. Melissa was a good cook. I don't know how because her mom is a horrible cook. She would season the turkey with all kinds of leaves and stuff, but it was always good." He smiled and shook his head.

"My recent Thanksgivings usually started with getting high, then going to whatever restaurant was open, then going home to drink until somebody got in a fight and the cops came," Debbie said. "I'm glad to put that in the old column."

"We can't cling to the dust." Everybody was surprised to hear Mike's voice and turned to face him. There were lines from the back of the recliner on his left cheek. "I said so at dinner. You have to let go of the past."

"When did you wake up?" Donnie asked.

"When you were talking about your mom," he said. "God bless her."

"Not everything has to go away," Donnie said. "Some traditions, the good ones, can just be adapted to fit. Like this movie. Only a person with a heart of stone could dislike *It's a Wonderful Life*. Let's make it our Thanksgiving tradition in honor of Wanda Wilder."

Josey's cheeks glowed as everyone agreed. She looked at Donnie and said, "Thank you."

"I think we need wine," Debbie announced, and she pushed herself off the sofa. She returned a few minutes later with a bottle of white wine, a corkscrew, and four stemmed glasses that she put on the coffee table.

"Uhhh," Donnie said. "Somebody here is underage."

"Don't be a stick-in-the-mud," Debbie scolded. "We ain't gonna get her drunk. She can have one glass. Those Europeans practically put wine in baby bottles."

"Yes, ma'am," Donnie said.

The wine was poured and Debbie looked to Donnie and said, "We need a toast, Mr. Writer-man."

Donnie thought for a minute. "I'll just build on what Dad said earlier," he told them, then raised his glass. "To the family we choose." Glasses clinked and they drank and settled in to watch the movie.

It was full dark out when the movie ended. Everyone pretended not to see everyone else wiping at tears as George read Clarence's note written in a copy of *Tom Sawyer*. Debbie refused to take any of the extra food home. Donnie sheepishly excused himself in telling Josey and Mike that he would be sleeping away from home that night. They both just grinned at him. Donnie gave the key to his pickup to Josey.

"I'll ride downtown with Debbie in the morning," he said. "You talked me into that Black Friday sale, so don't be late. Just in case people want used books as Christmas gifts."

On the drive to her trailer, Debbie said, "That was the best Thanksgiving I ever had. That Josey is just such a special girl."

"She is," Donnie agreed. "I'm pretty sure she's lying about her age because she's afraid of being put in state custody."

"Oh my Gawd," Debbie said, and covered her mouth with a hand. "I hadn't even thought about that. Nobody wants to be there. I had friends put in those state homes. It ain't good."

"No," Donnie said. "I'm sure it's not."

"I'm so glad she's here," Debbie said.

"Me, too," Donnie agreed.

The love making was slow but passionate, each clinging to the other, relishing the feeling of skin on skin, of taste, touch, smell, and the soft or loud sounds of the other. When it was over, they lay beside one another, Debbie on her back, Donnie pressed against her side, one of his ankles crossed over one of hers, the top sheet and quilt twisted but partially covering them. Outside, the wind pounded grit and leaves against the metal side of the mobile home.

"Can I ask you somethin'?" Debbie asked.

"Of course," Donnie answered in a whisper, his finger playing over her stomach.

"Your toast said family we choose," she said. "I know your dad is your dad, of course, and Josey lives with you, so that kinda makes her family. But what about me? How do I fit in?"

Donnie considered that. He had made the toast in the heat of the moment, with a familial feeling so thick in the room, it could have been stirred with a spoon. Of course he had included Debbie in that. He hadn't considered how, exactly, she fit, though.

"I love you," he said.

"I love you, too," she answered.

"I won't lie to you," he said slowly, his voice low. "I didn't think about the particulars. There was just so much love right then, you know? We felt like a family and it seemed right to say it."

"Family seems awful permanent," Debbie said.

"It does," he agreed. "I ... I'm not opposed to that."

"But do you want it?"

"There's still a lot to learn about each other," Donnie said carefully. "But I do love you and if things keep going like they are ... " He couldn't make himself say he would marry her. He had never even entertained the idea of getting married again. When she was quiet, he decided he had to tell her that. "I've never thought about getting married again. I thought I would always be alone."

"I always hoped I would someday," Debbie said. "A real wedding and a real marriage with a real preacher. Not somebody that got a license off the internet so they could charge fifty dollars to read out of a book."

Donnie had been watching his finger on her belly. He looked into her face and found that she was looking up toward the ceiling. He couldn't read her expression. "I promise that if we decide that's what we want, we'll invite the whole town and do it in the biggest church."

"Neither one of us is Baptists," she said. "I ain't. Are you?"

"No," Donnie said.

"We could get married outside in the spring or fall," she said. "If you decide you wanna marry me."

"You sound like you've already decided about me," Donnie said.

She looked at him then, and raised one hand to rest it on his cheek. "Donnie, I promised myself a long time ago that no man that wasn't worth marryin' would ever get in my bed again."

"Oh." It was all Donnie could think to say.

Debbie smiled at him. "I know our situations are different. None of my old relationships were worth stayin' in, and you feel guilty for how yours ended and you've been hidin' from the world for all these years. I'm not askin' you to get on your knees with a ring right now. But I want you to know that I consider this a serious relationship, and if you don't ... well ... " She lost her voice for a second and Donnie saw that she was about to look away from his face, but wouldn't let herself. "Well, then you need to go on home and leave me be."

Her hand on his cheek was the most comforting thing he could ever remember feeling in his life, with the possible exception of resting that same cheek against the heads of his babies. He was aware Debbie's breathing was short and shallow as she waited for his response. He considered making a joke about it being too cold and dark to walk home now, but he knew she wouldn't find it funny this time. He lifted her hand off his cheek, pressed her fingers together, and kissed them.

"I'm not leaving," he said. "I'm serious, too. So don't you even think about dating someone else."

She laughed, but there were tears, too, and she pulled her hand away and took his head in both hands and kissed him deeply.

They talked for a while about the dinner, about the movie, favorite movies, concerts they had seen and missed, and then, in a lull of the soft conversation, they both slept.

Chapter Twenty-One

From eight in the morning until noon, Lost Pages Bookstore ran a buy-two-get-one-free sale. From noon until close, the deal was buy two and get one book half-off. Donnie had been skeptical when Josey suggested the Black Friday sale. That was for big retailers, he argued. For stores that sold new merchandise. He'd never heard of a used bookstore having a Black Friday sale.

The grin never left the girl's face as she flitted around the store in her green elf's hat with jingling bells, but it got even bigger whenever her eyes and Donnie's locked. All he could do was grin and shake his head to show he had been wrong. In all the years he had been running the store, it had never been as full of people as it was right now. Townspeople he had only seen at the café or the few community events he'd attended were there, and he'd heard people telling Josey they'd come in from Buffalo, Waynoka, Fort Supply, and other surrounding towns.

And they were buying books! Lots of books. People were leaving with armloads of books and Donnie knew it would be the biggest sales day the store had ever seen, by far.

A man approached the counter with a stack of about ten paperbacks. He was a heavyset man with a scraggly brown beard turning gray, a receding hairline, merry little eyes, and fingers like thick pink sausages. "Yer datin' Debbie over at the café, ain't ya?" he asked Donnie with a grin.

"I am," Donnie said as he began sorting the books, determining which ones were free.

"I went to school with her," the man said. "Whoo! She was a wild one back in the day. I think she's settled down now, but man! There was a time."

Donnie glanced up and took in the man's ruddy cheeks and impish smile and wondered what he'd looked like as a teenager and whether Debbie had found him attractive. "Yeah, I think she's settled down. Age will do that, I guess."

"Gittin' married's what settled me down," the man drawled. "I got her pregnant, so we got married, and I went to work over to the grain elevator. Been married thirty-four years now. Three kids and one grandbaby."

"Marriage will do that," Donnie said. The man was buying detective and historical romance novels. "You like the romance novels?" Donnie asked as a joke.

"Oh, no, them're for my wife," the man said. "She reads and gets ideas. I like some of the ideas, if ya know what I mean. But then she asks me why I don't treat her like them guys in the books." He shook his head. "They ain't got jobs unloadin' train cars and checkin' wheat for rocks and stuff."

"We can't all be lords of Wales and England or Vikings on the high seas," Donnie said. "Somebody has to do the dirty work."

"That's purty much what I tell'er," the man said. "I like the myst'ry books. Sometimes I know who dunnit before I get to the end, but usually it's a surprise. I like these with the tough detective. I kinda wanted to be a cop before I got Linda knocked up. I usually buy a new book when I go to the Wal-Mart in Alva or Woodward, but I'll start comin' here now."

"I appreciate that," Donnie said, as he scanned the barcodes to take the books out of the store's inventory, thankful again for Josey's computerized system, and told the man how much he owed. The customer paid with a debit card and Donnie put the books in a paper bag from a stack he'd talked Roger at the grocery store into selling him for this day. Again, on Josey's insistence that they'd be necessary. He waved good-bye back at the man, who waved at him as he pushed his way through the front door, and thought again how Josey would never let him forget how she'd been right about this sale.

Omar and Austin were in the store and Donnie had been watching them as they watched Josey, and he knew she was deliberately going over and checking on them once in a while just to be teasing. She went back over after Debbie's classmate left, her bells tinkling as she bounced on springy steps.

"You only have about ten minutes left to get one for free," Josey told them. "Then you'll have to pay half price for that third book. Are you reading books about being a mother?"

Donnie had to clear his throat and cough to smother a laugh. Josey had caught them in the small section of books on pregnancy and motherhood. He was sure the boys hadn't realized where they were, as they'd just been moving around to get a better view of Josey. Omar blushed from the collar of his black T-shirt to the roots of his black hair, but his friend recovered quickly.

"I feel like it's a man's duty to understand what his woman is going through during that magical time when she's pregnant," Austin said in a very serious voice. Omar gaped at him while Josey sucked her lips under her teeth and nodded knowingly.

"I'm sure when the time comes, your wife will appreciate your knowledge and attention," she said.

"I hope you do," Austin said.

Donnie couldn't stifle the bark of laughter that time and several other customers looked at him, and some others were grinning because they'd heard the young people's conversation, too. When Donnie looked back at the group, he saw that it was Josey's turn to be startled and blushing. He felt a weird sense of satisfaction that somebody had finally gotten to her.

"I, umm ... I don't know about that," Josey said. "But happy reading." She turned away, giving Donnie a wide-eyed "What-the-hell-was-that?" stare before moving to a group of older women as far away from the teenage boys as she could go.

"Man! How could you say that?" Omar hissed at his friend as the boys moved back toward the fantasy section.

A few more customers checked out and as the clock moved past noon, the number of customers in the store dwindled. Then Donnie's phone rang and he saw that it was LizBeth. Josey looked over at him when the phone rang and he asked her quickly to take over the counter, then he headed for the back room.

"Hello," he said into the phone as he got into the storage area.

"I didn't think you were going to answer," LizBeth said.

"I'm sorry. I had to get to the back room. We're having a sale today for Black Friday," Donnie explained.

"Who's 'we'?" she asked. "Don't you run the store by yourself?"

Donnie considered how to answer. He said, "I have some volunteer help sometimes. Are you doing okay?"

"Yeah. Yesterday was lame. Are you still coming on Sunday?" she asked.

"Yes. Absolutely," Donnie said. "If you still want me to."

"I do. It'll be weird but good to see you again. I'm sorry I've been a bit– I mean, a brat for so long," LizBeth said.

"It's understandable," Donnie said. "I have a lot to tell you. I was also wondering if you'd want to come up here for a little while during your Christmas break."

"That might be cool," she said. "Wait. Do you have internet up there?"

Donnie laughed. "Yes, we have internet. There are a couple of town mules that turn a wheel to keep the receiver working."

"Ha-ha, Dad," she said.

"What are you doing today? I thought you'd probably be out shopping with your mom," Donnie said.

"I am. She's helping Brian with something. What do you want for Christmas?" she asked.

Donnie immediately got that lump in his throat and felt his right eye threaten to leak. He made a fist and pressed it into his thigh and cleared his throat. Neither of his kids had given him any kind of gift since he and Melissa split up. The most he could hope for was a card with no personal note, just a signature.

"You don't have to get me anything," Donnie said.

"Dad, don't do that. I haven't given you anything in years. I need to make up for that," she said.

"If I tell you what I want, will you not roll your eyes and tell me no?" he asked.

"I can't answer that," she huffed. "What is it? A new Ferrari?"

"No," Donnie laughed. "I want an eight-by-ten picture of you in a nice frame."

"Daa-ad," she complained. "What kind of gift is that?"

"Someday, when you're a parent, you'll understand," he told her. "I'd like one of Brian, too, if he'd allow it."

"Yeah, I can do that," she said. "But I'm getting you something else, too. What size underwear do you wear?"

Donnie laughed again, then told her his size. "But I need socks more than underwear. Thick ones. It's a lot colder up here."

"Mom and Brian are coming. I guess I better go," LizBeth said.

"Does your mom know you're talking to me? That I'm coming on Sunday?"

"She knows. She said it's my decision," LizBeth said.

"Okay. I did all the sneaking around I ever want to do," Donnie said.

There was a moment's silence, then LizBeth laughed. "Too soon, Dad. Too soon. I'll see you Sunday. Bye."

"Bye."

She was gone. Donnie wasn't usually a religious man, but he whispered a quick prayer of thanks, then pocketed his phone and went back to the front of the store. There were two Styrofoam containers on the counter and Josey was off helping an elderly lady in the true crime section. Donnie peeked into the top container and recognized the gravy-covered chicken-fried steak with a side of fries from Annie's Cafe.

"Debbie brought those over," Josey said, her bells ringing as she rocked back and forth on the other side of the counter. "She's a keeper." She gave him a wink.

"Yeah? Is Austin still in here?" Donnie asked.

"Oh. My. God!" Josey punctuated each word, then laughed. "I was so shocked when he said that, I didn't know what to say."

Donnie chuckled. "You handled it pretty well. It was kind of fun to see you get thrown for a loop, though."

"They both bought six books. Well, bought four and got the free ones," she said. "It was so awkward checking them out."

"When do you want me to admit that you were totally right about this sale?" Donnie asked.

"Every day, several times each day," she said. "What did she bring us?"

"The top one is chicken-fried steak. I haven't checked the bottom one," Donnie said. He did and found that it was chicken strips with fries and a cup of white gravy. He looked at Josey. "She knows us too well," he said.

"Keeeeeper," Josey sang.

"We kind of talked about that," Donnie admitted.

"Getting married?" Josey asked, her eyes bulging.

"Sort of. But I'm not ready," Donnie said quickly when he thought the girl was about to explode. Her smile faltered a little. "But we agreed it's a serious relationship and we don't want to date anyone else." He snorted. "Like that was even an option for me."

"It's a start," Josey said. "Then you had crazy sex, I'm sure."

Donnie cocked an eyebrow at her. "We'd already done that," he stage-whispered.

"Ewwww," she said. "Take your food and go eat, you filthy old man. I'll watch the store and eat when you're finished. But hurry up. I'm hungry."

"You go first," Donnie urged.

"No, I want to wait and see what true crime books Mrs. Schwartz gets," Josey said. She nodded toward the elderly lady she had been helping earlier. The woman had her gray hair in a tight bun on top of her head and was wearing a long denim skirt showing beneath her black wool coat. She currently held two paperbacks and was squinting at the shelves, looking for a third.

"Give her the third one for free, okay?" Donnie said.

"You're the boss, boss. Now go eat."

Donnie took his food and went to the back room. He sat at the little table that used to be his regular spot for eating his evening meals. The room was much different now. Josey had determined the bed was unfit to keep and it had gone to the dumpster behind the store. All his other personal belongings were now at the house. The room held this small table and the little microwave in the corner Josey called the break room. Otherwise, there were boxes of books and a couple of rectangular folding tables for sorting them. It looked the way a bookstore stockroom should look, he thought as he cut into his steak.

Donnie ate, then relieved Josey so she could eat. Traffic in the store was less in the afternoon, but business was still heavier than any other normal day. Donnie admitted to himself he should have sales more often. With the markup on the books -- many of which he got for free or very cheap at estate sales -- he could absorb the loss of giving away or selling one book at half price to bring in more business. Many of the customers had admired Josey's Thanksgiving decorations and the related book displays. She had cursed herself for not setting up Christmas displays the day before Thanksgiving Day, but Donnie had waved it away.

Josey reappeared and leaned on the counter beside where he sat in his usual chair. There was no writing going on at work today. "Wilson came in while you were on the phone earlier," she said. "I forgot to tell you."

"From the paper?"

"Is there another Wilson in town?" she asked.

"What did he want?"

"He took some pictures and asked me how business was going. He said it's been a long time since anyone on Main Street has had a Black Friday sale, but he bets other businesses will do it next year because of us."

Donnie nodded thoughtfully. "That's good. You might turn this whole town around before you're done," he said.

"Was it your daughter on the phone?" Josey asked.

"Yeah." Donnie watched her carefully for any reaction.

"She's calling pretty often."

"This is only the second time," he said.

"You're still going to see her on Sunday?"

"Yeah. Do you want to come? Anybody in Lawton you want to visit?" he asked.

"No, I don't think so. Besides, Mike might need me," she said.

That kind of surprised Donnie. "Why would Dad need you?"

Josey blinked as if she'd just realized what she said. She shrugged. "He's an old man. He gets lonely."

"Hmm." Donnie watched her, but she didn't give anything away. "You still don't want to tell me about his trip to Woodward?"

"Nope." She straightened and glided around the counter to go talk to a mom with two kids in the children's section.

Exasperated, Donnie shook his head, but there was nothing he could do about it. She had her own secrets and was privy to his father's secret, and he was out in the cold.

At about three o'clock, Debbie came over, her cheeks and hands red from the cold wind blasting through the street. Donnie was opening the door for a lady who had bought a dozen books; Debbie slipped in as the other woman went out. He let the door close and Debbie stepped into his arms and they hugged.

"You've been so busy over here today!" she said, her voice a happy gush. "People at the cafe have been talking about your sale all day, and most of them either had books with'em or they were talkin' about comin' here after they ate."

"It's been busy," Donnie agreed. "I'm glad Annie's got some business from it, too." Donnie knew people were watching them as they stood by the door, still holding each other. He could practically feel Josey's grin from wherever she was.

"I was thinkin' maybe I'd come over and get your key, then go to your house and have dinner made for y'all when you get off work," Debbie said. "I might use your shower, too. I smell like somebody done deep fried me and dipped me in gravy."

Donnie laughed. "I like that smell on you. But, I guess if you want to take a shower, I won't stop you. But really, you don't have to cook for us."

"Oh, it's just reheatin' stuff leftover from yesterday. It ain't no problem," she scoffed. "I promise I won't make a copy of your key."

"I don't care about that," Donnie said. "Are you sure you want to?"

"Yes. Now gimme the key." She held out her hand.

"It's in my coat pocket." Donnie gave her the house key, keeping the rest so he could lock the store and drive his pickup. They kissed quickly, then she swished out the front door and hurried back across the street to her own car.

"Public display of affection," Josey sing-songed behind him.

"Yep. And we'll have a hot dinner waiting on us when we get home," Donnie said without turning to face her smug smile. He went back to his chair and sat down.

The woman with the kids — a boy of about eleven and a girl that was maybe nine — came to the counter with three children's books and three horror novels. "You and the waitress from across the street are a cute couple," the woman remarked.

"Thank you," Donnie said. "She's really nice."

"I'm so sorry I haven't been in here before," the woman said. "I did come in just after you bought the store. I'd been a regular before, but, well, it just seemed so lifeless. I'm sorry to say it. I was buying my books online. But you've really turned the store around. It's more like it was before you came."

"Thank you," Donnie said again. "But you really need to thank Josey for that. She's been breathing new life into everything she comes in contact with."

"She's such a nice girl. Your niece, right?" the woman asked with a smile.

"Yeah," Donnie agreed.

The store closed at six, but the last customer didn't leave until about ten minutes later. As the young man left, Donnie tossed the keys to Josey and she locked the front door, then sagged against it.

"Whew," she said. "I'm tired."

"You should be. You were buzzing around like a bee in a field of daisies," Donnie agreed.

217

"We did good, though, right?" Her smile was just as bright as it had been early that morning.

"We did good," he agreed. "I'll figure up the receipts tomorrow, but I know it was the best day I've ever had here. Thank you. I couldn't have done it without you. I *wouldn't* have done it without you."

"Aw shucks, boss, it weren't nuthin'," she said. They laughed, then shrugged into their coats and went to the pickup.

They stopped off at the VFW and Donnie went inside to get his father. Mike was sitting at a table playing poker for toothpicks with three other men about his age. Donnie waited until the hand was finished, then said, "Dad, are you ready? Debbie's at the house making dinner for us."

"That's a good woman," Mike said. "Helluva good woman. She'll spoil us all." He rolled his remaining toothpicks under his fingers for a moment. "Well, boys, hot food beats taking your toothpicks. I'm out."

Another man said he needed to leave, too, and the other two grumbled about needing two more players. Donnie saw his dad hesitate as he started to get up, and a look passed over his face that might have been pain, but then it passed and he was up and coming around the table, but walking slowly and carefully.

"Are you okay, Dad?" Donnie asked. He was aware of several other men looking at them as he asked.

"Yeah, I've just been sitting there too long," Mike said. "My old bones get stiff as hell when I sit for too long."

They found his coat on the rack by the front door and he put it on slowly, then Donnie opened the door and they left.

The smell of a second Thanksgiving feast greeted them when they opened the front door of the house.

Chapter Twenty-Two

Donnie awoke early Sunday morning. He felt guilty about taking the truck and leaving his dad and Josey stuck at the house, but there was nothing to do about it. Then Josey pointed out they could always call on Debbie if they really needed to go somewhere, which they wouldn't. He ate some toast and shared an orange with Josey, then took to the highway, his truck's stereo speakers pumping the cab full of rock music from the 1980s.

It took him about three and a half hours to get to Lawton, and once he entered the city limits he realized he hadn't arranged a meeting point with LizBeth. Did she expect him to come to the house? He reached for the button on the steering wheel to make the command to call his daughter, then stopped. That would sound peevish. Maybe even cowardly. He gripped the wheel tightly, his knuckles whitening as he thought about seeing Melissa for the first time in many years. Maybe she wouldn't be home. If she knew he was coming, she would probably leave.

Donnie sighed, but found he could still remember every turn through his hometown to get to the brick house he had once shared with a wife and two children. He parked in the street and shut off the truck's engine. There were three cars parked in the double driveway and he knew his chances of Melissa being away were now incredibly slim. He could call LizBeth and tell her he was there and wait for her to come out ...

He threw open the truck's door and stepped onto the street his feet hadn't touched in seven years. The day was cold, but the wind wasn't howling here like it typically did in the northern part of the state. There was a breeze that rattled the remaining limbs of the big elm tree in the front yard, but otherwise the neighborhood was quiet. Donnie trudged up the edge of the driveway to the little walkway that led to the porch and then found himself standing before the front door.

He remembered being there a couple of nights after Melissa found out about the affair. She had shoved all his clothes into one huge trash bag and dragged it to the front porch. When he came for it, she yelled at and berated him, telling him how she and her mom had torn his office apart looking for other clues of his infidelity. When he finally got to go to his home office, about a week later, it was trashed. File cabinets had been pried open and folders emptied onto the floor so that he found himself walking over rejection letters and contracts dating back over three decades. The drawers of his desk were pulled out and overturned. Books torn off shelves and a poster of the rock band Kiss he'd had since his eleventh birthday was ripped and hanging in tatters from the inside of the door.

Donnie tried blinking all that away, but it was like a weight on his shoulders and he straightened himself as if the guilt was a physical thing. He rang the doorbell. He hoped LizBeth would answer and they would be on their way. He feared Melissa would answer and he would have to endure her icy stare. Or Brian … Brian who had burst into tears and fled the house when Melissa confronted his father about the affair. But it was a man he didn't know who answered the door.

The two men stared at each other for a moment. Then the stranger said, "You must be Don."

"Yes," he said. He guessed he should ask who this man was, but he knew. LizBeth had told him the man's name, but he couldn't remember it. "You're marrying Melissa," he said.

"I'm Alan. Alan Richards," the man said and he stepped out onto the porch and pulled the door closed behind him. He held out a hand and Donnie numbly shook it. "And yes, I'm marrying Melissa. Can we talk for a minute?"

"Sure," Donnie said, and the memory of that last talk with Melissa on this porch came back to him again.

"Melissa thinks LizBeth has reached out to you as a sort of rebellion against her remarrying," Alan said. He was a tall man, well built, trim, with a short thick beard of dark brown with just a few threads of gray in it. His hair was short, combed back from his forehead, and his hands were manicured and soft. His dark eyes were serious.

"I don't know anything about that," Donnie said. "I was just glad to hear from her."

Alan lifted a hand and rubbed the back of his neck, his brow furrowed. "Let me just come to the point, Don. I hope you're not here to cause any trouble."

"What trouble?" Donnie asked. Deep in his heart, a pilot light was lit and his blood began to warm. He didn't like this smug, serious, well-groomed man. What was he? A realtor? Maybe a car salesman?

"About the marriage. Or trouble with the kids," Alan said. He glanced back toward the door as if afraid someone would open it.

"Alan," Donnie began, "I want Melissa to be happy. I hurt her. I know that. If you make her happy, I'm glad. If LizBeth or Brian want to spend time with me, even as a form of rebellion, I'm going to make sure that happens. They're my children as much as they are hers. I've stayed away because that's what they've wanted. If that changes, I will be in their lives as much as they'll allow."

Alan must have sensed the rising passion in Donnie's tone. He held up his hands, palm forward in a gesture of peace, and then Donnie *knew* he was a smarmy car salesman. "I understand that. It has to be hard to be estranged from your children. I wouldn't come between you and them."

Donnie barked a short laugh, and suddenly he felt the spirit of Bolkar, his primitive mercenary, fill his mind. "You're damn right you won't."

Alan studied him for a long, silent moment. "You're not like she ... You're not like I expected."

"You thought I'd just roll over and give up and do and say whatever you wanted so I wouldn't cause trouble?" Donnie asked. "Maybe turn around and get back in my truck and leave without seeing my daughter?"

"I thought that might be for the best," Alan admitted. "She's said some things lately that have upset her mother."

"That's between them," Donnie said. "Are you going to tell LizBeth I'm here, or ... " He almost asked if he was going to have to forcibly move the other man, but he held back, not quite that bold. Yet.

"Will you promise me you won't cause trouble?" Alan insisted.

"I have no interest in you and Melissa," Donnie said. "I'm not taking my daughter out to tell her that her mother is horrible or that she shouldn't get married. But speaking of trouble, let me tell you this: I better never find out that you are trying to come between me and my children, that you are putting me down or refusing to let them call or see me. Do I make myself clear?"

Again, Alan looked at him for a long moment before slowly nodding. "I was told you were a passive guy eaten up with guilt who would agree to anything."

Donnie nodded now. "Those days are behind me. I'm more like my father now." And then it hit him, so hard that it almost rocked him on his feet, that Bolkar's personality had always been based on his father's. Usually quiet, brooding, but never one to put up with another's agitation, and ready to be irreverent or philosophical if the occasion called for it.

The door opened behind Alan and LizBeth came out wearing skinny jeans, ankle boots, a rust-colored sweater and a white down coat that was unzipped. Her hair was shoulder-length and wavy, dyed dark brown with streaks of gold through it. Her face was radiant with a big smile. "Hi, Dad," she said, and slipped around her future step-father and into Donnie's waiting arms. They hugged briefly, but tightly. "Are you ready?" she asked.

"Yes," Donnie said, holding her by the elbows and looking into her big gray eyes. He remembered how her large pupils would always catch the light from a camera flash and her pictures would come back with glowing orange demon eyes.

"That's your truck?" she asked, starting toward the pickup.

"That's it," Donnie said. He clicked the button on his key fob to unlock the doors, then turned back to Alan. "Which dealership do you work at?" he asked.

"What?"

"Car dealership. Which one do you work for?" Donnie repeated.

"How did you know that? Did LizBeth tell you?" Alan asked.

"It was your manicure and your greasy personality," Donnie said. Bolkar would have then planted an axe in the man's chest, but some things just weren't proper in the real modern world. Donnie turned and followed his daughter to the pickup.

"I heard it all," LizBeth said breathlessly once Donnie was in the truck.

"Did you?" Donnie asked, watching as Alan disappeared into the house.

"You really put him in his place," she said.

Donnie started the truck and pulled away from the curb. "Is what he said true?"

"What?"

"Did you get in touch with me as a way to rebel against your mom getting married?" Donnie asked.

"No, Dad. I promise," LizBeth said. She fidgeted with her fingers in her lap, then looked out the passenger window. Donnie waited, knowing she would say more. "I just see how Mom is with him. She's always holding his hand and hugging him and saying she loves him. She has pictures of them all over the house. She was never like that with you. She never treated you like that. I know ... I know, well, you're a writer and writers are sensitive and you probably needed to be treated like that and she wasn't doing it, so you let somebody else do it."

Donnie drove on, chewing that over in his mind. "You have writers stereotyped?" he asked, but he smiled as he said it.

"I might have done a little research on it," she answered.

He looked over at her. She was looking ahead of them, but her face was serious. "Really?"

"Yeah."

He thought about asking her to discuss her research, but let it go. She was right, at least about him. "Look," he said, "There is no excusing how I hurt your mother. What you say is true, but I should have been man enough to divorce her instead of sneaking around and cheating."

"I agree," she said. "But you didn't like confrontation. At least, not back then. I thought you might punch Alan back there."

"Thought about it," Donnie said, and grinned at her. She smiled back. "How's Brian?"

"He's good. He wants to see you before you go home. He would have come with us, but I didn't invite him. He was in his room playing video games with his friends. I heard him yelling something about getting a sniper. His room stiiiiinks!"

"Where do you want to eat?" Donnie asked.

"Can we do Pholicious at the mall?" LizBeth asked.

"Sure," Donnie agreed. He had heard of pho, but had no idea what it was.

It turned out pho was basically expensive and better quality ramen noodles with better seasoning. It wasn't bad, but nothing he would buy on his own. They sat in the mall's food court and LizBeth told him about her classes, the hot gossip about her friends, other students, and some teachers.

"Tell me about you," she said at last. "You live in that tiny town nobody's ever heard of."

"Sagebrush," Donnie reminded. "I've told you most of it. The store is doing well. I'm working on a new book and that's going well. I'm waiting to hear from my agent."

"Is the book about Bolkar?" LizBeth asked.

"You know about him?"

"Duh," she said, then paused and her face kind of scrunched up. "Did you think I never read your books?"

Donnie shrugged. "I wouldn't have blamed you."

"I've read them all," she said, then pulled a chunk of meat from her noodles with her fingers and popped it into her mouth. It was a motion that made him think of Josey and how much the two girls had in common. "Is the new book part of the series?"

"Yes," Donnie said. "I hadn't written anything since the divorce."

"What made you start this one?" she asked, pulling a wad of noodles up with her chopsticks. She put them in her mouth, but had to suck up a dangler. Donnie smiled at her and she laughed.

"I have a story to tell you," Donnie said. "I maybe should have told you when you called the other day, but what you said surprised me. I need you to promise you'll keep it just between us for now."

She looked at him dubiously. "You're seeing someone?"

Donnie laughed softly. "I actually did just start seeing someone recently, and that's part of the story. That part you can talk about to other people."

He could tell she struggled to keep her face expressionless. "This sounds juicy," LizBeth said cautiously.

"It's complicated and, honestly, I'm a little worried about it. Do I have your promise?"

"Sure," she said. "I promise."

Donnie absently stirred his bowl of noodles and green leaves and bits of chicken. Or was it fish? He couldn't remember. He took a deep breath, looked up at his daughter, and began, "You know I was here back in October for Mrs. Wilder's funeral." LizBeth nodded, still eating. "At the cemetery, the reporter who'd called and told me she died tried to interview me about where I was living and why I wasn't writing and all that. I was trying to get away from him and practically ran to my truck, and there was my dad. He was supposed to be in that assisted living center, you remember?" Again, LizBeth nodded. "He insisted I take him home with me. So, here's this reporter chasing me, and your grandpa demanding I take him to Sagebrush, so I gave in and let him in the truck and we took off."

"This is weird and a little paranoid and agoraphobic, Dad, but not some big scandalous secret," LizBeth said. "But I didn't know old people could just walk away from those homes."

"Same," Donnie said, and she smiled at his use of teen slang. "But that's not the real issue. You see, I didn't notice that there was a rolled up blanket in the bed of my truck at the cemetery. I didn't know that was there until we got back to the store and it sat up and started talking."

LizBeth froze, chopsticks dripping broth from noodles suspended just outside her mouth. "It did what?" she asked, then slowly pushed the noodles between her teeth.

"Mrs. Wilder's granddaughter stowed away in the bed of my truck," Donnie said.

LizBeth blinked at him a few times. "That weird Josey girl hid in your truck and you took her all the way home and didn't know?"

"It was all very confusing," Donnie said defensively. "The reporter and my dad and just trying to get away. I had no idea she was back there."

"She's still there, isn't she?" LizBeth said, and now there was a slight accusatory tone in her voice. "Oh God, Dad, she's not who you're seeing?"

"No!" Donnie said, so loud and sharp that people at other tables glanced over. "Good Lord, LizBeth, she's your age. Although she claimed she was eighteen and I just accepted that. That was stupid of me. I talked to your grandpa about that in the beginning and we agreed that if we heard somebody was looking for her, we'd know she was lying. But nobody ever looked for her, so I assumed she was eighteen and had the right to make her own decision until you called and said she was missing from school."

"Don't you live in the back of your store?" LizBeth asked. "Where is she staying? Where's Grandpa staying?"

Donnie sighed and stirred his noodles some more. "There's a lot more to the story," he said. "I'm going to deal with Josey. I don't know how yet. I need to find out why nobody is looking for her. But that's the part I'm asking you to keep to yourself, that she's with me."

"This is weird, Dad," she protested.

"Will you hear me out? Listen to the rest of the story?"

"Yeah. Okay."

He explained how they'd spent that first night in the store, then how his dad and Josey had helped rent a house, how Josey was working in the store and had instigated him dating Debbie and how sales in the store were up and everything was working better. Then he told her about the Thanksgiving dinner.

"Wow. I guess she's just what you needed," LizBeth said, and Donnie heard a note of jealousy in her voice.

"No," he said. "Every day, her presence reminded me of what I was really missing in my life."

"What's that?"

"You, LizBeth. You and Brian," he said. "I missed you both every day, anyway, but having her there made that pain even sharper. And then you called, and here we are. After all those years, it's like someone has decided my penance is over."

She gave him a look that said she thought he was being overly dramatic. "What are you going to do about her?"

"I don't know," he said. "Debbie and my dad both say I shouldn't do anything, that she has her reasons for hiding the truth, and since there's no indication anyone is looking for her, I should just wait until she's ready to tell me."

"She was always weird," LizBeth said.

"Tell me about her," Donnie urged. "What was she like in school?"

"Well, for one thing, everyone knows her mom is a dead crack whore and her grandma was a teacher at the school and all our parents loved her," LizBeth said. "Josey was always involved in everything. Student council, yearbook, band ... I don't even know. At spirit games, she was always running around organizing things and bossing people around. She'd come to class late and say it was because she was doing some activity. And she'd change her hair color every few weeks, and it would always be some wild color or combo."

Donnie listened quietly, thinking mostly of the first part of what Josey said. "Everyone knows about her mom? And her grandma?"

"Yeah. People used to tease her about her mom when we were kids," LizBeth said.

Donnie nodded. "I bet that's it."

"What?"

"Maybe, just maybe, she did all this to get a fresh start where nobody knows what her mom was or who her grandma was," he said. He sighed. "I went to Sagebrush to get away from everybody who knew who I was."

"Maybe," LizBeth said. "It's still pretty weird she'd just hide in the back of your truck."

Donnie chuckled. "There is no doubt about that."

"Changing the topic," LizBeth announced. "Tell me about your girlfriend. You're not going to get all weird about her like Mom is with Alan, are you?"

"I can promise you this," Donnie said solemnly. "I've spent too much time without you and Brian in my life. No woman – no person – will come between us again. Not on my side, anyway."

LizBeth gave him a little smile and nodded. "Tell me about her."

Donnie described Debbie's physical characteristics to his daughter, trying hard to keep his voice neutral and use few adjectives. "She grew up in Sagebrush and left for several years, then came back," he said, leaving out why she left and came back. "She's a good cook and really nice. Oh, and she's got a really strong Okie twang."

"More than you?" LizBeth asked.

"I dunt know whut yer tawkin' 'bout," Donnie said in an elaborate drawl.

"She sounds okay," LizBeth said. "I guess I'll meet her at Christmas? If you don't run her off."

"You'll really come?" Donnie asked, and he didn't care that his voice gave away his excitement. LizBeth smiled at him.

"Yes. But it's going to be really awkward for Josey," she said.

"Hopefully that'll all be resolved before then." He looked down at his soup. It had gotten cold. He stuck his chopsticks into the noodles and let them go. "I think I'm done with this."

"You didn't really like it, did you?" she asked.

"Not my favorite thing in the world."

"I suppose you'll want steak for dinner."

"I mean, I wouldn't say no," Donnie said in an innocent voice.

"I bet you eat too much red meat," his daughter said.

"No comment," he said. "What do you want to do now?"

"I want to look at shoes," she said.

"Of course. Women and shoes," Donnie said and rolled his eyes.

The mall had a couple of shoe stores in it. LizBeth bought herself a pair of sneakers in one and a pair of boots in the other. Donnie carried her bags and they wandered through different stores, just looking at things. She was tall and graceful, with long, easy strides to her walk, her hair bouncing softly, her eyes reflecting the lights of the mall or glowing with an internal light. Donnie was very aware of teenage boys and young men giving her second and third looks. A few people her age greeted her and gave him a strange look as if they didn't know LizBeth even had a father. He didn't blame them. He felt like a lucky pauper walking beside a princess.

They left the mall and got back in his truck. "What's next?" he asked.

"You'll think this is weird," LizBeth said, and she actually blushed.

"What?" Donnie asked, intrigued.

"Let's go to the park like we used to," she said.

Donnie thought something – or everything – inside him might melt at that suggestion. "So I can push you in the swing?" he asked.

"Maybe," she said.

They went to the park, and he did push her in the swing. For about twenty minutes, it was like the past eight years hadn't even happened. She was his daughter and he doted on her and it was like it was when she was just starting elementary school and would burst through the front door calling for him after school to show him her papers and tell him about her day.

"Let's walk around the lake," LizBeth said when she was tired of swinging. They walked to the edge of the water. Donnie saw that there was a fixture for a fountain in the middle of the pond, but it was off for winter. There was no sidewalk, so they walked around the bank, their hands in their coat pockets for warmth.

"You haven't told me much about yourself," Donnie prompted. "I saw guys checking you out in the mall. Do you have a boyfriend?"

"No. Not anymore," she said. She pulled a hand free to draw hair from her mouth after a gust of wind blew it there. "I had a boyfriend named Jackson. We were together for a while, but it didn't work out."

"You're young," Donnie said. "You don't want to get committed yet."

"You and Mom started dating young, didn't you?"

"Yes," he said.

"You outgrew each other?" she asked.

"I guess so," he said.

"You loved each other in the beginning?" she asked. "Did you love each other when ... when me and Brian were born?"

Donnie stopped walking and she stopped, too. He pulled his hands from his pockets and wrapped his arms around her and hugged her tightly, then let her go and looked her in the face as he answered truthfully. "Yes," he said. "We loved each other when we made you. She ... she had changed, but she still loved me, and I still loved her."

"Changed how?"

Donnie sighed and thought about how to answer. He stepped close to the water's edge and kicked some rocks into the waves. "She changed right after we got married," he said. "She was girlish and affectionate before, and then right after, she was just different. Like getting married aged her twenty years, or ... "

"Or what?" LizBeth urged. She stood beside him, waiting.

Donnie looked at her. "I tried to talk to her about all of this a long time ago. She told me I was wrong, that she hadn't changed. But it was almost like marriage was her goal, and once she got it, she didn't have to be affectionate anymore. She treated marriage like a business. We had income and expenses, and that's what she talked about."

"I asked her once if she supported your writing before you got famous," LizBeth said. Donnie remained silent, but in his mind he pictured himself offering her his first completed manuscript and remembered her rejecting it. "She said she did. That she let you buy a typewriter and then a computer and you were always mailing stuff and needing money for postage."

Donnie nodded slowly. "That's all true."

"I asked her what she meant about letting you buy that stuff," LizBeth said. "I asked her if you were working a regular job back then."

"Um-hmm," Donnie said into the pause, knowing what was coming.

"She said it was money she could have used on other stuff," LizBeth said. "I asked her like what, but she just said bills."

"She always handled the bills. I'm no good with numbers," Donnie said.

"But why did you have to ask for your own money?" LizBeth asked.

Donnie felt his eyes watering and he wanted to blame it on the breeze coming off the water, or maybe old age just made people cry easier. He sighed. "That's just the kind of relationship we had after the wedding," he said.

"I don't think that was right," LizBeth said.

Donnie didn't say anything, just looked across the water to the far bank where a small flock of ducks were pecking at the winter grass.

"Dad?"

He turned to face her.

LizBeth's eyes widened in surprise. "You're crying," she said.

"Sorry." He wiped quickly at his eyes.

"Writers really are sensitive," she said, and her tone was cautiously joking.

"Some of us are," he agreed.

She threaded her arm between his elbow and torso and shoved her hand back into her pocket. "I'm sorry I never asked for your side of the story," she said.

"Honey, you were eight when it happened," Donnie said. "But thank you. And no matter what else was going on, what I did was wrong and I don't want you to ever think I believe differently."

"We all make mistakes," she said quietly. "Dad. I'm ... pregnant."

It was as though a hand reached into Donnie's chest and just crumpled everything up and dropped it somewhere deep and dark. His vision narrowed with a field of black closing in around a telescopic view of a world he no longer really saw. He stood motionless and wondered if he was still breathing. He couldn't tell.

"Dad?" It was his daughter's voice. His baby girl with the big gray eyes and the outstretched arms running to him for a hug. The little girl he had brought to this park to swing and slide and feed breadcrumbs to the ducks. She was – "Dad? Did you hear me?"

Donnie turned to face her. "I heard you, honey," he said. "Tell me about it."

Her face reddened, but she didn't back away from what she had to say. "Jackson wanted to try sex without a condom. I didn't want to, but he kept asking and I finally gave in but told him ... " She paused and blushed deeper. "I told him he had to take it out before he finished, but he didn't."

"You're not on birth control?" Donnie asked.

She dropped her eyes and her voice. "I forget to take it sometimes."

"Did he break up with you when you told him you're pregnant?"

"He doesn't know," she said. "I broke up with him because I realized how selfish he was. I don't want him to know."

Donnie nodded. "I understand. You haven't told your mom?"

LizBeth shook her head. Now it was her turn to cry. Tears rolled down her cheeks. "She'll get so mad. She'll say I did it to mess up her wedding."

Donnie pulled his hands from his pockets and wrapped his daughter in his arms again. She sagged into him and broke down into sobs.

"I don't know what to do," she said several times. Donnie didn't answer, just hugged her and stroked her hair and promised it would be okay.

When her sobs had dissolved into hiccups and sniffles, Donnie pointed to a nearby bench and suggested they go sit down. Seated, he kept an arm around her shoulders and held her close to him. "What do you want to do?" he asked.

"I don't know," she said.

"Do you want to keep the baby?" he asked.

She picked at her fingernails in her lap. "I used to say women had the right to do whatever they wanted with their bodies, but when it's my body. My ... baby." She said the last word softly, as if just realizing what was growing inside her. "I don't think I can end it," she said.

"You want to have the baby?" Donnie asked. "And keep it?"

"I couldn't give it birth, go through all that, and then give it away," she said quietly.

"I understand," Donnie said. "How far along are you?"

"About two months. But I'm already getting sick in the mornings," she said. "Mom's going to figure it out soon."

"Do you want me to be with you when you tell her?" Donnie asked.

She rested her head against his shoulder. Her voice was little more than a whisper. "Would you?"

He gave her a side hug. "Yes, baby girl," he said.

"She's going to be so mad. She's always yelling at me about my birth control, but I just forget," LizBeth said. "I get up too late, I guess."

"Have you taken a test?" Donnie asked.

"Yeah."

"Been to a doctor?" he asked.

"No."

"Do you want to do that and be sure before we tell her?"

She seemed to think about it. "I guess I should."

"Let's go back to the truck," Donnie suggested, and helped her to her feet. They walked back quietly and he opened the door for her, then got behind the wheel, but didn't start the engine. Instead, he got out his phone and did a Google search.

"What are you doing?" she asked.

"Looking for an urgent care clinic that'll do a pregnancy test," he said, then pushed a button to make a call. On his second try, he found a clinic that was open on Sunday and would do a pregnancy test. He hung up and started the engine.

"I'm scared," LizBeth said.

Donnie reached over and took her hand and held it as they drove.

At the clinic, LizBeth was taken back almost immediately and Donnie sat alone in the lobby, flipping through a magazine he wasn't even seeing. He tried to fight back the thoughts about what a pregnancy would mean for LizBeth's future. College? A decent career? Would she even finish high school? And then there was the idea of facing his ex-wife and supporting LizBeth as she told Melissa she was pregnant. His mind was a whirlwind of dark thoughts with his daughter's sad face and tear-filled eyes at the center of the maelstrom.

LizBeth came out of the exam area. He knew from the fresh tears what the results were. "Probably nine weeks," she said and fell into her father's arms. "My life is over."

Donnie shushed her and petted her hair and promised her that her life was not over. He hugged her, then guided her to the checkout counter and paid the bill for the test and led his daughter back to the pickup.

"Do you want dinner before we go tell her?" Donnie asked.

"I couldn't eat," LizBeth said in a choked voice. Donnie started the truck and began backing out of the parking space. "Dad? Are you mad at me?"

Donnie stopped the truck right where he was and reached over and took her hand again. "I'm not mad at you, sweetheart," he said. "I promise. We're going to make the best of this." He made himself smile at her. "I'm going to be a grandpa."

She gave up two hiccups of laughter, then began crying again. Donnie drove back to the house he had given up without a fight in the divorce. "Alan's still here," LizBeth said.

Donnie parked the truck and turned to face his daughter. "How do you want to do this?"

"What do you mean?" LizBeth asked. Donnie could see the fear in her wide eyes.

"Do you want Alan in on the conversation?" Donnie asked.

"Mom will let him stay."

"It isn't about what your mom wants. This is family business. Do you want him in on it?" Donnie insisted.

"I guess it's okay," she said. "Mom will tell him, anyway."

"If it gets nasty, if your mom isn't supportive, you can always come live with me," Donnie said.

"Won't that be a court thing?" she asked after chewing her lip for a moment. "I don't want to cause all of that."

"I doubt it would come to that," Donnie said.

"Okay," she agreed.

"What about Brian? Do you want him to hear it?"

She chewed her lip again. "I guess I'd rather him hear it from me."

Donnie nodded and tried to think of any other questions, but he couldn't come up with anything. "Are you ready?"

"No." Her voice was small and quiet, the voice of the little girl who once dropped a glass of milk and tried to say it hadn't been her who did it.

Donnie unbuckled his seatbelt and took his daughter's small hands in his own. He squeezed them. "It's going to be okay, Lizzy. One way or another, it will be okay."

"Everything about this scares me," she confessed.

"I know." He let her go and got out of his side of the truck and went around to hers. She hadn't moved, so he opened her door and reached in and took her hand and gently coaxed her out of the truck. Holding hands, they walked up to the porch. LizBeth pushed the door open and Donnie followed her inside.

The smell of the house was different. Donnie couldn't describe it, really, but when he had lived here the house had smelled one way, an aroma he recognized as home, and now it was different. The entryway had three photos hanging on the left side, one of LizBeth wearing a sweater and sitting in a pile of autumn leaves, and one of Brian in a football uniform, holding his helmet under one arm. The third picture was of Melissa and Alan, him standing behind her with an arm protectively – or possessively – around her waist; they were both smiling.

LizBeth pulled Donnie forward. Alan's voice called from the living room, "LizBeth, are you home already? Did he –" The man stopped speaking as he stepped forward and his eyes locked with Donnie's.

"Where's Mom?" LizBeth asked.

"I don't think she wants to see your father," Alan said.

"We need to talk about LizBeth," Donnie said. "Where's Melissa?"

"I'm here." Melissa stepped out of the living room to stand beside her fiancé. She had cut her hair short and it was gray at the temples. She wore dark blue jeans, a long-sleeved red shirt, and gray socks. She crossed her arms and faced Donnie and he knew that accusatory look. "What about her?"

"I think we should sit down," Donnie said. "LizBeth said it's okay for Alan to stay, and she'd like Brian to be with us."

Melissa's defiant stance faltered a little and Donnie saw a flicker of worry pass through her eyes, but then it was gone and she was the stony woman he remembered. She raised her voice and called for Brian to come downstairs, then she turned and went back into the living room. LizBeth followed her, still holding Donnie's hand, so he followed and Alan came after. Brian's feet thundered down the stairs.

Melissa sat on the sofa. Donnie noted that all the furniture was different from the last time he'd been in the room. There were more pictures of the kids, including their most recent school photos, and more pictures of Melissa and Alan. LizBeth settled into a recliner and Donnie sat on the bricks of the fireplace's raised hearth while Alan sat on the sofa with Melissa. Brian barged into the room.

"What – ?" He stopped and stared at Donnie. "Dad. What are you doing here?"

"Hi, Brian," Donnie said. "LizBeth wants to tell everyone something. Will you sit down?"

Brian dropped into a wooden rocking chair Donnie knew used to belong to Melissa's mother. Everyone looked at LizBeth, waiting.

"It's okay, honey," Donnie urged.

LizBeth inhaled a deep, shaky breath, and just came to the point. "I'm pregnant."

"Oh, God. I knew it. I fucking *knew* it!" Melissa shouted. "You never take those fucking pills like you're supposed to." Her face was hard and angry, just as it had been the night she found out about his affair.

"How could you do this?" Alan demanded. "Doesn't your mother have enough to deal with?"

Donnie pointed a finger at him like a gun. "No," he said, his voice strong and loud and full of authority. "You can listen, but this is a family issue and we don't want to hear from you."

"He's going to be her step-father," Melissa screamed at Donnie. "He's already been a better father than you ever were, you cheating piece of shit!"

Before Donnie could respond, LizBeth let loose an ear-splitting screech that made everybody else stop talking and stare at her. When she lowered her head and closed her mouth, tears streamed from her eyes. "I knew this would happen," she sobbed.

"Was it Jackson?" Brian asked it in the calmest voice the room had yet heard. LizBeth nodded her assent and Brian nodded his understanding.

"I broke up with him, though, because he's a selfish ass," LizBeth said.

"He has to be held accountable," Alan said as if that was the final word on the matter.

Donnie started to remind the man to keep his mouth shut, but LizBeth reached over and put a hand on his arm. "No," she said. "He's out of my life."

"Well, you can't keep this baby," Melissa said. It was the tone she'd used when she told Donnie there was no money for the convention he wanted to go to or that she had already made plans on a night he wanted to meet with his few literary friends.

"I am," LizBeth said.

"You go to school and work part-time at Braum's and you think you'll have time to take care of a baby?" Melissa asked as if her daughter had taken leave of her senses.

"I'll find a way," LizBeth said.

"You think you can just have this baby and live in my house rent free? And I'll buy diapers and everything the baby needs?" Melissa demanded.

Donnie ground his teeth, wanting to shout his own responses, but he held his tongue. LizBeth was doing well and he was proud of her.

"This is my home and I would like to stay," LizBeth said. "But it's your house. You've been very clear that you own the property, Mom. If you don't want us here, we'll live somewhere else."

"Where would you ... " Melissa trailed off and her hard, angry gray eyes snapped toward Donnie. "*This* is why you're here!" Her voice was almost a hiss.

"Dad didn't know until just over an hour ago," LizBeth said, again speaking before Donnie could.

"But he used it as a way to get you to side with him," Melissa accused. "To go live with him so he won't have to pay child support on you."

This time LizBeth couldn't silence him. "Is that still all you care about? The fucking money?" Donnie snapped at his ex-wife.

"You can't talk to her like that," Alan said, his own voice rising.

Melissa told him to hush, but Donnie was more forceful. "Shut your mouth, you sleazy asshole, or I'll come over there and shut it for you. This is about *my* daughter."

Alan's dark eyes burned with anger, but he sat still.

Donnie said, "I've told LizBeth she can come live with me if she wants to, but I don't think that's what she wants. But she *will* live somewhere that she is loved and supported."

"Are you saying I don't love my daughter?" Melissa asked.

"You always go to the extremes," Donnie accused. "I did not say you don't love her. But you are not being understanding and loving right now."

"She's sixteen and pregnant," Melissa said.

"And she's our daughter and she needs us," Donnie countered.

"Please stop," LizBeth sobbed.

Everyone was silent as Brian pushed himself from the rocking chair and walked across the room to lean over LizBeth. He put his arms around his sister's shoulders and hugged her. She buried her face against his shoulder and cried.

"This is what she needs," Donnie said, but he said it quietly, without accusation. "Can we give it to her?"

"What about adoption?" Melissa asked.

Donnie shook his head. "She already told me no. She wants to keep it. We'll be grandparents."

"It's too soon," Melissa said, defeated.

Donnie shrugged, then reached over and rubbed his daughter's back. He faced his ex-wife. "I know you have a lot going on with your wedding coming up. I don't know what your plans are for living after that. If this is too much for you, she can come live with me."

"You live in the back of a used bookstore," Melissa said as if he'd forgotten his situation.

"No," Donnie said, shaking his head. "We got a house."

"We?" Melissa asked.

"My dad is living with me and another friend," he said. "We share the rent."

"She's not going to go live with three men while she's pregnant," Melissa said emphatically.

"I'm not going to fight you on it, Melissa," Donnie said. "As far as I'm concerned, the decision is LizBeth's. If she decides she wants to come live with me, I'll take her in, and if it means a court fight, I'll do it."

LizBeth's sobs had stopped and she was sitting up, though with her elbows on her knees and her chin in her palms. Brian stood beside her, his hand on her shoulder.

"LizBeth, where do you want to live?" Melissa asked.

She cleared her throat, gave Donnie a thankful look, then said, "Here. All my friends are here. But I want Dad in my life. I want him to feel comfortable visiting me and my baby." She paused and looked at her brother. "And hopefully Brian. And I want to go visit him sometimes. But I don't want you two to fight."

There was a small pang of disappointment that she'd chosen to stay with Melissa, but overall, Donnie felt a huge surge of pride in the way LizBeth spoke up for herself and what she wanted. His hand still rubbing her back, he looked at Melissa, and asked, "What do you think?"

"This isn't like that hamster you had," Melissa said to LizBeth. "You have to feed it. Babies are a lot of work."

LizBeth offered a weak smile. "I know, Mom. Will you help me?"

"You're too young," Melissa said, and she broke down in tears. Donnie looked away as Alan moved closer and took her in his arms. His gaze met LizBeth's.

"I'm proud of you," he mouthed. She smiled weakly. Donnie winked at Brian and his son gave him the first smile he'd given his father in years.

Then, suddenly, Melissa was off the couch. She moved quickly across the living room and fell on LizBeth, hugging her and sobbing, and LizBeth hugged her back and cried with her mother. Donnie knew then it would be okay. He shot a look at Alan and knew that Melissa's soon-to-be-husband also had read the signs. They nodded at each other.

Peace was established and a truce existed. Donnie stayed for a while and he and Melissa talked civilly, if distantly and in vague terms, about how things were going with them. Donnie focused mostly on how business was improving, how he was writing again, and his relationship with his father.

At last, Donnie said it was getting late and he had a long drive to get home. He stood up and reached into his pocket for his keys.

"You haven't eaten," LizBeth said. "You hardly ate anything at lunch." She looked at the others and told them, "I made him eat pho."

"He wouldn't have eaten that for anybody but you," Melissa said, and she said it with the faintest of smiles.

"I'll pick up some chicken nuggets and fries to eat while I drive," Donnie said. "Do you want to walk me out? Both of you?" He looked at his children. They both stood up and he told Melissa and Alan good-bye and went out the front door with LizBeth and Brian behind him. They stopped beside his truck.

"Thank you, Dad," LizBeth said. She threw herself into his arms and hugged him tightly around the neck. "I couldn't have done that without you."

He hugged her back and kissed her on the cheek. "You've got a long, hard road in front of you," he told her. "But I know you're strong enough to do it. I love you, LizzyBeth."

She smiled at the old nickname. "I love you, too, Daddy," she said.

Donnie turned his attention to his son. "Brian, I wish I could have spent more time with you today, but I guess it was best it was just me and your sister this time."

"That's okay," he said. At fourteen, he was taller and more muscular than Donnie had been. His dark hair flipped out around his ears and generally looked shaggy, but Donnie had never been a fan of haircuts, himself.

"LizBeth wants to come up to Sagebrush around Christmas," Donnie said. "I'd be glad to have you, too."

He nodded. "That'd be cool," he said.

"Can I hug you?" Donnie asked.

Brian shrugged. "Yeah. I guess so."

Donnie hugged his son and Brian put one arm around his father's shoulder to let his arm rest on his back for a moment. Donnie held him tightly, then let him go, but couldn't resist ruffling his hair just once. Brian grinned as he put the hair back in some kind of order that seemed like it was still chaos to Donnie.

"Well, I guess I'll go before I start crying again," Donnie said. "It is so good to see and talk to you both again."

"Dad?" Brian asked. "Did you and Mom always fight like you did tonight?"

"No," Donnie said. He didn't add because he had always been too cowardly to stand up to her. "We didn't, and I'm sorry you had to see it tonight or ever."

Brian just nodded but didn't say anything.

Donnie told them bye again and got into his truck. They waved as he pulled away from the curb. Driving home was like floating on clouds and he didn't even think about food until his stomach growled very loudly about an hour from home.

Chapter Twenty-Three

Life was full and good for the next couple of weeks. Josey worked tirelessly on holiday displays at the store, trying to include December celebrations from all cultures, or at least all of them the store had books about. She called the local elementary school and arranged to set up a Christmas tree in the store with the wishes of children who otherwise might not have a merry holiday. Wilson Pepper, editor of *The Sagebrush Democrat* newspaper and reader of detective novels, showed up to take pictures of the tree and do a story.

"You're making this store a regular community hub," Wilson said to Donnie. "Why was it important to you to set up this tree and work with the elementary school?"

Leaning on the counter, watching an elderly lady holding three paperbacks and looking at the white cards on the green tree, Donnie thought about all the platitudes he could offer. "Like almost everything else that's happened here since October, this was Josey's idea," he said. "I loved it and agreed to it, of course, but it's all been her."

"Have many people come in and claimed tags off the tree yet?" Wilson asked, scratching down notes on his pad as Donnie answered.

"A few. I'm hoping more do," Donnie said. "There were about forty-eight or so cards on there when we started."

"What are some of the things being asked for?" Wilson asked with only a quick glance up at Donnie as he continued to write.

"It's a variety. Bicycles, video games and consoles, a Peppa Pig playhouse was something I saw and had to look up to see what it was," Donnie said. "I saw one girl asked for a guitar. Lots of stuff."

"Will you be claiming a tag?"

"Yes," Donnie said. "We've actually arranged with the bank to jointly take care of unclaimed tags. But don't put that in, okay?"

"Right, right," Wilson said, adding an asterisk. "That might make an interesting piece after Christmas. What about your store becoming such a hub for the community?"

"I'm all for it," Donnie said. "You don't have to buy something to come in. There's always free coffee and people are welcome to come in, sit a while, read, or hang out. We have a book group and can start others if people are interested. We want to be a part of the community."

The lady with the books came to the counter and put her books down. They were all Andrew Greely novels, Donnie saw. She had a tag for an eight-year-old girl from the tree.

"Mrs. Wagner, I see you took a tag from the tree," Wilson said. "Would you like to tell readers of the *Democrat* why you're interested in that?"

"I still don't like that our town newspaper is named *Democrat*," she said in a voice raspy with age. "It should be neutral. I'm a Ronald Reagan Republican and I don't like reading my news from a paper called the *Democrat*."

Donnie picked up the novels and turned away to hide his grin. Wilson Pepper took the criticism in stride. "Yes, ma'am, I hear that a lot. I don't own the paper. I'm just the editor. Will you tell me about the Christmas tree tag?"

Florence Wagner picked up the tag in her wrinkled, arthritic fingers. "It's for a little girl. Eight years old. She wants coloring books, crayons, and a sketchbook. I loved to draw when I was a little girl, so this speaks to my heart. I want to encourage that creativity in a young person."

"That's beautiful," Wilson said, scribbling on his pad just as fast as he could.

"How much do I owe you, young man?" Mrs. Wagner asked Donnie. He told her the total and she paid him in exact change from a small clasp wallet she took from her purse. Donnie thanked her and she took her books.

"I love people like that," Wilson said as he finished writing down her quote. "They say the best things, and readers love seeing that someone else said just what they would have said. How about a picture of you and Josey by the tree?"

241

Donnie called for Josey, who was going through boxes in the back room, hoping to find a book about Kwanzaa. She came to the front and he told her what Wilson wanted. She immediately began straightening her hair and slapping dust off her sweater. They went to the tree and stood awkwardly in front of it.

"Josey, how about if you act like you're showing Donnie one of those cards at just about your shoulder level," Wilson said as he lifted his camera. "Donnie, you're interested in what she's saying."

They did the pose and he snapped a few pictures, checking them on his camera's screen. "Got it," he said. "This'll be in the paper Thursday. Front page above the fold."

Donnie laughed. "We're big news in Sagebrush," he joked to Josey.

Wilson was almost to the door when Donnie's cell phone rang. Donnie hurried behind the counter to grab the phone that was beside his computer, shooting a glance at Josey as he did and saying, "It's Gene." He picked up the phone and answered it, barely aware that Wilson had stopped by the door and Josey was whispering that it was Donnie's agent.

"Donnie, are you sitting your ass down?" Gene asked. His tone was peppy and Donnie figured he had good news.

"I'm standing up," Donnie said.

"Put your ass in a fuckin' chair," Gene said.

"Okay," Donnie said. He continued standing.

"A couple of days ago, Sara Castlebury, the editor of a new fantasy line, made an offer based on your partial and outline," Gene said.

"Really? How much? Why did you wait to tell me?" Donnie asked.

"They want to buy out your backlist and repackage the old Bolkar books with new covers," Gene said. "But only if you're agreeable to the next part."

"Spit it out, Gene," Donnie said excitedly. "What is it?" He was vaguely aware of Wilson edging back toward him.

"There's this producer who worked on Netflix's *The Witcher* series. He's got some financial backing and some interest from Hulu and he wants to adapt Bolkar's story," the agent said. "He wants you to sign an option giving him the rights to film one season, with an option to continue if the series is a success. There are clauses that give you more money if the first and successive seasons are picked up."

Donnie dropped into his chair. "You're kidding," he breathed.

"The fuck I am," Gene said and laughed. It sounded like he had a cigar in his mouth.

THE LOST PAGES BOOKSTORE

"How much?" Donnie asked.

"The deal is set to go with your okay on the backlist," Gene said. "You're not getting much for those. Five thousand per book and three percent royalty."

"Okay, okay. What about the new one?" Donnie asked.

"Sixty-five K advance, half on delivery of the manuscript and half on publication," Gene said. "The percentages vary based on sales, but the average will be about five for royalties. It'll be in the contract and we can negotiate if you're not happy with it."

"Okay. Good," Donnie said. "And the Hulu thing?"

"It's hard to say for sure how much it might be, but this producer is offering a nice option," Gene said, and quoted Donnie a high five-figure number. "That's all payable as soon as you sign the contract. Minus my fifteen percent, of course."

"Of course," Donnie said, laughing.

"How's the writing going, by the way?" Gene asked.

"Good," Donnie said. "I think I'll have a draft finished by Christmas."

"That's good to hear," Gene boomed. "Are we happy?"

"We're happy," Donnie agreed.

"If you're happy, I'm happy, Donnie-boy," the agent said. "I gotta go, but I'll send those contracts. Look 'em over and get back to me A-SAP."

"I will. Thanks, Gene," Donnie said, and put the phone down.

"Sounds like good news," Wilson said. "Anything the local readers of our fair city might be interested in?"

Donnie gave him what he knew had to be the goofiest of grins. "Not yet," he said. "Not until contracts are signed."

"Contracts usually mean money," Wilson mused.

"You are right about that," Donnie said. He saw that Josey was bouncing on her toes, about to burst, waiting for him to spill the details. "This isn't for the paper. Not yet," Donnie said. "It could all be nothing if the contracts aren't right, but Gene, my agent, wouldn't tell me about an offer unless it was legit. Do you promise not to print anything yet?"

"As long as you promise to let me be the first when the time does come," Wilson said.

Donnie nodded. "I promise." He took a deep breath, then said, "The new book I'm writing just sold. They're going to reprint all the old books. And there's a producer that wants to adapt the novels for a TV series."

Josey squealed so loud that the few customers in the store all jerked their heads up and looked toward the counter where she was jumping up and down. She ran around the counter and threw herself at Donnie and hugged his neck so tightly it almost cut off his oxygen. "I knew you'd do it," she gushed.

"That's great news, Donnie. Congratulations." Wilson extended a hand and Donnie shook it. "Did I hear you say you'll have the new book finished by Christmas?"

"Yeah. Hopefully sooner. Especially now," he said.

"With the storm we're supposed to get this weekend, it'll be a good time to stay inside and write," Wilson said. "As long as we don't lose power again."

"I haven't kept up with the weather," Donnie admitted. "Another big storm?"

"One of those polar vortex things," Wilson said. "It's in Canada but is supposed to charge down the Great Plains like a herd of freezing buffalo and cross into Oklahoma on Friday. They're saying Friday afternoon right now, but that could change a little."

"Ice and snow?" Josey asked.

"Lots of it," Wilson promised.

"You haven't been here for a big storm," Donnie said. "We get it worse than you're used to, even as close as Lawton. There's nothing to break up that wind and we're at a higher elevation."

"There's already a run on groceries," Wilson said. "If you haven't stocked up, you better do it."

"We just went to the grocery store a couple of days ago," Josey said.

"We might get a few more things," Donnie told her. "Thanks for the heads up, Wilson."

"Spreading the news is my job. Look for your Christmas tree story on Thursday. I have to go get the paper to bed," he said, gave a salute, and left.

"I'm so excited!" Josey said, her eyes wide and glowing. "How are you going to tell Mike and Debbie? Are you going to tell your kids? Will your ex want some of the money?"

"She won't get any of the money," Donnie said. "As for the rest, I have to think about it. LizBeth and maybe Brian will be here during Christmas, so I might wait and tell them then. I'll tell Dad when we pick him up from the VFW after work."

"Invite Debbie over for dinner," Josey insisted. "I want to see her face when you tell her. Oh, but she'll probably want to celebrate with sex."

Donnie laughed at her and looked around the store. "We don't need to announce that to the customers," he said quietly. "And she's not an animal that would attack me on the dining room table."

Josey shrugged. "If you say so," she said.

Donnie hadn't said much to Josey or his father about his visit to Lawton. With Josey, it was because he didn't want to put her on her guard about knowing her true age. He'd decided he'd just wait until LizBeth came for her visit and let the issue work itself out. He wasn't sure how his dad would react to the news his sixteen-year-old granddaughter was pregnant, so he didn't mention it. He'd simply told them it was a good visit and that they'd eaten and gone to the park and that he'd met Melissa's soon-to-be second husband. Debbie was the only one he'd told the entire truth to, and she had been supportive and said he'd done the right thing by not getting upset at LizBeth.

"It's a traumatic thing, gettin' pregnant that young, and it made her realize she needed her daddy," Debbie had said.

"Did she just use me as a buffer between her and Melissa?" Donnie asked.

"Have you talked to her since you left Lawton?"

"We've texted," Donnie had said. "She texted and asked if I got home okay and I asked if things were still good there."

"Personally, I don't think she would have kept the conversation goin' if she'd just wanted you there when she told her mom she was pregnant,' Debbie said. Donnie agreed with that assessment.

The text messages continued, too. He sometimes heard from LizBeth a few times a day. She usually texted early to report on her morning sickness, and sometimes during the day to complain about school, and they always told each other good-night now. Donnie had texted Brian to say it had been good to see him, and the response he got was short, but not rude, and Brian hadn't sent any other messages. Donnie mentioned it to LizBeth and she told him Brian never sent long messages, so Donnie didn't worry about it too much.

Donnie texted Debbie, who was off work now, and asked if she'd come to the house for dinner because he had news to share with her. She said she would, so he told Josey he was going to the grocery store to get some things for dinner and for the storm.

As he got in his truck, Donnie decided he and his dad hadn't really had much time together lately. His father had been going to bed early and had become unusually quiet during breakfast. Some days he went to the VFW post while Donnie and Josey went to the store, but most days he stayed home and said he just napped and watched TV. He never wanted to come to the store anymore. He was most talkative during dinner, making his usual irreverent jokes and telling stories about his past, then he'd go to the living room with them for a while, but pretty soon he announced he was tired and went to bed. Donnie pulled into the VFW parking lot and turned off the truck's engine.

Major Jack Schwartz greeted Donnie when he entered the low building. There was the usual sound of clicking dominoes and elderly men joking and cussing at each other. "Donnie," the Major said, extending his meaty hand. "How have you been?"

"I'm good, how about you?" Donnie asked.

"Can't complain," Major Schwartz said. "What brings you in?"

Donnie thought that was an annoyingly stupid question, but he kept that to himself. "I need to do some grocery shopping and thought Dad might want to go with me."

"Mike's not here," the Major said.

"But I dropped him off here this morning," Donnie argued.

"Yeah. He was here. We had pizza brought in for lunch and I guess it didn't agree with him," Major Schwartz said. "He got to feeling bad, so I drove him home."

Donnie studied the man's wide, wrinkled face. "He didn't call or text me," he said. The Major shrugged his shoulders. "What was wrong with him?"

"Just some indigestion. Heartburn," Schwartz said. "He ate some Tums here but wanted to go home and rest. I'm sure he'll be fine, but he's probably asleep. I'd just let him be if I was you."

"He's sleeping a lot lately," Donnie said. He said it more to himself, but the other man took it as part of their conversation.

"It comes from living in that old folks' home," the Major said. "He told us he was always bored there and he slept a lot just so they'd leave him alone. Still in the habit, I guess. And, sometimes, us old guys just like to sleep."

"I guess," Donnie said, but he wasn't so sure. "At least he's not in Woodward again." Schwartz only smiled and nodded, so Donnie excused himself and left.

He drove on to the little grocery store and was shocked despite Wilson's warning to see the parking lot was almost full of cars. Inside, the store was buzzing with mostly women who pushed full carts of food. As he pushed his own cart past an aisle, he saw two women jerking back and forth on a box of Cap'n Crunch cereal. Donnie knew he was going to be too late, and sure enough, when he got to the bread aisle there wasn't a single loaf of white bread left on the shelves. He took one of the remaining three loaves of generic wheat bread, then went to the refrigerator section and grabbed three cans of biscuits. Most of the beef was gone from the meat section, but he found a couple of packages of chicken breasts for that night's dinner and some pork chops to supplement what they had in the freezer at home.

Roger, the short, mustached store manager, was putting jugs of milk in the refrigerator when Donnie left the meat department. He saw Donnie and held up one of the jugs. "These are all we have left. If you want one, you better grab it now."

Donnie took the jug and put it in his cart. "This is crazy," he said. "Is the storm really supposed to be that bad?"

Roger put the last two jugs in the refrigerator, then shrugged. "You know how those TV weathermen like to predict the end of the world a few times a year," he said. "I don't know. I wish they'd tell grocery stores a few days before they make their forecast so we could stock up."

"Roger!" They both turned to find a woman in a long red coat and garish makeup standing behind a loaded cart. "Do you mean to tell me you're out of toilet paper?" she demanded. Donnie noted that she had a sixteen-roll package in her cart already.

"Every package we had in stock went on the shelf this morning, Mrs. Bertram," Roger answered calmly.

"Well, I never! How can people be so selfish?" She heaved her cart into a turn and stomped away.

Roger shook his head. "People get crazy," he said. "How are your dad and niece?"

It took Donnie a moment to process that. He kept forgetting that most people in town still thought Josey was his niece. "They're good," he said. "Josey has more people coming into the store than I ever dreamed of."

"I've heard," Roger said. He started to say more, but another woman rolled up and demanded toilet paper.

"I'll see you later," Donnie said, and slipped away. He stocked up on facial tissue, a worthy backup if their home supply of toilet paper ran out, and got some canned goods and microwave popcorn.

He found his dad asleep in the recliner in the living room, his face turned to one side and his mouth open as he snored. Donnie paused, his hands full of grocery bags, and looked at his father. The older man's face seemed thinner, almost sallow, and the fingers of his hands on his chest jerked and trembled in his sleep. He saw there was a prescription pill bottle on the end table beside the recliner and decided to take a look at it after he put the groceries down.

In the kitchen, he raised the bags to the counter, but one caught the edge and ripped enough to allow a can of vegetable stew to slip out and crash to the floor, just missing Donnie's foot.

"Who's that?" Mike's startled voice demanded from the living room.

"It's just me, Dad," Donnie answered. "I got some groceries. Debbie's coming for dinner."

"Oh. Okay," Mike said. Donnie heard the faint rattle of pills and knew his father was hiding the bottle that had been on the table.

"I'll be in there in a minute," Donnie called, and began putting the groceries away. When he got to the living room, he noted the pill bottle was indeed gone, but his dad didn't look any better for his nap. He settled onto the end of the sofa nearest the recliner. "Major Schwartz told me he brought you home because some pizza disagreed with you."

"Oh. Yeah," Mike said. He nodded and rubbed his stomach. "It went right through, though. I thought I was gonna blow the toilet apart." He laughed at his own joke, but it wasn't very convincing.

"Dad, are you okay?" Donnie asked. "You look thinner than you were when you forced your way into my truck in Lawton."

"I'm fine," he said. "Just old. Getting ready for that long sleep beside your mother."

"Don't talk like that," Donnie said, frowning. "I need you to stay around for a long time. We still have a lot of catching up to do."

Mike smiled at him for a moment, then looked toward the window and the tree in the front yard. "I guess my soul will cling to this dust a little longer," he said. "I had to look that up after it came to me on Thanksgiving. It's Psalm one hundred-nineteen, verse twenty-five."

Donnie laughed softly. "I never thought I'd hear you quoting scripture."

Mike pushed himself up a little straighter in the chair. "I've always been a believer," he said. "Just never felt the need to push it on anybody. I know your mom made sure you got to church. I never could tolerate all that singing, myself."

"Well, you make sure you cling to the dust for a long time," Donnie said. "What were those pills I saw when I came in?"

"Oh, just heartburn medicine," Mike said, waving the question away as if it were a summer mosquito.

Donnie almost asked if he could see the bottle, but knew that would be pushing a boundary, telling his father he didn't believe him, and he wasn't ready for that conversation yet. Were the pills connected to the secret trip to Woodward?

"There's a storm coming," Mike said.

"Yeah. Wilson Pepper told me," Donnie said.

"Who?"

"The newspaper editor. He's doing a story on the Christmas tree for needy kids we have in the store," Donnie said. "I picked up some extra groceries and stuff. There wasn't much left. I hope your bowl-busting shits are over, because the toilet paper in the house is all there is."

"I think I'm good," Mike said.

"Dad, there's something I should tell you," Donnie said. "It's about my trip to Lawton."

"You were pretty evasive about that," Mike said. "Did you and Melissa get into it again?"

"We did, but it's the reason we did that I wanted to tell you about," Donnie said. He paused, trying to think of a way to soften the news, but there really wasn't a way to do it. "LizBeth is pregnant."

Mike was quiet for a long moment, then he nodded his head slowly twice. "She's only, what, about seventeen?"

"Sixteen," Donnie corrected. "She wants to keep the baby. She broke up with the guy she was with."

"A lot of girls are having babies in high school," Mike said. "Lots of single moms. I don't think it's smart, but if they can do it, I guess LizBeth can."

"I thought you'd get mad and want to go kill that boy," Donnie admitted.

Mike shrugged. "What good would it do to get mad?"

"Melissa blew up, of course, but she came around," Donnie said. "LizBeth wants to come up and visit over Christmas break. I think Brian might come, too."

"That's great," Mike said, and now his face did light up. "I haven't seen them since you and Melissa split up."

"Of course she never brought them to visit you," Donnie muttered. "Dad, there's something else. If I tell you, do you promise not to say anything about it?"

"Scout's honor," Mike said, raising two fingers.

"LizBeth had a class with Josey," Donnie said. "Josey is supposed to be a junior in high school. She's not eighteen. She's a minor."

Mike was quiet for a long moment. Finally, he asked, "Does she know you know?"

"No."

"Donnie, we've talked about this before," Mike said. "That girl's got a good head on her shoulders. If somebody was looking for her, I think we would have seen her face on the news. I still say to just let it be."

"It's going to be awkward when LizBeth comes to visit," Donnie said.

Mike smiled. "Yeah. That it will. But we'll cross that bridge when we get to it. Now, is there a reason Debbie is coming to dinner so unexpectedly?"

"There is," Donnie answered. "I invited her, and you can find out why when she gets here."

"I'm old. My heart might not handle a surprise," Mike warned.

"You'll be fine. I need to get back to the store. Do you need anything? Do you want to come?"

Mike seemed to consider it, then said yes, he would come and sit in the back and drink some coffee and read for a while. He was slow to get up from the recliner and blamed it on old bones, but it seemed to Donnie that it hurt his dad to walk.

"You're sure you're okay?" he asked as he opened the front door.

"I'm fine. Just old and stiff. This cold weather gets in the bones," Mike insisted.

When they got to the store, they found Josey playing peek-a-boo around the end of a bookshelf with a toddler in a thick pink coat. The child squealed in delight every time Josey hopped into view and said, "Ahhh, peek-a-boo!" The little girl's mom was the only other customer and she was browsing the horror section. Josey saw the men and offered a quick wave before jumping out at the toddler again.

Mike chuckled at the girl, slapped Donnie on the arm, then made his way to the Queen Anne chairs and the coffee pot. Donnie went to his seat and opened his computer. There was an email from Gene and he opened it eagerly and found two contracts that he began reading intently.

With Josey filming him on her phone and Mike, who found out early what the surprise was, grinning broadly behind her, Donnie signed the book and film option contracts. He put them in an envelope – again while Josey recorded the act for publicity and posterity – and hurried over to the post office to mail them back to his agent, then they closed up the store and went home.

Donnie began cooking, and when Debbie arrived, he sent her to the living room with his father and Josey. He fried the chicken, thankful for a real stove instead of the hot plate burner he'd used for so many years at the store, and made mashed potatoes and corn and baked one of the cans of biscuits. He set the table and called everyone to come eat.

Josey waited until everyone had filled their plate before blurting, "Tell her now!"

"Can't I eat first?" he asked.

"No!" She said it like she was offended he would even ask. Her face glowed with excitement and Donnie couldn't help but grin at her.

"My agent sold my new book," Donnie said as if he was announcing the time.

"Say it with enthusiasm," Josey insisted. "Tell the rest."

"They're going to republish my back titles, too," Donnie deadpanned.

"Uh! You're infuriating! There's gonna be a TV series!" Josey crowed over the table.

"Really?" Debbie asked, then she jumped out of her chair and ran to hug Donnie where he sat in his, squeezing him hard and planting a big kiss on his cheek before going back to her own chair. "I'm so happy for you."

"It's funny how people get happier over the possibility of a film than of the original book," Donnie said.

"No," Debbie argued. "I didn't mean it that way."

Donnie grinned at her. "I know. And the film business is where the big money is. And this film deal right now doesn't mean that the books will actually become a TV series. I just gave a producer the right to shop them to studios."

"It's still exciting," Mike said.

"It is," Donnie agreed. "So is this perfectly golden-brown fried chicken that is still hot from the skillet."

They ate and talked about the progress on the new book, how many episodes each volume might make when filmed, and who would play the major parts. Through it all, Donnie watched his father, and could tell when the older man's energy began to flag.

Mike's face lost its animation, his eyes lost their sparkle, and a few minutes later his complexion seemed to turn gray.

"Donnie, this was an amazing supper," Mike said. He wiped at his mouth and put his napkin down with a shaky hand. "I'm feeling kind of tired, though, so I'm gonna go ahead and go to bed." He nodded at Debbie and Josey and told them, "Have a good evening. I'll see you both later." Then he left his chair and the dining room; Donnie noted that he put a hand on the door frame for support as he passed.

The table was very quiet. No one ate, drank, or spoke.

"I'm worried about him," Donnie said quietly.

"I'm sure he's just tired," Josey said, but her voice lacked conviction.

Donnie wanted to plead with her again to tell him what his father's secret was, but now wasn't the time. He looked down at his food and no longer felt hungry. "I guess I'm done, too," he said. "I'm sorry I didn't get anything for dessert. The place was almost sold out and I just didn't think of it."

"It's okay," Debbie said, and she reached over and squeezed his wrist.

"I'm full, anyway," Josey said. "I'll help you clean up."

Donnie allowed them to help clear the table and store the leftovers, then they pulled out the *Life* board game and played two games before Debbie said she needed to go home. Donnie walked her to her car.

"I'm sure he's okay," she said as she leaned against her car door and Donnie put his arms around her. She hugged him back. "Old people get tired easy."

"I guess," Donnie said, unconvinced. He kissed her forehead.

"Congratulations on the book and TV thing," Debbie said. "I knew you'd find success. You deserve it."

"Hmm," Donnie hummed into her knit cap as she laid her head against his chest. He wasn't convinced of that, either. "Thank you," he whispered.

They kissed and he watched her drive away, then he went inside. Mike was already asleep, so Donnie went upstairs and showered and got into his own bed.

Chapter Twenty-Four

Thursday came, and with it came the newspaper article and a stream of people, most of whom worked downtown, to pluck wishes off the Lost Pages Bookstore Christmas tree. When Sherry Brown came by at lunch, she took two of the cards, saying, "Just in case there aren't any left for the bank." That inspired Josey to take one for herself and one for Donnie. One thing Donnie was very proud to see was Omar and his band come in and each one of them took a wish; Donnie knew that all four of the boys weren't so far from qualifying to have their own wishes on the tree. By noon on Friday, all the cards were taken and a few people had already brought back their purchased gifts.

The store became quiet after Sherry left with a few books for her weekend reading. An hour later, Donnie noted that the world outside was as dark as if it was late evening. The wind was picking up, too, blowing dirt and trash down the street, north to south. As he watched, his neighboring business owners were shutting off lights and locking doors. He saved his book file and opened a weather radar on his computer. The polar vortex was bearing down on northwest Oklahoma.

"It's really dark out there," Josey said. As Donnie was checking the radar she had wandered up from the back room to see why the store was so quiet.

"Yeah," Donnie agreed. "Lots of people are closing up for the day." As he said it, he watched the door of Annie's Cafe open and Debbie let three farmers out, waving at them as they left. She turned the sign on the door to read CLOSED, then looked across the street and waved to the bookstore. Donnie and Josey waved back.

"It's gonna be bad, huh?" Josey asked.

Donnie read from the computer screen. "'Expect up to a half inch of freezing rain followed by eight to twelve inches of snow. Snowfall could be more in isolated areas. Temperatures will drop below zero tonight and won't get above freezing for at least five days.'" He looked up at her.

"I guess we'll probably be closed tomorrow," she said.

"I'd say that's a safe bet," Donnie agreed. "It's that freezing rain that worries me."

About fifteen minutes later, the first fat drops of rain splashed onto the street and sidewalk outside. A minute later and it was raining for real. Donnie packed his computer and locked the front door and together he and Josey went to the truck and drove home. The raindrops were turning to ice on the windshield before they got there. Josey got out and ran inside to check on Mike while Donnie stayed in the truck and called Debbie.

"Hello?" she asked.

"Hi, honey. It's me," Donnie said. "Have you left work yet?"

"I'm just about to," she said.

"It's starting to freeze. Are you okay to drive in it? I can come pick you up. I just dropped off Josey," Donnie said.

"Are you gonna stay with me during the storm?" she asked teasingly.

"I'd like to, but I can't leave Josey and Dad alone. You could stay with us," he offered.

"If the power goes out in the trailer park, I'll definitely be there," she promised.

"I'm worried about you being able to get there if that happens," Donnie said. "You do know that Josey already knows we have sex, right?"

"That don't mean she's gotta hear you moanin' and gruntin' like a stuck hog in the bedroom right next to hers," Debbie said and laughed. Donnie heard another woman, probably Annie, laughing in the background.

"There's a bathroom between the rooms," he said weakly.

"Baby, I'll be alright," Debbie said. "If I need to come over, I will. Or you can drive that big ol' truck over and pick me up."

The truck's windshield wipers were pushing slush across the glass. Donnie sighed. "Okay. You're as stubborn as you are pretty. It's starting to get bad, so please leave soon, be careful, and let me know when you get home. Please?"

"Okay, you ol' worry-wart," she said, laughing again. "We're all leavin' now. I love you."

"I love you, too," Donnie said. "Be careful!" She was gone.

He shut off the truck's engine and went inside and got an old blanket and used it to cover the truck's windshield, then he went back inside and took the cup of hot chocolate Josey offered him. The three of them stood by the big window of the living room and watched the rain fall for a while.

Donnie turned on the television and they all settled down to watch a very excited Oklahoma City weatherman describe what was happening across the street. Storm trackers were out and, to the surprise of the viewers, they showed a shot of deserted downtown Sagebrush as the meteorologist said businesses were closing early and people were preparing for the worst.

"It's Lost Pages Bookstore!" Josey cried out as the storm tracker's camera swept down Main Street. The white lettering on the plate glass window looked faded and the store was dark behind the glass, but all the downtown shops looked the same. "We need to repaint the name," Josey said.

"We do," Donnie agreed.

"It's the end of the world again," Mike said as he dropped into his recliner. He gave a snort of laughter and opened yesterday's newspaper with the picture of Donnie and Josey and the Christmas tree on the front page.

Josey brought out the chess set and she and Donnie placed their pieces, but neither was really in the mood for a game, so she went to the kitchen and heated up leftovers. Everyone ate at the dining table, but there wasn't much conversation. Even Jasper, who watched them intently for dropped food, was quiet.

"I hope this doesn't keep people from buying the gifts for the kids from the tree," Josey offered.

"There'll be plenty of time after this storm blows over to get those," Mike assured her.

"Yeah," Donnie agreed. "There's time."

By nine that evening, there was a glaze of ice on the front porch steps and the branches of the elm tree in the front yard. Donnie kept texting Debbie, who had gotten home and eaten dinner. She said she was going to bed to fall asleep to the sound of freezing rain hitting the metal top and sides of her trailer. Donnie, Mike, and Josey watched the beginning of the ten o'clock news, hoping for something other than storm coverage, but there was nothing. Mike excused himself and went to bed.

"I think I'll go watch TikTok videos in bed before I go to sleep," Josey announced.

Donnie texted LizBeth and Brian and told them what the weather was like where he was and asked if they were ready for the storm. Brian said, "Yeah" and that was all, but LizBeth told him she'd gone shopping with her mom after school and they were all set to stay inside for a few days. "Alan's here," she added. Donnie said he was sorry and told her to stay warm.

Finally, Donnie turned off the television and went to the dining table with his computer and wrote for about two hours before he got frustrated with the mistakes his tired mind and hands were making and shut the computer down. He went to bed and was soon asleep.

He awoke to what sounded like a gunshot. Then there was another one and the sound of ice tinkling through tree limbs. His room was abnormally dark. Donnie looked at the alarm clock and saw that it was off.

"Shit," he cursed. The power was off. Most likely a tree limb fell and pulled down a line, maybe even blew a transformer. There was another sharp crack and more tinkling ice and a crash as a big tree limb hit the ground outside. Donnie checked his cell phone and saw that it was just after three in the morning.

He went to his bedroom window, but all he could see was the roof of the house next door, so he pulled his socks and sweatpants back on against the chill and made his way down the stairs. There was absolutely no light from any appliances in the house or street lamps outside. Donnie wondered about Debbie and if her power was out and if she was still asleep. He was thankful he had plugged in his cell phone before going to bed, although there was no way it could have charged completely.

At the bottom of the stairs, he realized there was a strange smell, like sewage. He looked quickly out the front window. The elm had lost some limbs, but none had hit his truck. He supposed he should have thought of that possibility and decided he would brave the cold and move it to the street in front of the neighbor's house where no tree limbs would hit it.

"What is that smell?" he whispered. He made his way to the kitchen and opened the cabinet under the sink and found the cheap blue plastic flashlight. He flicked it on and the beam was strong and steady. He looked under the sink, but there was no leak and the sinks themselves were dry. He started toward the downstairs bathroom.

He was several feet from the door when the beam of light brushed over the outstretched hand. Donnie froze, petrified, holding the light so that the hand was in the center of the circle of illumination, a bare forearm going back into the darkness. The hand wasn't moving.

"Oh, God, no," Donnie whispered.

He forced himself to move the beam of light up the arm. His father's head rested on the hard tile floor of the bathroom. There was a big purple lump on his forehead and a trickle of blood that led to a small pool of deep red that formed around the place where his eye met the floor. Donnie groaned and moved the light some more. Mike's light green pajama pants and white underwear were around his ankles. His legs were thin and white in the yellow glow of the flashlight. There was something about the underwear. Donnie focused the light. There was blood staining the bottom of them.

"Dad?" Donnie asked, his voice trembling. "Dad? Dad!" His father didn't move. Donnie ran into the bathroom and instinctively tried to flip the light switch. It was already in the on position, but there was no light except what the shaking flashlight offered.

Donnie shone the light into the toilet and saw that the water was thick and red. He moved the beam back to his father and saw that Mike's buttocks were smeared with crimson and, to his horror, there was another pool of blood where his pelvis rested on the floor.

"Dad!" Donnie wailed.

Upstairs, Josey called out, "Donnie?" Jasper, who slept in Josey's room, began barking. Outside, another tree limb exploded away from its brothers and crashed to the frozen ground. Josie called again.

"Down here," Donnie called. "It's Dad. He's ... He's really bad."

Donnie put a hand on his father's shoulder and shook the man gently. There was no response. He picked up the arm he'd first seen in the light and tried checking for a pulse with his own shaking fingers. Josey's slight figure stepped into the bathroom doorway. Jasper tried to get around her to investigate.

"Oh no," she said, her hands rising to cover her mouth. "Oh no," she repeated, then saw what Donnie was trying to do. "Check his throat," she said. "Jasper, no! Go lay down." The dog reluctantly moved away.

Donnie looked at her, helpless and not understanding.

Josey knelt beside him and pressed two of her slender white fingers against Mike's whiskery, wrinkled throat. She held them there for a minute. "There's a pulse," she said. "He's alive."

They looked at each other.

"We have to call nine-one-one," Josey told him.

Donnie nodded, then his senses flooded back. "They'll have to come from Alva or Woodward," he said. "It could take hours in this weather."

"It's all we can do," Josey argued.

"No," Donnie said. "I'll take him there. I'll take him to the hospital in Woodward. I can get him there faster than they can get here and take him back."

"But they can treat him in the ambulance," Josey said. She grabbed his arm with the hand that held the flashlight. "Donnie. We have to call."

Donnie shook his head. "No time," he moaned. "He's bleeding out of his butt. So much blood ... " He looked around him, but Josey still held his arm with the light and the blood was just darker blotches in the dim room. "Stay with him while I get dressed."

She continued to protest as Donnie pulled his arm free and flew up the stairs. He dressed quickly in jeans, boots, an undershirt, and a hooded sweatshirt. Downstairs, he pulled on his coat, then realized Josey wasn't in the bathroom. He shook that away and went to his father's bedroom and stripped the blankets off his bed and spread them on the floor beside the bathroom door.

Carefully, Donnie stepped inside the bathroom and gently rolled Mike onto his back, then pulled up the man's pajama bottoms and underwear. He carefully lifted his father from the floor, having to step in blood as he did it, and carried him to the blankets, where he lay him back down and wrapped him as tightly as an infant.

"I'm going with you," Josey said. She was beside him, dressed and wearing her coat, gloves, and hat. "I started the truck and put your seat forward so we can lay him on the back seat. But it's really, really slick, Donnie. You might fall on the porch and that would make everything worse. Please call."

Donnie shook his head and went for his own coat and gloves. He lifted his father in his arms and pushed through the front door. It was like stepping into a deep freeze. Ice was thick on the edge of the porch, the steps, and the walkway leading to the driveway.

"All I have to do is get off the porch, then walk through the yard," Donnie said to himself.

"Be careful," Josey said behind him.

Donnie took a deep breath and moved one foot, then the other to the ice edge. He stepped down with his right foot, then put his left beside it. Right foot down. Left foot down. He was on the walkway. Left foot forward. Right foot beside it. Left foot forward onto the grass; it crackled and crunched under his weight. Right foot forward. Donnie breathed a little easier. Ahead of him, his truck idled, steam rising from the tailpipe, the driver's door open and the dome and headlights beckoning him forward. Still being careful, he covered the distance until he was standing on the icy driveway beside the open door.

Josey got in on the other side and took Mike's head and shoulders and guided them onto the narrow back seat. Donnie tucked the blanket-wrapped feet onto the seat so that they were behind him, then dropped his seat into place and raised a foot to get into the truck.

The other foot slipped from under him and he crashed to his knees, his face slamming against the door handle.

"Donnie!" Josey cried and leaned across the front seats to check on him.

Donnie pulled himself up by holding on to the door handle and the steering wheel. He held himself in an upright position, breathing heavily. He tasted blood and knew he'd bitten his tongue. He turned his face and spat, then noticed the edge of the blanket over his windshield. He pulled it away and let it drop into the yard, then eased himself into the truck.

"This is a bad idea," Josey said.

"It's the fastest way," Donnie repeated. He dropped the truck into reverse and tried not to notice how they mostly slid out of the driveway. He got the truck straightened out and drove slowly through the neighborhood, coasting through stop signs, until he was on Main Street, then through town and on the open, frozen highway.

All around them, strands of barbed wire, naked tree limbs, dead grass, wheat stubble, mailboxes, and dark streetlights were shiny with ice, and it kept falling so fast the truck's defroster and windshield wipers struggled to keep up.

"So much blood," Donnie kept saying in almost a moan as he hunched over the steering wheel to watch the road. "He was bleeding from his butt. Why? Why from his butt? So much blood."

"I'm going to call the hospital and tell them we're coming," Josey said. "They can at least be ready."

"Yeah. Yeah, good idea," Donnie said without looking at her.

Josey took a minute to look up the number on her smartphone, then dialed. She put it on speaker. Someone answered. "Hi. My name is Josey Wilder," Josey said. "I'm with my uncle and his dad. We're coming down from Sagebrush. Mike Nelson is seventy-nine years old with prostate cancer. We found him unconscious and bleeding from the rectum on the bathroom floor."

Donnie's head snapped around and he gaped at Josey. The girl refused to look at him. "Prostate cancer?" he demanded.

"Why didn't you call nine-one-one?" the female voice in Woodward asked.

"My uncle said it would take too long for the ambulance to get to us," Josey answered.

"We could have begun treatment in the ambulance," the nurse said. Donnie saw Josey's jaw muscles clench and he knew she wanted to look at him and say, "I told you so," but she was afraid to face him.

"Prostate cancer?" he said again, helplessly, and returned his attention to the highway.

"What is Mr. Nelson's condition right now?" the nurse asked.

"He's unconscious in the back seat," Josey said. "It looked like he fell off the toilet and hit his head on the sink. There's a big bruise on his forehead. It bled a little, too."

Donnie slowed to a crawl and eased the truck through the turn from the eastbound highway to the southbound, the one that would take them to Woodward. He pushed the speed back up to thirty. There was not another vehicle anywhere to be seen. The slush kept falling from the sky, sounding like a heavy metal drummer pounding all over the truck.

"You say he was bleeding from the rectum?" the nurse asked.

"Yes. There was a pool of blood under him and blood in the toilet," Josey answered.

"Do you know what stage his cancer is in?"

"I don't know," Josey said. "He just told me it's advanced."

Donnie felt tears stinging his eyes. "How could you keep that from me?" he asked without looking at her. He swallowed more blood from his tongue.

"How far from the hospital are you?" the nurse asked.

"Donnie?" Josey asked. "Do you know?"

He swallowed hard, tasted his own blood. "Maybe thirty miles," he said. Josey repeated that to the nurse.

"Is Mr. Nelson still bleeding?"

"I don't know," Josey answered. "We've got him wrapped up pretty tight in blankets."

"Okay. He's still unconscious?" the nurse asked.

"Yes."

"Did you try to wake him?"

"Yes."

"There was no response?"

"No."

"None at all?" the nurse asked.

"None," Josey answered. "Even when Donnie picked him up and carried him out of the bathroom, wrapped him in blankets and carried him to the truck. Mike didn't even moan."

"What are the road conditions where you are?" the nurse asked.

"Bad," Josey said. "It's raining ice and the road is really slippery."

"Do you know who Mr. Nelson's primary care provider is?"

"No," Josey said. "I know he had an appointment for a test at this hospital a few weeks ago."

There was the sound of computer keys. "Do you know his birthdate?"

"Donnie?" Josey asked.

"August fifteen, Nineteen-forty-two," he said. He had to wipe at his eyes again.

"I found him," the nurse said. "I will notify Dr. Pastorini and we'll be ready when you get here. Can I get a phone number to call you back?"

"Do you want to give them your number?" Josey asked.

"I left my phone at the house," he said.

Josey gave the nurse her number and the nurse advised them to drive carefully, then they hung up.

"Debbie tried to call while I was on the phone," Josey said meekly. "Do you want me to call her back?"

"Yes, please," Donnie answered stiffly.

"Donnie, I'm sorry," she pleaded. "He made me swear I wouldn't tell you or anybody. He came to live with you because he wanted to be with you at the end. Please don't be mad at me."

He risked a glance at her and thought about what she'd said. It wasn't good enough. He turned his attention back to the road. "You hid that from me just like you hid that you're supposed to be a junior in high school. What else, Josey?"

She didn't answer. There was the sound of her phone dialing, then Debbie's scared voice. "Josey? Are you okay? Why won't Donnie pick up?"

Josey didn't answer. Donnie looked over at her and saw that her face was crumpled, broken, leaking snot and tears as she held the phone extended toward him in a shaking hand.

"Debbie," Donnie said. "My dad has prostate cancer. Fucking prostate cancer. And they were hiding it from me. He collapsed in the bathroom and he's bleeding from his ass and has a knot on his head and we're taking him to the hospital in Woodward."

"Cancer?" Debbie asked. "Oh, Donnie. I'm so sorry. How is he right now?"

"Unconscious," Donnie answered.

"Why are you driving? Why didn't you call for an ambulance?" she asked.

"It would have taken them too long to get him and take him back to the hospital," he answered, and he knew his voice gave away his irritation.

"Are you okay?" she asked.

"I'm just pissed off that nobody told me my father is dying of cancer," Donnie snapped. Josey's phone shook violently in her outstretched hand. Ahead of them was an underpass where a train could cross over the highway. Someone had spray-painted "Class of 2019" on one of the concrete flanges that held back the banked earth. "I can't believe I didn't know," Donnie said.

"He didn't want to die alone in a nursing home," Josey sobbed.

"Donnie! Did you make her cry?" Debbie asked.

More tears filled Donnie's eyes. He took a hand from the steering wheel to swipe at his face.

The steering wheel jerked in his one hand and suddenly the truck was spinning, spinning, spinning on the icy highway. Josey screamed. On the phone, Debbie screamed. Donnie cursed and fought for control, but the back of the truck was off the highway and they were sliding at an angle into a drainage ditch. The pickup began to pitch to the right and Donnie knew they were about to roll. He looked out the passenger window and saw the ice-covered concrete of the railroad overpass a moment before it caved in his door.

His body filled with sudden, burning agony. He thought he was choking on his tongue as he tried to scream. He didn't know if he was making any sound or not. There was blood running down his face and his nose hurt and the airbag from the steering wheel was deflating in front of him.

They were stopped.

Donnie looked toward Josey, but his eyes couldn't focus. He tried to say her name, but his eyes rolled up and he collapsed forward onto the steering wheel. Blackness took away the pain.

Chapter Twenty-Five

Cold. A rushing sound. A voice. Pin pricks cascading onto his face.

... sorry ...

Donnie tried to open his eyes, but the lids wouldn't raise. He sank back into darkness. Something was pulling at him. The pin pricks stopped. There was the voice again.

... sorry

so sorry ...

promised

The blackness surged up from his feet and swallowed him again.

Lights flashing against his closed eyelids. Something touching him. Red. Blue. The lights were insistent. Important.

Donnie ...

... hear me ...

He forced an eye to open. One of them wouldn't open. Left? Right? He wasn't sure. A giant black face loomed inches above his and Donnie wanted to shrink away, but he didn't have that much control. A blinding light flashed into his one open eye.

Concussion

He knew that word. Connnn ... cussion.

His eye closed and there was the sensation of floating, then a bump and a slide to a stop. The red and blue lights weren't flashing anymore. It was warmer here. A slamming noise, and then more motion.

Donnie welcomed the darkness back.

The next time he opened his eye, he was warm and sitting upright. The pain was still there, but it felt far away, muted. He knew from the smell that he was in a hospital room. Then he noted the steady beep of a machine tracking his heart rate. Fluorescent lights shone down on him and somewhere in the distance he heard the muted tones of conversation.

"Josey?" He formed the word, but nothing came out of his throat. Donnie licked his lips and tried again. "Josey?" It was only a croak.

"She's not here."

A thick-waisted nurse wearing a pink sweater over her white scrubs adorned with teddy bears said as she came into the room. Before Donnie could ask where Josey was, the nurse kept talking.

"You have a concussion, Mr. Nelson," she said. "You also have a huge deep tissue bruise on your left thigh. Dr. Gonzales was shocked the bone wasn't broken, so you got lucky there, but you won't be putting any weight on that leg for a while. We picked some glass out of your scalp, neck, and face. You're going to be okay." She smiled at him.

"Where's Josey and my dad?" he asked.

"Your dad is in ICU," she said, her smile slipping away. "I'm not the kind of person to sugar coat it, and I think you probably already know that his prognosis is not good. The last I heard, he was still unconscious."

"Josey?" he insisted.

The nurse blew out her breath and looked away, and for a moment Donnie thought she might be wishing that she was the kind to sugarcoat the truth. "A social worker took her."

Donnie stared with his one open eye as he tried to comprehend what he'd just heard. "Social worker?" he asked.

The nurse reached up and fluffed an IV bag hanging from a pole beside his bed. Donnie saw that there was a tube running into his arm. "I heard a little bit of that conversation," the nurse said, dropping her hand back to her side. "She said she told you she was eighteen so you'd let her live with you, but she's only sixteen and turned herself in so you wouldn't get in trouble."

"No," Donnie said. Then he was sobbing. "No, no, no, no."

"There's a police officer who'll want to question you to see if your story matches hers. He's here now." The nurse stepped out of the room and spoke to someone Donnie couldn't see. "He's awake and coherent now."

She left the room and was replaced by a short, stout man with sandy blond hair and a big semi-automatic revolver in a black holster. He pulled a chair beside Donnie's bed and took a small notebook from his shirt pocket. "Mr. Nelson, I'm Officer Denham. I need to ask you about the girl, Josey Wilder. Can you tell me how she came to be living with you?"

Tears still spilling from his eyes, Donnie started at the beginning, with Mrs. Wilder's funeral, his dad, and Josey hiding in the bed of his truck. He told how she worked in his store and they all got a house together. "She got to be like a daughter to me," he finished.

"I'm unclear yet as to why there was no Amber alert issued for her," Officer Denham said. "Your story matches hers and there was no indication of abuse on her. I doubt you'll be charged with kidnapping or worse."

"Worse?" Donnie asked.

The policeman cleared his throat. "Sex trafficking, Mr. Nelson. Statutory rape. There are a number of possibilities."

"You're crazy," Donnie said. "There was nothing like that. Nothing at all."

He shrugged. "I believe you, but I have a report to write."

"Where is she?" Donnie asked.

"All I can say is state custody. The social worker that picked her up will find her a bed in a facility or maybe with a foster family," Officer Denham said. He reached into his pocket and pulled out a business card. "This is the social worker who took her. I don't know for sure what the protocol is, but she can probably at least tell you the girl is safe." He put the card on the tray beside Donnie's bed, then took out another card, flashed it at him, and said, "This is my card, if you need to tell me anything else."

Donnie nodded, and the cop excused himself and left. He expected the nurse to come back in, but instead Debbie rushed into the room. She stopped just inside the doorway. Her eyes widened and she covered her mouth.

"Debbie," Donnie said. "They took her."

"Oh, baby," she said, hurrying to him and sitting on the edge of the bed. She gathered one of his hands into hers and held it tightly. "Your face is all swollen and purple on one side."

"I figured," he said. "They took Josey. I was awful to her. I yelled at her for lying to me. She knew about Dad. I yelled at her for that and for lying about her age, and now the state has taken her."

"I know," Debbie said quietly. Donnie looked at her questioningly, so she continued. "She called me back after the accident. She called for help, then called me back. She talked real fast and wouldn't let me get a word in. She was cryin' and talkin' fast, sayin' how she'd been lyin' to ev'rybody and she was real sorry and she knows she shoulda told you how sick Mike was but he made her swear she wouldn't. She said she was turnin' herself in."

Donnie turned his head away. The feeling of the pillow against his injured face was like fire, but he couldn't bear to face Debbie. More tears flowed from his eyes. "We have to get her back," he said quietly but resolutely.

"We'll do what we can, honey," Debbie promised. "The state ain't gonna wanna keep no sixteen-year-old girl."

"I hate myself for what I said to her. I was just hurting and scared," Donnie said. "Dad is really bad off."

"Josey told me that," Debbie said. She hesitated, then added, "I got another call, too."

"Who?"

"LizBeth," Debbie said. "Josey got ahold of her and told her you were in an accident and hurt pretty bad. She told her how you don't have your phone, but gave her my number. She wants you to call her." Debbie rummaged in the small brown purse she wore slung over her shoulder and pulled out her cell phone. She poked and slid some things, then the phone began to ring and LizBeth's voice answered.

"Hello?" she said.

"LizBeth," Donnie said. "It's Dad."

"Are you okay?" she asked. "What happened?"

Donnie told her about finding her grandpa on the floor, the ride to Woodward, and the wreck. "I have a concussion and I think she called it a deep tissue bruise on my left thigh. I'll be okay."

"What about Grandpa?"

"I don't know yet. The nurse said he's in bad shape," Donnie said.

"Mom won't let me come see you," LizBeth complained.

"No," Donnie said. "She's right. It's way too dangerous. I'll be okay."

"How long will you be in the hospital?"

"I don't know," Donnie said. "I just woke up a few minutes ago."

"Josey said she was leaving," LizBeth said. "She told me that you love me and that I'm lucky to have you as a dad. What happened? I didn't even know she had my number."

"She's very resourceful," Donnie said. "I yelled at her. I was scared, but that's no excuse. She turned herself in to the state as a runaway, I guess. A social worker took her before I woke up."

"I'm sorry, Dad," LizBeth said. "I know you cared about her."

"Yeah."

"Your girlfriend seems nice," LizBeth said. "Oh shit, this is her phone. She's listening, isn't she? And I just cussed."

Donnie laughed, but only a small one. "She is listening, and she's pretty incredible." He winked at Debbie with his one good eye. She wore a huge smile.

"I hope to meet her soon," LizBeth said. "Is there anything I can do for you?"

"No, honey. I'll be okay, but thank you," Donnie said. "You stay inside where it's safe and warm."

"I love you, Dad," she said. "I'm going to go tell Mom and Brian you're mostly okay. Bye."

"She seems like a nice girl," Debbie said, putting her phone back in her purse.

"She is," Donnie said. "Josey contacted her. She did everything. She ... " He couldn't go on.

"She told me your dad left a letter to you in your mom's Bible on the dresser in his room," Debbie said. "But I was already on the road and, well, I don't have a key."

"You will," Donnie said.

"Josey said it was important, that your dad carried it with him during the day and put it in the Bible at night," Debbie said.

"Shit," Donnie muttered. "That doesn't sound like a letter I want to read. Where's that nurse?"

Debbie found the corded remote and pushed the call button for the nurse. A voice responded through the little speaker on the device, "Yes?"

"I want to go see my dad," Donnie said. "And what is this stuff you're pumping into me?"

"That's saline to keep you hydrated, Mr. Nelson," the female voice said. "I'm afraid you can't leave your room yet. I'm sorry. Is there anything else?"

"I need to know how my dad is," Donnie insisted.

"I'll see if I can find out anything," the voice promised.

Donnie looked up at Debbie. "Do you think you could go to intensive care and find out anything?"

"I'll sure try," she said, and leaned over and kissed the uninjured side of his face, then left him alone in the room.

With no one to distract him, the pain surged up. Donnie's head throbbed, and his leg felt like someone was digging into it with a cold pickaxe. He didn't dare look under the thin sheet and blanket to see the injury. Not yet. He thought back to the accident, the tires slipping, the truck spinning. He thought it was going to roll over, but then ... He remembered the train overpass and sighed. He supposed his truck was probably totalled. He wondered where it was.

A nurse passed by without looking in. Donnie realized he had no idea how long he'd been out. He looked around the room and found a clock. It had probably been close to five a.m. when they wrecked. It was now after one p.m. He wanted his phone. He wanted to try to call Josey. He had to apologize to her, and get her back.

Debbie stepped back into the room. Her red eyes told him most of what he needed to know. She came back to her chair and sat down and took his hand. "It's bad," she said. "He's not conscious. He's hooked up to all kinds of machines, baby. They're goin' to ask you what you want to do."

"What I want to do?" Donnie asked.

"The life support. If you want to unplug it."

Donnie couldn't respond. That wasn't possible. His dad had been perfectly fine a month ago. Even a week ago. Well, maybe not a week ago. When had he slowed down and started sleeping so much?

"I feel so bad we didn't notice what was happening," Debbie said. "I distracted you."

"No," Donnie protested, and he squeezed her hand. "I'll want to talk to the doctor before I make any decisions."

"Of course, baby," she said.

"Debbie, will you call Josey? I wish I had my phone. Will you call her and see if she'll answer?" Donnie asked.

Debbie withdrew her hand and took her phone from her purse again. She called and put it on speaker. The phone rang once and went to voicemail. "Hi! This is Josey. I'm really sorry I missed your call. Leave me a message if you want me to call you back. Thanks!"

"Josey, hon, this is Debbie and I'm here with Donnie and we really wanna talk to you," Debbie said. "Please give me a call back." She looked at Donnie and shook her head, then put the phone back in her purse.

"Jasper," Donnie said. He sighed again. "I'm sure he's messed in the house. He's probably hungry. And there's the mess in the bathroom from Dad. Our power went off and limbs were snapping off like cannon shots. That's what woke me up and how I found him."

"My power was out, too. I woke up real cold and called you but you didn't answer, so I called Josey," Debbie said.

"She was on the phone with you when we crashed."

"Yeah," Debbie said. "I was so scared. She hung up on me, then called me back after she called for help. She was so upset, but was such a little trooper. She told me you were knocked out and hangin' out the smashed door with blood runnin' down on the ground and freezing there and she had to drag you back into the truck so your face wouldn't freeze."

Donnie couldn't respond, but just hung his head in shame at the memory of her face all crumpled and wet as he yelled at her for lying to him. "She's an amazing kid," he mumbled.

A doctor came into the room, along with the original nurse. "Mr. Nelson, you're awake," he said. He was a tall man with a ring of gray hair around an otherwise bald and shiny dome of a head. He wore gold-rimmed round glasses, like John Lennon or Harry Potter, and he smiled and smelled of expensive aftershave. "I'm Doctor Rasmusin, the attending doctor here today. How are you feeling?"

"I hurt," Donnie said. "It's getting worse. It wasn't so bad when I first woke up."

"That would be the demerol wearing off," the doctor said. He held an electronic tablet and began tapping at the keys as he talked. "You were mostly unconscious when you came in, but thrashing around in obvious pain, so you were given the pain medication and we did a CT scan to make sure there was no bleeding in your skull." He looked up at Donnie, his glasses flashing in the light. "You took a heck of a bump to the head, but it's going to be okay. There was no internal damage. I'm going to do a cognitive and neurological test with you in a few minutes."

"What's that?" Debbie asked.

Dr. Rasmusin gave her a quick look. "For the cognitive, I'll ask him some questions, check his memory. The neurological will check his balance, coordination, vision, hearing, and reflexes."

"Okay," Donnie said. "I think I'm good on all of that. I mean, I remember the wreck and how it happened."

The doctor only nodded. "Your leg is a concern," he said. "I probably can't really check your balance because of that. How that bone didn't break is beyond me. You'll need to be monitored as the bruising heals."

"When will I be able to leave?" Donnie asked.

"That depends on the tests," the doctor said. "Are you ready?"

He had Donnie read an eye chart, touch the tip of his nose with the index fingers of each hand, asked him questions about his childhood and what he ate for dinner yesterday and the names of his kids and their birthdays. All the while, he tapped away at his tablet.

"You seem to be okay," Dr. Rasmusin said. "But I would like to keep you overnight. I mostly want to make sure you sleep and wake up on your own and be sure nothing gets worse. If everything looks good in the morning, we'll let you go. The roads will probably be better by then, too."

"I have to stay overnight?" Donnie asked. He was disappointed.

"That's my recommendation," the doctor said.

"What about the pain?" Debbie asked.

The doctor thought about it. "I'd rather not do intravenous unless we have to. I'll prescribe some Percocet. You understand those can be addictive and you should only take them as needed?"

"I understand," Donnie promised.

"What would you say your pain level is right now?" he asked.

Donnie considered. "Seven. Maybe an eight."

The doctor nodded and banged on his tablet. "Okay, then, one of the nurses will bring you that pill and I'll be back to check on you later." He left, the nurse in tow.

Donnie dropped his head onto the elevated pillow behind him. It wasn't a smart move, as it brought a stab of pain and made his vision swim for a moment. "I want to go home," he said.

"I can go to your house and take care of Jasper and get you some fresh clothes," Debbie offered.

"The roads are too bad," Donnie said. "Is it still sleeting?"

"No. It was snowing pretty hard when I got here," Debbie said. She got up and went across the room to a big window, pulling back the curtain to let in the muted afternoon light. They both saw that snow was falling in huge, soft flakes. "I can drive in snow," Debbie said.

"No, I don't want you to," Donnie said. "I've caused enough trouble. I couldn't live with myself if anything happened to you."

"I got here without runnin' into a railroad bridge," she teased, leaning over and kissing him on the mouth.

"That's a low blow," Donnie accused.

"I'll bring your phone and your computer, too," she said. "No sense you layin' here not workin' on that book that's gonna make you rich and famous again."

"Please don't go," Donnie said. Then he remembered something. "You don't have a key."

She smiled sadly at him, then reached to a low shelf on the bedside table and brought up a Ziploc bag with Donnie's keys and wallet in it. She opened it and took out the keys, then resealed it and put the bag back on the shelf. "Your bloody clothes are in another bag down there. I think you oughta throw them away."

"Don't go," Donnie said.

"Honey, that poor dog needs to be fed. It'll be okay," Debbie said. She leaned over and kissed him again. Donnie grabbed at her hand, and she squeezed his fingers, then slipped away. "I'll be back before ya know it. And hey, they got lights and heat here, so I'll be spendin' the night, too."

Donnie couldn't help but give a little laugh at that. Debbie blew him one more kiss, then left. A few minutes later, the nurse returned with a pill in a little white paper cup. She brought a gold pitcher of ice water and a cup and poured him a drink for the pill.

"Thank you," Donnie said after taking the pill. He felt tired. "Is it okay if I sleep? Are people with concussions not supposed to sleep?"

She gave him a smile. "As long as you're hooked up to all these monitors, you'll be okay. If anything goes wrong, it'll let us know and we'll take care of you. Go ahead and get some rest, Mr. Nelson."

"You can call me Donnie," he said. "Will you keep me updated on my dad?"

The smile fell away from her face. "They're doing all they can for him, but it isn't likely he'll leave this hospital. They hope he might regain consciousness for a while."

"You mean ... " Donnie couldn't make himself say that his father was near death. "How did he hide it from us? How does anyone hide being that sick?"

"Those are questions I can't answer," she said softly, and there was real tenderness in her voice this time. "I am sorry, though."

"Thank you," Donnie said weakly. He put his head back against the pillow and closed his eyes. He was aware of the sound of the nurse's shoes walking away, and then nothing.

When he opened his eyes again, Debbie was in the room with him. "You didn't go?" he asked.

"Look out the window," she said, grinning at him.

Donnie turned his aching head and saw that the pane of glass was black, except for the steady, thick snow falling in a slant from north to south. "How long was I out?"

"The nurse said you fell asleep right after I left," Debbie said. "You've been out for about eight hours. I've been back for a couple."

"Did you have any trouble?" Donnie asked.

"No. It's slick, but the snow makes it easier to drive than on my first trip down here," she said. "Your computer is there on the window ledge. I put your phone on the charger over there, too. It was about dead. You have messages. And ... " She lifted something from her lap and put it on the rolling tray with the gold pitcher of water and the cup. "I brought this."

Donnie recognized the wrinkled faux leather black cover and red-edged pages of his mother's Bible. It was the one she had carried with her to Sunday morning church services every day of his life until the end of her own. The top corner was curled up a little from her fingers diligently opening the book to follow whatever passages the preacher was using as a lesson. Sticking from a place just shy of the middle of the book was the top edge of a white envelope. Donnie reached over and took the book and put it in his lap. He opened the Bible to the place with the envelope, noting that it was the book of Psalms. The envelope had his name on it in his father's handwriting.

Donnie stared at the envelope as if it was The Hanged Man in a deck of Tarot cards. He couldn't bring himself to touch it for a long time and just sat propped in the bed, staring at it. Debbie remained quiet in her chair beside the bed. There was no possible way that letter would say anything good. It was a death letter. A good-bye. He knew it. He wasn't aware of the tears running down his face until his breath hitched in a sob. Debbie's warm hand filled his.

"Do you want me to read it to you?" she asked.

Donnie shook his head. "I'll read it." He pulled his hand free and lifted the envelope from its place between the pages of his mother's favorite book. He tore an end off the envelope and shook out a folded piece of light blue legal paper. With shaking fingers, he unfolded it and began reading to Debbie.

Dear Donnie,

If you're reading this, you know that I'm very sick. Maybe I'm already dead. The cancer came fast and showed no mercy. I refused to die in that fucking old folks' home. I wanted to be with family, and I wanted to see if I could do anything to help bring you back into the world before I left it. I don't know if I could have done it, so thank God for that angel that hid in the back of your pickup.

Josey knows I'm sick. I had to tell her. I made her swear she wouldn't tell. You've come back, Donnie. You're writing and you're happy and you're in love and now you even have your own kids back, plus Josey. I've seen everything I hoped to and I'm ready to go. When the end comes, I hope I go quickly. Please don't let them hook me up to a bunch of machines. Donnie, I'm begging you, let me go to your mother.

Donnie broke off and dropped the letter back onto the Bible and cried for several minutes over the thought of his mom and dad being reunited somewhere beyond death, but also at the realization he had to be the one to tell the hospital to let him go. He dried his eyes with a tissue Debbie handed him and resumed his reading.

Don't be mad at Josey for keeping this secret. I sure as hell didn't want to spoil your happiness by making you worry about me being sick. There's not a damn thing anyone can do about it. Don't hold it against the guys at the VFW, either. They were a big help to me and good company when I was well enough to be sociable.

My will is on file with the family lawyer in Lawton. There isn't much left to inherit, but I did leave some trinkets in a safe deposit box at our bank. They're in envelopes labeled for the people who should have them.

Tell your sisters I love them and forgive them for putting me in that center. I wish I could have seen them before the end came, but they are doing well and didn't need me like I hoped you did. Don't forget to tell them their old man loves them, and all his grandkids, too.

You remember at Thanksgiving I mentioned Psalm 119:25. The full verse is "My soul clings to the dust; revive me according to your word." You revived me from the dust of that retirement center and I'm going to the grave believing I helped to revive you so that you found your words again. Let go of the past, Donnie. You've punished yourself long enough.

Forgive me for not telling you all of this in person. I was never very good at all the mushy stuff. I love you, son."

Love,

Dad

The signature came at the bottom of the page, as if reaching that point was a signal that he had said enough. Donnie cried openly. He heard a nurse come in, pause, ask Debbie what was wrong, then leave although Debbie didn't say anything. He was aware of Debbie taking the letter from his hand and heard her folding it and putting it back into the torn envelope and the envelope back between the pages of the Bible. The weight of the book was lifted off his lap. She sat beside him and held his hands while he wept.

"I love him," Donnie sobbed.

"I know," she said.

"I don't want to lose him."

"He's in pain, Donnie. He's ready to go. He wants to go to your mom. I think that's so sweet," Debbie said.

Donnie had no answer. Debbie leaned forward and kissed him. The nurse came back in. It was a different nurse now, a young Hispanic woman with dark, flashing eyes and high cheekbones.

"Are you okay, Mr. Nelson?" she asked, her voice musical with its Spanish accent.

Donnie gave Debbie a meaningful look that she understood and she slipped off the bed and back into her chair. Donnie faced the nurse. "My dad is in ICU," he said. "I just read a letter he wrote to me. He doesn't want to be on life support. What do I need to do? But I don't want it done until I can get out of this bed and be there with him."

"I know about your father," the nurse said. "I am so sorry. To end life support, there are legal papers you have to sign. I can start that process for you, if that's what you want."

Donnie tilted his head to look at the ceiling. He fought his internal battle again. Could he do it? It's what his father wanted. He looked back at the nurse and nodded. "Yes, please."

"Okay, Mr. Nelson," she said. Then she held up a little white cup. "I brought this for your pain. It will be morning when the papers are ready. You can take this and sleep."

Donnie nodded again.

"Miss?" Debbie said as the nurse gave Donnie the pill and a fresh cup of water. "Can I stay with him in here tonight?"

"Yes," she said. "Are you his wife?"

"Girlfriend," Debbie said.

"That's fine. The chair by the window folds out into a bed," the nurse said. "It isn't very comfortable, but it's okay. I can bring you a pillow and blankets."

"Thank you," Debbie said.

The nurse left. Despite all the sleep he'd had and all that was on his mind, Donnie felt himself growing heavy and drowsy. He wondered when he had last urinated. Oh God, had they put a catheter in him? He couldn't tell. He knew he was slipping in and out of sleep, between memories and dreams about his parents, about his boyhood with his sisters. He came fully to wakefulness one time, calling out, "Dad!" as he sat up.

"Baby, are you okay?" Debbie asked from her made-out bed near the window of the dark room.

"Ummhmm," Donnie murmured and sank back into his own darkness.

Morning came with the hospital's attorney, a frumpy woman in a gray pantsuit with a folder full of papers that used a lot of words to say Donnie gave the hospital permission to let his father die. He signed with a trembling hand.

Chapter Twenty-Six

Donnie sat in a wheelchair beside the bed in which his father lay. He held Michael Marion Nelson's hand while the hospital staff went about the task of shutting off the machines and removing the tubes that kept him alive. Debbie stood behind him, her hand on his shoulder. The only sound came from the monitor that tracked the dying man's heartbeat. After a moment, the chief of surgery spoke.

"There's no way of knowing how long it will take," he said. "It could be minutes, but might be hours."

Donnie nodded without taking his eyes from his father's face.

It took two hours and twenty-eight minutes. Mike Nelson gasped suddenly, sucking in a huge breath and jerking in the bed. The hand Donnie held clamped onto him for a moment, then relaxed. The air came out of the deflating lungs, the body became limp, and the heart monitor changed from a steady beat to a continuous scream of death. A nurse in blue scrubs rushed in and turned off the machine. She hesitated.

"I'm very sorry," she offered, then slipped out of the room.

Donnie sat and stared at the still face of the man he had tried all his life to please. All that was over now. Another chapter of his past had come to an end. The hand he held was dust, and the owner of it had bid him let it go. Donnie raised the hand to his lips and pressed a kiss onto the knuckles, then placed the hand carefully on the bed. Debbie's hand tightened on his shoulder.

"I have to call my sisters," Donnie said. "Will you close the door?" Debbie did as he asked while Donnie pulled his phone from beneath his uninjured thigh. He called

Margaret first, kept his voice calm while he told her he had to connect Gina to the call, and he called his youngest sister.

"What's this all about?" Margaret demanded. "You're scaring me, Donnie."

His eyes fixed on his father's lifeless face, Donnie began. "I found Dad on the bathroom floor." He told them about the blood, about leaving home in the ice storm, finding out their father had hidden the fact he had prostate cancer and was dying, and about the wreck. "I have a concussion and a hurt leg. I'm in a wheelchair right now. Dad left a letter. He ... " Donnie's voice faltered for the first time. "He did not want to be on life support."

Gina was sobbing. Margaret said, "Don't you do anything until we get there."

"Dad passed away a few minutes ago," Donnie said. "I was with him."

There was only the sound of Gina crying. Then she lashed out, but not at Donnie. "I hate you for how you made us put him in that home, Maggie. You just wanted that house."

"No!" Donnie's voice was cutting. "Dad forgave all of that. I'll send you a picture of his letter. We're not going to blame each other for what happened. He was our dad and in the end, he did exactly what he wanted to do. You'll see."

Margaret spoke quietly. "All his final expenses are paid," she said. "He bought the plot next to Mom's and paid for his funeral when he paid for hers. How do we get him home?"

"Can you call the funeral home and ask that?" Donnie asked her. "Like I said, I'm in the hospital myself. I think they'll release me today. My truck is totaled, I think. I have to call the insurance company. I'm on some strong pain meds, too."

"Are you okay?" Margaret asked. "How bad is it?"

"I'll be okay," Donnie said. "I also have to find Josey. The state took her."

"Explain to me again who she is," Maggie asked. Donnie did. "And you're going to try to find her right now? With Dad's body still warm?"

"Yes," Donnie said. He remembered again his father's Thanksgiving prayer. "She's become part of the family. Even Dad said so. I can't just give her up to state custody."

"How will you get here for the funeral?" Maggie asked.

"I'm hoping Debbie will drive me down."

"Who's Debbie? Donnie, what is going on up there?" his sister asked.

Donnie looked up at Debbie, then reached out and took her hand. "Debbie is my girlfriend."

Gina beat Margaret to the next words. "You have a girlfriend? That's good, Donnie. I'm glad for you."

"Yes," Maggie agreed.

"We have arrangements to make up here," Donnie said. "There's a dog, too. And Debbie will have to see about taking off work. If she wants to come ... " He looked up into her brown eyes.

With her free hand, Debbie swiped at his shoulder. "You know I'm takin' you home and stayin' with you until you're okay."

Donnie smiled up at her. Into the phone, he said, "I suspect they'll want to come in and take Dad ... somewhere else. Let me know what the funeral home says."

"Donnie," Gina said quickly, as if afraid he was about to end the call. "Don't leave us in the dark anymore. Please? We barely know you anymore. We're family, too. You're the head of the family now. You have a girlfriend and a dog and you had a runaway living with you and we didn't know any of it. Please, talk to us more."

Donnie opened his mouth to tell her the phone line ran both ways, but he stopped himself. He could almost see the reproach on his father's face. "Okay," he promised. "I will. But you have to do the same."

"We'll do better," Gina said "Won't we, Maggie?"

"Yes," Maggie said, her voice soft, maybe even contrite.

"I'll see you both soon," Donnie said, and now he did end the call. He looked at Mike's face one more time, and made a final promise. "I'll get her back, Dad. I'll find her."

Debbie pushed his chair back to his own room, where Donnie snatched up the card for the state worker who had taken Josey from the hospital. The name on the card was Krystina Briggs. He dialed the number and was a little surprised when a female voice actually answered. He expected voicemail.

"Is this Krystina Briggs?" Donnie asked.

"Yes."

"My name is Donnie Nelson. I'm calling about Josey Wilder. You picked her up at the hospital in Woodward yesterday," he said.

"Yes, Josey told me all about how she stowed away in your pickup after her grandmother's funeral," Krystina said, and she chuckled. Donnie found that irritating.

"Do you have her?" Donnie asked. "I mean ... I ... " He rubbed at his forehead in consternation and his fingers pressed on the edges of the swelling there, sending a jab of pain all the way down to his groin. "I want her back," Donnie said. "She's become family."

"Mr. Nelson, I know she cares a great deal for you, too," Krystina said. "She was crying the whole time she was with me."

"She's gone?" Donnie asked, his voice defeated. Debbie, sitting in the chair beside him, took his free hand in hers. Her own face gave away her feeling of loss.

"I'm afraid so."

"She's ... where? A state facility? A foster home? What can I do?" Donnie asked.

"It's a unique case, Mr. Nelson," the woman said. "Unfortunately, I'm not able to give you any details because she is underage. I can promise you she's safe, though."

"You won't tell me?" Donnie knew his voice was too close to a whine. He cleared his throat. "You can't tell me anything? Did she leave a message for me?"

"I'm afraid not."

"Can you reach her? Can you tell her I'm sorry?"

"I couldn't do that, Mr. Nelson. I'm sorry." She wasn't. Donnie could tell. He thanked her curtly and ended the call.

"Check your phone, honey," Debbie said quietly. Donnie looked into her eyes and she smiled sadly at him. "I didn't listen, but I saw a notification that you got a message from Josey."

Donnie went to his voicemail and saw that he'd missed a call from Josey early yesterday morning, probably right after they'd gotten to the hospital. He looked at Debbie again, remembering his fear of opening his father's final letter. This couldn't be that bad, he hoped. He pressed the button.

"Donnie, it's me," Josey's voice said. "I'm sorry for everything. I've been a burden from the minute I sat up in the back of your truck. I should have told you about Mike right after I saw him taking those pain pills, but he was so desperate and begged me not to bother you with it and said you'd find out when you had to. I'm sorry for that. And I'm sorry I lied about my age. I didn't think you'd let me stay if you knew I was only sixteen. That was wrong. I should have trusted you and been honest with you. I told a hospital worker that I'm a runaway and they called somebody and the state is sending somebody to get me. I won't be a bother anymore. I hope you'll keep Jasper and take good care of him. Tell Mike ... " Her voice stopped and he heard a distant sniffle as if she'd held the phone at arm's length from her face. "Tell Mike I love him. I hope he survives a while longer. Thank you for everything. I loved being with you guys and look forward to reading your new book. I love you. Bye."

Donnie leaned his head back and cried openly for a long time. When he was finished, he hurt everywhere and felt empty and dehydrated, as if his insides were filled with Sahara sand and pain. "I'm the biggest piece of shit ever," he said.

"No, baby," Debbie said. "You yelled at her in the heat of the moment. It was justified. I wish you hadn't, but nobody can blame you for it. This ain't over if you don't want it to be."

"I don't know what to do," Donnie said. "I want to go home."

"I'll go see if I can find out when you can do that," Debbie said. She got up and kissed the top of his head, then left him.

Donnie held his phone in his lap, the screen blank, and thought about playing Josey's message again. He didn't. He couldn't. He put the phone on the rolling tray table where his meals were served.

"Let's get you dressed," Debbie said as she came back into the room. "Your dismissal papers are almost ready. The doctor said you can go, as long as you have someone to help you. That would be me. He said you'll need to rent a wheelchair, or at least crutches. He'll come and tell you all that, but the nurse said you can get dressed first."

Putting on a shirt was no problem, but Donnie nearly passed out from the pain of lifting his injured leg long enough for Debbie to pull up a pair of gray sweatpants. He collapsed back into the wheelchair, sweating and heaving.

"I'll let you rest a minute before we put on your shoes and socks," Debbie said, her face full of concern. "That leg is frightful lookin'."

"That's how it feels, too," Donnie panted. "Go ahead with the shoes. I want out of here."

While Debbie was knelt before him putting on his socks, Dr. Rasmusin came in and asked how he was feeling. Donnie told him he just wanted to go home.

"I understand, but how's the pain?" the doctor said.

"If I tell the truth, are you going to make me stay?" Donnie asked.

The doctor laughed. "No. You're free to go after you sign a couple of papers. The nurse will give you a prescription for Percocet. There are no refills. You'll need to make an appointment with your primary care provider within a few days to be checked again.

The paperwork to get a wheelchair or crutches is there, too. Just take that to a medical equipment provider."

"Thank you," Donnie said. "I know I haven't been a very good patient."

The doctor waved away his complaint. "Under the circumstances, you've been very good. I am sorry about your father."

"Doctor, can you tell me about the girl who came in with us?" Donnie asked. "Josey. She had blue-and-silver hair. Was she hurt?"

"A few bumps and scratches. Nothing serious," Dr. Rasmusin said. "Her injuries seemed to be emotional."

"Yeah," Donnie muttered.

"Have a safe drive home," the doctor said, then excused himself.

A black nurse Donnie hadn't met before stepped up and smiled and pointed him through the papers he had to sign and showed him the prescriptions. "Do you have any questions?" she asked in a soothing but somehow still bubbly voice. Donnie said he didn't. "We have to have an orderly wheel you out to your car," the nurse said.

"I'll go pull up to the door," Debbie said. "Oh! Your coat." She had put the plastic bags of Donnie's bloody clothes in the suitcase she'd used to bring their fresh clothes, but his blood-stained coat hung on a hook by the window. She looked at it dubiously and Donnie followed her gaze.

"It's all I've got," he said. He asked the nurse, "Can you help me put it on while she gets the car?"

Ten minutes later, Donnie was sitting in the passenger seat of Debbie's cold car with hot air blowing onto his feet. The world was a dull white earth and gray sky. He reclined his seat because it hurt to sit up straight. Debbie drove them to a Wal-Greens store first and told Donnie to stay in the car. She went inside and came out carrying a white prescription bag and a pair of silver aluminum crutches that she put in the back seat.

"You didn't have to do that," Donnie protested. "I'm going to pay you back for all of it."

"I know," she said as she started the car again. "I got generic pills. It was a lot cheaper."

Donnie chuckled. "You're an amazing woman," he said as Debbie began the drive home, staying well below the speed limit because there were still patches of ice on the highway. Donnie dozed.

He dreamed he was going home, but home was in the back of his store again. There was no bed. All the stuff he'd used to make the back room home was gone and he was going to have to sleep on the Queen Anne chair cushions again and that meant his butt falling between them and he would wake up hurting, hurting, hurting.

Donnie woke up, thinking he had fallen between the cushions, but they were still driving and he just hurt from his injuries. Debbie had turned the radio on and classic country music was playing softly and she was humming along. Donnie relaxed and told himself he didn't live in the store anymore.

The house ...

Something about the house.

The rent. He couldn't afford the rent. Mike's retirement paid part of the rent. And Josey paid the rest. But he didn't pay Josey to work in the store. Where did she get the money?

Donnie sat up so suddenly that Debbie cried out in alarm. She took her foot off the accelerator and looked at him. "Are you okay?"

"Sherry Brown," Donnie said. "She knows where Josey got the money. I'd bet anything she knows."

"Hon, what does that have to do with anything?" Debbie asked, speeding the car up again.

"If Josey was really a runaway – if nobody knew where she was – how did she get part of her inheritance sent to Sagebrush?" Donnie asked. "She went to the bank and talked to them about it, and then she had the money. Somebody who controls her money knew where she was."

"Okay," Debbie said, her tone saying she still wasn't following.

"She was never reported missing and somebody was okay with her being in Sagebrush and asking for access to the money her grandmother left her," Donnie said. "That Krystina Briggs said Josey was an unusual case. Whoever she called to get the money probably took custody of her from Briggs."

"But who?" Debbie asked. "She doesn't have any family. Her mom and grandma are dead and she doesn't know who her daddy is."

"Who would control the money for an estate?" Donnie asked.

"A lawyer?"

"A lawyer," Donnie agreed. Donnie pulled his phone from the pocket of his bloody coat and looked up the number for Sagebrush's only bank. He made the call and Sherry Brown answered.

"Mrs. Brown, it's Donnie Nelson," he said.

"Donnie! How are you? I heard about your father and the accident and we've all been so worried about you," Sherry said.

"I've got some injuries, and Dad passed away this morning," Donnie said. "But I'll tell you all about that later. I need your help. I know Josey came and talked to somebody at the bank about money before we rented the house. I've got to know who she talked to."

"Donnie, she swore me to secrecy," Sherry said as if it was the most obvious thing in the world.

"Mrs. Brown, please," Donnie begged. "I'm sure you know she isn't my niece. I yelled at her and she turned herself in to the state and somebody took her while I was unconscious and that person doesn't have her anymore. I think she called her grandmother's lawyer to get her money and I think that's who has her now. Please, I'm begging you. Can you tell me who it is?"

"Josey's gone?" Sherry asked, her voice revealing surprise and fear. "Oh, Donnie, that's awful."

"Mrs. Brown, I love her like she's my own daughter. I need her back. Will you help me?" Donnie asked.

"Donnie, ever since you took over that store, I've asked one thing from you and you've never given it to me," she said.

Donnie pressed the phone to the uninjured side of his head, his mind racing. Then he grinned. "Sherry, will you help me?"

"It's about time," she said, and Donnie could hear the triumphant smile he knew she had on her grandmotherly face. "Now, you know I'm not supposed to release this information, so you didn't get it from me."

"No, ma'am," Donnie agreed.

She told him the name of a law firm he recognized from his hometown. "I don't know who she talked to there, but I heard her promising she was okay and needed the money to help rent a house. There was some arguing, but you know our Josey."

"That I do," Donnie said. "Knowing Mrs. Wilder, I'm sure it was no less than the senior partner there. Thank you so much, Mrs., I mean, thank you, Sherry." He hung up and looked at Debbie. He felt better than he had for a while. "I think we're on the right track," he said.

Sagebrush's landmark grain elevator was a dirty finger rising from white snow into the gray sky ahead. Donnie decided to try texting Josey, hoping she would respond to that if she wouldn't take his call. He told her he was sorry and that his dad had passed away that morning and that he wanted her to come back and live with him again.

Debbie pulled into the driveway of the house where once three people had lived. She helped Donnie get his crutches adjusted and walked slowly behind him as he struggled through the snow to the front porch. Someone, probably Debbie, had shoveled the ice and snow off the steps. Donnie guessed she thought she'd catch him if he fell, despite them both knowing he was too heavy. He could only use one crutch and Debbie did help pull him up the steps onto the porch. Donnie paused there and looked around. The elm tree had lost several big limbs that lay in the yard, shrouded in heavy white snow.

"I wonder who shoveled these steps," Debbie said as Donnie looked around.

"It wasn't you?" he asked.

"No, I didn't have time for that," she answered. She smiled and winked at him. "People 'round here are gettin' some strong feelin's for you, I guess."

Debbie opened the front door and shooed him inside, closing the door behind them. Jasper came running from the kitchen and Debbie had to intercept the big dog before he jumped on Donnie and sent him sprawling. She held him and roughed up his thick neck fur and told him he was the best dog ever while he wiggled and licked her. With the dog calmed, Debbie stood up and faced Donnie.

"Let's get you out of that bloody coat. I'll put it in the washer ... " She trailed off and looked around the living room. "Well, shoot, there still ain't no power, so I guess I won't be washing anything." She peeled the coat off him and dropped it in a corner. "Now you go sit down. I'll find something for us to eat and you can take one of your pills."

Donnie looked at the sofa, then at the recliner that his father had claimed as his own. Beyond that was the short hallway with Mike's bedroom, and the bathroom. Donnie remembered the floor.

Debbie's hand closed on his arm. Donnie turned to face her. "Hon, I cleaned all that up when I was here yesterday. I couldn't let you come home to that."

Donnie nodded slowly and sadly, fighting hard against the tears. He had cried too much already. "I love you," he said.

"I love you, too. Now go sit," she said.

Donnie made his way to the sofa and fell onto it. Jasper came over and jumped up beside him and licked his face before Donnie could block his tongue. He hugged the dog close, burying his face in the thick fur while Jasper did all he could to lick anything he could slap his tongue to.

Debbie came back with a plate that held a peanut butter sandwich and some barbecue potato chips with his pill. She had a can of Coke in her other hand. "Get down, Jasper," she commanded, and the dog obediently got off the sofa and slunk away, but not too far.

"Before I take the pill, I want to call that lawyer," Donnie said. "Where's your food?"

"I'll be right back," Debbie said, putting his food and drink on the coffee table. She was back and sitting beside him, holding her own identical plate by the time Donnie had the phone number.

A receptionist answered and Donnie asked to speak to the attorney who had handled the estate of Wanda Wilder. "That would be Mr. Henthorn," she told him. Donnie asked to speak to him. "May I ask what this is about?"

"My name is Donnie Nelson. Wanda Wilder's granddaughter hid in the back of my truck after Mrs. Wilder's funeral."

"One moment and I'll see if he's available," the receptionist said. Donnie waited, and after a couple of minutes a man's voice came on the phone.

"This is Nathaniel Henthorn, Mr. Nelson. How can I help you?"

"I'm trying to find Josey," Donnie blurted.

"For what purpose?" the lawyer asked.

"To apologize, for starters," Donnie said. "And to ask her to come back to Sagebrush. I need her. Hell, we all need her up here."

"You realize she is only sixteen years old?" Nathaniel Henthorn asked.

"She only just told me that yesterday," Donnie said, and wondered that it had really only been one day ago. "She told me first that she was eighteen and we – me and my dad – went with it because there was no Amber alert or anything like that."

"I see," the lawyer said in a flat tone that told Donnie nothing.

"Is she with you?"

"She certainly is not here in my office, no," Mr. Henthorn said.

"Do you have custody of her?" Donnie asked.

There was a long moment of hesitation. "I'll answer this only because I know she cares for you a great deal. Yes, Mr. Nelson, I have custody of her. She technically has been in my custody since her grandmother passed on."

"I thought so," Donnie said. "Can I talk to her?"

"She has her phone, Mr. Nelson," the lawyer said. "If you've tried contacting her and she hasn't responded, that's her decision. I hope you will understand that."

Donnie felt his insides sagging. "I understand," he said. "Please tell her I miss her and I'm sorry."

"I'll pass that along. Is there anything else?"

"No," Donnie said, completely defeated. The attorney thanked him and hung up. Donnie stared at the plate of food. Debbie hugged him.

"Give her time," Debbie urged. "You have to eat, hon. Eat and take your pill and I'll help get you to bed. Do you ... Can you sleep down here?"

Donnie looked at the stairs and measured the torture of going up them verses the emotional distress of sleeping in his father's bed.

"I changed the bedding," Debbie said, reading his thoughts.

"You're perfect," he whispered. At her urging, he swallowed his pill with a drink of Coke and chewed listlessly at the food, not tasting anything. Then she helped him to his father's empty bed and he fell onto it. She pulled the covers up and went to let Jasper out to relieve himself, then she came back, stripped off her jeans and got in the bed with Donnie. Her body was warm and soft in the cold room and the pain and the pill was pulling him back into darkness.

Chapter Twenty-Seven

"I guess I'll be moving back into the store," Donnie said as he sat at the dining table watching Debbie make gravy on the gas stove. Buttered bread she'd browned in a skillet, and a plate of bacon were already steaming on the table with cups of hot tea. Jasper sat near Debbie, hoping she would drop more scraps and tell Donnie it was an accident.

"If you'd rather," Debbie said without turning around.

"What other choice do I have? I can't afford to stay here without the help on rent," he said.

Debbie poured the white gravy into a bowl and brought it to the table. She gave him an exasperated look, then sat down across from him. "You could move in with your girlfriend."

"Oh," Donnie said, stunned. "I didn't presume ... I mean ... do you want me to?"

Debbie shrugged and pulled apart a piece of bread. "You're not a bad cook. You're a decent lay. Your dog is kinda cute. I guess it wouldn't be too bad."

Donnie laughed. "Thank you. I don't want to impose, so if you're not ready for that, I understand."

"Are you ready, Donnie?"

He studied her for a minute and thought about it. "I am," he said. "But I may need some more training. I've been on my own for a long time. Do you mind me drying socks over the toaster?"

"Eww. They go in the oven, dummy."

"Aren't we fancy," he said as he put gravy over his own toast. He added some bacon to his plate and started eating.

"What do you have planned for today?" Debbie asked.

"Call the insurance company about my truck first," he said. "Then Dad's lawyer. There's a will, but I can't imagine there's much left to inherit. Maggie is handling the funeral home, so I hope to hear from her. I wish I could get out and buy a new truck. I hate that you'll have to drive us all the way to Lawton."

"I wouldn't let you drive with that leg, anyway, mister," Debbie said. She had a tiny spot of gravy just beside the corner of her mouth and it was adorable and Donnie wished he could slip over and kiss it away, but moving would be agony. His head felt better, but his leg was worse. It was a black-and-purple knot of pain from his hip to his knee.

"I suppose not," he agreed. "Other than those calls, I guess the pain pills will pretty much knock me out again."

"What would you think of me picking up the afternoon shift today?" Debbie asked.

"That's fine with me," Donnie said. "I don't want Annie mad at you over me."

"She'll be fine, but I wanna help out as much as I can before we have to leave," Debbie said.

Donnie sighed. "I figure we'll be gone two days and one night for the funeral and the reading of the will," he said. "Do you think somebody would watch over Jasper for us?"

"I can prolly find somebody," she said.

They finished their breakfast and Debbie took the plates away and cleaned up from the meal while Donnie downed his pill. He called his Farmer's Insurance agent and explained about the wreck. His truck was at a salvage yard in Woodward. The agent said they'd have someone go look at it that afternoon. Donnie admitted there was still a lien against it and the agent said, based on what he said about the damage and airbags deploying, the vehicle likely would be considered a total loss.

Next, Donnie texted Maggie and asked if she'd heard anything from the funeral home. She texted back, "With them now."

Donnie pushed himself up from the table and went to the sofa, where he lay end to end, propped up on pillows and covered with a quilt. Using the crutches was still difficult and left him tired and sweaty and hurt his armpits. He could already feel the effects of the pain pill, though. Debbie came in from the kitchen and adjusted his blanket and pillow and kissed his forehead.

"Do you have your phone?" she asked.

Donnie held it up for her to see..

"How much battery?"

"Seventy-eight," Donnie said. They'd left his phone charging in her car overnight and planned to charge hers there today.

"I'm gonna go to the trailer and get dressed for work, then go on in. I'll prolly work until about seven. Is that okay?" she asked.

"You're too good to me," Donnie said.

She smiled at him. "You're already high and slurring your words. Are you warm enough?"

"Ummhmm," Donnie said. He was wearing sweatpants, a T-shirt, a sweatshirt, wool socks, and had the thick blanket over him. "You're too good for me," he said again and grinned at her.

"My God, you're such a lightweight," she teased, then kissed him again and went to the door to put on her coat. Jasper came over and stood beside her, wagging his tail happily. "Nope, you have to stay here and take care of Daddy," Debbie told him. Jasper whined and wagged his tail faster.

"If there's a woman around, he likes them better," Donnie said, and now he heard the slur in his voice. He giggled. "He loved Josey more than me. Slept with her." He paused and his mind drifted toward sleep. "I miss her," he said.

"I know, baby," Debbie said. "Go to sleep."

Sometime later, Donnie was jerked out of sleep by the ringing of his cell phone. Bleary-eyed and barely coherent, he grabbed it off the coffee table, dropped it, almost fell off the sofa picking it up from the floor, and finally swiped the button to answer it.

"Donnie? Are you okay?" Margaret asked.

"Yeah," he said. "I was asleep. The pain pills knock me out."

"Are you okay with the funeral being the day after tomorrow at ten in the morning?" she asked.

"Yeah, that's fine," Donnie answered. "I have to call the lawyer. I fell asleep before I did that. What time is it?"

"It's a little after three," she said. "I can call, if you want."

"I'm the executor," Donnie said. "I think I should call. Did you ... Do they have Dad there?"

"Yes."

"How's Gina?" he asked.

"She's sad, but she's pulling it together," Margaret said. "Her and Dad weren't that close, but I guess just knowing he was alive was a comfort to her. She kept saying she's an orphan now and I had to point out she's a grown woman with a husband and daughter of her own."

Donnie smiled, but it was a sad smile. "I know," he said. "I never even considered the possibility of him dying. Until the last few weeks, he was just like I remembered. He had energy and he was cussing and telling me how to fix my life. But there was a seriousness to him, and a ... I don't know. Like a philosophical side I'd never seen before."

"He was coming to terms with it, I guess. I wish he had told us," Maggie said. "Anyway, unless he had some fortune hidden away, I can't imagine reading the will can take very long."

"Who knows, with Dad," Donnie said. "Maybe he had a secret life as a pirate."

"Save it for your books, Donnie," she said.

The call ended and Donnie reclined in his place on the sofa. He looked out the window. The sky was blue and clear, but without the low cloud cover, the day was even colder. He wondered how long it would be until the power was back on. Jasper lay on the floor in the doorway of the hall leading to the master bedroom. His brown eyes were open and watching Donnie.

"I wish I had your coat," Donnie said. The dog thumped his tail once against the floor. "Do you miss going to work?" Another single thump. Donnie wanted company, but didn't dare call the dog over for fear Jasper would jump on his hurt leg. Instead, he called his father's attorney and explained the situation. They could only schedule the reading at two in the afternoon the next day. Donnie agreed to it, then texted the information to his sisters and Debbie.

Bored, he grabbed the television remote and hit the power button three times before he remembered there was no electricity. He put it back on the table and wished for his laptop, but again, no power, and he was pretty sure the battery was nearly spent. And, he reasoned, he was probably too woozy to write coherently.

He slept again.

He awoke to the sound of the front door opening and Debbie came in with a whirlwind of freezing air. The house was dark and the window showed only the blackness of night.

She closed the door and shivered, then smiled at him. She was holding a paper bag and Donnie could smell cooked food. His mouth began to water.

"Chicken strips and mashed potatoes," she said, putting the bag on the coffee table. Jasper sniffed at it and looked from Donnie to Debbie hopefully. Debbie laughed. "And there just might be a box of scraps for the bestest doggie in the whole wide world," she said, ruffling the thick golden fur around his neck as his tail fanned the air.

Debbie lit some of the scented candles Josey had loved and they ate at the coffee table, taking turns tossing scraps from a third Styrofoam box to the happy dog, clapping when he snatched the morsels from the air.

"Wilson Pepper came in today," Debbie said. "He'd heard about Mike and the accident, of course. That man knows ev'rything. I asked him if he knew of anybody who'd watch Jasper for a couple of days and he volunteered to do it."

"Really?" Donnie asked, surprised, though he couldn't really say why.

"Yep. Said to bring him by the office before we head out in the morning," Debbie said.

"He's a good man," Donnie said. "I owe him an interview."

Debbie's musical laughter filled the room. "Yeah, he told me to remind you."

They finished eating and Debbie suggested they shower. Fortunately, the house's hot water tank was also heated by gas, so they could at least have hot showers, even if it was by candlelight.

"Don't get any ideas," Debbie warned him. "I say we shower together so I can soap you down without you falling over and hurtin' yourself worse'n you already are. No shower sex."

"I get to watch you lather yourself up," Donnie said. "That might inspire something."

"Then you can stand there on your one good leg and take care of it yourself because I ain't stayin' in there longer'n I have to. That hot water ain't gonna last forever and it'll be cold enough gettin' out without the water goin' cold."

She washed them and Donnie behaved. He had no choice. The pain was flooding back and he spent most of the time with one hand on the wall for support. After the shower, they dressed in sweats again, Donnie took another pill, and Debbie helped him into the bed. She got in beside him and cuddled next to him. They talked for a while until Debbie fell asleep. Donnie was afraid that after sleeping all day, he would remain wide awake, but the pill, the warm blankets, and Debbie's steady breathing helped him drift off.

They got an early start the next morning, dropped off Jasper, and picked up breakfast from a McDonald's in Woodward to eat in the car. Once they got to Lawton, Donnie gave directions to get to his childhood home where Maggie now lived with her husband and kids. They found his sister was home alone and she and Debbie made a big fuss about getting Donnie and his crutches inside and settled, then the two women talked as if he wasn't there. He wanted to roam around the house and see his boyhood bedroom, but getting up the porch had taxed his strength. He fell asleep to the sound of Margaret telling Debbie a recipe for green bean casserole.

When he awoke, Gina was there, sitting beside him on the sofa, and she'd joined the conversation about domestic activities. Margaret and Debbie sat in chairs across the coffee table from the sofa. Donnie kept his eyes half closed and studied the sisters he hadn't seen in over seven years.

Margaret was still tall and thin. Her dark hair was gray at the temples and at the edge of her forehead. Her face looked even thinner than he'd remembered and her glasses had big lenses in white frames. She had a narrow mouth and used a lot of hand gestures when she talked. She had on a yellow shirt covered with a long forest green sweater and tan slacks with yellow socks.

Gina, on the other hand, was short and had gotten plumper since the last time he'd seen her. Her wavy brown hair framed a jolly face and twinkling eyes and full lips. She was wearing a red sweatshirt and blue jeans with Uggs boots.

Donnie was amazed at the ease with which Debbie was already talking to his sisters. Nobody looking on would have guessed that they'd only just met. Finally, Margaret said, "It's almost time. I guess we better wake him up. It'll take a while to get him back in the car. We can take my van. Maybe that'll be easier for him."

"Donnie?" Debbie called. "Honey, it's time to wake up."

"I'm awake," Donnie said. "Have you hens laid any eggs yet?"

"I'll put another egg on the other side of your head," Maggie joked.

Donnie reached up and touched his injured head. Instead of the headwrap he'd worn when he woke up in the hospital, he now just had a giant adhesive bandage over the swollen knot. "I think one is enough," he said. "Who's gonna pull me to my feet?" Margaret and Debbie helped him up and got his crutches in position. The three of them helped him out to Margaret's green minivan.

Debbie gave Donnie a kiss, then said, "I'll go get us a hotel room while y'all take care of this."

"You're not coming?" Donnie asked, then shook his head. "I guess it's just immediate family. Let me give you my credit card."

"You got enough to worry about," Debbie said, and closed his door, gave him a final wave, and went to her own car.

"I like her!" Gina said from the front passenger seat.

"I do, too," Margaret declared. "She's so friendly. You can't help but like her. Was she up there all the time you've been there and you're just now going out?"

"Not the whole time," Donnie sulked.

They drove to the lawyer's office and found themselves in a conference room with a man who looked way too much like Ray Bradbury with his thick white mutton chops, short stature, and thick glasses. His name was William McNeal and he constantly took off the black-framed glasses to twirl them or suck on the end of an arm.

"When your father first came to me, there was a good deal of money," McNeal said. "But his time in the assisted living facility and his medical treatments depleted his resources considerably." He sat sucking on his glasses and looking at a thin sheaf of papers in a file folder.

"Do you know how long he was sick?" Donnie asked.

The lawyer put his glasses on and peered over the top of them at Donnie. "He was diagnosed about eight months ago. He never liked going to a doctor. He did some early treatments, but when they began talking about chemotherapy, he said no. He told them he wanted medicine for the pain. He talked a lot about wanting to see you again, Donald."

Donnie nodded. "I'm glad he forced himself on me," he said.

"Well, I'm sorry to say his entire holdings come to only twenty-three thousand, eight hundred fifteen dollars and seventy-two cents. As the executor, Donald, you can decide what to do with that money," McNeal said. "There are also three envelopes, one for each of you."

"Can you divide the money between us?" Donnie asked. "Three checks?"

"I can do that," McNeal said as he handed Donnie a small white envelope with his name written on the front in his father's handwriting. He gave one to Gina and one to Margaret.

Donnie opened his envelope and found a thin pen knife with a wooden handle worn smooth from years of use. He recognized it immediately as a knife his father had seldom carried with him, but kept on his dresser. It had belonged to his own grandfather, who had given it to Mike on his seventh birthday, when he felt the boy was old enough to have a pocket knife.

Gina opened her envelope and immediately began to cry. She reached in and pulled out their mother's wedding ring. Mike Nelson had put back money from every paycheck for almost a year to afford a ring he thought was good enough for the woman he wanted to marry.

"There's nothing lumpy in my envelope," Margaret said. She tore it open and pulled out a single small sheet of paper. She read it aloud, "You already got my house. Make sure you fill it with memories and live well. All is forgiven and I love you." She folded the paper and held it in her lap with one hand, dabbing at her eyes with a tissue.

William McNeal wrote each of them a check, expressed his sympathy, offered his services if they were ever needed, and wished them well. Donnie and his sisters left.

"Are you up for lunch?" Gina asked him.

"Sure. If you don't mind Debbie joining us," he answered. His leg hurt, his armpits hurt, and he was beginning to get a headache, but it wasn't time for another pill. He hoped eating would help. They settled on a restaurant and he texted directions to Debbie.

After they ate, Debbie took him to their hotel room and helped him into bed. They had power in Lawton and Donnie marveled at the electric lights and the glowing clock beside the bed.

"I want to call LizBeth," Donnie said. "But my head hurts so bad."

"You're not supposed to take that pill for another hour," Debbie said. "But I guess it wouldn't hurt to take it now. Go ahead and call her."

Donnie called and LizBeth picked up immediately. "Hi, Lizzy Bee," Donnie said, but his voice wasn't right and she knew it.

"Are you okay, Dad? You don't sound good."

"I'm kind of hurting," he said. "But I'll be okay. I'm about to take my pain pill and that'll put me to sleep, but I wanted to call and let you know we're in town. I wanted to see you this evening, but I just hurt too much."

"I understand," she said. "Will you be okay tomorrow?"

"I'll manage," he said. "How are you? And everyone?"

"We're good. You know Mom plans to come to the funeral, right?"

"That's fine," Donnie said. "I'm glad."

"Really? I thought it would be awkward," LizBeth said.

"Funerals are a time for forgiving," Donnie said. "Too late, I guess, but I'm glad she's coming. Alan?"

"He offered to, but Mom said no."

"Good," Donnie said. He knew it sounded mean, but he wasn't part of the family. Had never met Mike Nelson.

"Get some sleep, Dad. You sound really bad and it's a big day tomorrow. I love you," LizBeth said.

"But how are you?" Donnie insisted. "Are you still sick in the mornings?"

"Yeah, but I'm okay."

"Okay. I love you, too," Donnie said.

The day of the funeral dawned bright and bitterly cold. Debbie helped Donnie into his best suit, which was black because he was practical that way, knowing black would work for any occasion. She wore a black dress and he warned her that her legs were going to freeze. She checked them out of their room and they drove to the funeral home.

Donnie crutched his way up to the open casket and looked in at his father, who seemed to be resting peacefully in a bed of white satin. His face was so lifelike that he might have opened his eyes and asked if breakfast was ready. The viewing was anticlimactic to Donnie, who had held the man's hand while his last breath shuddered out of him. With Debbie's help, he made his way to a pew in the chapel and sat down.

Melissa came in with LizBeth and Brian. Whispered introductions were made and Debbie insisted they all share the bench, so LizBeth sat next to her father, then Brian, then Melissa.

The chapel quickly filled and Donnie was shocked to see so many people sitting behind him. He hadn't realized his father had so many friends.

A tall minister with a pot belly stepped to the pulpit and spoke generally about life and death, said a few things about the number of people and how many lives one life can touch, then asked if anyone wanted to speak a memory about Michael Nelson. Donnie was about to struggle to his feet, but someone beat him to it.

"I worked with Mike for thirty years," a short bald man in a brown suit declared. "Nobody could have a better friend. He loaned me twenty dollars when I lost my wallet in nineteen seventy-three. I needed that money more than I could tell him. My baby needed medicine and I was desperate. He loaned me that money and told me I didn't have to pay him back, but by God I did. It was two years later, but by God, I paid him back the money. I could never thank him enough." The man dropped back into his seat, wiping at his eyes while a woman comforted him.

A man about Donnie's age stood up next. "Mike mentored me in the shop," he said. "I was just a dumb kid and almost electrocuted myself standing in a puddle of leaked water and trying to plug in a conveyor belt. He stopped me, and after that day, he was always there to help without me ever needing to ask. I've been shop foreman for ten years because of him."

More and more people, mostly men, stood up and talked about how Mike Nelson had made a difference in their lives. And then a voice spoke that sent gooseflesh down Donnie's spine.

"I never had a father and never knew my grandfather, but for the past two months Mike Nelson and his son Donnie were those things for me when I didn't have any other family in the world. I can never thank them enough for taking me in and making me feel like family."

Donnie twisted in his seat and found her near the back of the chapel. Her hair was no longer blue and silver, but was now orange with purple undertones. Her pale oval face was streaked with tears and she was looking straight at him. He mouthed her name and she smiled, then sat down.

"Help me up," Donnie whispered. Both Debbie and LizBeth helped him get to his feet and position his crutches under his arms. Donnie looked over the gathered mourners. "I'm Donnie. Until a couple of months ago, I didn't realize how lucky I was to be Mike Nelson's son. When I woke up this morning, I thought I had learned that, but seeing all of you here today and hearing how my father made a difference in your lives, shows me that there was so much more I didn't know about this great man. I was living an empty existence, and he made the decision to spend his final days dragging me back into a real life and I am more thankful than he could know." Donnie paused, thinking, but there was nothing more to say. "I love you, Dad." He sank awkwardly into his seat.

Margaret rose and talked about how her father had pushed her on a swing and played dolls with her when she was little and how he had a huge heart and forgave her for the worst thing she had ever done.

297

Gina stood up and tried to speak, but could only cry and say, "I love you, Daddy" before sitting back down.

A few others spoke, then the minister read Psalm Twenty-three and led them in a hymn. People filed out, many to line up their cars to proceed to the grave site. Donnie looked desperately for the orange hair of a young woman, but couldn't find Josey. He got into Debbie's car and they drove to the cemetery behind the hearse. Again, Donnie looked for Josey among the smaller crowd there, but saw mostly hats and hoods and scarves. The minister spoke some more about life everlasting and how Mike was now with his wife in the arms of Jesus and the funeral was over. People drifted back to their cars to get out of the biting wind.

Disappointed, Donnie swung on his crutches back to Debbie's car, LizBeth and Brian walking beside him and Melissa a little off behind them.

"Where are you going now, Dad?" LizBeth asked. "Mom said you can come to dinner."

Donnie looked over at Melissa, who gave a short nod. "That's very kind, but I'm really hurting. I'll probably sleep all the way home, then take my afternoon pill and sleep all night."

"The bump on your head is huge," Brian said. "How much worse is your leg?"

"A lot," Donnie said. "It would be inappropriate to drop my pants and show you."

"You'd freeze your dinger off," Brian said.

"Brian!" Melissa snapped.

"Sorry, Mom. Bye, Dad. I'm sorry about Grandpa." Brian stepped forward and gently, awkwardly hugged Donnie, then went to stand with his mom.

"Bye, Dad," LizBeth said. "I'll see you soon." She hugged him and Donnie kissed her forehead.

"Bye, sweetheart," he told her.

"Dad, I have to say something," LizBeth said. Donnie looked at her inquisitively. "I'm not jealous. I was a little bit before, but after hearing how Grandpa helped all those people, I understand it now. It's okay."

"What do you mean?" Donnie asked.

"You'll find out." She stepped up on her toes and kissed him quickly on the cheek, then he and Debbie watched his children and ex-wife go to her car.

Margaret and Gina stopped, their families hovering nearby, and the siblings hugged and promised to stay in touch better from now on, then they, too, moved away.

"I'm freezing," Debbie said.

"I told you," Donnie teased. He pushed forward on his crutches, but a figure stepped in front of him and looked up at him with innocent green eyes.

"Do I have to stow away in the back again?" Josey asked.

Donnie dropped his crutches and grabbed the girl so she couldn't drift away like smoke this time. "Oh my God, Josey. I thought I'd never see you again," he said.

She hugged him back and said, "I guess I was a little melodramatic." They released each other, but then Debbie was there to hug the girl. After the hug, Debbie picked up Donnie's crutches and gave them back before he fell over.

"Are you really comin' home with us?" Debbie asked.

Josey dropped her gaze to the ground for a moment. "That depends on a few things," she said.

"Anything," Donnie said. "What is it?"

"You have to forgive me," she said.

"That's done," Donnie said, and Debbie agreed.

"Then there's this guy," Josey said, lifting her head and waving stiffly at another figure who had moved close.

Donnie turned and found himself facing a tall, elderly man in a black suit, with dark eyes that somehow made him think of snapping whips. He immediately knew who it was.

"Mr. Nathaniel Henthorn, I presume," Donnie said. He held out his hand and the lawyer pumped it once, very firmly.

"Mr. Nelson," the man said. "As I told you, Miss Wilder is in my care. She has filed the necessary paperwork for emancipation and I suspect the judge will grant it to her. However, it was a requirement of her grandmother that she not only finish high school, but get a college degree with the trust fund established for her. Because of the deception she engaged in, I understand she has not been attending school."

"No," Donnie said. "She hasn't."

"She has asked my permission to return to Sagebrush with you," the lawyer said. "I am willing to grant that permission on the condition that you send me documentation proving that she is enrolled in the local high school by the end of the week."

Donnie thought his grin might split his face into two separate parts. "I'm more than agreeable to that," he said.

"Very well, then," Henthorn said. "I'll be calling to make random checks on her wellness, but I trust she will probably be running your house and business even while attending school. She's like her grandmother that way."

"She certainly is," Donnie agreed.

"Good day," Henthorn said, and shook Donnie's hand again. He tipped his fedora to Debbie, and gave Josey one last hug, pulling her tight against his expensive wool coat while saying, "No more lies, Josey Wilder. You have too much to live up to." He released her, turned, and walked away with long, graceful strides.

Debbie helped Donnie into the passenger seat while Josey got into the back. Debbie slipped behind the wheel and they started for home. Donnie didn't feel any pain in his head or leg. He looked into the back seat and said, "You told LizBeth what you were doing, didn't you?"

"I did," Josey said. "I had to. You're her dad. I couldn't let you be responsible for me if it was going to hurt her just as you two were finally talking again."

Donnie and Debbie looked at each other and smiled. Donnie felt so happy that he wanted to shout or cry or run in circles like a happy dog. He craned his neck to look back at the orange-haired girl.

"Something's different about you," Donnie said over his shoulder. "Did you get a new shirt?"

They laughed the way a family laughs at an inside joke.

About the Author

Steven E. Wedel began craving fame and fortune in the literary world when he was in high school. After writing his way through careers as a machinist, journalist, corporate writer, public relations specialist, and retiring as a high school English teacher, he's decided to keep writing despite the lack of wealth and notoriety.

Wedel has published over 30 books, mostly in the adult horror genre, but he's also written for the young adult, children's, Western, and thriller markets. He's dabbled in other genres using pseudonyms. His non-fiction writing includes how-to articles for writers, literary criticism, and hundreds of articles for print newspapers and online sites.

In 2004 Wedel earned a master's degree in liberal studies, creative writing emphasis, from the University of Oklahoma. He earned a bachelor's degree in journalism from the University of Central Oklahoma in 1999, and graduated from Enid High School in 1984. He is a lifelong Oklahoman, father of four, with three grandsons. He currently lives in central Oklahoma with his dogs Bear and Sweet Pea, and a cat named Cleo.

He'd still take the fame and fortune if it comes his way ...

Be sure to visit him online and sign up for his newsletter: www.stevenewedel.com

Wide

Also by Steven E. Wedel

The Werewolf Saga

Shara

Ulrik

Nadia's Children

First Born (coming soon)

The Werewolf Saga: Apocrypha

Call to the Hunt

Murdered by Human Wolves

Cody Treat Series

Afterlife

The Saga of Tarod the Nine-Fingered

The War Lord

The Puppet King

The Nine-Fingered

The Death Merchant

Volume 1

The Travels of Jacob Wolf

The Broken Man

Standalone Novels/Novellas

A Light Beyond

Amara's Prayer

Inheritance

Little Graveyard on the Prairie

Love Curse

Mother

Orphan

Seven Days in Benevolence

Shim and Shay's Wish

Songbird

The Prometheus Syndrome

The Teacher

Yes or No

With Carrie Jones

After Obsession

In the Woods

Sleeper (coming soon)

Short Story Collections

Darkscapes (third edition coming soon)

The God of Discord and Other Weird Tales

The Zombie Whisperer and Other Weird Tales

Unholy Womb and Other Halloween Tales

Non-Fiction

You Want to Do What? Things I've Learned as a Teacher

As Editor

Tales of the Pack

Milton Keynes UK
Ingram Content Group UK Ltd.
UKHW020820110823
426718UK00014B/511